DAW BOOKS PROUDLY PRESENTS THE SCIENCE FICTION NOVELS OF W. MICHAEL GEAR:

The Donovan Series

Outpost
Abandoned
Pariah
Unreconciled*

The Spider Trilogy

The Warriors of Spider
The Way of Spider
The Web of Spider

The Forbidden Borders Trilogy

Requiem for the Conqueror
Relic of Empire
Countermeasures
*
Starstrike
*
The Artifact

*Coming soon from DAW Books

ABANDONED

DONOVAN: BOOK TWO

W. MICHAEL GEAR

DAW BOOKS, INC.

DONALD A. WOLLHEIM, FOUNDER

1745 Broadway, New York, NY 10019

ELIZABETH R. WOLLHEIM

SHEILA E. GILBERT

PUBLISHERS

www.dawbooks.com

33614081543398

First Paperback Printing, November 2019
1 2 3 4 5 6 7 8 9

TO
RED CANYON JAKE
SHETLAND SHEEPDOG EXTRAORDINAIRE
AND MY
BEST FRIEND, BUDDY, AND PAL.

ACKNOWLEDGMENTS

This book would not be possible without the encouragement and enthusiasm of the good people at DAW Books. My thanks to Sheila Gilbert, Betsy Wollheim, and the remarkable team at DAW.

To my beloved Kathleen O'Neal Gear I extend my love, appreciation, and gratitude. Every day that I wake up with her in my life is a miracle.

Finally to Theresa Hulongbayan and the ever-effervescent **Facebook Gear Fan Club: Book Series First North Americans**, I thank you all for the support, enthusiasm, and encouragement. You remain a constant reminder that nothing is as pitiful as an author without readers!

Like a weary Hercules, Mark Talbot hunched in his battle armor. He perched on the rounded stone outcrop deep in the forest and stared up at the night sky. A combat-hardened Corporate Marine private—supposedly the toughest of the tough—he fixed tired eyes on the patterns and swirls of stars. Wondrous stars. A sparkling, frosty hoar that glittered against the soot-black sky.

God, he wished he was out there.

He took a deep breath, caught the rank odor rising from inside his armor, and wrinkled his nose. He stank like shit in a toilet. He had lost count of the days that he and Shin had been living in their protective gear. Thirty? Forty? Hard to tell since he'd left his personal com back on the doomed aircar. Somewhere along the line, one day had merged into another and they'd lost count.

Propped back in the shadow of the rocks, Shin gasped in pain. More than a week had passed since the slimy leech thing had bored its way into her foot. After weeks in armor, Shin had wanted a bath. They both had. They'd drawn lots. She'd won.

At the pool of clear water they'd found, she had stripped off her armor and waded out. Splashing and scrubbing, she'd laughed, squirted water at him as he stood guard and swapped banter.

The squishy creature had waited until Shin stepped out on the muddy bank. She'd been too busy drying her hair to notice when the thing came wiggling out of the mud. Didn't feel it until it pierced her skin. Had barely had time to look down before it had burrowed into the bottom of her foot. Even as she shrieked it was inching its way under the skin of her ankle and deep into her calf.

Looking back, he should have amputated her leg at the knee. She'd screamed at him not to. Said it would have been a death sentence. Pleaded that the thing would probably emerge on its own. That it probably couldn't survive in a human.

He should have done a lot of things differently.

That was Donovan.

A person did a lot of looking back on Donovan.

Talbot tensed as a strange, piercing whistle sounded from the forest. Massive trees surrounded Mark's stone outcrop; they rose up in a black wall. Trees on Donovan were like nothing he'd seen on Earth. These were giants, four and five hundred feet tall; high overhead the triangular branches interlocked, and the leaves were huge. Walking beneath them was like traveling through an immense cavern. And the roots, they were the worst of all. Tarry too long in one spot and they'd slither out of the ground, seek to wrap around a foot, ankle, or calf. Get caught by the roots and within an hour they would completely engulf a person to the point that not even powered combat armor could break free.

Safety could only be found on one of the stone outcrops. Chunks of bedrock, they jutted up like islands in the ocean of forest. Talbot and Shin had made their way north, traveling from outcrop to outcrop. For whatever reason, the roots avoided solid rock.

The weird, piercing whistle sounded in the forest again. This was something new. Yet another horror in Donovan's endless parade of terrifying creatures and plants, no doubt.

For the most part he and Shin had grown used to the sounds, the constant chirring, clicking, singing, and chiming of the wildlife. He didn't know if any of the creatures even had names—though some must have been cataloged by Donovan's colonists over the colony's thirty-year existence.

The house-cat-sized, four-winged fliers were the worst peril, but they couldn't penetrate armor when they swarmed him and Shin. Then there were the sort of dinosaurian bipedal monsters; the smaller clawed creatures; the leechlike sucky things that had burrowed into Shin and slipped out of the mud to try and pierce his armored feet and ankles; and the list went on. Vine-like hanging predators would swing out, only to scrape along his impregnable and slick-sided armor. The firehose-thick snake creatures that whipped sideways to tangle around his feet might not be able to penetrate his protective shell, but they'd trip him. And falling was always precarious because of the roots.

That was another thing about Donovan; the damn plants moved. One way or another, everything on Donovan would try and kill you. As Garcia had found out, and Shin, dear Shin, was even now experiencing.

"You all right?" he asked, annoyed by the hypocrisy of the salutation.

"One of the things is wiggling in my stomach, Mark. I feel . . . like I want to throw up. But it's . . . numb. I'm . . . falling, spinning. Endless damn vertigo. God, so . . . sick."

She'd told him that there were several now, eating their way through her body. Either the first had divided, or there had been more than just that one that had gotten under her skin.

Talbot leaned his head back and imagined himself flying off his solitary stone perch and soaring up, up into the night sky. Burning his way out of the gravity well. Past atmosphere into the vacuum. Then on beyond the orbit of Donovan's moon. Out away from the star they called Capella. Clear out to the inversion point.

He closed his eyes, let the fantasy possess him as he floated there in space. As if in a trance, he would clap his hands, invert symmetry. Godlike, he'd pop out of the universe and navigate his way back to Solar System some thirty light-years distant.

Home. Blessed, wonderful home.

What he'd give to walk the avenues of Transluna, to peer into the shops, walk into a food stand and eat sausage, donuts, tacos, red beans and rice, Szechuan shrimp, couscous, chocolate cake. Or anything for that matter. Home food.

But when he opened his eyes, it was to stare up at the alien sky that had become too familiar. No Orion, no Coal Sack, or Big Dipper. Just the whiter, brighter smear of the Milky Way, and clusters of stars for which he had no names.

The servos whined in the night as Talbot resettled himself atop the stony outcrop. He checked his charge: barely twenty percent. Come morning he'd have to clean the voltaics. Take enough time to let Capella recharge the power pack. Fact was the suits wouldn't take a full charge anymore.

One of the night creatures flew past in a whisper of wing beats. The dark form blotted the stars as it slowed, circled, and decided he and Shin weren't food.

Shin made a deep-throated gargling sound, kicked her left leg out, and tensed. He waited out the spasms, then asked, "I could end it. Want me to?"

She swallowed hard, kept panting for breath. Had there been light he would have seen the sweat pouring down her round, brown face. The terrified quivering of her eyes as they jerked about in their sockets.

"Maybe." She sucked another frantic breath. "Can't feel a thing below my chest."

Nothing had prepared them for Donovan. It was one thing to read that the planet was dangerous. Another to have its jaws snapped shut around you.

"We were screwed the moment we lifted off from Port Authority," Talbot whispered to the night.

"What the hell were we thinking?" Shin asked.

"Garcia's idea." He smiled bitterly. "I still remember how he looked at us over the rim of that beer mug in the tavern. 'Do you really want to space back to Solar System without going out there?' Remember, Shin? That look in his eyes?"

She tensed so quickly her armor clattered on the underlying stone. When she finally managed to relax and catch her breath, she said, "Yeah. And he was the first to die. Walked under that droopy looking tree. With the big floppy leaves and all the weird vines."

"And the vine wasn't a vine at all," Talbot finished, remembering how Garcia had tried to bat one of the hanging "vines" to one side only to have it whip back and shoot into the gap between Garcia's collar and his neck. Even as Garcia screamed he was being lifted. Lifted! Heavy combat armor and all, right up into the tree.

"How did that thing do that?" Talbot asked.

"No wonder the Donovanians call it a nightmare," Shin whispered. "We couldn't even get a fix on him up there. Couldn't put him out of his misery."

Talbot made a face in the night. Word was that a nightmare devoured its victim alive. Sent shoots inside a person's body to slowly digest him from the inside out. Like the things inside Shin's body were doing to her.

They'd flown south from Port Authority in their jury-rigged aircar. Traveled just over six hundred kilometers, deep into the forest beyond the southern extent of the Wind Mountains, and set down in what looked like a clearing in the trees.

As they leapt out, they'd noticed the thick root mat squirming under the aircar. Wiggling roots. Wow. That was new.

Didn't matter. They'd been too busy bragging about being the first humans to ever set foot on that spot. Laughing, staring around at the universe of huge trees rising up to majestic heights around them. Odd trees, with triangular branches, weirdly shaped green, turquoise, teal, and lime-colored leaves.

Not to mention the noise: a cacophony of singing, clicking, rattling harmonics.

And they'd started their circle, clambering over the root mat. They proceeded with their helmets hung on belt clips, sniffing and remarking at the exotic perfumed odors. They carried their rifles at the ready. Each had his heads-up display monitoring for movement, heat signatures, and any threat.

But damn, the whole place was alive. Flashes of gaudy color flickered among the branches as Donovan's peculiar Technicolor creatures vanished in pell-mell flight.

"Wish we could go back, Shin. Slap ourselves silly before we jury-rigged that aircar and flew south."

"I'd be happy . . ."—she sucked a pained breath—"to be put on report. Scrubbing toilets never . . ." Again she tensed and grunted in pain.

"Looked so good?" he finished for her.

He thought back to Garcia. How they had shot futilely up into the branches. If they stepped underneath, the whipping tentacles would try and catch them. And if they stood still, the roots would inexorably begin to feel their way up and around their armored feet. And all the while, high in the tree, they could hear Garcia screaming.

"I keep seeing the aircar," Shin said through shallow

breaths. "Remember, when we got back. It was just a thick ball of roots. What stupid . . ." She stiffened, groaned.

"Can't believe we left our coms in the aircar," Talbot whispered. "What a bunch of fools."

"It's the smart way to do it," Garcia had assured them. *"Can't disobey an order if we're not around where we can hear it, right?"*

"Must have been an equipment malfunction," Shin had joked.

The massive woody strands had crushed the aircar as if it were a foam cup.

Mark Talbot stared out at the night, his heart like a leaden anchor in his chest. At least twenty days had passed, and probably more, since he and Shin last heard a shuttle, which meant *Turalon* had long since spaced for the Solar System.

As far as Talbot knew, it was just him, Shin, and Donovan. God help them.

The odd rattle in Shin's throat made him turn. "Shin?" Nothing.

He shifted, raised his thumb light, and flicked it on. Shin's almond eyes were wide, sightless, the pupils fixed. Her mouth hung open, caught in a silent scream. Threads of her black hair shifted with the breeze.

A mouse-sized bulge appeared under Shin's skin where her neck cleared the armor. Horrified, Talbot watched it make its slow way up and around under her jaw. He tried to imagine what it would feel like to have something eating out the inside of his tongue.

God, I can't stand this.

"Good bye, old friend," he whispered. Weary to the soul, he stood, grabbed Shin's booted foot, and rolled her unceremoniously down the steep slope. Her armor clattered hollowly as it bounced its way down the rocks and into the forest below.

No way was he going to sleep next to her corpse when those *things* might slip out and take a try at him.

Tilting his head back, he looked up at the stars again.

I am alone.

2

"**S**upervisor?" Lieutenant Deb Spiro's voice brought Kalico Aguila awake. Kalico blinked, sat up, and as she did the lights illuminated her personal quarters.

Such as they were.

Once—back before she'd been abandoned on Donovan— Kalico would have considered the notion that she'd actually sleep in such squalor to be a bad joke. She'd lived like a god, a Corporate Supervisor, privy to the inner workings of the Board. A contender for an eventual seat and the honored title of Boardmember. Powerful people feared her for her political skills and her ruthless ambition.

And then she'd asked for the Donovan assignment. A high-risk gamble, a shortcut that would assure her final triumph. These days, the sight of her quarters acted as a spur to focus her dedication to the task at hand: she had to amass a fortune for the time when, hopefully, another ship would arrive from Solar System and get her off Donovan.

If—and it was a big if—another ship was coming.

She ran fingers through her midnight-black hair and glanced around her plastic and featureless white-walled room. A duralon chest of drawers, an improvised wardrobe, a cushioned recliner, bedside table, and sialon desk composed her furniture inventory and held all the personal items that remained to her on Donovan.

Back in Solar System, her luxurious apartment at Transluna awaited her return. What a wonderful dream, with its high-glassed walls and incredible views of the city. Talk about a distance beyond comprehension. Sometimes she wondered if Earth, Solar System, and Transluna actually existed, or if, during the transit to Donovan, she and *Turalon* had come out in some alternate universe.

The thing was—given the mathematical and statistical modeling that underlay space travel—neither the alternate nor null hypothesis could actually be proved. This might indeed be the same universe into which she had been born. It might, with actual greater statistical probability, be another universe entirely. It all depended upon which definition of "reality" a person chose to believe among the various hypotheses floating around in theoretical physics.

The default response was "just deal with it."

She shot Lieutenant Spiro an irritated look, threw back the bedding, and swung her feet to the smooth floor. "What's wrong, Lieutenant?" she asked as she padded over to her wardrobe. Checking her naked body in the mirror, she winced. The perfect figure she'd maintained for years had grown gaunt, the ribs too deeply outlined, toned muscles now thin, her belly too hollow.

The lieutenant's square face, heavy jaw, and black eyes had a grim set—not that she ever displayed anything more animated than mild disapproval. The word "dour" might have been coined specially for Spiro.

"Deserters, ma'am. Two of them. Talovich and Cabrianne. Security Officer Perez just delivered them from Port Authority. Turns out they shipped themselves out in a tool chest. Pamlico Jones collared them as they were trying to sneak through the gate at the shuttle field."

"This has got to stop," Kalico said bitterly. "That's the second time this month. The threat of work details doesn't seem to deter them anymore."

She slapped a hand against her wardrobe. "Don't the damned fools understand? They *signed* a contract. They *knew* what they were getting into."

"Did they?" Spiro asked softly. "Did any of us have the slightest idea what Donovan was really like?"

"No." Kalico shot the lieutenant a sidelong glance. "We had no idea that six ships were lost somewhere in inverted symmetry. Or that *Freelander* would show up like some sort of *Flying Dutchman* with its crew dead and out of phase with time."

Kalico paused as she pulled on her black pants suit, then added, "Nor did we know just how incredibly rich this ball of rock was."

"What are all the jewels, rare-earth elements, gold, platinum, and silver worth if you can't get them back to Solar System?" Spiro asked.

Good question.

When it came to Lieutenant Spiro, Kalico figured she needed all the insight she could get. The woman was too brittle, a sort of Corporate manikin. Spiro liked her world ordered—and her place in it well defined. She functioned best when she was a particular part in the machine. Following precise orders, seeing to the letter of their implementation.

Donovan was anything but ordered.

In the beginning, Kalico's Marines had been under Captain Max Taggart's command. Spiro had loved the guy in her own inflexible way—and his betrayal had broken something deep in Spiro's rigid psyche.

Damn it, Cap Taggart might have pissed Kalico off when he walked away, but compared to Spiro, the guy had been solid. She missed him. Longed for the man's resilience and intuition. Then the son of a bitch had "gone native" and it got him killed.

Deb Spiro was the wrong woman, in the wrong job, in the wrong place. Not that Kalico had a choice. But what if Spiro couldn't adapt in the end? What if she snapped under the pressure?

Then I'd better know sooner rather than later, because I've bet everything on this.

That included more than her opulent lifestyle as a Corporate Supervisor back in Solar System. She'd wagered her brains, ambition, drive, and talent. In getting the Donovan assignment she'd used her wits, played every card. Compromised her integrity, prostituted her body, and sold her soul.

If she could save the Donovan project, it would fast-track her right into a seat on the Board, and—if she were clever and ruthless enough—ultimately into the Chairman's seat. At which point she would become the most powerful woman in the universe.

A marvelous dream. Right up until the day she'd set foot on this reprehensible ball of rock and watched it all come crumbling down.

"The fact, Lieutenant, is that we're here. The contract is the underlying fundamental of The Corporation, and we're essentially on our own. This mine, this compound, is our single hope for the future. I can't maintain it—let alone save us all—if people think they can turn their backs on their obligation to the job. Their obligation *to me*."

In the mirror, Kalico watched for Spiro's reaction. Couldn't tell if the obtuse lieutenant understood the nuance. Why did the woman have to be a blunt instrument when Kalico needed a fine scalpel? In irritation Kalico brushed flecks of dust from her shoulders, then nodded to Spiro. "Proceed."

She followed the lieutenant out and into a short corridor that led past the administrative offices, such as they were, and past the mess hall doors.

At the dome's main entrance she waited while Lieutenant Spiro opened the double doors, then stepped out into the glare of the yard lights. Sunrise was still several hours away. She could see the perimeter fence glowing silver in the lights; the buildings, haulers, and excavating equipment were parked in neat rows in the yard lot.

Privates Michegan and Anderssoni stood over two men wearing dirt-smudged overalls. Both were on their knees, ankles and hands bound behind them. As Kalico stepped out, they looked up, hope fading.

"Talovich and Cabrianne," Kalico said flatly. "Didn't learn a damn thing from the others before you?"

"Look, Supervisor Aguila," Cabrianne said in a desperate attempt at reasonableness. "My contract was for five years as a hydraulic systems specialist for agricultural sprinkler systems. They've got me down in a tunnel in the ground sticking explosives into holes in rock. I didn't come here to be a dumb shot jockey like that. I've got rights that—"

"You are charged with desertion in a hostile environment. Section fifteen, paragraph three. You want me to recite the clause to you in full?"

Cabrianne winced. "I know. You have full discretion in the range of punishment." He chuckled humorlessly. "If I didn't have bad luck, I'd have no gagging luck at all."

Kalico scrolled through her implants, pulled up his file. "You have a reputation as a troublemaker. Your crew chief down-hole rates you as more trouble than you're worth."

Cabrianne lifted a suggestive eyebrow. "Maybe it's just a point of reference, but given that, what do you want to put me down-hole again for? After a couple of months of cleaning toilets, packing shit to the gardens, and mucking around in the sewage, it's not like I'm going back underground motivated. You know what I mean?"

Talovich had been silent the whole time, gaze fixed on the ground before him. She scrolled through his file. "Says that you're a structural engineer. But we have you running a mucking machine. Your crew chief has you labeled as insubordinate."

For the first time Talovich raised his eyes. "I don't mind working, Supervisor Aguila. I do mind working for a guy who's so dumb he couldn't prop his eyelids up with toothpicks."

"What does that mean?"

"I'm running a mucking machine, and he's sitting on his ass, drinking coffee, and farting around telling the shoring crew where to put timber. The guy doesn't have a clue. I don't want to be in that damn hole when it all comes tumbling down."

He narrowed an eye. "And it's going to fall. Maybe not for a month, or a year, but structurally, that timber they've put in the Number One is worthless."

Talovich shrugged. "So, yeah, I ran. Better cleaning toilets than buried alive under a couple million metric tons of rock."

She studied his file. "Your expertise is in bridge building. We are not crossing rivers or gorges here."

"Supervisor, building a bridge, shoring up a mine, it all comes down to bearing a load, right? You're still holding something up. In this case, the roof of the mine. Same principle."

Dawn was just graying the eastern horizon. Her people should be waking up in the barracks, griping about the coffee ration, pulling out their overalls, and shuffling to the bathrooms.

"Lieutenant Spiro?"

"Ma'am?"

"Your pistol, please."

Both men looked up, horrified, as Spiro laid her side-arm in Kalico's hand. Fitting her palm and fingers around the grip, Kalico hefted the heavy weapon.

"I must have discipline," she said firmly. "The desertions have to stop. Now. If they don't, it will be but a matter of months and we're all dead. Punishment, up to now, has proven ineffective. Therefore, I'm going to have to resort to something different."

Cabrianne cried, "Look, I was wrong. You let me get down into that hole again, and I swear, you'll never hear so much as a peep out of me again."

"Not a peep. In that, you are correct." She shot him through the head.

The man's corpse flopped limply onto the ground. His limbs twitched; a gasping rattle sounded deep in his throat.

Talovich sucked a panicked breath. The muscles at the corners of his mouth were quivering; his jaws bunched as he clamped his eyes shut in anticipation.

Kalico handed the pistol back to Spiro, saying, "Mr. Talovich, after breakfast you will give me a personal tour of the Number One mine. You will show me where the crew chief is in error. Assuming I agree with your analysis, and if I give you a crew and the authority to do so, how long will it take you to properly shore the Number One mine?"

Talovich swallowed hard. "I uh . . . ma'am?"

"Is something wrong with your hearing?"

"N-No, ma'am."

"How long?"

"T-Two weeks. Maybe three." He was staring in horror at the bloody remains of Cabrianne's head.

"If you convince me that you are right, you will have two."

"Yes, ma'am," he whispered, horrified gaze torn between her and Cabrianne's still-twitching corpse.

"Lieutenant Spiro, see to Talovich's bonds. My records indicate that Anderson has experience in building and construction. Have him accompany me and Mr. Talovich when we take our tour."

"Yes, ma'am. And Cabrianne?"

"Strip his coveralls and have them washed. It's not like

we can requisition new coveralls from stores. As to the corpse? Toss it over the fence. Donovan can dispose of it."

At that, she turned on her heel and headed back into the dome.

Damn it! She'd been wasting a structural engineer on a mucking machine? What the hell else had she missed that might end up dooming them all before this was over?

Think, Kalico. A mistake won't just destroy you, but every man, woman, and child under your command.

3

Breakfast wasn't up to Security Officer Talina Perez's standards. Compared to the tasteless pap they served at the Corporate Mine cafeteria, her usual fare of chamois steak, potatoes, and jalapenos, all seasoned with achiote, was a royal feast. Supervisor Aguila's miners were fed re-hydrated rations. Additionally they got a single, small cup of coffee. Or they would until the last of the supply of freeze-dried packets ran out.

Talina's gut squirmed uncomfortably. Her quetzal made its presence known. The thing presented itself as a foreign body in her belly, turned out it was just the alien creature's molecules playing with her brain. Flowing through her blood and tissues. Back in Port Authority, Cheng was still trying to figure out the biochemistry.

She glanced around the cafeteria, took in the distribution of coverall-dressed men and women. These were transportees: contract labor who had spaced from Solar System on *Turalon*. Most were bound to The Corporation for a five-year contract, some for ten. Three quarters of them had arrived on Donovan to find their job didn't exist, that the machine, animals, or study they'd hired on to take care of had vanished during the long years before *Turalon*'s arrival. Never one to waste a human body, The Corporation reserved the right to reassign a person to whichever profession was in need.

Supervisor Aguila had decided they would be miners. And she had the marines to back her decision.

To Talina's way of thinking, the transportees were still "soft meat." Skulls—so named for the shaved heads they had sported upon arrival—who hadn't a clue about how to survive on Donovan.

Rather than accept their fate, each and every one could have opted to ship back on *Turalon* when she spaced for Solar System. True, they'd have lived the rest of their lives in debt to The Corporation, but the overriding fact was that most had been too afraid to make the trip. Especially after learning how many of the big cargo ships had vanished in transit over the last fifteen years. The list was impressive: *Nemesis, Governor Han Xi, Tableau, Phoenix, Ashanti,* and *Mekong.* And before that, four of the smaller survey ships had vanished in the early days of Donovan's exploration.

Even as they were trying to assimilate that chilling fact, *Freelander* had popped into orbit. A mere three years out of Solar System, her crew was dead of mass murder, old age, and insanity. Three years. But according to the ship's clocks, she'd spent one-hundred-and-twenty-nine years in transit through whatever reality, universe, or physics she'd inverted to.

Everyone knew that spooky shit happened when a ship inverted symmetry. Until *Freelander,* no one had known just how spooky.

All of a sudden, life in a mine on Donovan didn't look so bad.

Talina had originally come to Donovan under a ten-year contract. That had been eleven years ago. At this stage, she figured she didn't owe The Corporation a damned thing. She spooned up another heaping of rehydrated ration and wished she'd thought to bring a bottle of Tabasco. It wasn't the real thing, of course, but in Port Authority they made a palatable substitute from the variety of different pepper plants that thrived in the gardens.

A door in the rear opened, and Supervisor Aguila entered, followed by Lieutenant Spiro. At sight of Spiro, Talina's gut tightened, and a cool rage built under her collar. She and the lieutenant had way too much bad history for the short time they'd known each other.

The quetzal coiled into an angry ball below Talina's heart and hissed its rage.

Aguila glanced around, spotted Talina, and started toward her. The woman wore a natty black pantsuit, her thick black hair gleaming in the light. Behind her, Spiro was in shining combat armor, as if about to engage in a firefight.

"Oh, joy," Talina whispered under her breath and surreptitiously reached down to unsnap the strap on her pistol. Her vision sharpened—colors leaping out vividly and shading into the IR and UV ranges. Her hearing grew more acute, registering every sound, the clinking of utensils, whispers of conversation, the shuffling of feet on the floor.

That was the quetzal's doing as it played with her senses.

Aguila seated herself unceremoniously across from Talina and straightened her cuffs. The woman fixed steely blue eyes on Talina's. "Unusual, isn't it? Flying solo at night?"

"Couldn't sleep," Talina told her. "Not only that, but we opened a crate that contained upgraded night vision screens for the aircars. We've been looking for an excuse to try them out. Your deserters gave us the opportunity."

Talina let her gaze slide sideways to Spiro. "How you doing, Lieutenant? Ducked out of any fights lately?"

"Been saving myself to beat the crap out of smartasses." Spiro's blocky face broke into a thin grin. "Know anyone who might fit the bill, smartass?"

Talina picked the spot on Spiro's high forehead. Right there at the point of a squat triangle drawn between the woman's eyes and just above the nose. That's where she'd put the bullet.

Aguila waved Spiro down. "Enough, Lieutenant. At ease." To Talina she said, "Thanks for bringing my two misguided wanderers back."

Talina leaned forward, fully aware that all eyes in the place were on her and Kalico Aguila. "We made a deal. When a person gives their word on Donovan, they mean it. I would have figured that you'd been here long enough that you'd be picking up on that."

"Any sign of my missing marines?" Spiro asked through gritted teeth.

"Nope."

"Like so many of my contractees," Kalico said, "they're absent without leave. Just so we're clear about who they belong to."

"Nothing's changed," Talina said coolly. "We haven't seen so much as a footprint. Haven't heard a word. And if Garcia, Talbot, and Shintzu were wearing battle tech, someone would have said something."

Kalico nodded as one of the kitchen staff—a young man wearing an apron—brought her a bowl of the same ration the rest were eating. The Supervisor shook a fork out of the rolled napkin and took a bite.

Swallowing, Kalico gestured with the fork. "Dismaying as it is to both sides, we need each other. We're on our own, Perez. Your people and mine. Maybe *Turalon* gets through. Makes it back to Solar System. Captain Abibi and her crew are outstanding. And the math worked to get *Turalon* here in the first place. Reverse it, and they should pop back into Solar System space where they initially inverted."

"Didn't work with *Mekong,* if you'll recall. She made it to Donovan, then vanished on the way home." Talina scraped the bottom of her bowl clean.

They ate this same bland shit at every meal? No wonder they were deserting like flies.

Kalico gestured with her spoon. "I can give you a couple dozen hypotheses to explain why *Mekong* didn't get back to the Solar System that have nothing to do with inverting symmetry or probability statistics. Could have been an atmosphere plant malfunction, disease, hydroponic collapse, mutiny, generator malfunction, hull breach, and on, and on."

Kalico arched a challenging eyebrow. "Space isn't a safe place to travel. But that's not the point. Fact is, we need each other."

"Maybe. I still remember that you wanted to put Shig, Yvette, and me up against a wall and order a firing squad to blow us apart."

Spiro's expression turned gleeful at just the mention.

"You shot a Corporate Supervisor in the head. What was I to think?" Kalico waved it away. "I know, I know. Maybe we both made mistakes. Donovan has a way of changing the rules."

Like killing Cap Taggart?

Someone had murdered Cap as he lay helpless in a hospital bed back in Port Authority. Whoever it had been had turned a drug-dispensing valve wide open and overdosed him dead.

Talina shot another cold glance at Spiro. One of the prime suspects.

To change the subject Talina said, "I left the latest inventory from the *Freelander* cargo with your office. Pamlico, Chaco, and Toby Montoya are sorting the goods and equipment based on utility. If it's even got a chance of being operative, it goes in one pile. After that they try and figure out if there's any of it that's salvageable. That goes in another pile. And finally, if it's just junk, that goes in a third."

Talina paused. "And there's another thing. Some of the guys, they say the equipment is haunted. Possessed. That it has a sort of eerie feeling, makes their skin crawl. That weird shit happens around the crates, and they get the shivers at odd moments."

"After one hundred and twenty-nine years of sitting aboard *Freelander*, what can we expect?" Kalico frowned in irritation as she chewed. "What about the seed packets?"

"Cheng and Iji are working with them." Tal gave the woman a smile. "Here's a ray of good news. He figures ninety percent will germinate. Best of the best news yet: The coffee beans sprouted."

"Perez, that bit of cheery sunlight might have just secured our future." Kalico laughed softly. "Who'd have thought? Just the promise of coffee makes me feel like I've got a blood-rotted chance of pulling this off."

"How's your farming and field clearing progressing down at the smelter site?"

Kalico's gaze hardened. "Your people said the soils were good, but we're having a hell of a time with the jungle. It fricking moves. We've cleared close to a hectare out of the forest, but how do we keep the trees out? As soon as you clear a patch of ground, the closest trees start shooting out roots and crawling over to take it back. A four-hundred-foot-tall tree with a bole five meters in diameter . . . and it can move ten meters in a day?"

"We've never tried farming in thick forest before." Talina considered the problem, thinking back to when she and Cap had survived on their own in the forest. But that was much farther north, different species of trees, and even then they'd barely made it.

Cap. She ground her teeth, feeling that spear of grief.

The quetzal inside her began to gloat. Piece of dung that it was.

Talina flicked her gaze to Lieutenant Spiro, wondering if she really was the murderer. She'd hated Cap.

For that matter, it could have been Kalico Aguila herself. The Supervisor hadn't made many bones about her disdain for Cap Taggart.

Spiro—through the entire conversation—hadn't shifted her black-eyed glare. Hard to think that two people, anywhere, hated each other more than she and Spiro did. As if it wasn't bad enough that all of Donovan was already out to kill them.

Tal gave the armored bitch her most antagonistic smile.

The woman looked like she wanted to swallow her tongue in response. Talina's quetzal-enhanced vision could see the heat rising in her cheeks.

Kalico had missed the undercurrents as she said, "As to the farm, I don't want to plant critical crops there until we know we can keep it from being overrun. If you could see to shipping us lettuce, beans, peppers, and cabbages, we'd appreciate it. Maybe some corn and other high-yield grains, too?"

"Yeah, I'll have some of the farmers start packaging seedlings." Talina shoved her bowl to the side and sipped the last of the weak coffee in her cup. "I heard the smelter is coming together."

"All but the power." Kalico studied her over the breakfast bowl. "The radioactive cores decayed over the century that they were stored on *Freelander*. We're working on it. Call it a week to reradiate using the shuttle's reactor. After that we should have both heat and power."

"And the mine?"

"Number One is producing nicely. We've built a crude stamp mill to break up the ore. The europium, holmium, and terbium deposits we're finding are remarkably pure. Gold is wonderful stuff when it runs in threads as wide as we're getting. Number Two is looking very good, the vein widening the deeper we go. But it's sulfated. We'll have to rely on the smelter.

"Getting the ore to the smelter's a problem, since we

can't cut a road through forest that moves. We're thinking of an overhead tram to carry the ore down to the smelter."

Aguila tapped a finger in emphasis. "I'll have my people get in touch with your Toby Montoya about buckets. Maybe he can make something from the metal in *Freelander*'s junk pile?"

"And the cable?"

"We're considering extruded carbon fibers. But we're still working on that. Have to manufacture them in vacuum."

"Good thing you've got the shuttle, huh?"

"Even better, I have an industrial chemist with a background in fabrication. Cable like that gives me something to trade with you people."

"It would indeed." Talina slapped her hand to the table. "Anything else you need from us? Anything I should take back to Shig and Yvette?"

"Just my thanks for bringing Cabrianne and Talovich back."

"How's their day going?" Tal stood, happy to depart.

"I shot Cabrianne through the head and had his body tossed over the fence." Kalico fixed Tal with a cold stare. "Talovich got a promotion."

"Funny world we live in."

"Yes it is, isn't it?" Kalico's hesitant gesture of the hand betrayed embarrassment. "If you wouldn't mind, Tal. We charge a half-SDR for breakfast here. I wouldn't bring it up, but, well, you know how it is with a market economy."

"Yeah." Talina tossed out one of Port Authority's silver one-SDR coins, saying, "Keep the change."

Then she shot one last derisive glance Spiro's way and flicked an insolent salute. The lieutenant appeared to be smoldering on the inside like an overstuffed volcano.

With a final nod to Kalico Aguila, Talina turned on her heel and strode toward the door.

She knew that every eye in the place was following her.

The quetzal seemed oddly satisfied.

But then more than anything, it wanted her dead.

4

Trish Monagan had bootstrapped herself into a ring-tailed fit as she stomped down Port Authority's main avenue. Capella hung more than a hand's height above the eastern horizon and illuminated the weathered white domes interspersed among the stone and chabacho-wood structures.

As she went—cursing the entire way—her shoulder-length auburn hair swung with each step. The few who encountered her took one look at the fire in her green eyes, nodded, and ducked out of her way.

Damn it, she was newly turned twenty, second in command of security at Port Authority. Donovan born and raised, she'd never had the luxury of a carefree childhood. Young people got old fast. Or they got dead. Maybe when she hit old age, like twenty-five, she'd get her temper under control. Until then, if she wanted to vent over unadulterated stupidity, she'd damned well vent.

Trish picked up her pace until her scoped rifle bounced on her back, sending shimmers of color through the quetzal-hide jacket she wore. The same splash of color rippled up her boots with each heel strike on the hard gravel that paved the avenue.

"Coming through," she snapped as she approached the high perimeter fence. One of the guards jumped to swing the smaller "man gate" open where it had been built into the main gate.

Trish stormed through. Out of second nature, she glanced around the aircar field, one hand going to her rifle. It would have been better to have had the aircar field enclosed by a nice, safe perimeter fence. The Corporation, however, had never bothered to send them enough fencing material.

Well, in fairness, they had, but failed to realize that fences on Donovan had to be fifty feet high to keep out the most lethal of Donovan's predators. Meanwhile several containers of electric fencing that had been aboard *Freelander* suggested that, perhaps, when they finished sorting the piles of cargo, some augmentation of the town's protection might be possible.

Assuming they could adapt the solar panels and regulate the voltage through the wire. Everything about Donovan was complicated given that they were mostly creating it *ad hoc*. The colony was a slapdash mixture of nineteenth and twenty-second-century technologies all cobbled together in the hopes of survival.

Having spotted no dangers—and seeing several people already working on the vehicles—Trish relaxed. Taking a stand in the center of the packed-clay lot, she pulled her binoculars around and raised them to her eyes. She fixed on the southern sky above the far tree line beyond the agricultural fields.

"Two Spots?" she accessed her com. "Is Tal on schedule?"

"Roger that. About fifteen klicks out."

As Trish waited, she ground her teeth. Shit on a shoe, Talina knew better. It was originally her rule, after all.

There!

Trish picked up the black dot in the southern sky. Definitely an aircar. None of the larger flying species living in this part of Donovan flew that straight.

In the couple of minutes it took for Talina's aircar to approach, circle, and drop to a landing, Trish rehearsed several verbal assaults.

When Talina finally shut down the thrusters, grabbed her pack and rifle, and stepped out to solid ground, Trish opened with: "Of all the stupid, irresponsible, and dumb-assed stunts to pull. I ought to smack you up alongside of the head. What the hell were you thinking?"

Talina shrugged one strap of her pack over the shoulder of her ragged and patched black security uniform. Her rifle, she let dangle from her right hand.

"Someone needed to test the night vision. Montoya's people got it wired in yesterday. After bagging those two deserters, it seemed like a perfect opportunity."

"Broke your own clap-trapping rule, Tal." Trish lifted an angry finger. "Scared hell out of me when I heard you'd flown off in the middle of the night. Why didn't you give me a heads up?"

Talina's midnight eyes lit with no little amusement. "You were asleep. It was close to two."

"And you think *that* makes it all right? What if you'd gone down?"

"I'd have climbed a tree." She pointed at her pack. "Night vision goggles. New ones from *Turalon*. Not military quality, but good enough get around the forest at night. Even have a thermal detector should the spare quetzal or bem be lurking in the shadows. What's got your tit in such a wringer?"

"Tal, I'm barely over the last time you were lost in the bush. People *die* out there."

"Yeah, I broke my rule. What are you going to do, Trish?" The mocking smile was back. "Shoot me?"

"Talina, damn it, you—"

"I'm your boss. Back off!" Talina stepped past her, heading for the gate. "Besides, I was on the com to Two Spots the whole time. I was even sending telemetry, giving him readings from one of the remote sensors we found in *Freelander*'s cargo. If I'd gone down, he could have scrambled half the town to come get me."

She glanced sidelong. "Maybe even you, if you weren't in the middle of your beauty sleep. It's doing wonders for you, by the way. Love that cherubic red in your cheeks. Or is that just 'cause you're pissed off?"

Trish felt some of her mad leaking away as she matched Talina's stride, heading for the gate. "Two o'clock in the morning, huh? You weren't sleeping again, were you? The nightmares . . . That quetzal inside you."

"Yeah, he's a real jewel. Got an appointment with Cheng and Dr. Turnienko tomorrow. See if they're closer to figuring out how to get the pus-sucking beast out of my bloodstream. It's screwing with my dreams. I mean, vivid. I'll be in the bush, camouflaged, waiting for chamois, and bam! I'm in a chase, running full-out."

Talina shook her head. "Weird, I tell you. We never think about it, because we're built the way we are. But the feeling of air streaming through a quetzal? Wow. Are they ever efficient compared to Earthly lungs: Suck. Stop. Exhale back through the same passage. Stop. Inhale. Do it all over again. All that time we're exhaling, we're losing peak oxygenation."

Trish and Talina nodded to the guard, passed through the man gate, and back into Port Authority.

"Do you know how bizarre that sounds?"

"Oh, yeah. You ought to see from my side."

As they proceeded past the warehouse district, Trish asked, "So, who'd you see at the mine? I'd guess Lieutenant Spiro wasn't there, or there'd be blood spatters on your uniform."

"Had breakfast with Aguila and Spiro. Aguila kept a leash on the lovely lieutenant. Probably because she didn't want unnecessary violence disrupting her people's breakfast."

Trish raised an eyebrow. "Yeah, a lieutenant's bleeding and dismembered corpse lying on the cafeteria floor can have a dyspeptic effect on the average Corporate employee's digestion."

"Funny how some people are, huh? Anyway, Aguila says they're having a terrible time keeping farmland cleared. As soon as they cut it, the forest starts moving in. She says they're picking out free gold from the Number One. Going to build a tram to get ore down the hill to the smelter."

"And the two guys you took back?"

Talina arched an eyebrow. "One ended up as a corpse on the other side of the fence. Aguila shot him herself. Said she promoted the other one."

"Right. Promoted. And how does that work?"

"Got me."

They had made their way to the admin dome. The building, once a brilliant white, had taken on the tint of aged ivory, and Donovan's version of microbial life shaded places on the outside with darker patches. These were now vying with terrestrial fungi the humans had imported from Solar System.

No one knew what long-term effects any of the terrestrial plants, microbes, or humans themselves would have on Donovan. Or vice versa, as Talina's "infection by quetzal" had made abundantly clear.

The Corporation—despite cries, pleas, and barely inhibited outrage from environmental scientists—could have cared less. To The Corporation, Donovan represented an exploitable source of immense wealth and power. One which was far from the public eye and academic scrutiny, and access to which they controlled with an iron hand.

Talina led the way into the main hallway, leaned her head into Shig Mosadek's office, and asked, "You and Yvette got a minute?"

Shig looked up from his desk, a faint smile on his broad lips. The man pushed back and stood. All five-foot-three of him. He ran a hand through his unruly mop of thick black hair.

"Have a nice flight?" he asked as he wiped at his pug nose; it seemed to have been squished onto his brown face as an afterthought.

"The night vision gear's great," Talina told him. "Looking at the way Sheyela wired it in is a little scary, but even in the dark of the moon, visibility is like daylight."

"Had to be jury-rigged," Shig told her, leading the way to the conference room. "The power packs had degraded to the point they wouldn't take a charge. Nor did the connector plugs match. Like so much of *Freelander*'s cargo, we're left making do as we can."

At Yvette Dushane's door, Shig called, "Talina's back. Want a report on what the spider queen is up to?"

Trish grinned. The spider queen? Not a lot of love was lost between the Supervisor and Port Authority.

Trish stepped back as Yvette emerged from her office, a coffee cup in hand. Physically, she was Shig Mosadek's opposite. Where he was short and brown, she was tall—six feet—pale and thin. Her narrow face and severe nose added to the wolfish effect animating her green eyes. Slightly silvered ash-blonde hair topped her head.

They were just as different by nature. Shig's personality reflected the tranquility and introspection you'd expect from his previous life as a professor of comparative religions. Yvette came across hard—almost cutting and acerbic in her take-no-prisoners approach to life.

Yvette fixed her green eyes on Trish, asking, "So did you tear Talina a new one when she landed?"

"Thought of it," Trish told her back. "But she was

armed. And after dealing with Kalico and Spiro, I figured she'd be desperate to shoot someone. Anyone. So I best not make myself a candidate."

The junior member, Trish followed in the rear as they filed into the conference room. She took a chair off to the side and watched the others seat themselves.

Essentially, Shig, Talina, and Yvette were the leadership. Supervisor Aguila called them "the Triumvirate": the established ruling power in Port Authority. Some years back they had declared independence from The Corporation. Executed the then-Supervisor, a man named Clemenceau. In the absence of The Corporation, they had started running Port Authority on their own. That had been in the dark days before *Turalon*'s abrupt arrival in orbit had changed the entire political equation.

New people—not the least of whom was Supervisor Aguila—had since dealt themselves into the fray. The most loathsome was the recent transportee Dan Wirth. If that was even his real name. Since his arrival on *Turalon*, the psychopath had taken over Port Authority's only bordello and established a gambling house that offered additional prostitution, questionable loans, and violence for hire. Through acumen and unsavory deeds, Dan Wirth had become the largest single property owner in Port Authority. He even insisted on, and got, a seat on the town's "council."

Trish's parents had been "second ship," arriving just after the colony had been established. Trish had been born in Port Authority, part of the first generation of true Donovanians, though there had only been five of them in her age group who'd survived to adulthood. Her peers, two females and two males, had since married, moved out into the bush, and were having kids of their own.

Trish had been six when her father disappeared during a survey expedition in the southern hemisphere. Her mother had died when Trish was twelve. Not that she'd ever have suffered, but Talina had taken her in. Treated Trish like a little sister, and gave her a direction during those wild years when Trish was finishing her education. Fact was, Trish Monagan worshipped Talina. Would do anything for her. And had done so in the past, though God help her if Tal ever found out.

"How did things look?" Yvette asked, elbows propped as she cradled her coffee cup with both hands.

"They're making progress." Talina sat back in her seat. "They've got a hauler operational to remove ore from the Number One and Two mines. Aguila has built a stamp mill that is running on steam power, of all things. The ore is being piled just outside the main gate. Waste is being dumped down the side of the ridge and bladed flat to create additional level ground.

"As I flew out, I could see that she has a team logging chabacho and stonewood lumber. With that shuttle of hers, she's setting up towers in the forest for her tram. Says she's figured a way to make carbon-fiber cable in orbit."

"How's that coming along?" Shig asked, fingers laced before him on the table.

"It's theoretical. If she succeeds, she wants to trade cable for things we make that she needs. The smelter itself has been assembled on a flat by the river down below the mine. Looked to me like crews are still building the power plant. Running pipes from the river to the reactor. Said she'd have it up and running in a week. Somebody on her crew must have figured out how the thing works."

Shig was smiling, his expression placid. "A fascinating enterprise, don't you think?"

"How's that?" Yvette asked.

"After years of surviving, cut off from The Corporation, *Turalon* makes planetfall. We come within a whisker of going to war with the Supervisor and her marines, and end up as two mutually exclusive societies and settlements, both inextricably linked at the hip for our very survival. She and her people depend on us for food, medical care, maintenance, and technical expertise. We depend on her for a share of the largesse taken out of *Freelander*'s hold."

He chuckled his amusement. "All this effort to accumulate wealth, and there's no telling if we're ever going to see another ship from Solar System again in our lifetimes."

"Aguila has bet everything that they're coming back." Yvette sipped her coffee. "You ask me, *Turalon* was the last hope. And let's face it: Chances are that she's not going to make it back to Solar System. I've got better odds betting on black at Dan Wirth's crooked roulette wheel than I have of ever seeing another ship from Earth."

"I'm with Yvette," Talina said wearily. "Our best long-term strategy is figuring out a way to stay self-sufficient. With *Turalon* and *Freelander*'s cargo, our chances are a hell of lot brighter than they were six months ago."

Trish studied her friend's face, seeing the fatigue lines, the sorrow. Not only was Talina grieving over burying a man she'd loved, but the quetzal inside her rarely left her any peace. That reality lay behind the dark circles under her eyes and the tense lines at the edges of her mouth.

Talina had always been a tough woman, resigned to deal in the most expedient way with whatever problem arose. On Donovan, as head of security, she literally had the power of life and death. As well as being a living legend, she was in some ways Donovan's ultimate survivor: capable of coping with both the realities of Port Authority as well as the exigencies that arose out in the bush.

She and Cap, after all, miraculously walked out of the forest after two weeks of being lost without a trace. A feat that not even the Wild Ones—humans who'd moved out into the hinterlands—would attempt.

"So," Shig mused, fingers stroking his chin. "She's ready to plant her first crop. Very well. We'll send her seedlings. Our best interests are served if her people can figure out how to make a farm thrive in the middle of the forest down there. That's another source of food in case something disastrous happens to our farms here."

"She really shot that deserter, Cabrianne?" Yvette mused.

"And said she promoted that guy Talovich. I saw Cabrianne's body where they had tossed it on the other side of the fence." Talina shrugged. "Sounds like a sort of mixed message, don't you think?"

"Clever," Shig countered. "Talovich must have been more useful to her. Structural engineer, wasn't he? Want to bet but that he's substantially more motivated to help her succeed from here on out?"

"Are we going to keep honoring this agreement to return her deserters? Especially if she's going to start shooting them?" Talina asked.

Shig laced his fingers together. "We've built a society on

contracts. Keeping agreements. If we start violating them, where does it end?"

Yvette said thoughtfully, "We got lucky the first time we crossed swords with Aguila. And then it was only because she didn't understand Donovan or its people. Underestimating her would be a mistake. She will go to any lengths to save herself and her mine."

Trish studied Talina from the corner of her eye. She wouldn't underestimate Supervisor Aguila, for sure. But when it came to dangerous women? She'd put her money on Tal.

The problem was, her old friend and mentor had a quetzal inside her—and she'd been kicked too hard by life in the last months. All of which made Talina Perez a sort of ticking time bomb.

Just got to figure out how to keep you from going off.

5

The power pack indicated a twenty percent charge. Talbot slapped it, but the readout remained the same. He glanced up at Capella; Donovan's sun was as high as it would get in the turquoise sky. Twenty percent. That was all the charge his dying suit voltaics could produce.

Clouds were building off to the west, towering columns of fluffy white. Stoked by the moist breezes blowing in from the Gulf, they fed the constant afternoon cloudbursts.

None of which helped Talbot's current problem.

The miracle was that his solar chargers had worked for as long as they had. No one had ever pushed combat armor this long or under such extreme conditions in the field. Operational conditions in Solar System had dictated the suit's design. Tactical combat realities in the Corporate world rarely required a marine to be armored for more than three or four hundred hours at a maximum. The suit had been designed to function for a thousand hours of continuous operation before being returned to the unit armorer for refit and servicing. As if anyone would be expected to live in his suit for more than a month.

Talbot had been in his now for way more than two thousand hours. Not to mention that Donovan's day was about 25.5 hours long. The miracle was that the unit had lasted as long as it had without servicing.

Moisture, mud, debris, biofilm—not to mention that he lived in the suit—all had a detrimental and corrosive effect. Only seven of the photovoltaic cells still worked. But it was the battery pack that was finally wearing out, taking less and less of a charge as the days went by. In a unit armorer's workshop, the battery no doubt would have been a simple fix. Lost in Donovan's wilderness? Without tools, let alone the training necessary to service the thing? No way.

He would have expected the servos that worked the

joints to have gone before the power pack. That they hadn't was a fricking miracle.

Talbot took a deep breath and sighed as he looked out at the vast green-blue panorama that spread before him. He'd found the next rocky outcrop—upthrust bald stone that so resembled the *kopjes* he had known in South Africa during his training days there. Like islands, they stuck up from the endless forest.

A flock of scarlet fliers burst from the treetops in the distance to the south. They wheeled, jinked right, and then left as a mob of the vicious four-winged predators chased after them.

For a couple of seconds the pursuit zigzagged above the highest branches. An instant later, the scarlet fliers shot down into the trees, taking their pursuers with them.

Talbot licked his dry lips and ran dirt-encrusted fingers over the armored carapace where it lay charging on the stone beside him. Should he put it on? Just the sight of the four-winged predator flock sent a shiver through him. The first time they'd attacked, he'd been on the forest floor. Had barely had time to fasten his helmet before they were pressing around him, biting, slashing, and beating.

As with so many of the threats he'd survived, his armor had proved impenetrable. In the end, the beasts had lost interest in slicing impotently and breaking their teeth on his hard exterior; they'd flown off in search of easier prey.

He couldn't constantly live inside his helmet, but he kept it ready along with his rifle, and could clamp it on his head in a fraction of a second.

Like the time the monster had magically appeared from the very roots he walked on. A huge, three-eyed, dragon-like giant of a thing. It had flared a wide collar in a dazzling ruff of laser-bright colors. Then it let out a screech that half-paralyzed Talbot in his tracks.

He had barely clamped his helmet down before the thing leaped full onto him, tearing with claws, clamping fang-filled jaws around his helmet and shoulder.

Pinned in the beast's jaws as he was, Talbot nevertheless had managed to claw his sidearm from its holster. Three rapid shots had sent the creature stumbling back. As the thing had screamed its rage and pain, brilliant bands of awesome yellow, black, and indigo rippled down its hide.

In a parting move, it had leapt high, hammered Talbot in the chest with both hind feet. Blasted him backward into the root mass. Despite the armor, the blow had stunned him. Without it, his chest would have been crushed. He'd barely crawled away from the roots that wiggled out of the ground and sent filaments out to discover the source of their disturbance.

I didn't even see the thing!

How could a creature that big have been so well camouflaged that he'd almost stepped on it?

He ran his fingers lovingly across the scarred and filthy armor. But for its protection he'd have been dead more than a dozen times over.

"Not that it helped Garcia," he whispered, remembering how the dangling creepers had shot down between the man's neck and the suit collar. "What toilet-sucking fools we were."

He shook his head as he stared off at the northern horizon. Up there—an impossible distance across that sea of forest—lay Port Authority. A place he'd never see again.

The power pack for his armor would never last that long. Without it to power the servos, he'd never be able to move, let alone use the suit's ventilation and cooling systems, or the heads-up display that allowed him to avoid hazards, see at night, and detect threats.

The towering thunderheads in the west had marched even closer. He had perhaps an hour before the first downpour.

Talbot's stomach growled, reminding him that he needed to shoot something with one of his last three bullets. Then, in the aftermath of the rains, he'd have to find fuel dry enough to cook his catch.

And when the last bullet was spent?

When the batteries refused to take even a residual charge?

"Donovan will win," he whispered dryly.

Closing his eyes, he wished himself back in Devonshire. Put himself in his parents' house. A place with clean water, dry linen bedding, and hot meals cooked on the stove. How he'd laughed with Brenda, his little sister. School days. He and his good friends: Matt, Riley, and Derek.

Cricket. He'd played cricket.

The bat's grip clung to his palms like yesterday's memory. He could see the ball as it was bowled, feel the swing, the vibrating crack.

Distant thunder broke the reverie.

Time to go. The charge was as high as it was going to get. By the time he'd donned the armor, climbed down off the rocky knob, the storm would have come.

Talbot stood, wondering—not for the first time—how Cap and Perez had crossed virgin forest without armor.

"You're a tougher, smarter man than I ever gave you credit for, Cap," he whispered as he clamped the carapace over his shoulders and watched his lower armor energize.

Then came the arms, and he stood.

He had just slung his rifle and reached for his helmet when he saw the faint hint of brown rising above the forest to the northwest.

But what would make . . . ? Shit on a shoe, it couldn't be.

He blinked, clamped on his helmet and chinned the magnification in his face shield. At the maximum twenty power, he couldn't believe what he was seeing: a column of smoke.

Someone was burning something.

Targeting on it, he hit the rangefinder.

Forty-four kilometers.

Talbot fixed the coordinates in the navigational system.

It couldn't have been a natural burn given how water-logged the forest was from the daily rains. As far as he knew, the only creatures on Donovan who kindled fires were humans.

Forty-four kilometers.

Maybe three days' travel if he didn't hit a major obstacle.

Assuming his armor power pack lasted that long.

And if it wasn't human? But turned out to be a volcanic vent? Some curious natural phenomenon?

"Then at least I'll have a warm place to die," he told himself as he started down the steep slope.

6

A piece of transparent plastic tarp had been taped over the hole broken in Talina Perez's living room wall. Once a couch had rested in the middle of the floor; after a raging quetzal had batted it through the wall, the couch's splintered remains had been hauled off. But not before one of the women had salvaged the upholstery for its fabric.

Nothing was wasted on Donovan. No telling if there'd ever be another ship from Solar System. And the textile industry in Port Authority remained in its infancy.

When she had awakened that morning, Talina had splurged, brewed a cup from her stash of coffee. Doing so was a reckless indulgence, given that she only had a few packets left. So far no one had found an equivalent to caffeine on Donovan.

"Please, by all the powers of the universe, let those coffee trees survive and flourish," she said, lifting her cup in a toast to the heavens. Then she savored the last, wonderful, rich swallow.

Setting her cup in the sink, she took another glance at the damage to the side of her dome. A reminder that no place on Donovan could ever be considered safe.

The quetzal had sneaked in past the shuttle field gate— apparently rode across town atop a shipping container— and managed to get inside her house undetected. Then it had taken Cap prisoner, used him as a shield in its attempt to kill her.

The plastic flapped back and forth in time to the breeze outside. A sort of reminder of futility.

The quetzal inside her coiled and tightened around her stomach.

"Yes, you piece of shit. That was your brother, lover, or whatever." She still wasn't sure which, but the quetzal that had invaded her house had come strictly for revenge. The only logical conclusion was that it had loved the one that now resided in Talina's gut.

"Close."

"Yeah, it came close, all right. But I killed it. Just like I killed you."

She shook her head, grabbed her jacket, and flipped it across her shoulders before she slung her rifle.

Stepping out the door, Talina looked up and down the street. She lived in the residential section. When Port Authority was originally laid out, the land had been cleared and surveyed. Polymer-fiber domes were then placed and inflated in nice orderly rows. Kitchen modules and walls were erected inside, and the whole thing sprayed with a catalyst that hardened into a shell. Quick and easy housing. The hacks at the time had called them "instant igloos."

Originally, according to plan, they'd been laid out in a perfect Cartesian grid. What Talina looked upon that morning as she stepped out into the street still echoed that original plan, but additions, sheds, ramadas, and small houses built of local stone and wood had created a jumbled clutter between and around the domiciles.

Call it a metaphor: The Corporation had arrived all tidy, ordered, and set in ranks. Then Donovan mucked it all up into a chaotic, but utilitarian, functionality.

Talina sighed, the coffee buzzing her brain.

She set off down the avenue, possessed as she was with a sense of weary frustration. How did a woman get her life back when an alien was lurking inside her? She could feel the beast, as if it were plucking emotional strings that sent vibrations of irritation through her.

She passed the education building where the children were locked away with their lessons. In addition to basic science, math, reading, history, social science, mining, mineralogy, agricultural science, and genetics, they were taught survival skills. How to cope with Donovan, recognize its plant and animal threats, and purify water of the heavy metals found in just about everything but rainwater.

The kids spent ten hours a day, six days a week, having their heads crammed full. On Donovan, only the smart survived.

Talina waved to Inga Lock as she approached the town's large-domed tavern. Inga was an imposing woman in every aspect: big-boned, with silver-blonde hair. Tall and busty. For whatever reason, she was sitting on the bench out front, thick arms crossed, enjoying the sunshine.

The large dome behind her hid the tavern's actual size. Mining colony, right? It had been dug out underground to accommodate more patrons.

"Hey, Tal," Inga called. "I'm tapping a new brew tonight. A heavy, thick, rich stout. You come try one."

"Wouldn't miss it."

The tavern's official name was The Bloody Drink—a moniker that derived from Port Authority's early, more sanguine days. Most folks called it Inga's. Behind it stood the two-story, stone-and-log building where Inga kept her brewery, distillery, and winery. The second floor had been partitioned into rooms she mostly rented out to Wild Ones who traveled into Port Authority to sell their harvest, hides, and the fruits of their various mining and prospecting ventures.

Just past Inga's came the assay office, the various small workshops, spare parts warehouse, the weapons factory, sawyer's, the hospital, and finally the admin dome where it backed onto the shuttle field fence on the east side.

Talina opened the door to the hospital and started down the hall. Donovan had one physician: Raya Turnienko, a forty-five-year-old Siberian woman with almond eyes, straight black hair, and a no-nonsense disposition.

As the population had dwindled, the back of the fifty-bed hospital had been converted into labs. The domain where the chemist Lee Cheng and his assistant Mgumbe, the exobotanist Hiro Iji, and the exozoologist Step Allenovich conducted constant research on Donovan's plants, animals, and microbial life.

If survival on Donovan depended upon a single person, it was Lee Cheng. In the years before *Turalon* finally popped into orbit, Cheng had been called upon more than once to save the day and the colony.

Cheng had somehow managed to synthesize everything from aspirin, antibiotics, psychotropic pharmaceuticals, anesthetics, salves, antivenoms, poisons, glues, and, well, just about everything under Capella's shining rays that humans found themselves out of and had to try and manufacture.

Nor were Cheng's days of weary toil over. Odds were good that *Turalon* would not make it back to Solar System. And even if she did, it would be at least another five years before The Corporation could possibly outfit and send a return vessel.

Donovan was on its own, abandoned. What both Port Authority and Supervisor Aguila had on hand would have to last them. What they didn't, they would have to try and fabricate. Like rubber. That was Cheng's latest challenge.

Talina made her way to Turnienko's office. Found it empty, and proceeded down the hall. Four of the remaining twenty hospital beds held patients: three were injuries; one was a guy named Mullony who was recovering from a fair fight stabbing at The Jewel.

"Tal?" Raya called from a doorway down the hall. "Down here. Cheng and I were just going over notes."

Talina averted her eyes as she passed the room where Cap had been murdered—as if, by not looking, she could somehow ignore that pain.

In the conference room, Cheng, Mgumbe, and Raya had already taken seats at the battered table. Talina's old friend, Hiro Iji, sat beside Cheng, eyes closed as he scanned something on his implants.

Only two of the three light panels still worked, and of those, one was flickering on its last legs. Apparently, like so many of Port Authority's failing parts, either replacement light panels hadn't been included in *Turalon*'s cargo, or the parts The Corporation had sent didn't fit, were the wrong model, or were somehow incompatible.

A holo projection glowed in the air above the table, displaying lines of data as well as a hovering three-dimensional molecule of some sort. The thing reminded Talina of a short, thick, three-strand section of rope.

"Have a seat," Turnienko told her.

Talina slipped into the chair, giving Mgumbe a nod and a smile. "How have you been?"

"Up to my ears in emergencies," the big African told her, flashing a tired smile. "You?"

"About the same."

Turnienko settled into the seat next to Talina and pointed at the molecule. "There's your beast."

"That's a quetzal genetic molecule," Cheng added as he fingered his chin and stared at it. "One taken from your blood. Deconstructed and catalogued. Fascinating, actually. We'd never have taken the time to unravel—"

"How do we get rid of it?" Talina interrupted what she knew was going to be a long and complex lecture on a quetzal's unique biochemistry that she'd never have a prayer of understanding.

Into the sudden silence, she added, "I want every trace of the quetzal gone. All of it. It's messing with my head, Lee. Fooling with my body. Granted, I'm stronger, more agile, and I can see and hear like never before, but this thing's talking to me. Screwing with my dreams. It did its best to kill me that night its partner got into my house."

She felt the beast smugly rearrange itself against her backbone, as if proud.

Cheng turned his dark eyes her way. "Tal, we're working on it. To be honest, we haven't a clue. Hell, we can't even explain how these molecules have managed to establish themselves in your system. Normally, foreign molecules trigger an immune response, T cells are activated. Antibodies lock on, triggering the body's defenses. Your white blood cell count isn't even elevated. We can't find any trace of a titer in your blood that would relate to the quetzal molecules."

Turnienko added, "Either they somehow manage to suppress an immune response, or they are recognized as either friendly or neutral."

"It sure as hell is *not* friendly. It tried to paralyze me when I was fighting with its mate." Talina narrowed an eye, remembering the incredible stab of pain her quetzal had sent through her body.

A sudden hot flash left her uncomfortable, and she could feel the quetzal's hand in it, as if the beast were reminding her of its presence.

Cheng nodded toward the molecule. "It is a really a fascinating molecule. The more we study it, the more amazing we discover it to be."

On the screen the three stands of the rope began to unwind and fray, each strand separating into fibers.

Cheng said, "Think of it as an analog to our DNA. It's the coding molecule for Donovanian higher life. Our DNA resolves into two strands, the Donovanian equivalent into three. We currently hypothesize that as happened on Earth, life here began in the seas. In Donovan's unique evolutionary history, some ancient adaptation selected for an ancestral morphology that consisted of three conjoined organisms. The adaptation was so successful that, like the vertebrates on Earth, they proliferated into the dominant phylum. Trilateral symmetry—that is, having three sides—isn't a handicap in a liquid environment. But when life moved on land, some lucky adaptation—perhaps a parallel to methylation in our own DNA—stifled ontological development of one of the TriNA strands. Allowed the development of what we perceive of as bilateral symmetry, which was the key to land adaptation and subsequent species radiation."

Iji spoke for the first time. "Though it doesn't look like it, the plants are still trilateral. That's why the branches are triangular. So are some of the stems. When we look closely at the physiology of the trees, they may have round trunks, but cross-section them, and you can see the three divisions in both the cellular structure and circulatory systems."

Mgumbe then said, "All of which makes our classification of 'plant' and 'animal' on Donovan suspect. Working out the cladistics for speciation is going to be fascinating and complex."

Iji shook a finger. "If 'speciation' even exists as we think of it in the Terrestrial sense."

"That's all nice and interesting, but what does it have to do with me?" Talina leaned forward.

"We think the quetzal you killed that day in the canyon purposely infected you." Raya crossed her arms. "Given the subsequent actions of its mate, it wanted to mark you for later revenge. Easy to track. Have you dripping scent, if you will."

At the hesitation in Cheng's eyes, she asked, "But?"

He shrugged. "It could have had other motives as well. We're just not sure."

"Lee, if it has other motives, I don't want to find out what they are. Get it the hell out of me."

"We're not sure how to rid your system of the quetzal TriNA, if we can call it that. We could filter some of it out of your blood, but we can't figure out how to flush it out of your tissues. And Talina, it is changing your body, slowly and surely. Vision, hearing, taste, musculature, they're incorporating Donovanian cells. But it's being done selectively. Why just those organs? Why not your hair, fingernails, skin?"

Turnienko added, "It's as if there's a logic behind what's being enhanced. My tests show no modification of your liver, spleen, or kidneys. What's going on in your brain? That, too, is targeted to the sensory areas of the brain, the language and imaging centers, but not the neocortex, the frontal lobes, any of the reasoning or memory centers."

"In short," Mgumbe added, "you're not going insane. Nor is it fooling with the personality centers. It's as if it wants to leave you, you."

"Why? It wanted me dead."

Three shrugs around the table were hardly encouraging.

"Tal," Cheng said wearily, "at this moment, there's nothing any of us can do to rid you of your parasite."

Iji added, "We're off the maps here. Tal, since you were infected with this thing, our knowledge of quetzals and their capabilities has grown exponentially. We now know that the beasts communicate, and how they do it. Even have a handle on how they think. Why this particular one chose you, who knows?"

"It wanted me dead," she repeated doggedly.

"But you say it talks to you?" Turnienko asked.

"Single words, almost like an impulse. Like a whisper in my mind. Or I'll have a flash of intuition. A 'don't go that way,' or maybe a 'danger is lurking there' feeling. Sort of like a sixth sense. It's not like we're discussing the philosophical meaning of the multiverse. Mostly it reacts to emotions."

"Somatic reactions rather than cerebral," Cheng noted, eyes going vacant as he made some sort of notation in one of his implants. "Makes sense. Any kind of limbic response releases adrenaline, lipids, and other compounds into the blood. Nerves are aroused. Those are old vertebrate responses, and we now know that quetzals communicate by means of chemistry as well as visual displays."

"Isn't this a lot to be hanging on one little molecule?" Talina asked.

"A molecule with a lot more storage space for information than you'll find in your own DNA," Cheng countered. "Remember, DNA codes for all of you, how to construct, maintain, and run your body, not to mention a host of innate behaviors. It took quantum computers to finally sort it all out, and years of research. There's no telling what's in that lump of quetzal TriNA. Which is a misnomer since it may be an acid, but it's not nucleic. Donovanian cells don't have a nucleus."

"I want it out," Talina insisted. "I want to be me again."

Cheng rubbed his eyes. "Mgumbe, Iji, Raya, and I are doing the best we can. Personally, I'd love to turn you into my very own fascinating research project. But I've got the whole damned colony asking me to perform miracles. Love and respect you as I do, your case is way down the list. Right now, rubber is at the top."

She read the exhaustion in his eyes. Nodded. "Yeah, Cheng, I know. I'm sorry."

She'd seen him before when she asked for a cure. Had seen the look in his eyes when he hadn't been able to formulate or manufacture antibiotics in time to save Mitch's life. Or medicines for the kids who succumbed to simple diseases. Cheng had suffered with them, empathetic, working without sleep until he finally unlocked enough secrets from Donovanian plant chemistry to synthesize a suitable replacement for something as simple as megacillin.

"Sorry, Lee." She leaned back and closed her eyes, aware of the beast huddled so smugly inside her.

"You can control it, right?" Mgumbe asked. "Didn't I read somewhere in your report that you just imagine yourself drowning, and the creature desists?"

"It panics," she told him. "Almost goes catatonic. Quetzals are totally terrified of drowning."

"I know how hard it is for you to hear this, Tal." Raya had on her "doctor" face—the one she adopted when she was telling someone they were dying. "But for the time being, you're stuck with your beast. I'm sorry, but you're our guinea pig, our test case. So we want to monitor you every couple of days. If it happened to you, it will happen to someone else."

"If it hasn't already among the Wild Ones," Iji retorted, a frown on his broad forehead.

"Great." Talina scowled down at her gut. "Just what I wanted to be: a monument to science."

"Beats being a partially digested corpse in a grave," Turnienko shot back. "Which is what you'd have been if you hadn't killed that creature whose remains are inside you."

7

The way Dan Wirth was looking at Trish just made her fume all the more. The guy had that smirking superiority virtually leaking from his plastic smile, as if to offset the steely set of his brown eyes. She sat across from him at one of the gambling tables in The Jewel. One hand rested suggestively on her pistol as she glared, the tabletop between them like a battlefield.

Dan Wirth had arrived aboard *Turalon*. A transportee. Sent by The Corporation to herd cattle. Since no one back in Solar System had heard that the last cow on Donovan died eight years ago.

Instead, Wirth had built The Jewel in an old core drill warehouse that Thumbs Exman owned up until the night he lost both the warehouse and his life in a card game with Dan Wirth.

Trish had never been able to prove that Wirth had been Exman's killer. Thumbs' body had been found in a farmer's field out beyond the fence.

Wirth was in his thirties; the three-month growth of curly brown hair atop his head barely masked his newcomer status. Trish had been there the day the guy stepped off the shuttle. She'd been instantly dazzled by his ladykiller smile, that sparkle in his eyes, and those charming dimples.

"*Quetzal*," Talina had warned her, seeing through Wirth's roguishly charming personality to the cold and calculating predator beneath. Talina had an eye for monsters, no matter how beguiling they might appear on the surface.

"That's all I can tell you, officer," Wirth now told Trish, his voice reeking of false sensitivity. "If I'd had the slightest clue that Jay and Mullony were going to get into it, I'd have had Art toss them out forthwith."

She glanced behind Wirth to where his enforcer, Art Maniken, sat smiling and playing with a long-bladed knife at the back bar. Art had been around. Arrived at Donovan on *Mekong* as a Corporate-trained accountant. He'd played at the farce for a couple of months, chafed under Clemenceau's stern hand. Not that there had been much accounting to start with. Then he'd deserted into the bush in the company of a couple of miners.

Art Maniken had thrived on the fringes of Port Authority. A natural hunter and tracker, he made his living shooting chamois and crest for the hides and meat, and trading them for as many wild nights in town as his credit would allow. Then he'd head back to the bush.

Art had taken to Dan Wirth the moment he met him, figured him for a kindred spirit. Tough, willing to kill on command, Maniken had found his niche. Wirth let Maniken indulge in enough sex, drink, food, and good times to keep the man lapdog loyal.

Trish refocused on Wirth. "This is the second guy Jay Cates has knifed. Back before *Turalon* spaced, he knifed a guy in Inga's. Killed him."

Wirth's smile might have been filled with sunbeams. "Officer Monagan, I can't deny a man access to my establishment just because he has a checkered past. That's half of Donovan. Even Shig. Didn't I hear he shot a man in the back of the head?"

"Tambuko. Yeah. We tried him for rape. Convicted him. That was an execution, Dan."

"Precisely." Wirth thrust out a finger as he leaned forward, a carnivorous grin on his full lips. His quetzal-hide vest flickered in the light. "Where's the moral prerogative? Let's not fool ourselves with hypocritical little games, Officer. We both know that some problems are best dealt with permanently, and quickly, for the good of the community. Heaven forbid a Tambuko, or let's say a Fig Paloduro, or an Abdul Oman be allowed to rile up the good citizens of Port Authority."

He spread his arms wide, head back as if in rapture, saying, "Praise be, how joyous the light that brings us comfort with the timely departure of black brigands of their like."

Then he was in her face again, eyes narrowed. "But Cates and Mullony, after a few drinks, get cross-wise over a game of cards. In a fit of passion, they both leap to their feet as they shout insults so dastardly and vile they're fit to shiver the dead, and lay into each other. Fair fight, no less."

He paused. "And for that, you're in here busting *my* balls? I'm the guy who had to clean the bloodstains off my floor, chairs, and tables."

"You always have the answer, don't you?" Trish took a deep breath and slapped the tabletop with an impotent hand.

"Officer Monagan," Wirth said, overacting his feigned weariness. "When you have proof of my craven disregard for the lives, wealth, and health of our beloved community, please, come clap me in irons. Until then . . . ?" He tilted his head as if to invite comment.

At that juncture, Allison Chomko walked over wearing a slinky and low-cut dress. Was this still the same woman Trish had known back in school? Allison was older—had been a couple of years ahead of Trish in school. She was second ship, arrived as a child, but still in that limited first group of children raised on Donovan. That Allison had been shy, dominated by a tyrannical father, and blushingly in love with Rick Chomko. A man she married within weeks of her father being killed by a bem out in the bush.

Allison had always been a tall beauty with pale-blonde hair and a complexion like fine porcelain. Now she looked absolutely gorgeous; the thick wealth of her hair fell over her shoulders, the skintight dress accenting every elegant curve in her perfectly proportioned body. Word on the street was that if a man could meet Wirth's price, Allison would take him back for an extended session of sex and drugs.

That Wirth had convinced Allison to prostitute herself was just another measure of how thoroughly she'd fallen under his spell.

Trish could see it in the woman's eyes, which looked wistfully vacant, dreamy blue, as though hallucinating some lovely thing beyond this world.

"Yes, my darling?" Wirth asked, grinning up at his prize.

"I have a man with a nugget, Dan." The dreamy smile widened. "Almost two ounces. He'd like to cash it out."

"Safe's open," Dan told her.

"Oh. It is?" A slight frown crossed Allison's smooth forehead, wrinkling her golden eyebrows. "I should have remembered."

Then she turned and crossed the floor in a perfectly balanced undulation, moving like a gentle wave among the tables. Every male eye in the place followed her.

"Is that how you turned her into a whore?" Trish asked acidly. "Drugged her?"

"Do I ask if the men in your bed are stimulating their erotic tendencies?" Wirth arched an inquiring eyebrow. "Or are we instituting a moral inquisition in Port Authority that I didn't know about?"

"The Allison that I used to know, that I grew up with—"

"Is an adult, making her own decisions. I'll assume the root of your jealousy stems from your inability to lure a man of any sort into your bed."

Trish wrinkled her nose. "God, you really piss me off sometimes, you maggot."

Wirth laughed from deep in his belly, the lady-killer grin back. "Not that it's any of your business, but the glassy look in Allison's eyes? She fell the other morning. Wrenched her back. Not enough to take her to Raya, but the painkillers keep her up and enjoying life."

Trish stood. "Yeah, right."

"Heard the good Supervisor shot a deserter down at the Corporate Mine the other morning."

"That's what Talina tells me." Trish paused. "You worried Aguila might be coming after some of the transportees you've taken on?"

Wirth leaned back in the chair and straightened his colorful vest. "Me? I'm not so worried. My people are making wages. The ones who hired on as indentured, I'll take good care of them. They came to me. Asked me for a contract. We've been all through that."

He studied her thoughtfully. "But, Officer, if you ever hear that slit's going to move on my people? You let me know. ASAP. Ricky tick."

Trish shrugged her rifle over her shoulder, glanced around at the gaming tables, the bar, the cage in the back of the room where a prospector was even now getting Port Authority coin for his gold nugget.

Wirth was making a fortune, had a couple dozen men and women working for him here, at Betty Able's brothel, and at the other "businesses" he'd managed to gain control of. Not to mention that he had his name on titles and deeds all across Port Authority.

"I'll think about it, Skull."

"All of which brings me to another problem. I've got missing people. Three of them. The ringleader's a fellow by the name of Petre Howe. Rita Valerie and Ashanti Kung are with him. They were crew on *Turalon*. Didn't want to space on what was sure to be slow suicide trapped in that bucket. Signed an indenture for ten years to work for me. So I sent them out to Tosi Damitiri's mine outside of town."

"Out at Tosi's place?" Trish shrugged. "You checked all the piles of quetzal crap out there for bits of uniform? Maybe the odd shoe?"

"I think they're all alive and well," Wirth said with a smile. "I just thought I'd take this opportunity to let you know that when I find them, it won't be murder, but an execution for contract violation. Call it a heads up. Just so you don't waste your time coming to interrogate me for the 'facts.'"

"Yeah. Sure. As if you gave a damn about facts." With that, she gave him a mock salute and headed for the door.

Behind her, Wirth broke out in amused laughter.

8

Talina sat on a large wheel rim. It had been unbolted from the hub on one of the haulers that had been brought planetside from *Freelander*. The original tire had been dismounted; the thing had cracked and deteriorated during the hundred and twenty-nine years in *Freelander*'s hold. The original synthetic rubber compound had barely lasted long enough to get the hauler across Port Authority and to the vehicle lot before coming apart in hard chunks.

Cheng had convinced some of the miners to sculpt a mold fitting the tire's specifications. They'd used local clay. Then they'd baked the mold sections into a hard ceramic.

The wire and cable had been stripped from the old tire's carcass and inserted in the mold. Then the various sections of the mold had been fitted together. Today was Cheng's first attempt at making a tire from his mundo-leaf rubber compound. Cheng's previous experiments had produced promising results; buffers, bumpers, and small parts were now being manufactured without issue down at the foundry.

A tire—especially one for a big, heavy piece of equipment like a hauler—posed a considerable challenge. Cheng had heated his compound in a giant mixing vat, and then used compressed air to inject the goo into his mold, watching the little relief holes to ensure that his mundo rubber completely filled the mold cavities, especially the critical bead area.

Now Cheng, Toby Montoya, and a host of people waited for the casting to cool.

"What if it really works?" Montoya asked as Cheng paced anxiously back and forth. "We can get back to really digging clay again. Fill up all those containers we've been emptying on the shuttle field."

Cheng spread his hands wide. "For all I know . . . assuming we can get it out of the mold in one piece . . . the tire might mount all right, then fall apart within the first hundred yards once a load is on it. People take tires for granted, but going all the way back to iron rims, a huge amount of know-how has gone into building one. This could just be the first step in a long and arduous learning process."

"That's Donovan," Talina whispered under her breath, then glanced up at the puffy clouds rolling in from the gulf. She knew the signs: rain this afternoon.

Trish came sauntering out of the gate, her jaw cocked, a glint in her eyes. She plodded her way to Talina's rim, unshouldered her rifle, and sat, hands braced on the warm steel. "How's it going?"

"We're waiting for the rubber to cool."

Trish looked at the hulking compressor, the heating vat where the compound was cooked and mixed. Then there was the injection piping, all of which had been fabricated from salvaged scrap and machinery. Call it a monstrous mishmash of a machine. A plumber's nightmare. The words *ugly*, *cobbled together*, and *junkyard crap* came to mind.

"Yeah, the engineers back in Solar System would wince, wouldn't they?"

Trish shook her head. "If this works we're going to be in need of a lot more mundo leaves. That's a dangerous flight south." Then she hopefully added, "Cheng really thinks he's got it figured out, huh?"

"Says the long molecules in the leaves straighten when they're heated and wind together when they cool, a lot like the sap they first made rubber out of back on Earth. The difference is that here we've got whole, endless forests of mundo trees."

"Yeah, and about a third of them have nightmares hiding up in their branches." Trish blinked, as if in revelation. "Wonder if I can interest Dan Wirth in going mundo tree hunting. Get him to check out a couple for us. You know, wander underneath, look up, and call, 'Hey! Any nightmares up there?' at the same time he's wondering what those tentacle things hanging down are all about."

"You pissed off because that soft meat, Mullony, got himself stabbed in a fight?"

Trish shook her head. "I could give a rat's ass if some Skull got cut over a poker game. But anytime something happens at The Jewel, at Betty's, or one of Wirth's 'enterprises' I want to know about it."

"Even Mullony said it was a fair fight."

"Yeah, yeah. It's just that it's Wirth. What a mud-crawling slug. He knows how to push my buttons. All holy and righteous. Smiling. And what really pisses me off is that he knows that I know how much I'm being played."

"You should have let me shoot him that day."

"Tal, you were going to pick him off from a rooftop. In the middle of the avenue. In the middle of the day. Bang. Blood and brains blown all over the street."

Talina gave Trish a grim smile. "If you hadn't stopped me, who would have known? One minute he's there, the next he's dead. Before anyone would have thought of the assay office roof, I'd have been gone."

"That's out-and-out murder."

"Yeah, and I still wonder if he wasn't the one who turned up Cap's medicine dial. Everyone who was in The Jewel that day told me Wirth and Cap faced off, said that they hated each other. That Wirth promised he'd be getting even."

"You really think he did it?"

Talina shrugged. "A lot of folks had it in for Cap there at the end. The Supervisor, Spiro, half the marines, Wirth, Paloduro, Oman, some of the rioters. But Wirth is right up there as a prime suspect."

Trish softly said, "Could have been something else, too, Tal. Did you ever think it could have been someone who didn't want to see him suffer anymore? The guy wasn't ever going to walk again. I wouldn't have put it past Cap to have begged, pleaded, to have someone open that line. Perhaps one of his marines who stopped in to see him? Might have even been Raya. Maybe Felicity. Even Shig would have done something like that, figuring it was karma or some such."

Talina rubbed her hands together, her hard palms rasping. She gave Trish a pensive sidelong glance. The young woman was one of the few survivors of the first generation. One by one, her childhood friends had been killed until only four of Trish's friends were left. And they'd married and moved away.

Then had come the tragic deaths of Trish's parents when Talina had stepped in, given the twelve-year-old a home, guidance.

But what did that kind of trauma do to a kid? Trish might have been a Donovan-hardened twenty, but deep down she wrestled with her own demons. She wouldn't think murder for a good cause to be a prohibited act.

Could Trish have . . . ? No. Nevertheless, Talina said, "I have nightmares thinking that whoever did it might have done it on my account. To save me from having to take care of a cripple for the rest of my life."

Trish stared up at the clouds, her jaws clamped tight, eyes squinted as if in pain. "If I could pick who did it, I'd pick Wirth. Didn't they do that back in the Middle Ages on Earth? Choose someone they didn't like to blame all the bad stuff on? Hang everything on his neck and then burn him at the stake? We could do that here. Start with Wirth."

Talina smiled warily, unable to scry out the meaning behind Trish's expression. "Oh, sure. And the next person on the list would be me. If you'll remember your history, they also burned witches. I'm the one who's possessed by an evil demon." She tapped her breast. "Got a quetzal running around in my blood and bones. Giving me visions. Talking to me. Tell me that's not witchery."

Trish playfully punched Talina in the shoulder. "You're right. I should have let you shoot him that day."

Wirth had been centered in Talina's optical sight as she braced her rifle on the assay office roof. Just the slightest pressure . . .

The image broke, and she sighed.

"By the way," Trish said. "He's missing three people. *Turalon* crewmen that deserted. Wirth hid them out at Tosi Damitiri's mine. Asking around, I've learned that hard rock mining didn't sit well with them. They want out."

"I can't imagine having Tosi for a boss. The guy's a mess, but he's got a paying claim out there. Must be nice having that many people making hole for him. But what's Wirth say?"

"Says he'll execute his runners when he finds them. Not murder, mind you, but execution. He quoted both Shig's execution of Tambuko and Aguila's execution of Cabrianne as legal precedents."

Talina shot her a sidelong look. "Who the hell does he think he is?"

"The guy who got rid of Paloduro and Oman for us." Trish's expression pinched. "No questions asked."

"Suck a slug, what did we get into?"

"Trouble. Tal, trust me. This is just beginning."

Cheng bent over the ceramic tire mold, took a temperature reading with his thermometer. "All right, people. Let's see if we've really made a tire."

"And if you have," Talina called, "what's next?"

"Got to figure out how to refabricate power modules for these big hauling trucks," Tyrell Lawson called from where he was undoing the fasteners for the tire mold. "If we can make the seals and tires, all we have to figure out is how to get the power packs to take and hold a charge again. The motors are essentially brand-new. Do that, and we've got a whole new fleet of vehicles."

One thing at a time.

That could have been Donovan's motto.

Today a tire.

Tomorrow a power pack.

The day after that, I find Cap's killer. And when I do . . .

S itting in her chair at the end of Inga Lock's long bar, Talina nursed her mug of stout. Inga reserved the mug especially for Talina. It was one of the first crafted by Tori Ashan when he set up his glassworks a decade back. He had only gotten better with practice, and the demands Port Authority made upon his time were legion. Even better, Pete Morgan's hydrocarbon well was not only producing crude oil, but natural gas, the first of which had been bottled, compressed, and delivered to Tori. The quality of his work, so Tori claimed, was about to skyrocket with his new source of heat.

As Talina slipped her fingers along the mug's surface, it acted as a reminder that, as filled with trouble as her days were . . .

"Mind if I join you?" Shig's voice caught her by surprise.

She'd completely blocked the tavern's sights and sounds. A measure of her level of distraction. With Shig's interruption, it all came crashing back: the raucous laughter; the banging of cups, mugs, and glasses; the rising and falling babble of conversation at the heavy chabacho wood tables; or the scraping of a bench or chair.

Inga, at that moment, was writing a charge under Tyrell Lawson's name on her big board at the far end of the bar. Out in the main room, perhaps fifty people were clustered here and there among the tables, most dressed in chamois hide with quetzal vests and boots, various styles of hats pulled back on their heads. And mixed in were the soft meat who'd arrived on *Turalon*. At least the ones that had evaded Aguila's net or had found employment suitable to their contracts before the Supervisor had been abandoned by *Turalon*'s departure.

Inga's served as the social heart of Port Authority. The admin dome might have been the brain, and the cafeteria the stomach, but here Talina sat in the beating center.

Shig climbed onto the chair next to hers and shrugged his quetzal-hide cape off. She could see it was spotted with water.

"Raining out there?"

"Just started," he told her, propping elbows on the polished chabacho wood bar. "Still light and misty. Perfect for the crops. Trish is making her rounds. Ensuring that the compound is buttoned down tight and the guards are alert. Night like this, well, it's a quetzal kind of night. They'll be hunting."

"Haven't had a sighting since I killed that last one. Three months. Call it a record."

He nodded, lifted a finger when Inga glanced his way. Then he turned his soft brown eyes on Talina. "You've been unusually quiet these last couple of days."

"I took a deserter back to Aguila, and she shot him. The combined brains of Turnienko, Cheng, and Mgumbe tell me I've got to get used to this beast in my blood. And all these months on, I haven't solved Cap's murder. What's not to love?"

Shig smiled and inclined his head as Inga brought him his half glass of wine.

"New vintage, Shig," the bluff woman told him. "Small batch, special. I've had it buried in the cellar for a year now. What do you think?"

Shig lifted his glass, sipped, and nodded. "Most agreeable. Hardly a trace of that acidic aftertaste. Gentle on the tongue. If wine were a sutra, this would be the White Lotus."

"Oh, great," Talina growled. "How's it feel to know you're brewing Buddhist wine, Inga?"

"The White Lotus sutra is Hindu," Shig corrected mildly.

Inga threw her hands up, laughing all the way as she retreated down the length of her kingdom.

Shig glanced sidelong at Talina as he set his glass down.

"What?" she demanded. "Let me guess. Given the mood I'm in, and since I brought it up, you're going to give me a lecture on overcoming selfishness, transforming my mind, and achieving nirvana like a good little Hindu?"

Shig winced, as if in pain. "Nirvana is a Buddhist concept."

"Whatever."

"My, but we're testy tonight. I heard that Cheng's experiment was a success. That he not only molded mundo-leaf rubber, but was able to mount and inflate his tire on a rim."

"Yep. But let's see if it's still holding air come morning, shall we? And then, if it is, if it will roll all the way to the clay pit and back."

Shig nodded, turning his wine glass. "Tal, there are times I wish I could step inside and massage your soul with perfumed oils. I understand that you are our warrior, but for the moment, you are drowning in *krodha*." He paused. "*Krodha* has its uses for a warrior, but when it dominates your *dharma* it will destroy you."

She squinted an eye. "Enough with the Buddhism, all right? I get your point."

"If you did, you'd know that was Hindu. It's your dharma to be our strength, passion, and spirit. That's who you are. You've lost your *Tao*. That's your way, or path. Correct words state the contradiction. And your Tao is in many ways, our way."

"Are all Hindus psychotic?"

"Absolutely not. And the secret to the Tao, which is related to both Hindu and Buddhist philosophies, is in many ways the unity of opposites."

Talina sucked down a gulp of her stout. "Why do I constantly wonder if you were dropped on your head as a baby? And why do I think it was a lot more than once?"

Shig's smile grew into a grin. "Because at heart I follow the path of a bodhisattva. A teacher. And one who seeks to alleviate the miseries of others by helping them to find their way. For the moment, you've stumbled off the path. Alone as you are—you cannot strike back at the source of the pain. Can't kill it so that you can get back on your path of being the invincible Talina Perez."

"Shig, if I shoot you dead, right here, you're not, like, going to be reincarnated in the next baby born and continue to irritate me, right?"

"It's a distinct possibility. Nothing I can think of in physics would preclude it. Reincarnation is a major tenet in the religions to whose precepts I adhere."

"Well, shit."

"I just figured I'd come remind you that you're so busy

staring at the impenetrable forest, you can't see the trees closest to you. Let alone the fact that many of them are your close friends who would offer shelter as you seek to find refreshment and rest in their shade."

Talina granted him a slight smile. "You're forgetting. If Buddha had lived on Donovan, he'd have plopped himself down under the Bodhi tree . . . and as soon as he lost himself in meditation, the roots would have tangled around, crushed him, then slowly digested his corpse."

Again, Shig winced. He lifted his wine and sipped daintily.

Talina reached out, laying a gentle hand on his shoulder. "Okay, reality aside, I realize I'm just being crabby. Part of it comes from the new people. A lot of them don't want to be here. They'd a hell of a lot rather be back in Solar System, and they're delighted they're not sitting in *Turalon,* counting down for two years to see if they pop back into solar orbit, or if they're lost. Talk about a living hell. But, really and truly, they don't want to be on Donovan either."

"They're still locked away in culture shock." With ultimate precision, Shig replaced his wine glass on the bar.

"Yeah. Makes it harder with Wirth and his people stirring the pot. He's the moral equivalent of my quetzal, but he's infecting the whole of Port Authority."

"The serpent we've nurtured to our breast. We've had this argument about ethics before, along with the ensuing discussion of what our moral values should be in a free society."

"At what point do libertarian values become nihilistic chaos, Shig?"

"At what point do *your* values become the arbitrator for the behavior of others, Tal?" Shig spread his hands wide. "We could, of course, create a direct democracy; unleash the tyranny of the majority to dictate its will upon the minority. Direct democracy, you will recall, is the worst form of government ever implemented and to which humanity has ever been subjected." He smiled, lifting a finger. "Except, of course, for all the others."

"We've got a population of roughly four hundred people in Port Authority." Talina rocked her mug of stout back and forth. "Aguila's got another three hundred down at

Corporate Mine. And who knows how many Wild Ones are scattered around out there in the bush? Maybe another five hundred? Seems to me we ought to be able to figure things out between ourselves with a such a small population."

"Not much to bet the future of the species on, is it?"

"Not with Donovan against us."

"But is it? Donovan I mean," Shig mused. "Is it Western or Eastern?"

"Excuse me?"

"The Western religions, Judaism, Christianity, Islam, all worship the same books, with some exceptions the same holy figures, the same roots of tradition, and the same god. Yet they are mutually exclusive. Often to the death. Sometimes just over the interpretation of the tradition itself.

"In the east, Taoism, Buddhism, Hinduism, Confucianism can all become mixed and blurred. Hopelessly syncretic. Maybe that's what that quetzal in your gut is all about. Donovan's way of trying to blur with us, seeking what it can use, and in the process, creating something new."

The quetzal stirred down beneath Talina's sternum.

"Oh, screw you, you piece of shit," she growled down at it.

"Got a reaction, did I?" Shig smiled. "Perhaps that shot was not so far off the mark." He paused. "What does it tell us about quetzals, when yours reacts to my words? Does it monitor your interactions that closely and intimately?"

Talina lifted a suggestive eyebrow. "Now you know why I'm really anxious to get this damn thing out of me."

"I think I'm getting more than a glimmer. But consider this: We're born, live, and die entirely alone."

"I wouldn't go quite that far."

"Oh, shared thoughts with anyone lately? Entwined your soul around Trish's? Found humor in her innermost thoughts? Or she yours?"

"Don't be ridiculous."

"I'm not. My question is: What if that's how life on Donovan experiences normality? The sharing of molecules, essences of beings, exchanging and interacting? Multiple personalities inhabiting the same tissue?"

"What keeps it from becoming chaos?"

"What keeps our libertarian society from degenerating into the same? Perhaps Donovanian biology smacks of an eerie similarity to human society?"

Talina made a face, unsettled at how much his words had mirrored some of her most secret fears. "If you ask me, you really were dropped on your head too many times as a baby."

"Perhaps, but you'd be surprised how much sense can get knocked into a person's soul."

"If this is true, why didn't Raya, Cheng, or Mgumbe think of it?"

"Scientists are into understanding the intricacy of process. How things work. Philosophers, however, are obsessed with understanding meaning. The bigger picture, if you will."

"And you think this is the bigger picture?"

Shig took another sip of wine. "It could be. But then, I'll bet you never considered the lessons the floor learned when it was being hit by my head, either."

10

The *Turalon* and *Freelander* cargos had made a remarkable difference for Port Authority. Granted, most of it— on the first inspection at least—was useless. What good was a condensation module for a 75-16-A566 Series II atmospheric evaporation unit? Especially when no one on Donovan had ever laid eyes on a 75-16-A566 Series II unit? Like so much of the equipment and supplies, they were for devices or machines that had vanished with the previous six ships.

Not that the Corporate planners and procurement officers were entirely to blame. They were more than thirty light-years away. Beyond communication, on the other side of a minimum four-year round trip. The Corporation's planning for Donovan went back ten to fifteen years. They had laid out the strategy to exploit the planet, designed and built the equipment, produced and dispatched it, only to have most of it disappear "outside" the universe when the ships inverted symmetry just beyond Jupiter's orbit.

From the various bits and pieces, however, and given the native ingenuity of people like Sheyela Smith—their best electrical technician—they'd been able to adapt, concoct, jury-rig, and somehow cobble together enough disparate parts to reactivate the motion detectors on the perimeter fence. Another fortunate bit of luck had come in the form of light bulbs for the tower lights. Once again, the fields beyond Port Authority's defensive fence and moat were illuminated at night.

For Trish—born and raised on Donovan as she was— that didn't mean squat. She'd been six when her best friend, Jeanne, had been eaten. Within a month, her father had vanished in the forest. A slug had killed her friend, Marco, when she was seven. She lost her mother at twelve. And of the sixteen children her age she'd started school with, only four were left.

Donovan was a harsh taskmaster. And even more to the point, she wasn't about to let the rest of her team bathe in a sense of false security. Just because they had their surroundings awash in light didn't mean that quetzals wouldn't still try and infiltrate the town.

Not after what they'd learned from Talina's latest attacker. The beast had planned, hidden among the shipping containers, eaten four people, and ridden past the shuttle field gate *in the cargo*. Only then had it managed to somehow make its way to Talina's, undetected, and attempt to kill her.

No one had anticipated that quetzals had that kind of intelligence. How many other forms of Donovanian life had they underestimated?

Walking down the main avenue, Trish stared up at the night sky, where patchy clouds blacked out large swaths of the stars. The evening felt cool, damp, with the promise of more rain.

Having checked each of the perimeter positions, she had all of her sentries on their toes. Now she passed through the residential area, flashing her light and thermal detector this way and that, knowing from hard-earned experience which places quetzals instinctively tried to hide themselves.

How had Talina's attacker—over five meters in length, two meters tall at the shoulders—managed to reach Talina's house in midday, no less?

That had puzzled her for months now.

Even as she brooded over the problem, she illuminated Talina's dome with her light. She climbed the steps and checked the latch. Locked. As it should be.

A gust of breeze flapped the plastic taped over the hole in the dome's side.

Stepping down, Trish rounded the curve and shone her flash on the damaged wall. It took a lot of force to break the duraplast coating on a dome. Talina's quetzal had knocked quite a hole in . . .

The plastic flapped again, clearly displaying a long slit.

"Bite my damned ass," she growled, then accessed her com. "Two Spots, you there?"

"Gotcha, Trish. What's up?"

"Got a cut in the plastic they taped over Talina's broken wall." She stepped close to inspect the long cut.

"Quetzal? Should I sound the alert?"

Something about it . . .

"No." She fingered the cut. "This is too clean, sliced by something really sharp. Quetzal claws would have ripped it unevenly. My guess is human."

"Roger that. You want back up?"

"Not yet. But stay on the line while I check it out."

Thievery was uncommon in Port Authority. They really didn't have enough people—not to mention that everyone pretty much knew who owned what.

She backed around to the door, drew her pistol, and eased up the steps. With a finger, she input Talina's security code. The lock clicked, and Trish let the door swing open. Her thermal scan suggested the room was unoccupied, and she hit the lights.

Opulence wasn't a common theme when it came to personal quarters in Port Authority. Yvette's place was about as fancy as domestic furnishings got, and it was mostly handwoven rag rugs, lacy curtains, and embroidery. As tough and cutting as Yvette's personality was, who'd have ever suspected she was into crocheting doilies?

Talina's home was as Spartan as a place could get. Just the essentials: breakfast bar with four stools, an easy chair with reading light. Stack of books on the floor. Empty spot where the couch had been. Dirty dishes sat in the sink, counter clean.

And to her immediate right . . .

"Shit." She accessed her com. "Tal? You have your bolt-action rifle with you? You loan it out?"

"Negative on that, Trish."

"It's not in the rack."

"Roger that. Watch your ass, Trish. I'm on the way."

Trish flipped the pistol's safety off, every sense on alert.

"Just hold it right there, Officer Perez," a voice called from the darkness beyond the bedroom door. "I've got this gun pointed right at your chest. We're not here to hurt you. So, please. Don't make us. We just want to talk. Now, holster your pistol."

Trish took a deep breath and slipped the pistol back into its holster. "So talk."

She watched as a dirty man in overalls stepped out, the rifle held awkwardly in his hands. Two women, one red-headed and freckled, the other slim and dark-skinned, emerged behind him. Like the man, the women were dressed in worn overalls that didn't fit so well. They looked hungry and lean. Trish could see ground-in dirt in their hands, the corners of their eyes, and the lines where the skin on their necks creased.

"I don't recognize any of you." Trish kept her hands open, palm out.

"We came off *Turalon*." The man told her warily. "Didn't want to space back. So we signed an indenture with that scum-sucking Dan Wirth."

"Ah, you're his missing indentures." Trish filled in the pieces. "You're working Tosi Damitiri's claim about twenty klicks out."

"Yeah," the dark woman said. "And we're not going back."

"Thought you signed a contract." Trish cocked her head.

The man's expression almost broke, eyes pleading. "You don't know what it's like. We're not animals!"

"Hey, okay, ease down." Trish made a patting motion with her hands. "Just tell me your side of the story."

"There's work, and there's work," the slim black woman told her softly. "Petre, Rita, and I, we're willing to work. But not fourteen hours a day. Not in conditions like Damitiri has us living in. We get fed crap. We get locked in a shed at night to sleep on mats on the floor. We think Ngomo's dead. Got his leg crushed in a rock fall. Damitiri said he was taking him to town. So he locked us in the shed, was gone for two days, came back hungover to beat hell, and said Ngomo died at hospital."

"Two Spots?" Trish accessed her com. "Check with Raya, see if some guy named Ngomo was admitted for a broken leg?"

"Roger that."

"So, what are you trying to do here?"

"Officer Perez," the redheaded woman, Rita, began, "we want a hearing, as is our right, to declare our contract with Dan Wirth to be null and void."

"You signed this under duress? He had a gun to your heads? Threatened you?"

"As good as," the thin black woman almost spat. "It was that or die in space aboard *Turalon* or *Freelander*. And when it comes to *Freelander* we'd have rather been spaced than set foot on that dead man's bucket again."

"You signed the contract," Trish told them softly. "You've got your copies?"

All three reached into breast pockets, producing folded papers. "Right here."

"And there's more," Petre told her. "You don't know Dan Wirth like we do. We demand a hearing, but more than that, we want to be alive to attend it. We also—as is our right—demand legal representation. We want protective custody and a lawyer. Now."

"Look, we don't really have a contract lawyer."

"Well, who hears your legal cases, Officer Perez?" the black woman asked.

"What's your name?" Trish lifted an eyebrow.

"Ashanti Kung. Atmospheric Tech, third class. This is Rita Valerie, Engineering Tech, third class. And this guy is Petre Howe, Hydroponics Specialist, third class." Ashanti stepped forward, reaching out with callused hands.

"Officer Perez, we're counting on you."

"Why'd you come here?"

"Because, ma'am, you're the only person on Donovan that Dan Wirth fears. If you can't protect us, you just go ahead and shoot us down right here."

Trish wrinkled her nose. "Officer Perez, huh? Well, if you think I'm Talina Perez, I'd say you are off to a rocky start, 'cause you're not exactly blowing my skirts up with your competence."

"Then, who are you?" Rita asked uneasily.

"Officer Trish Monagan." Dan Wirth might not fear her like he did Talina, but she could throw a couple of obstacles in the bastard's way. After all, Wirth had said he'd murder these three for crossing him. Maybe this was a chance to pay the son of a bitch back. So she took the out-standing option, saying, "You three are under arrest for criminal trespass, destruction of private property, and theft of a weapon."

At the shock in their eyes, she added, "All of which means that you must be placed in protective custody, under Talina Perez's control, until such time as all complaints are satisfied."

She smiled and extended her hand. "Now, do you want to give me Talina's rifle so we can eventually drop the charge of theft?"

11

If there were a nerve center in the town of Port Authority, it would have been the multifunctional, rectangular, four-by-ten-meter room just off the admin dome's central corridor. Dominated by a single sialon-topped table surrounded by mismatched plastic chairs, the conference room was contiguous to the communications center and radio room, next door to the armory, and across the hall from Shig's and Yvette's offices and the records and documents room.

It even had a window—though the sills tended to seep during heavy rains, and a slight tinge of green terrestrial mold now crept down the duraplast wall to mark the moisture's path.

As a measure of the serious nature of the meeting, a pot of the precious coffee had been brewed by Millicent Graves, who ran the cafeteria. It steamed in the center of the table as Talina stared out the smudged window at the morning beyond.

Capella stood a couple of hand widths above the eastern horizon, rays of light beaming through the patchy clouds. Beyond the perimeter fence, the shuttle field still sported mud puddles from a heavy predawn downpour.

Pamlico Jones and his crew were already at work, sorting through shipping containers. To the north, empty containers had been stacked seven high until they resembled a drunken ziggurat. In the coming years, they would be filled with clay and the rare-earth elements that made Donovan so remarkably valuable.

The work would all be done on faith, of course. Faith that *Turalon* would make a successful return to Solar System, that The Corporation would eventually send another ship.

The last time, that had taken a full seven years.

How long would it be this time? Especially if *Turalon* vanished into inverted symmetry, never to return. Never to report Donovan's fantastic riches to the scum-sucking Board of Directors.

Behind her at the table, Shig yawned audibly; as Talina turned, Yvette entered the room, a notepad under her arm, her coffee cup dangling by its handle where she'd hooked it with a finger.

The clutter of maps, containers, and chairs shoved against the walls didn't so much as distract Yvette as she set her notepad down and dipped a cup of coffee from the steaming pot in the middle of the table.

"So, we're pitched headfirst into another mess," Yvette muttered as she parked her tall frame in a chair and rubbed her hatchet of a face. She fixed her green eyes on Tal and asked, "Couldn't Trish have just shot them as burglars and saved us the shitstorm this is going to cause?"

"Trish is funny that way," Talina said. "She might be the best marksman on Donovan, but she's squeamish about blowing holes in people. I hope that doesn't turn out to be a long-term character defect."

"It just might," Trish called as she burst through the door. "It's a terrible failing I have. I like to know who I'm shooting, and for what reason."

Talina watched her friend toe a chair out before flopping into it as if collapsing. Trish's faintly freckled face had a drawn look, and her shoulder-length auburn hair was unkempt, in need of a wash. She flashed her gaze around the table, taking in Shig, Yvette, and Talina, where she stood before the window. Dark circles and puffy eyes added to her fatigued appearance.

"If they'd been anyone but Wirth's slaves, I'd have slapped them in cuffs and sent them back."

"They are indentured, not slaves," Shig reminded, stabbing a finger into the middle of the contract copies that lay on the table before him. "Ten years? What were these people thinking?"

Talina stepped over and used her cup to dip out coffee before seating herself next to Shig. "They were thinking that spacing back to Solar System on *Turalon* was a death sentence."

"And to escape the fire," Trish added, "they sold their souls to Dan Wirth. Jumped into his frying pan, condemning themselves to be worked to death, crushed in mining accidents, and slowly starved."

Yvette asked, "But Tosi's in charge of them, right? How does that work?"

Trish rubbed her face, leaned forward, grabbed a cup, and scooped out coffee. She sniffed it, eyes closed, expression heavenly, then sipped. "God, I needed that. Okay. Here's how it works: Tosi bet his holdings against a throw on the craps table. Lost, of course. Idiots never learn, and Tosi's never been mistaken for bright.

"So Wirth gets the claim, but gives Tosi back fifty-one percent interest. Why? Because Wirth is no one's fool. As long as Tosi's claim is producing, Wirth wants Tosi working it, and not going out to find another one. And, it's rich enough that Wirth wants to increase production. Just as Wirth is wondering how he can get more bodies into the mine, in walk four deserters from *Turalon*."

"So what's the problem?" Talina asked. "A lot of people work in mines. It's what Donovan is all about."

Trish arched a thin brow. "Not all of them are treated like slaves, locked in a shed, forced to sleep on pallets on the floor. Nor are they working fourteen-hour days. Raya's just finishing up with the physical, but we're talking underweight and malnourished."

Trish smiled humorlessly. "And then there's the matter of the missing man, Ngomo Suma. Their story is that a big chunk of rock crushed his leg. Tosi supposedly flew him in to Raya, but Ngomo never got here. Tosi told them that Ngomo was here, healing."

"Where's Tosi now?" Shig asked, thoughtful eyes on the contracts before him.

"I don't know." Trish stared down into her coffee. "Out at his claim? Confabbing with Wirth? Searching for his lost slaves? I thought I'd better give you an update before I brought him in."

"What do these runaways want?" Yvette asked.

"They want their contracts and indenture declared null and void. They want to get away from Tosi and Wirth, but they're scared to death that Wirth is going to have his goons kill them before they can make their appeal."

"I wouldn't put it past him," Talina agreed. "He's not

going to take this lying down. He'd rather they ended up as corpses than freed of their contract obligations. First, he can't allow that precedent to be established, and second, he won't stand for the loss of face. It will make him look weak, and as I know Dan Wirth, he'd burn Port Authority to the ground before he'll let that happen."

"It would appear that our Mister Wirth has once again placed us in an intolerable position." Shig touched his fingertips together, eyes thoughtful. "Indenture cannot be allowed to become slavery. Nor can the state be given the power to intervene in contracts entered into by consenting adults."

Shig tapped the contracts again. "And, given the wording here, all parties freely admit to participating in these instruments without duress."

"They were scared to death," Trish countered. "And this is Wirth that we're dealing with."

"That is always the problem." Yvette's expression betrayed distaste. "Just when people are on the verge of a workable system that guarantees liberty, along comes a psychopath to exploit it for his own gain."

She glanced at Shig. "It is inevitable, you know. We have to intervene."

"And start the process of authoritarianism?" Talina asked. "Loosen that first stone from the top of the hill, and it will gain momentum until government's first and consuming purpose is the perpetuation of ever more government."

Shig asked, "I am wondering if there is a way to handle with this without making a scene. Perhaps deal with Wirth privately, seek a way that allows us to remove . . ."

"Get out of my way!" came a cry from down the hallway, and within seconds, Dan Wirth—dressed in a black tailored business suit—bustled through the door.

Talina's first response, as always with Wirth, was to drop her hand to her pistol and flick the retaining strap off. She felt that frothing of rage the man always incited deep down inside her.

Her quetzal—for the most part quiet this morning—now took notice. She could feel her senses warming, an involuntary charge running through her muscles. Her vision sharpened, and her hearing became acute. Energy began to charge her muscles.

Well, at least when it came to Dan Wirth, she and the beast could agree on something.

"Where are my people? I want them. Now." Wirth stormed up to the table, fists knuckle-down as he placed them on the sialon. He glanced from person to person, and fixed on Trish Monagan. "You did this, didn't you? Connived and set this up?"

"Sorry, Dan. Caught them breaking and entering, destruction of personal property, trespass, and theft of a firearm."

"Where?"

Trish inclined her head toward Talina. "At Officer Perez's private residence. They slit their way through the plastic to gain entry. No way I could turn them over to you with those kind of charges standing against them."

Wirth smiled, a curious light dancing behind his disconcertingly soft eyes. "Ah, yes. But what else could we expect? Very well. What are the fines?" He was reaching for his belt pouch as he spoke.

"No fines," Shig said amiably. "This isn't The Corporation. Nor are we Corporate officers who could impose a fine. Actually, until you forced us into a cash economy, we hadn't thought in those terms. Rather, transgressions were accommodated by different forms of restitution, such as labor, a share of the crop, a percentage of mineral, or what have you."

Wirth's smile pulled his lips tight. "But of course." He clapped his hands and, with a flourish, pulled out a chair. Seating himself, he leaned forward, expression intense. "So, good people of mine, let us bargain. Now, the fine and upstanding Officer Perez—having suffered the grievous personal injury of having her personal quarters disturbed, and her irreplaceable plastic violated—is in need of restitution. What can I do to be accommodating, given the heinous disregard shown for life and limb by these miscreants in my employ?"

Talina narrowed an eye, fully aware that Wirth never once made eye contact.

"I mean it," he declared passionately. "I won't have my

people acting irresponsibly and soiling my good name. By all means, let us bring this to a satisfactory conclusion here. Now."

"So far they have only been charged," Yvette told him, voice deliberate. "They've asked for a hearing."

"Bah." Wirth waved it away. "They were caught red-handed, yes? They're my people. I plead guilty on their behalf. In redress for the *good* Officer Perez's personal injury"—he inclined his head her way—"I'll make sure to have her wall fixed permanently and professionally. Not to mention the replacement of any articles which might have been misused in her house."

Talina's jaw muscles began to cramp as she ground her teeth. She felt her pulse settling into the slow and intense beat that presaged violence on her part. "They have a right to a hearing."

As if he could sense the magnitude of her growing rage, Shig lifted a calming hand in her direction. "Unlike The Corporation where bureaucrats make decisions based on ruthless authority and whatever interpretation of facts they deem sufficient for their causes, your people ask for a fair hearing. We will give it to them."

"They're *my* people, bound and contracted," Wirth countered. "I withdraw their request."

Shig lifted the contracts. "Nowhere in these documents does it say that they have surrendered their legal right to self-determination over to you. Only that they will labor for your sole benefit for ten years. In short, you have the right to utilize their labor, and to determine where they labor. Nothing more."

Wirth's smile turned radiant, his posture softening and the lady-killer dimples in his cheeks forming. It didn't matter how many times Talina had seen it, the way Dan Wirth could just dial on that boyish, almost innocent charm, amazed her. It always took a moment to remember that it was an act, that beneath it the man remained a cold-blooded reptile.

"You're right," Wirth agreed. "As soon as you've charged them, arraigned them, whatever we do here, I'll have one of my people drop by to pick them up. No reason you should have to keep them under lock and key until the hearing. I'll deliver them to whatever place, I assume Inga's, whenever you want them there."

Yvette said, "Why bother waiting?" She glanced at Trish. "Have Two Spots put out a call on the radio. Set a meeting for eighteen hundred hours at Inga's. Announce that we've been asked to make a decision on criminal charges against three *Turalon* crewmen, and at the same time, announce that they, in turn, want to challenge a contract of indenture against Dan Wirth."

"What?" Wirth slapped a hand to the table, his charm vanished in an instant, the serpent beneath baring its fangs.

"It's their right to challenge a contract," Shig said mildly. "However, unless you did something fraudulent, or they did, I doubt they have a legal leg to stand on." Shig paused. "You didn't force them to sign under duress, did you?"

"Do you think I'm an idiot?" Wirth asked in a cold whisper.

"Anything but," Talina told him, leaning forward so that he had to meet her eyes this time. "But we're holding that hearing. All charges will be heard, all matters brought to an *impartial* conclusion. You have my word."

"Your word?" Wirth seemed to have gone unnaturally calm. And all the more dangerous for it.

"My word," Talina repeated. "Just like you have my word that if anything happens to any one of those three people between now and six tonight, I will hold you personally responsible for murder. And I will kill you dead."

12

"That's thirty-five hundred degrees," Aurobindo Ghosh, the engineer, shouted over the furnace roar. The cramped control room barely had enough space for the three people crowded into its confines.

Kalico Aguila nodded as she watched the holographic readouts glowing on the control panel before her. Separate screens displayed visuals of various workings as the smelter finally hit operating temperature.

On another screen, a loader began feeding ore into the bin-shaped hopper. That in turn gravity-fed to a conveyor that dropped the crushed rock into the furnace.

Heated to thirty-five hundred degrees Celsius, the rock melted, running down through ceramic grating to sonic agitators which turned the liquid to mist. Centrifuges then separated the elements based on atomic weight, spinning off the heaviest first until only the lightest remained to be vacuumed away. Electromagnetic fields then further separated the metals, diverting them into separate channels that were subjected to various electrical charges that continued to sort the metals into finer and purer streams.

At the end of the process, compressors filled tanks with gases, while the liquid metals poured into molds. By mixing the flows, various alloys could be tailored to order. The tailings were dumped to cool. Afterward they could either be carted off as waste or further processed for their elements.

All in all, the smelter was a masterpiece of engineering and design—assuming she and her people could keep the complicated piece of equipment running. The technicians trained specifically for its operation had died on *Freelander*. Kalico's two engineers were making it up as they went along.

On the monitors she watched as the first streams of white-hot metals emerged from the big machine's convo-

luted innards and began running down channels into bar
molds.

"By all that's holy and wonderful," she whispered under
her breath, "that's the most beautiful sight I've ever seen."

"Power's down a quarter," Desch Ituri, her second engineer told her. "By God's ugly ass, Supervisor, this thing
eats energy like a shark."

"How long can we run before we have to start shutdown
procedures?"

"Ten minutes?" He shrugged. "Not more. Not this first
time. All of the channels and orifices must be clear when
we shut down. None of the metal can be allowed to cool
and harden in restricted places or it will plug the works.
Even then, Supervisor, we're just hoping we get the shut-
down correct."

Kalico took a deep breath, tension rising to vie with her
feeling of success. The problem would be the power source.
Her people had recharged the reactor cores to the best of
their ability using the shuttle's reactors. Where could she
get the power she needed?

Freelander?

Even if she could remove one of the ship's reactors, how
would she ever get that kind of bulk and mass down to the
planet? Besides, the reactor's structural supports and cas-
ing were designed for freefall. They'd collapse under Donovan's gravity.

Or am I fooling myself?

Odds were that it would be a decade or more before
anyone from Solar System came looking. More than that if
Turalon didn't make the return trip in one piece, or in a
timely fashion.

Maybe she had time to recharge the cores, even build a
facility to manufacture new ones. Donovan was rife with
rare-earth elements and radioactive ores. Her smelter had
just proved that it was capable of separating metals, including promethium and uranium. Lead for shielding? That
was a byproduct of the ores from Number Two. Her reactor
would be a primitive thing to begin with. Dangerous. But
she had a whole, empty planet to store the radioactive
waste on. That, or just shuttle it to orbit and plot a slow
spiral into Capella where it would burn up. No one had

figured out how to pollute a star. Maybe she could be the first.

Like an overprotective mother she watched the shut-down procedure as Desch carefully let the smelter's functions run their full terms. The white-hot streams of metals slowed, thinned, and finally trickled their last.

On the collection floor, she saw molds filled with cooling gold, silver, lead, zinc, tungsten, molybdenum, manganese, and other metals. The tanks had taken partial charges of hydrogen, helium, argon, and other gases.

This is the key. This one piece of machinery. If I can just keep it running, I have the future clenched right here. In my fingers.

Desch might have been in another universe, so intently did he watch his displays, fingers flicking this way and that as he worked the interactive holo to shut down the reactor.

"Supervisor?" Spiro's voice interrupted in Kalico's ear com.

"Go."

"I think you need to come to the radio room. Got a hit on one of your high-priority concerns."

"And what would that be?"

"Supervisor, with all due respect, I think you'd better come up here and listen for yourself."

Kalico said, "Roger that. I'm on the way."

She left Desch to his monitors and Ghosh to his readings, stepped out through the control room door, and closed it behind her. The big sialon structure seemed to hum, as if it were oddly happy, alive.

That had to be her imagination.

Kalico made her way out into the flat yard, the soils baked hard by the shuttle's exhaust. The front-end loader stood beside a pile of ore, the operator already climbing down from the cab. She could just see the corner of the hopper she'd watched being fed.

The reddish earth, so recently wrested from the forest, now had rows of terrestrial crops that stretched out a couple of hundred yards beyond the smelter aircar lot. They wouldn't plant more until she was sure she could protect her farm from the forest. A fact that rankled, since in a few months her ration packs would be exhausted; she'd be completely dependent upon Port Authority for food.

Where the piping ran from the smelter into the river, steam was rising at the point boiling water discharged from the cooling pipes. Nothing could distract from the fact that she'd made the raw materials for success.

But what could have put that tone in Spiro's voice? *Come up and see for herself?*

She nodded to her aircar pilot as she climbed over the side and seated herself. As the vehicle rose, it blasted out the barest cloud of red dust, then circled, gaining altitude as it headed south toward the ridge where her mines could be seen on the skyline.

She glanced down as they followed the line of towers that would power her tram. Her industrial chemist, Fenn Bogarten, insisted that with a source for carbon, he could fabricate cable to carry the buckets. Now that the smelter worked, she could capture the carbon.

"So what the hell is so important, Spiro?"

Out of pure instinct, Kalico glanced up at the late afternoon sky. Had Spiro just heard that another ship had popped in? Now that she had one triumph, she was itching for others. If it was a ship, it had to have come from the past, one of the missing vessels, for Solar System would not send another until they had some word from *Turalon*. That fact had been understood from the beginning.

Her driver carefully flew wide of a flock of scarlet fliers, the creatures flashing warning colors and diving for the treetops below.

Passing over the fence, the aircar descended and touched down on the main lot in front of the entrance to the great dome. Her driver immediately shut the aircar down, leaped over the side, and offered a hand as she stepped out.

Accessing her com, she asked, "Spiro? Where are you?"

"Radio room, ma'am."

Kalico pushed through the double doors, passed the mess hall, and took the third right.

In the cramped radio room, an operator sat at the single chair, her head back, face thoughtful. Spiro, dressed in fatigues, arched a questioning eyebrow and handed Kalico a headset.

"Thought you might want to hear for yourself, ma'am. This is a recording."

Kalico placed the headset to her ear, a slight smile coming to her lips as the voice announced itself.

13

The thick root mat sank under Talbot's feet as he plodded through the forest's shadowed depths. Around him the boles of trees rose in gargantuan columns. Trunks of ten, fifteen, even twenty meters in diameter went soaring up into an infinity of intermixed branches, hanging vines, and impossible heights. Call it a cathedral of the gods. A place where even giants might have strode in awe.

He could have imagined nothing like it short of a VR holo fantasy come to life. The stuff of dreams and exotic special effects.

In passing through the forest depths, he had long since grown used to the occasional tree caught in the struggle of being uprooted by several of its fellows. He could find no other explanation except that several of the arboreal monsters had banded together and acted as a team to lever the offender from the ground in which it was rooted. The struggling victim—thick stalks of root diving down to cling to the soil—knotted its peripheral roots into those of its unkind neighbors. Even its branches were interlocked, struggling with its mates to stay upright.

Inevitably some lost the battle, their tremendous lengths thrown flat onto the forest floor where they became interlaced and covered by the victors' roots. Their trunks would be mottled with fungal-like growths, wood riddled by insectoid creatures that chirred and clicked as Talbot passed by. And there, too, were swarms of flying and scurrying creatures, of shapes, colors, and designs that bordered on the fantastic.

Despite the months he'd been marooned here, he still remained awed by the variety of life, the phenomenal diversity. So much, so different, that he couldn't even begin to place the creatures into categories.

One eye continually on his compass, he realized that the ground had begun to incline. Step by step, he labored his way up. Couldn't stop. Couldn't pause to catch a breath. To do so would mean that the roots would wind their way around his boots. In the past he'd used his laser to cut them away, but the charge had long since been exhausted. The suit no longer had the capability to recharge it.

A flicker of fear teased at his heart as his suit dropped to four percent. When it hit two, the servos would kick off. Essentially, he'd be immobile. Strong as he was, he'd barely be able to take a step in the heavy duraplast armor. The only choice would be to quickly abandon it to the roots, and hurry on before he, too, was engulfed.

Thinking back he wondered if he shouldn't have kept Shintzu's carapace. Tried to figure a way to remove her power pack. Doing so took specialized tools and was relegated to the unit armorer. Something about how they didn't want fumble-finger marines either electrocuting themselves, causing fires, or frying expensive equipment.

Maybe, if he survived this, he'd have a talk with the commandant, perhaps give the fine old gentleman a word or two on keeping the suits active when pushed well past their design parameters.

Yeah. Right.

Talbot smiled to himself and kept his eye on the power monitor. The slope was steeper here, eating power. The gauge flashed three percent. And there, up ahead, he could see a rock outcrop protruding from the root mat. Additionally, the trees were smaller: only five or ten meters in diameter, more widely spaced. Somewhere along the line, he'd figured out that it meant there was less dirt between the ground surface and bedrock.

What to do?

Reluctantly he slogged his way over to the outcrop and inspected it. Black, angular stone jutted from the slope. Maybe a couple of meters high. Some of the little bug things skittered away, clicking and chittering.

He climbed out onto the stone beyond the last of the wispy, thin roots. According to his suit monitors, he should be within three kilometers of the smoke. The source was just up there, somewhere in the high country beyond.

Not enough charge. He wasn't going to make it.

He powered down his suit.

"So what do I do?" Talbot whispered as he unsnapped his helmet and lifted it off. The forest's remarkable perfume of subtle, sweet, and tangy odors filled his nostrils.

If he dropped his armor here, reassembled it, locked it together with the last of the photovoltaics facing up, it would recharge over the next few days, even in the indirect forest light. But if it lost charge while he was on the root mat, he'd barely get out of the suit before the roots took it. And if he lingered, they might get a grip on him, too.

Talbot wasn't sure what it would be like to be imprisoned by the roots, slowly suffocated as they wound into his eyes, nose, ears, and mouth. Figured maybe he didn't want to find out.

Nor did he want to leave his precious armor behind. That was like walking naked out into a zoo full of starving predators. He had one round in his rifle. One. After that, the weapon's only use would be as a club. He'd shot his pistol dry days ago.

"Three kilometers." He pointed in the direction, as if to reassure himself. "That way."

Cap Taggart and Talina Perez had walked out of the forest and didn't have armor.

But the only time Shin had been out of hers, that leech-slimy thing had speared its way into her foot. Could one of those same things pierce his boot and pants leg?

And what of the hundred other creatures he'd encountered over the last months? The side-whipping tube things, the hook-covered vine creatures, the three-eyed dragon beast with its remarkable camouflage?

"I've been able to spot most of them first," he told himself. And he had. At least when he was paying attention. Over the weeks, he'd learned. Developed a feel for the predators, knowing where they'd be lurking. Even made a game of teasing them, getting them to strike his armor.

He took a deep breath. "Have I learned enough? Am I smart enough? Quick enough?"

Face the fact: Either he was, or this small, black, rocky outcrop was the end of the line. He could starve to death or die of thirst right here. He'd be in one piece, safely encased in armor, but just as dead.

"This is cucking frazy," he muttered, reaching up and

flipping the latches on his arm pieces. He caught a good whiff of himself as he unlatched the carapace and set it down. Then came the pelvic piece and both legs. He emptied the waste containers and carefully put the suit back together, positioning it so the photovoltaics could begin to charge. As dim as the light was, with few working voltaic cells, and as poorly as the suit functioned, it might be weeks before the charge was up to ten percent.

Talbot patted it, saying, "Hopefully I'll be back, old friend. If not, have a great life."

That amused him. Unless some creature rolled it down into the roots, the suit would lay there, propped in its niche, maintaining itself for a couple of years until the power pack completely deteriorated. The duraplast would last for centuries.

Talbot stared down at his sweat-stained coveralls, discolored by his body's oils and salts. When he pulled the arms straight, flakes of dead skin puffed out. The garment hung lose, proof of the muscle mass and fat that he'd lost on his diet of Donovanian meat. The discoloration of his nails, the loss of hair, he suspected came from heavy metal poisoning from eating the wildlife.

"Okay, buddy," he told himself. "Let's see if we can stay alive for the next three kilometers. And if that smoke turns out to be a volcanic vent? Might just as well throw myself in as an offering. At least it will be quick."

That said, he buckled his utility belt with its knife, survival kit, and empty pistol around his too-thin hips. Slung the remains of the meat from last night's kill over his shoulder. The meat had a sweet, tangy odor. He'd grown adept at contriving a pack from the hide to carry the boned-out bonanza.

With the point of his knife, he scratched "All things end" into the rock. A reasonable epitaph for his beloved suit, and perhaps for himself as well. He wondered if human eyes would read it.

Lifting his rifle, he flicked the safety off and stepped down onto the root mat.

To his surprise, it didn't wiggle nearly as violently as it had when he'd been in his armor. With one last look at the thinning trees above, he started up the slope, fixing his direction on a spot as far as he could see among the tree trunks.

Glancing back, his heart sank. His armor perched there, looking for all the world like a broken and discarded doll.

"Farewell, old friend."

Possessed of a terrible sense of misgiving, he plodded wearily upward, every sense in his body on alert for the first sign of danger. Never, in all of his life, had he felt so vulnerable and alone.

14

To Talbot's surprise, the roots barely reacted as he climbed the long slope. But then, he weighed a quarter of what he did when armored, and his soft-soled boots didn't have the sharp edges that his armored ones did.

Unencumbered as he might have been, he was still winded in very short time. Damn, but he sure missed the movement-enhancing servos that made climbing in armor easier than walking.

As he pushed himself, step by step, up the slope, he kept his eyes on the trees, veering wide around the hanging vines and suckers. The hook-covered tendrils generally had less than a meter of reach.

Bypassing that, he spotted one of the side-striking tube creatures lurking in a hollow of the roots. That threat he avoided by taking a wide berth behind the thing.

Fact was, when he didn't upset the roots, he could go more slowly, pick his path. Pay more attention to the forest itself. While he missed the thermal and UV detectors in his heads-up display, he could hear better. Was more aware of the sounds and smells.

And yes, he knew that vinegary smell. Didn't know what to call the hunched thing that looked like a ball of roots rising from the forest floor, but knew it had two tentacle-filled "hands" and a two-meter reach.

Go wide around that one.

By the time he reached the top of the incline, he was awash with sweat and feeling the first tickling of thirst. In the past, his suit recycled his urine, sweat, and moist breath. Then, to augment the supply, he'd find a trickle of water cascading from the afternoon rains.

He paused to catch his breath on what was obviously a mesa top. Here, Capella's scattered rays of sunshine pierced the high canopy. The trees were more widely placed, the ground more open. Looking down, he found a thin trace of roots atop the black, cracked, and mostly level bedrock. Threads of white, gray, and wavy bands of glittering crystals ran through the stone.

Talbot took a backsight, fixed his direction, and started off. Without the suit's computational abilities, his path was mostly dead reckoning. The smoke had to be straight ahead, somewhere.

If it had been the work of men, there'd be a sign. Beaten trails, scarred trees, some evidence of human activity to tell him he was close.

No more than fifty meters across the flat, he found the first clue. A stump. Cut long ago, but nevertheless, sheared straight across. He blinked, fought his first instinct to reach out and touch the long-rotten wood. On Donovan, a person didn't randomly touch anything if he had any sense.

Again he fixed his direction, noting the angle of the sun. A twist of the breeze almost made him gag as it wafted his own stench to his nose. Smelled like something had crawled into his clothes and died. What self-respecting Donovanian creature would lower itself to eating anything as disgustingly unwashed and repulsive as he?

But then back on Earth, vultures, coyotes, jackals, and dogs ate even more vile stuff. Best not to project his finicky sense on thc hungry locals.

He kept sniffing, hoping for a hint of smoke or burned wood. Doing so, he again caught an off-vinegary whiff of something. Stopped short. Noticed the oddly shaped boulder, an identical match for the one beside it. Right down to the slash of white quartz-like mineral that ran across it. Two absolutely identical boulders? Not a chance.

Talbot stepped warily around it, realized the pattern was shifting slightly. But for a chance of the light, he'd have missed the three shining black eyes that seemed to flow across the beast's body as it tracked him.

"Mother, son, and child," he whispered, keeping well away. "What the hell kind of thing are you?"

Carefully, he retreated, trying to stare all the way around him, wishing he had eyes in the back of his head.

When something bolted away in the gloom to one side,

he almost jumped out of his skin. Might have been one of the iridescent-scaled leaf-eaters he'd been shooting and eating.

Think, damn it.

Which way? He didn't dare get turned around in the maze of similar-looking trees. He picked the shaft of sunlight, Capella light. Whatever. Matched the angle, and took his cue.

How far had he come? One kilometer?

He used to be so good at distances. On the training runs in South Africa, the Sahara, and northern Russia, he'd always been able to gauge the distance. Maybe a sort of subliminal count of his running strides.

Now, for whatever reason, he had no idea.

Warily, he kept his methodical pace, breath slightly labored, his rifle oddly heavy in his out-of-shape arms. One thing was sure, if the four-winged, fantastically colored, swarming predators found him like this, he wouldn't last five seconds before they carved and chewed him down to the bones.

But if he ran into one of the camouflaged dragon things? Well, that one shot in his rifle had better hit its mark.

One shot.

What if he missed?

Just the thought of it sent a slimy sensation down his backbone.

Careful.

And he was. Every sense hummed on alert. Eyes scanning, nose searching, head cocked to give his slightly better right ear a bit more advantage.

He hoped he was still on track, not veering away from the source of the fire. Damn it, with his suit, he'd have been directed to within meters.

Another stump. Cut cleanly across. A long time ago. This one, too, was mostly rotted out.

On he went, watching the angle of the sun through the high trees.

Then he found the trail. At least, it looked like one. A linear scar through the forest. A rut, though filled with root mat. An anomaly, different from the random jumble of forest he'd spent days living in. Nothing else he'd seen on Donovan left straight lines but humans.

"So, which way?" he wondered. "Go left? Or right?"

And the light was failing, slanting in the late afternoon. What did he have? An hour? Maybe a little more before darkness?

And then what?

He had to have a rock outcrop.

Not that he'd sleep, virtually naked and unarmed as he was.

Which way?

He closed his eyes, willing his heart to slow, and listened.

There, off to his right, a faint, barely perceptible static sound. Call it a white noise. Either it was wind in the trees or a river.

Turning his steps, he prowled ahead as rapidly as he dared. All it would take would be one mistake. A single misstep. A momentary lapse of attention.

Close. He had to be close.

Even then he came within a whisker of disaster. The three-lobed, meter-across leaves, the dangling vines that didn't quite reach the ground.

Some instinctive and primitive part of his brain caused him to throw himself backward. At the same instant, one of the dangling vines flashed through the space where his head had been but an instant before.

He fell hard on his butt. Crab-like, Talbot scuttled backward until he was well beyond the tree. Safe, he paused, panting, until the feather touch of the roots tickled around his fingers.

Crying out, Talbot lurched to his feet, eased away from the disturbed roots. He tried to swallow his heart back down to where it belonged.

Damn it! Just under the tree's hanging branches lay his rifle. Discarded in his haste.

"Clap-trapping hell," he cried.

That was a damned nightmare up there in the mundo tree's shady heights. Like the one that had caught Garcia. The kind that bored into a person's body. Yanked them up off the ground, and slowly devoured them from the inside out. For days, if the stories were true.

Somehow, Talbot suspected they were.

Donovanians didn't exaggerate. Nor did they make up scary fairy tales. They didn't need to.

From his survival kit, he pulled the small, collapsible grappling hook, quickly tied it onto the coil of thin cable. Designed mostly for freefall work, it nevertheless had a ten-thousand-pound tensile strength. More than enough to pull a rifle out from under a mundo tree.

But how close could he get? He had twenty meters of wire-thin cable.

Creeping forward, he shook out the hook and line. At the edge of the tree, he tossed the hook. Worse, he could see the first filaments of roots threading their way along the rifle's butt, action, and forearm.

"Screw me, no!" he bellowed, casting again and again, only to have the grapple hook in the roots.

He jerked it free, saw the growing irritation in the roots. The more the roots got jacked up, the quicker they were going to engulf the rifle.

And there, just above the weapon, hung the ever-so-innocent-looking nightmare's tentacle.

Some tough, toilet-water-sucking marine I am.

He was going to lose his gun, and all because a tree-clinging, man-eating alien had him buffaloed.

But then, that was the thing's nature, wasn't it?

"You attack other creatures." Talbot hung his coil of cable on his belt hook. "What happens if something attacks you? You used to that?"

He *hated* the idea that popped into his head.

He had to have that rifle.

Which was when something from basic training stirred down in his memory: "Sarge always said, 'Trust your training, ladies and gentlemen.'"

He slipped his long fighting knife from his belt. The only thing he'd been using it for was cutting up the creatures he'd shot for food. At night, having nothing else to occupy himself, he'd kept it honed to a razor edge.

Nightmares were the meanest beasties in the jungle. They did the attacking. Those were the rules they knew.

I'm out of my fucking mind.

His hammering heart and the jitters in his nerves proved he was right.

Still, if this didn't work. If the thing got him, jerked him up into the tree, he'd use his knife to sever a femoral artery. No being digested alive for Mark Talbot.

Step by step, he advanced, balanced, every sense on edge, his rapt gaze fixed on that closest tentacle. It hung there, for all purposes dull, dumb, and lifeless. A hairy, greenish-blue, plant-looking strand maybe two centimeters thick.

Damn. How close could he get? He kept his pace even, fought to keep breath in his fear-tight lungs.

"Easy. Easy," he kept repeating, his right arm tensed and at the ready. The knife handle felt snug in his grip.

"Nightmares do the attacking. Go on, twitch, you pus-sucking son of a bitch."

One more step.

He tensed, body coiled, and lunged. Slashed. The keen edge of his blade bit deep. Through it, Talbot felt the nightmare stiffen, helping his blade bite as he severed the tentacle.

In one swooping move, he tore the rifle from the roots, pouring every ounce of energy into his flight as he ran out from under the menace of those overhanging branches.

Stopping short, he bent double, the thrill of adrenaline coursing through his veins.

"Yeah? Take that, you piece of . . ."

Something moved behind him.

Talbot whirled, slapped the rifle's butt into his shoulder. He was drawing aim when he stopped short. Standing there . . . was *a little girl*?

A very human little girl. Blue-eyed, with tangled blonde hair. Talbot wasn't any expert when it came to children, but he guessed her at maybe nine years old. She wore a leather skirt, what looked like a thin-fabric blouse, and knee-high boots crafted of some soft leather.

Even more to his surprise, she had her arm around the shoulders of a miniature version of one of the three-eyed, dragon-dinosaur predators that had tried to kill him. The thing was perched on its back two legs, claws curled and ready on the three-fingered forefeet. Colors were flashing and rippling across its hide like a psychotic rainbow.

The little girl cocked her head skeptically. "Either you're trying to get killed, or you're really stupid." Then her nose wrinkled. "And you smell like rotten garbage."

15

The shuttle's whistling roar could be heard over the cacophonous babble that rose and fell in Inga's. The place was packed, the crowd drinking, discussing the reason they'd been called. Looking forward to the break from monotony.

From her position on the stairs, Trish instinctively glanced in the direction of the landing field despite being fully underground in Inga's subterranean tavern.

Odd. Trish didn't remember any scheduled arrival. But then the Supervisor didn't always communicate her comings and goings with either the triumvirate or Port Authority security. Besides, though the *Turalon* cargo had been deeded to the Donovanians, Supervisor Aguila was still the legal title holder to the *Freelander*'s cargo—though the precise legal limits of her control remained a bit fuzzy. The Supervisor often sent the shuttle, unannounced, to pick up the odd piece of equipment.

Trish stared around the room, reading the excitement. Shig had been brilliant when it came to packing the place. The charges against Howe, Valerie, and Kung were unusual enough to generate interest. That it was coupled with a contract challenge against Dan Wirth—of all people— added to the allure. And finally, that it dealt with *Turalon* deserters served as the topping to a special cake.

Shig had not only made sure that the place was filled to capacity, but the high profile undercut Wirth's incentive to have his three indentured workers eliminated. At least for the short term. Doing so now would inflame public opinion to the point it might destroy his businesses, his name, and maybe even his life.

"How are we doing, Two Spots? Anyone from that shuttle need my assistance?"

"*Doing well, Trish. No request from the shuttle. Supervisor Aguila just asked for permission to land and enter the compound. Other than that, the sentries are all at their posts. Bitching about missing the great event, but on deck."*

"Roger that. Let me know if Aguila needs anything or if something crops up."

"'Firmative."

She turned her attention back to the room, watching it as she did from a couple of steps up on the stairway. The tavern was awash with people, some dressed in worn orange, faded yellow, or tan coveralls. Others evoked Donovanian chic in their tailored chamois-hide shirts, pants, and smocks. Most wore hats of one sort or another, and a veritable host of quetzal-hide capes, boots, vests, and wide-brimmed hats glinted colorfully in the light.

Her old friend Stepan Allenovich came clomping down the stairs in his quetzal-hide boots. Big and bluff, Step was trained as an exozoologist, and his work with Donovan's wildlife had laid the foundation for studies that would take centuries to complete. That didn't mean that hunting, tracking, drinking, frolicking with females, the occasional brawl, and working as the number three in command of Port Authority security weren't as much a part of his life. Since the arrival of *Turalon*—and especially Dan Wirth— Trish wasn't sure exactly which side Step came down on anymore.

"How's it look?" he asked, taking a position beside her.

"Two thirds of the town's here." She pointed to the two tables on the left side filled with Wirth's people. Allison's gleaming blonde hair couldn't be missed where she sat slightly removed from the rest of the prostitutes. "There's Maniken, Wong, and Schemenski with the rest of Wirth's enforcers. We going to have any trouble from them if this goes south?"

Step grinned at the underlying tension in her voice. "Nope. Not here. Dan's nobody's fool. Whatever happens, he's not going to take any chances on the crowd. He saw what happened when the Supervisor almost lost it all in a riot that time."

"So, what's he going to do if he loses?" She shot him a probing glance.

"I know what you think. I can see it in your eyes. Take

a deep breath and relax. I'm not on his payroll. Don't mean I don't enjoy his wares, but Mama Allenovich didn't raise just anybody's fool. So as I see it, here's the play: If he loses this thing, if Shig, Yvette, and Tal declare the indenture null and void, you get those three *Turalon* deserters to the aircar port, posthaste, ricky tick. Then you use that new night gear and fly them out to whichever holding or research base you want, and drop them.

"Be back by dawn, and don't you tell me, Inga, Two Spots, or anybody but Tal where you dumped them."

"Got it." She shook her head. "Should have let Tal shoot him that day."

Step shot her a startled glance. "Tal was going to shoot Wirth?"

She nodded, letting her gaze drift over the crowd.

"Trish, I'll forget I ever heard that. And more to the point, you forget it too. And don't you tell another soul." Step pointed with a gnarly finger. "If Wirth ever hears that? Well, his relationship with Talina is strained enough."

"She thinks Wirth killed Cap."

"Wouldn't put it past him. But in all the time I've spent in his place, I've never heard so much as a hint that he did."

"You think that means anything?"

"Nope."

At that moment, Shig, Yvette, and Tal emerged from the door leading to Inga's storage room just off the north end of the bar. With them came Howe, Ashanti, and Valerie dressed in their filthy overalls, their faces and hands washed and oddly clean in comparison.

Shig, Yvette, and Tal walked behind the bar to where three stools had been placed in Inga's normal domain. The other three took chairs placed just out from the crowd and before the bar.

Shig's voice, augmented by speaker, called, "Quiet, please, I'm calling this proceeding to be in session."

"Point of order," Wirth called. "I ask that Talina Perez, an aggrieved party, be dismissed from this board. She cannot be relied upon to make judgment without prejudice. I call for a vote from the people."

Yvette called, "Those in favor, please rise."

Trish smothered a smile as only Wirth's people and a smattering of additional bodies, all Skulls, stood. The vote was woefully short from a majority.

"The point is defeated. Are there any additional points of order?" Yvette was quick in adding, "Hearing none, let us proceed."

"In the matter of the charges of trespass, destruction of private property, breaking and entering," Shig announced, "we have the three accused here before us. On the recommendation of the investigating officer, Trish Monagan, we have dropped the charge of theft of a weapon. Will the accused stand?"

The three rose.

"How do you plead?"

"Guilty." The answer was given in unison.

"So noted," Shig announced. He turned to glance past Yvette at Talina. "Officer Perez, as the aggrieved party, do you wish to make a statement?"

Talina's voice carried across the room. "As the aggrieved party, I request no more than a verbal apology from the convicted, provided they pay court costs."

"Is a verbal apology and court costs satisfactory to the board?" Shig asked, and received two ayes from Yvette and Talina. He added, "Do I hear an apology from the convicted?"

"We're sorry," the thin Ashanti Kung said, her voice remarkably strong for such a stick figure of a woman. "Officer Perez, we ask that you forgive us. We couldn't think of anyone else we could turn to. Our only chance to make it alive to this inquest was to put ourselves under your protection. That you, Officer Monagan, and the board have enabled us to speak, and openly air our abject slavery and exploitation at Dan Wirth's—"

"Objection!" Wirth cried, leaping to his feet. "These people are prejudicing the next case on the docket. An apology? Well, yes."

He turned to the crowd, adding, "Here's how you do an apology." Bowing low, he extended a hand, calling, "Yes, I'm sorry. Grievously and verily, my soul writhes with regret. I deeply abhor the vile actions that my wasted and tortured person inflicted upon such a noble and virtuous officer as Talina Perez. May my shame be manifest for decades. May ashes and urine be heaped upon my head. Let my name never more be uttered upon the ruby lips of children, virgins, and the holy."

He straightened from the bow. "Now that, ladies and gentlemen, is an apology."

The crowd broke into guffaws, whistles, and stomping feet.

At the bar, Talina rose to her feet, slamming her pistol onto the chabacho wood with a bang. "Shut it off! Now! I'll have order, or by damn I'm going to crack heads!"

At the snap in her voice, the room went quiet but for the occasional snicker.

Shig sighed. "Objection is sustained, though barely. Officer Perez, are you satisfied with the apology?"

"I am. It is my recommendation that this case be closed pending payment of court costs."

"Agreed," Yvette chimed in.

Where they stood on the rear stairs, Step leaned close and asked Trish in a low voice. "Court costs?"

"We're way ahead of you, Step. Afterward, Talina is going to lead them back into Inga's office to 'pay court costs.' She'll take them right out the back, and get them out of sight until we can get them someplace safe."

Step grinned in response.

"So be it," Shig announced. He took a breath, moving on to the next complaint. "Petre Howe, Rita Valerie, and Ashanti Kung, who are seated before us, have entered into a contract of indenture with Dan Wirth. They request that their contracts, which are here, before me, be declared null and void by this board."

Trish heard someone coming down the steps and turned. She was shocked to recognize Supervisor Aguila and Lieutenant Spiro. The Supervisor wore a natty black suit that emphasized her slim and fit body. The wealth of her long black hair was pinned at the nape of the neck.

Lieutenant Spiro, in a dress uniform, sidearm on her belt, rifle over her shoulder, walked a step behind, her hard eyes taking in the room. She barely granted Trish a nod as the two of them passed. At the foot of the stairs, they slipped back into the shadows.

"Wonder what she's doing here?" Step muttered from the side of his mouth.

"Two Spots?" Trish accessed her com.

"Roger."

"Supervisor Aguila just walked in with Spiro. Let Tal, Shig, and Yvette know."

"'Firmative." Patching into the net, Two Spots said, *"Trish wants you to know that Aguila's here with Lieutenant Spiro."*

Trish watched the subtle change at the bar as Talina and Yvette stiffened at sight of the woman. Shig paused for a second, a weary smile bending his lips. Trish had seen that look before when some sudden new inevitability had presented itself.

Nevertheless, Shig said, "The board would hear the petition to declare these contracts null and void."

"Objection," Wirth cried, rising. "The very notion that this board can declare a private contract null and void is outrageous. Or is the triumvirate seizing the power to paw into all of our private doings?"

He turned to the crowd. "Think about it. Is this the way you want to go? Back in Solar System, under The Corporation's thumb, government controls all business. Here, business is ours. Our contracts are between people. Agreements we broker with each other. Do we want government inserting its nose into our private, sometimes intimate affairs? I ask, what damned business is it of theirs?"

Whistles, stamps, and shouts erupted.

"Quiet!" Talina bellowed.

Again the room stilled.

Shig, shoulders slumped, pressed the fingertips of both hands together, almost as if in an act of prayer. "This board agrees with Mr. Wirth in absolute principle. We did not agree to hear this complaint without long, and I must say, somewhat acerbic debate. What is at issue here is not the inviolability of the contract, but whether the terms specified therein are being met and complied with in the spirit under which the contract was negotiated. The complainants in this case are arguing malfeasance, abuse, and nonperformance on Mr. Wirth's part. Based on those claims, we feel the board, and the entire community, has a right to hear this case.

"Therefore, the objection is overruled," Shig replied. "Besides, anyone may voice a petition. Whether it will be acted upon remains to be seen."

"The complainants may proceed," Yvette called.

The redhead, Rita Valerie, stood, artfully facing the crowd instead of the board. "You all remember what it was like in those last days before *Turalon* spaced? You've heard the stories about *Freelander*. You can see her when she passes overhead in orbit up in the night sky."

Valerie raised her hands, her filthy coveralls exposed for all to see. "We weren't going to space back on that bucket of death. Not after what happened to its crew getting here. *Freelander*'s a death ship. And the odds for *Turalon* making it home are just as grim. So, I ask: How many of you, whose contracts are up, volunteered to space back to Solar System on *Turalon?* It's a free ride home to friends and family, to a life of luxury. You fulfilled your contracts, had a fat bonus waiting back at Transluna. How many of *you*, like us, opted for Donovan? For a new life here?"

A few calls of "Aye" and "Here, here" could be heard interspersed around the room.

Valerie paused, as if in thought. "So, can you blame us for going to Dan Wirth? The marines were rounding up anyone who even looked like they might not want to go back. What do you do when you're being hunted? You go to what you think is the safest place. Take whatever terms you can for that one shot at survival."

She gestured to her overalls. "We don't mind work. Don't mind hard work. What we got was slavery. At Tosi Damitiri's mine we are locked in a shed every night. We have a bucket to piss and shit in. Our beds are thin mattresses on a wooden floor.

"Our workday starts at dawn. We cook the rations. Whatever Damitiri offers. Usually whatever was cheap at market, and sometimes what he happens to shoot. Then we go down in the hole, drilling, placing shots, blasting, mucking, sorting, processing. We get a third of a ration at midday and ten minutes to eat it, urinate, and get a drink from the water pail. Then it's back into the hole until Damitiri tells us to quit. We refused once. Asked to have a day off. He locked us in the tunnel for two days without food or water."

She cocked her head, expression wan. "There were five us in the beginning. Chan Tzu couldn't take it. He ran. Took off at first light for the bush. Damitiri says a bem got him less than half a mile from the claim. He brought the bones back for us to see."

Around the room, heads were nodding.

"A chunk of roof fall crushed Ngomo Suma's leg. Damitiri loaded him into the aircar, locked us in the shed, and flew to town. We spent two days in there, suffering in darkness without food or water.

"The morning Damitiri let us out, he was so hungover, he could barely walk. And today we have learned that our friend, Ngomo, never made it to the hospital." She paused for effect. "Wonder where he ended up? Perhaps tossed over the side? Dropped in thick bush somewhere? It's easy to make people disappear on Donovan."

Valerie tilted her head, hair falling back to expose her gaunt face. "We don't mind *honest* labor. We signed the contracts, figuring that we would be treated fairly, offered decent and reasonable work. Even work in the mine. But with clean beds, three solid meals a day, with occasional time off to relax and recoup. Back on Earth, slaves were worked to death."

"Objection!" Dan Wirth cried.

"Overruled, Mr. Wirth. You'll get your time to respond," Shig replied. "Go on, Ms. Valerie."

"Did I say slaves? Isn't that claim a bit extreme?" Valerie raised her fists, as if they were shackled. "But what else do you call it? Don't all of you here, working on contract, have your evenings and two days a week off? Don't you live in comfortable, if modest, housing with running water? Take showers? How many of you work fourteen hours a day, seven days a week?"

She took a deep breath. "How many of you are locked in a shed at night? Caged like an animal? Hmm? Anyone? How many of you have to escape, hide yourselves in Talina Perez's house, just to live long enough to testify at a hearing like this?"

She paused. "Is what I'm describing indentured labor? Or is it slavery?"

Valerie turned to face the panel. "That is why we ask

this board to declare our contracts null and void. We signed a contract to work for Dan Wirth. That he turned us into slaves is proof of his noncompliance. Which, when you get down to it, is pretty damn simple."

Around the room, angry voices began to stir. Someone shouted, "Null and void!" Another cried, "We don't need no slavery like that here."

"Hey! Bottle it!" Talina cried. "Quiet!"

People reluctantly complied, but a lot of heads were turned Dan Wirth's way as he rose, spreading his arms. "Can I respond?"

Shig told him, "The board will hear the defendant."

Wirth, perhaps not surprisingly, climbed up on the table where everyone could see him, arms still spread. "You all know me. I'm a businessman. I run a lot of businesses. The Jewel, a couple of workshops, an oil well, more than a dozen mines and claims, and I have my civic duties, serving on the town council with our esteemed board here." He gestured at the bar.

"That said, I am aghast." He turned, facing the claimants. "I didn't know! And I am ever so sorry. No, more than that. Appalled and mortified. And yes, this is my fault. My fault for being so busy, overwhelmed, and buried in so many concerns I never took the time to ride out to Tosi's to see what the conditions really were. And I will never, ever, allow that to happen again."

He turned back to the audience. "I am filing charges, here and now, against Tosi Damitiri for gross malfeasance. What he did to these people was *criminal*! For that, the man needs to be hounded, caught, tried, and punished. Yes, these decent people came to me in a time of need. And yes, I went out of my way to offer them what I considered help."

He paused, voice pleading, "And I am so sorry."

He turned, arms out to the three. "If you will let me, can I make amends? Can I redress the wrongs done to you in my name?" A pause. "Can I *make this right*!"

His passionate words echoed down from the dome.

The three glared at him, intransigent, unforgiving. Valerie said, "You can. Void the contracts."

"Not only will I void them, but let me offer each of you a substantial bonus along with my apology."

The three were looking nervously at each other.

"Hard for them to show up with their throats slit any-time soon," Step whispered.

"I think we still better get them the hell out of here. Wirth played this better than I thought he would."

Step crossed his arms. "Nope. It was Rita Valerie who made the difference."

Shig asked, "To the complainants: Do you wish to withdraw your challenge?"

"As soon as Wirth tears up the contracts," Howe called.

Shig had that thoughtful, musing look that Trish associated with his waiting for the second shoe to drop.

Wirth theatrically leaped off the table, grabbed the contracts down from the bar, and with a flourish, ripped them in two to the stomping and hooting of the crowd.

"Look at the complainants. Laughing, hugging each other. They are dead," Trish murmured. "All three of them. Don't they know that?"

"Maybe," Step replied laconically. "Who knows? Wirth might have another angle he's figuring to play with them."

By that time, Talina was pounding on the bar for order.

As soon as the din dropped, Shig asked, "Is there any other business to come before this board?" His eyes were on the shadows where Kalico Aguila stepped forward.

"There is," Aguila called, striding down the center aisle, Lieutenant Spiro at her heel. "I have a complaint."

"Come forward, identify yourself, and be heard," Yvette said warily.

The crowd was suddenly electric, heads turning, people realizing for the first time that it was Supervisor Aguila. Whispers and hisses could be heard, people shifting.

"I am Corporate Supervisor Kalico Aguila. I represent The Corporation's interests on Donovan. I, too, have a complaint. A violation of contract."

"The board recognizes the Supervisor," Shig said, the weary smile on his lips. "Please elaborate."

Aguila stood before them, hip cocked, almost insolent. "You used the term 'inviolate' when you described this board's reverence for the contract, did you not?"

"I did," Shig replied. "The contract is the basic and fundamental instrument for the conduct of our business relationships, as you well know from your own negotiations with us, Supervisor."

Kalico made an airy gesture. "If I might ask, had the inestimable Mr. Wirth not torn up the contracts, how would this board have ruled?"

Yvette said, "Given that the case—"

"Oh, come on!" Aguila cried, turning to face the crowd. "I'd like to know, wouldn't all of you? Can you tell me that you're not curious yourselves?"

Calls of assent came from the audience as Aguila wheeled back on her heel, asking, "It's not that difficult. You know the merits of the case, what would you have ruled?"

Trish watched Shig, Yvette, and Talina glance back and forth among themselves.

Shig said, "We would have ruled in favor of the defendant, with the stipulation that he immediately provide relief, redress for abuse, and establish proper and humane conditions whereby the complainants could fulfill the terms of their agreement."

"What?" Valerie cried, leaping to her feet.

Talina banged her pistol. "Out of order! Be seated."

Shig raised a restraining hand while the rest of the room quieted. "Ms. Valerie, you people willingly signed the contract. And you were right to bring your plight to the board. Just because Mr. Wirth was either negligent, or even purposefully abusive, doesn't merit nullification of the contract you signed."

"Why?" Valerie and the rest cried in unison.

"Because in the contract that you signed there is no clause for termination based upon nonperformance on Mr. Wirth's part." Shig again raised his hand. "That doesn't mean that workers don't have rights to fair, reasonable, and equitable treatment."

Shig raised his voice. "Which, in the future, this board will see that you adhere to with your other indentures, Mr. Wirth. Are we understood?"

At his table, Wirth stood, spreading his arms wide in that humble gesture. "This was an isolated incident, Shig."

"Yeah, in a quetzal's ass," Trish murmured out the side of her mouth.

"Returning to my complaint." Aguila stepped forward,

reaching a hand back to Spiro who slapped a sheaf of papers into it. These she placed on the bar before Shig.

As Shig took them, Aguila said, "Given that this board, and thereby, Port Authority, recognizes the primacy of the contract, I have come to ask that the contracts I have just proffered be honored by this board."

"What specifically do these refer to?" Talina asked where she leaned forward on her elbows, hard gaze flicking from the Supervisor to Spiro.

Aguila turned, indicating Ashanti, Valerie, and Howe. "I come before this board to claim these deserters. I have just provided you the terms of their employment by The Corporation. Terms in which they relinquish certain rights, including the right to terminate their employment. Cutting to the chase—as the old saying goes—these three, and any other *Turalon* deserters, are mine."

A ripple went through the crowd.

"Oh shit," Trish muttered.

"Now," Aguila continued, "does this board truly recognize a legally binding contract? Or was that all hot air, while beneath lies a certain amount of hypocrisy?"

Shig handed the contracts back to Aguila. "The board does indeed recognize the Supervisor's point. Your dealings with any *Turalon* crewmembers is not any concern of ours."

"Shig!" Talina cried.

Yvette shot Talina a hard look. "It is *not* our concern."

Across the room, Trish could see Talina boiling.

"Lieutenant Spiro," Aguila ordered. "You will place the deserters under arrest and escort them back to the shuttle."

Spiro turned, a twisted grin on her lips, her hand on her pistol, and gestured that Valerie, Howe, and Kung stand. Expressions shocked, they started for the door.

"So," Step asked. "Does this mean they're not paying court costs?"

16

I t took Talbot two blinks of his eyes to prove that he wasn't seeing and hearing things. Or, if he was, it had to be malnutrition—perhaps a toxic effect from the heavy metals that had to be rife in his system—because the hallucination was remarkably real.

The little blonde girl and the creature were still there, although the creature had spread its wide collar, ripples of red, yellow, and black rolling across it like angry waves. The serrated jaws parted and a darting, whiplike tongue flashed out.

Talbot knew the kind of beast it was; a big one had tried to eat him. Had smashed him backward into the roots, and would have crushed his chest but for his armor.

"Please lower your gun," the little girl told him stiffly. "You are upsetting Rocket. He knows what guns are."

Talbot gaped, sidestepped intuitively to avoid the now-questing roots, and, asked, "Who *are* you?"

"Kylee Simonov. Who are you? Where did you come from? And why are you so filthy?"

"I'm Private Mark Talbot. Seventh Corporate Marines. *Turalon* detail. Our aircar went down in the forest south of here about . . . Hell, I don't know. Three months ago? Four? I'm all that's left. But what's a kid like you doing out here? And what's with the creature?"

"I thought marines were soldiers." She cocked her head. As she did, the three-eyed Rocket mimicked her movements in perfect sync. The effect was just plain eerie.

"We are." He figured she wouldn't understand the difference between the superior qualities of a marine and a mere soldier. "Now, where are you from?"

"Mundo research base. Isn't that obvious?" Her blue eyes were taking on a suspicious cast. "Everybody knows where Mundo Base is. We're the farthest south research field camp on Donovan."

"Never heard of it," Talbot told her with a grin. "Look, I've got a thousand questions, and it's going to be dark real soon. How about you lead the way to your mommy and daddy's house. After what I've been through, I'd really like to see a human face."

She looked at the multicolored creature, and said, "A human face? He thinks I'm not human. Maybe we ought to leave him to the nightmare."

"Hey, did you hear me?" Talbot cried. "I've been lost in the toilet-sucking forest for months. I'm half-starved, and without my armor . . ."

"Such a crier. Don't bawl. Follow us. But stay back. I don't trust you. And if you try anything, Rocket will know."

"I'm not going to try anything. And what kind of animal is Rocket, anyway? It looks like something that tried to kill me."

"He's a quetzal." She glanced back at him as she turned away. "Don't you know *anything*?"

A quetzal?

Talbot warily inspected the creature as it turned to keep pace with Kylee. Sure enough, it was a miniature version of the thing he'd shot in the forest.

"Isn't it a little dangerous for you to be wandering around out here in the forest? With a, um, quetzal, no less?"

Again she shot that irritated glance over the shoulder. "I'm not the one who walked under the nightmare. It's not like anyone doesn't know about the nightmare. He's been there for as long as any of us remember."

"I'm not from here. Get it?"

"As Rebecca would say, no shit." She was headed slightly northwest, away from the direction he was headed when he encountered the nightmare.

"Which way is Mundo Base?"

"This way."

"How do you tell in all the trees?"

From the look she gave him, he might have been an idiot. The quetzal hissed, the sound almost like laughter.

"What were you doing out here by yourself?"

She reached in a pocket to pull out a data cube. "Rebecca asked me to collect the imagery from the Seven C trail monitor. And then we smelled that horrible smell. I mean, don't marines ever take baths?"

"Hey, listen, don't bust my balls, little girl. I've been living in combat armor for the last . . . Well, forever. Shin stopped to take a bath, and some slimy leech-thing ate into her leg. Crawled around her insides. Finally killed her. I wasn't going to take the chance."

"She was barefoot next to water?"

"Yeah."

"Slug. You should have used that knife to either cut it out or cut her leg off at the knee. Once they get inside they replicate and, well, like your friend found out, it's not nice."

"How old are you?"

"Nine."

"You don't sound nine."

"How does nine sound?"

"Well, like a . . ." He gestured futility, worried at the rapid pace the little girl and pet monster set through the trees. How would she spot the dangers before she was in the middle of them?

"I'm a microbiologist and psychologist like my mother," Kylee told him in no uncertain terms. "Watch out. That sidewinder's new. He wasn't there this morning."

He followed her finger to see one of the long, fire-hose-thick, whip things that liked to try and trip him. So that was what they called a sidewinder? Aptly named.

"Is it dangerous?" Talbot asked.

She turned to stare at him, her big blue eyes shining with disbelief. "Why are you still alive?"

"Up until this morning I was encased in combat armor."

"I don't understand this armor you talk about."

"It's a sort of protective suit." Then he asked, "How many people at Mundo Base?"

"Eleven. Rebecca's the team leader. Dya, she's my mother, and Su Wang Ho are the adults. Then there's us eight kids."

Kylee was trotting again, the quetzal keeping pace at her side. To Talbot's amazement, the two lateral eyes could swivel back far enough to keep him in the beast's peripheral vision.

"Yeah? Well I don't trust you either, buddy." He kept

his voice to a whisper. Louder, he asked, "How long have you been out here?"

"I was born here."

"You just mentioned three women. Where's your dad?"

"A swarm of death fliers caught him when I was three. At least we think it was death fliers from the way the bones were chewed."

He made a face. She'd actually seen her dead father's bones? "What are death fliers?"

"Have you told me the truth about anything? Or are you a pedophile?"

"A *what*? Of all the . . . What on Earth would give you that idea?"

Kylee tossed her long blonde locks over her shoulder as she glanced back. "Rebecca has stories about pedophiles who live in a far-off world called Solar System. They're adult men who lie and beguile young girls so they can abduct them and sexually abuse them. And you, mister, are definitely *not* from here. And you've been lying to me the entire time."

"No, I'm not from Donovan. And what makes you think I'm lying?"

"If you'd been in the forest for months, you'd have been attacked by death fliers. It was hard enough to swallow the fact that you didn't recognize Rocket as a quetzal."

"Okay. I'm not from Donovan. I arrived here on a starship called *Turalon*. You do know what a starship is, right?"

"Of course. They come from Solar System. Where pedophiles live." She stopped, began frowning. "Thinking logically, I'm wondering if I have a high enough statistical probability to indicate you really are a pedophile. Maybe I should just kill you now as a prophylactic measure?"

"Prophyl . . . What's that?"

"An action or procedure initiated to protect oneself from future injury."

"Are you *really* nine?"

"Do you *really* not know what a death flier is?"

"Hey, *little* girl, I've been attacked by every fricking living thing in this damn forest. I just don't know their names, got it? The worst were the four-winged flying things. A hundred of them, that fluttered, clawed, and beat at me."

"Death fliers." Kylee squinted, as if giving him the benefit of the doubt, and continued to trot along the now-recognizable path. Stumps had become common as they proceeded, the sky opening above them.

"Good name for them," he admitted. "Is there any protection from them?"

"Only if you drop and freeze," she told him. "They hunt by sight. Dya thinks they're limited to seeing light in the three hundred and sixty to six hundred and seventy-five nanometer range. It helps that they're not very smart. Easily distracted. No collective consciousness. Their success depends on movement by their prey."

"Okay, I'm not a pedophile, but there's no way you're nine, either. What are you? Some kind of dwarf?"

Kylee didn't even bother to look back this time, just shook her head in disgust. The quetzal, however, kept a constant watch on him.

They passed the first piece of equipment, a slim tower topped with weblike sensors on the top that turned with the wind.

Then came wooden frames, what looked like water collectors with piping that led down to tanks. They broke through the trees into a narrow open strip. It took Talbot a moment to recognize what he was seeing: terrestrial plants. Pine trees. Huge things. A solid line of them, brown needle mats beneath. Just behind them came a line of deciduous trees: oaks and maples. In their shadow grew fruit trees that gave way to blueberry, raspberry, plum and blackberry bushes. Finally came agricultural fields of corn, beans, various grains, cabbages, pepper plants, and a huge patch of giant prickly pear cactus. All in all, maybe thirty acres, if he had to guess.

At the far end stood the expected dome. But this one perched atop a hundred-foot-high tower, ridiculously reminding him of a monstrous, white mushroom. At its base were smaller domes, looking for all the world like freshly sprouted fungal caps. A series of towers, solar panels, collectors, and square wooden sheds were laid out in rows that backed against a distant line of pines. Beyond that, the land continued to rise until it formed an irregular series of low, thickly forested and rounded peaks on the northern horizon.

"Wow. Kylee, why wasn't this place on the record holos? How long has Mundo Base been here?"

"Fifteen years now. Originally it was supposed to be two smaller bases, but the designers didn't understand how implacable the forest really was. Not only that, but this location provided easy access to a geothermal source where the underlying rock is perfectly faulted for exploitation."

This kid couldn't be nine.

"How do you know all this?"

"Rebecca's husband was a geologist."

"What happened to him?"

"Cutthroat flower got him up on Rondo Peak. Rebecca named it after him." Kylee pointed to the tallest of the rounded summits on the northern horizon.

A slightly raised causeway led across the field to the collection of buildings. As they got closer, Rocket's colors began to soften, the creature turning a pearlescent pink.

As fascinating as that was, Talbot immediately fixed on the two aircars resting on blocks back under an equipment shed. "Those work?"

"No. The power packs were needed for more important things." Kylee shooed away a small flock of hopping creatures that vaguely reminded Talbot of mutant jackrabbits.

"What are those?"

"We call them roos. They're harmless, but beneficial. They let us know if any rogue predators are around."

"Rogue predators. Talk about an oxymoron." He shifted his rifle, seeing other creatures filtering away between the buildings and curious pieces of scientific equipment. The ground here was hard-packed, and paved with angular gravel.

Kylee led him right up to the base of the tower. Where, to his amazement, the hatch opened, and two women, each bearing a curious tubular gadget, emerged. The things reminded him of a piece of water pipe with a coil spring on either side.

The older woman, in her early forties, stood close to six feet tall, pale-skinned, with dark brown wavy hair, ample jaw, and penetrating dark eyes. She wore a simple smock woven out of some sort of ivory-colored fabric.

The second woman barely came up to the first's chest.

She was Asian, late twenties, her facial features delicate, perfectly proportioned, and topped by a wealth of shining black hair that spilled down her back. She, too, wore one of the smocks.

Both women were watching him with suspicious, slightly shocked eyes. Nothing on their faces hinted at so much as a polite hello.

And then there were the curious tubes they were pointing at Talbot's midsection. He didn't need an explanation to figure out they were weapons.

"Rebecca, Su," Kylee greeted. "Look what I found in the forest down by the old nightmare. He claims to be from Solar System. Given the things he says, I suspect he's a pedophile who came to molest us."

Talbot's gut tingled as the women raised their tubes, their expressions strained.

17

The thunder of conversation was so loud Talina, Shig, and Yvette could barely be heard over it; they sat at the end of the bar. Inga was doing a roaring business, glasses, cups, mugs, and jugs being handed across, filled, and handed back accompanied by the clink and clatter of coin, or Inga's calls of, "Half-SDR for Tony!" At which time young Micky would chalk it onto the credit board at the other end of the bar.

The cause célèbre, of course, was the big hearing, Supervisor Aguila's surprise appearance, and Dan Wirth's culpability. Wagers were being placed as to whether Tosi Damitiri would ever be brought up on charges of abuse. Most figured that Wirth was already taking steps to have Tosi's body "disappear" somewhere out in the bush.

Tosi, no matter what his dubious qualities might have been, was getting less than twenty percent odds of ever facing the board.

"The moment Kalico walked in, I knew it was all over," Shig said, his half glass of wine held delicately in his fingers. "And, at the same time, it was the answer to a dilemma."

"How to keep them safe?" Yvette asked. "Dan Wirth isn't known for forgetting a slight."

"I had an aircar ready to haul their butts out to Briggs' place. Chaco and Madison could have used the help." Talina glared angrily at her mug of stout.

Yvette laughed bitterly. "We all know they could have never come back to town. Even given what I suspect Aguila is going to do to them, I imagine it's better than what they had at Damitiri's. The man's a nut. What prompted Wirth to send them out there?"

"Unless she shoots them." Talina wrinkled her nose in disgust.

"That is her prerogative. Spacers take desertion seriously."

"Don't forget, we funneled a lot of *Turalon*'s crew through here," Yvette reminded.

"And they're all out in the bush." Shig lifted his glass to the light, studying the wine's deep red color. "In that regard, we were smarter than Dan Wirth."

"Going to have to put the word out." Talina shifted on the stool. "They come to town, we can't protect them."

"Careful," Yvette said. "Here comes Aguila."

Talina glanced over where the Supervisor pushed through the crowd, looking irritated that they didn't part for her. Behind came Lieutenant Spiro—and Private Dina Michegan was sticking closely to the lieutenant's heels while glaring daggers at the press of Donovanians.

Some, recognizing Aguila, stepped back with a slight nod. Others ignored her.

"So much for the vaunted privilege of the ruling class," Talina noted.

"Only through conflict and overcoming obstruction does the Supervisor find peace and illumination," Shig said thoughtfully.

"Great, here comes Attila the miner, and Shig's spouting Buddhism."

"That's more Tao than anything," Shig answered as Aguila stepped up and took the empty seat next to Shig.

Lieutenant Spiro leaned into Tyrell Lawson's personal space where he sat in the next chair in conversation with Hofer, and said, "Maybe you two scum-suckers might want to find more healthy surroundings, like away from here."

Talina started from her chair, only to have Shig drop a restraining hand on her arm. His bland smile was already in place to forestall her outburst.

Talina watched Lawson and Hofer as they disappeared into the crowd, shooting hostile glances back over their shoulders.

"Yes, Supervisor, do join us. It's been too long," Shig told the woman with a smile.

"How's the mine?" Yvette asked, voice neutral. "Making progress?"

"You might say that." She reached into a pocket and tossed a small ingot of gold to clunk onto the bartop. Talina guessed it at seven ounces.

"That's a sample from the smelter's first run this morning," Aguila added, arching her immaculately thin eyebrow. "Tonight's party is on me."

And with that, she signaled Inga, who strode down, demanding, "What'll you have, Supervisor? I've got a new stout, but if you're into something lighter, there's a bit of IPA left. And then, for a more refined palate, my latest red wine."

"Whatever Shig, here, is having." Kalico tossed Inga the ingot. "And another round of drinks. What's the word you use when I pay for my friends here? Tab? Is that correct?"

"That it is, Supervisor. I'll have you set up in a jiffy." She inspected the ingot. "And you'll get your change from this."

Aguila waved it away. "Keep it. Call it credit for some time when I'm in need."

"As if that will ever be the day," Yvette said with a chuckle. "Thank you for the drinks, Kalico. It wasn't necessary."

Talina fought to keep from lifting her lip. Wondered if she could leave Aguila's drink on the bar.

You are in the presence of the enemy. Use your head, fool woman. Maybe, if you can think for once, you can learn something to your benefit.

"Got your deserters all buttoned up in the shuttle?" Talina forced herself to ask politely.

"They are." Kalico fixed her cool blue gaze on Talina. "Oh, don't worry. I'm not going to stand them up against the fence and shoot them."

"Let me guess," Yvette said, "you've discovered the milk of human kindness, by the quart in every vein."

"Where did that phrase ever come from? Something ancient, no doubt." Kalico accepted the glass of wine from Inga. "How on Earth did people back then equate something like milk, a product for sustenance, with kindness?"

"Outside of offering our gratitude for picking up tonight's tab, is there something we can do for you, Supervisor?" Shig asked mildly.

Kalico, a curious tension in the set of her lips, said, "Officially I am here to announce the successful operation of my smelter. Unofficially I'm here to sit and drink and enjoy a conversation where every blood-rotted sentence doesn't end in 'Yes, ma'am.'"

Talina cocked an eyebrow when both Shig and Yvette laughed. But then, they'd always been more forgiving.

"We're not exactly your friends," Tal couldn't help but say.

Kalico chuckled at that. "Dear God. Since when has enjoying the company of peers ever had anything to do with friendship? You don't understand how the Board works, do you? Everything in the upper management of The Corporation is about power, position, ambition, and advancement. Who can play whom. When I was just a girl my father sat me down and said, 'Kal, never mistake anyone in administration as being your friend. In fact, if you ever feel you need a friend, hire an actor.'"

"And people say Donovan is heartless," Yvette almost snorted in derision.

Aguila took a sip of the wine. "Not bad, actually." Then she gestured. "Now, here's the ultimate irony: We four are the most powerful individuals on the planet. We may not like each other that much, but I know that—unlike after socializing with my fellow Board members—wherever I might spend the night tonight, I know I'll wake up alive in the morning."

She paused. "That, my friends—and I use the term advisedly—is a most peculiar circumstance to find myself in."

Talina exhaled a low whistle. "Wow. And you Corporate people think we're the barbarians?"

"Different universe back there," Yvette said. "Maybe even scientifically. Makes quetzals, bems, and nightmares seem almost benign."

"Lost a woman to some kind of creature out at the edge of the farm the other day. Looked like a rock. Grabbed her and stuck a big spike through her. She was dead and being eaten before we could get to her."

"Skewer," Talina told her. "Same as got Cap down below Briggs' place."

"Like bems, you know they're around because they

smell like vinegar," Yvette added, and took a sip of her whiskey.

"Are you having any luck keeping the trees out of your cleared land?" Shig asked.

Kalico shook her head, eyes fixed on some infinite distance behind the bar. "We've tried burning, ditching, nothing works. We've lost about a quarter of the land we originally cut. You're sure you don't have some clue about how to deal with this?"

"Not down south," Yvette told her. "Our forests here are primarily aquajade and scrub chabacho, probably even a different species than the kind of chabacho you have down there. The trees grow smaller, not as dense. The only real research in the south was done at Mundo Base Camp."

"What happened to it?"

"Abandoned," Talina said. "They got cross-wise with Clemenceau. Cut off communications."

"Is there anyone Clemenceau didn't get cross-wise with?" Kalico asked.

"It's a trait we've noticed when it comes to Supervisors." Talina kept her tone light, trying to hide the steel underneath.

"Oh, please," Kalico replied snidely. "Believe it or not, even Supervisors can learn from their mistakes." She smiled a plastic smile. "Up to a point. But let's get back to this Mundo Base. Where was it?"

"About two hundred clicks south and a little west of your mine." Yvette swirled her whiskey. "Science research station. Took a couple of tries to get it established. Like everywhere, it was a bitter learning process. Couple of months after they told Clemenceau to go screw himself in a dark corner, they sent a message saying they were abandoning the base. No telling what happened."

"You never went down to check?" Kalico asked.

"Not that far south," Talina told her, memories of two dead bodies lying in the street—and her own role in putting them there—playing through her mind. "That was eight years ago. Even then we were fighting a holding action. Who would risk a flight that far on precious equipment? Keep in mind, Cap and I went down on a milk run no farther out than Briggs' place. Trish looked for us for weeks. Imagine going down in deep forest? Instant death sentence."

Yvette added, "There are species down there we've never seen. Giant-sized fliers. Forest creatures beyond imagination."

"That's the whole planet," Shig reminded.

"I need your thoughts on something." Kalico leaned back in her chair. "My people have been working ceaselessly in an attempt to first build, then develop the mine. With the success of the smelter this morning, we have passed a milestone."

"Congratulations," Yvette announced. "To the smelter." She lifted her glass in toast.

Talina swallowed her pride and raised her mug. "To the smelter." It was, after all, an incredibly valuable asset.

"Who owns that two-story stone building behind the assay office?" Kalico asked.

"Hofer," Shig said. "The heavyset guy you had Spiro roust out of his chair so that you didn't have to rub elbows with the riffraff and hoi polloi."

"Would he sell it?"

"Hofer?" Talina smiled. "He'd sell his mother if the price were right."

"I want to buy it," Kalico announced. "But here's what I need to know from you: I would like permission to bring my people here in shifts for a change of surroundings. Before you object—Officer Perez—you should know that I've been giving this a lot of thought. First, I'd pay my people in SDRs. Coin from your mint in exchange for bullion. They can pay their way, market economy. Not only will it give my people something to look forward to, a way to relax and refresh, but it will provide a boost to your economy."

"What about discipline when they're here?" Talina asked. "Who keeps them in line?"

"Ten marines, to work in lockstep with your people. Lieutenant Spiro will be my—"

"No," Talina told her flatly.

Kalico arched a surprised eyebrow.

Yvette said, "Tal, in the long run, this is—for all of our

sakes—a good deal. We'll need to work out the details, but—"

Tal was still fixed on Kalico's cool blue gaze. "You promote Abu Sassi, Anderssoni, maybe Miso, and I'll work with them. They're solid."

Kalico glanced sidelong to where Lieutenant Spiro stood several paces away with Michegan, backs to them, a subtle reminder for the common folks to stay away.

When she glanced back at Talina—a thoughtful look in her eyes—she said, "I had no idea that you felt so strongly."

"Damn straight I do. You three work out the other details as you will, but that's my bottom line."

"And what about Dan Wirth?" Shig asked. "Supervisor, are you going to declare Betty Able's and The Jewel off limits?"

Kalico laughed bitterly. "I would if I could. Do you think there's any way this side of fire on Mercury that I'd have a chance to enforce that?"

"It sure didn't work last time," Talina noted sourly. "As today's hearing proved so well."

"There is a way." Shig finally lifted his wine, took a tiny sip, and then put it down. "Wirth is a psychopath, to be sure. Despite the grand show he put on here today, he hasn't a trace of empathy for any living being but himself. And ultimately, his only goal is his best interest. That, ladies, is what we play to."

"And Hofer's building?" Talina asked.

"I want to convert it to a dormitory. Can you negotiate for me with this Hofer?"

"How much do you want to pay?" Yvette asked.

"I have the most productive mine on Donovan. And a smelter. Do I care?"

Shig chuckled his amusement. "No, I suppose not. But I don't think it is in anyone's best interest to overinflate real estate values just because you can. Tal, could you talk to Hofer? Find a reasonable price? You and he have always had a certain rapport."

"Only because I've busted his head a time or two over the years." She smiled grimly. "But sure. I'll do it."

"And we have another, perhaps the most thorny, subject to negotiate." Kalico laid her slim hand on the bar. "I know

Wirth indentured more than just the three I collected to-day. I have prior claim on them given that they're deserters from *Turalon*. I'm willing to let that work out as it will, and over time."

"Go on," Shig said.

"I also know that sixty-some of *Turalon*'s crew deserted and are somewhere on Donovan." Kalico's gaze had grown frigid. "Most likely, they're sprinkled out among the Wild Ones. Maybe working on the surrounding claims. Perhaps hiding out on the farms just beyond the fence."

"Maybe," Tal granted, her own face gone flint hard. "It's a big planet."

Kalico's smile carried no humor. "Shig, you once told me that my dharma carried too much tamas, um, anger, rage, and discord. You also said that Donovan taught hard lessons. And, somewhat to my surprise, you're right."

"What does this have to do with the deserters?" Yvette asked.

"I didn't want to space aboard *Turalon* either," Kalico said. "I couldn't convince myself to give the order. Captain Abibi, bless her soul, understood my reluctance, so she took matters into her own hands."

"My, my," Talina whispered. "You're starting to sound almost human, Supervisor. Who would have thought?"

"Tal," Shig chided softly. "There are times your own tamas proves itself not only to be ugly, but ill timed." He gave Aguila an encouraging smile. "You were talking about the deserters, Supervisor?"

Kalico gave Talina a deadly squint, then said, "As you see them, let them know that if they're happy in their new circumstances, they are welcome to stay there. For those who—like the three today—would improve their lots, they are welcome to return to Corporate employment with only an 'unsatisfactory work' reprimand on their official record."

"That's unusually generous," Talina countered suspiciously. "Why?"

Kalico bit off what undoubtedly would have been a tart reply, smiled, and wearily said, "Play the odds, Officer Perez. Even with the best spin of the wheel, we're on our own. We may never see another ship in our lifetimes. None of us are in a position to waste talent, even when it cuts deeply against the grain to let bygones be bygones."

Sure, Kalico. As if I could ever forgive Cap's murder.

But rather than say more, Talina just tossed off the rest of her beer before standing.

"If you'll excuse me," she said. "I've got to make my rounds."

18

"**D**on't shoot!" Talbot cried as he faced the two women with their spring-loaded tubes. "I'm Private Mark Talbot, Seventh Corporate Marines, *Turalon* detail. I've never touched a child. We don't have pedophiles in Solar System anymore." He winced. "Well, there might be some out on the stations, but most are caught through Corporate psych screening. Weeded out. I swear. I'm not a threat!"

For long moments, the two women watched him, the tubes never wavering.

"What do you think, Su?" the tall, pale woman asked.

"I'd say we go ahead and shoot him," the petite Asian said, "but that would leave this incredible stink right here at our front door."

"Good point." The tall one—who had to be Rebecca—shifted her right foot forward. "If we decide to shoot you, would you do us the favor of walking out beyond the compound first?"

Talbot swallowed hard, that familiar sinking sense of impending disaster in his gut. "This can't be happening to me."

Rebecca couldn't hide the humor anymore. "You're right, Private. It's not," she told him as she flipped a lever that decompressed the springs and lowered her tube. Offering her hand, she said, "I'm Rebecca Smart. This is Su Wang Ho. Welcome to Mundo Research Base. From the looks of you, you must have quite a story to tell."

He shot a sidelong glance at the still suspicious Kylee. "Pedophile? Really?"

"Dya says—" she started.

Su interrupted. "Dya told you that story when you were a little girl to scare you into behaving, minding your manners, and to keep you diligently involved with your study. Now, can you tell me why she would have chosen that story to frighten you?"

Kylee wrinkled her nose, looking her age for the first time. "Because it's the one that yielded the most productive results."

"Ah," Rebecca said. "Illumination." She gestured to Talbot. "Come on in. Let's get you up to the main floor and check you over. You look just about all done in, Private."

He blinked, shook his head, struggling to synthesize this. "I'm not hallucinating, am I?"

"How long have you been in the forest?"

"Lost track. Seems forever."

Su said, "You didn't survive that long dressed like that."

"No. My armor ran out of charge this morning. Left it on a rock outcrop just down the hill, the other side of the nightmare."

"Good armor," Rebecca murmured as she led the way into the tower base. The round room had a duraplast floor, the tower rising high into the darkness above.

Talbot took in the crowded and stacked boxes—some sialon, others homemade-looking wooden crates. Unidentifiable pieces of equipment lined the walls between the heavy, internal structural supports. Just ahead was an elevator, the cage nothing more than an industrial wire-sided box.

Looking back, he watched Kylee kiss the quetzal on the lips and then wave the creature away before she closed the door and hurried to catch up.

"How does that work? The girl and the quetzal, I mean?"

Rebecca shot him an amused glance. "You came on that last ship?"

"The *Turalon*, yes."

"You're in for a real eye-opener, Private Talbot."

"Call me Mark, please. How'd you know a ship was here?"

Rebecca waited until Kylee charged in and slid the gate closed before engaging the lift. The cage shimmied in its tracks as it started to rise.

"You can hear the shuttles coming in over half the planet." Su and Rebecca had backed as far from him as they could, the slight quivers of their nostrils a measure of how used to his own smell he'd become.

"Why didn't you go into Port Authority? Lots of Wild Ones did."

"Wild Ones," Rebecca said softly, a smile on her broad lips. "That's what we're called now?"

Talbot, fearing he'd made a mistake, shrugged. Eyes on the structural members as they flashed past, he said, "Hey, I just got here. Since a nightmare got Garcia, the forest ate our aircar, and Shin was killed by a slug, I've been getting a complete education on how absolutely ignorant a man can be."

The lift rose through a sialon floor and into a foyer. One of the two light panels had been removed and replaced by a series of what looked like glass jars; they hung by the lids and had been filled with a light green substance that glowed. Homemade lights?

Rebecca pulled the door open, gesturing Mark out. "Shower's in the bathroom, second door to the right. You're about Rondo's size. How about you get cleaned up? By the time you're finished, we'll have food and something to drink ready. Then, while Dya checks you over for medical, you can start at the very beginning."

He took a deep breath, almost at the point of hysterical laughter. It hit him with unaccustomed ferocity: a sense of total relief that weakened his already frail muscles.

"I was ready to die today," he said, voice shaky. "You wouldn't believe what it was like out there. This . . . this . . ."— he gestured around at the white hall, hung as it was with work clothing and equipment—"is like a fantastic dream."

Rebecca crossed her arms. "Don't get too weepy with relief, Private. We're hanging on here, but don't get the idea that you're saved. You've just stumbled from one kind of desperate to another. Now, go get cleaned up, and we'll talk."

Chastened, he stepped into the bathroom, seeing a sink, toilet, and shower stall. Small, but utilitarian. Everything orderly. The brushes on the counter looked homemade, as did the folded fabrics that he assumed were towels. No sonic or pheumodrier. Call it rustic old school.

He wearily stripped out of his coveralls, nose prickling at the biting odor, the sloughed skin. In the reflective metal wall that served as a mirror, he stared in horror at his body. The sores were the biggest surprise. That and his half-starved appearance. When had his toenails grown so long?

"God, I'm a mess," he told himself hoarsely.

"We'll see what we can do about it," a voice said behind him.

Talbot whirled around, face-to-face with a blonde woman. In her early thirties, she had Kylee's eyes. A little shorter than he, she stood about five foot six, her face not unattractive with its upturned nose and good cheeks.

He should have reacted to the way she now studied his body, her critical gaze running down the length of him. "I have some salves that will help when you're finished."

He watched her scoop up his clothing, holding the coveralls out at arm's length. "We'll get these clean and see if they're even salvageable."

Then she turned and walked out. He noticed that she had broad shoulders, like Olympic swimmers did; her body carried muscle unusual for a woman.

Kylee was staring at him from out in the hallway, something thoughtful in her blue gaze. Maybe she was reconsidering her assessment of him as a pedophile.

"Screw vacuum," he muttered, stepping into the shower.

The controls were familiar, and within moments, warm water was cascading over him. The soap was an old-fashioned bar. And then came the agony of his open wounds.

You're a marine. Tough it out. Your whole hide is infected.

By the time he was finished, he stood panting, letting the water run over him. He should have stopped, but couldn't help lingering, arms braced against the walls to support him. The sensation of water running over his skin was like a drug.

When he finally opened his eyes, Rebecca and the blonde, who he assumed was Dya, were standing there, watching.

"Sorry," he told them as he shut the faucets. "I shouldn't have wasted the water."

Rebecca chuckled. "Water? That we've got plenty of. Well, along with problems." To Dya, she asked, "Where do you want to do this?"

"Work bench, solarium." The blonde beckoned with a flip of her fingers. "Step out here and let us dry you off."

"You're kidding."

"No. And this isn't the stuff of erotic fantasies. We're a

lot more practiced at treating wounds than you are," Rebecca told him. "I can hear the story you would tell now: 'And two women carefully patted down my wet skin with towels before leading me by the hand to the solarium. There, in the bathing light of Capella, they made me lay naked on a large table. And as they turned their supple fingers onto my body, I threw my head back and screamed as they took a wire brush to my open and oozing sores.'"

"You're right," Talbot told them. "Not the stuff of male fantasies."

Nor did he find anything erotic about their sober assessment as they patted him dry. Somehow it reminded him more of taking a Corporate Marine physical with the poking, prodding, and technical discussion of various lesions, swollen glands, and general emaciation.

They led him out into the hall, through a door, and into a large room that appeared to be nearly a quarter of the dome with a kitchen area, tables, a line of windows facing Rondo Peak, sofas, chairs, and desks . . . and eight large-eyed boys and girls of all sizes and ages.

A sight which stopped him cold. Somehow, the fact he was buck-assed naked before all these children wilted him on the inside.

Dya gave him a tug. "Come on, Private. You're surrounded by scientists, either budding or established. Beyond that, you're about to be a lesson."

"Lesson?"

She and Rebecca led him through a door into a transparent slice of the dome filled with sunlight and plants. The place smelled of rich soil, greenery, and the multitude of flowers. The central bench had been cleared of pots and jars, and a tarp laid out.

"Be our guest," Dya told him with a gesture.

Even as he swung onto the table, the children were filing in.

"This is Private Mark Talbot, a Corporate Marine from Solar System," Rebecca began her lecture. "He's survived in the forest for three months by wearing body armor. Designed for military combat, it has beneficial functions when it comes to Donovan. We will know more after we retrieve it.

"Because Private Talbot could not leave his armor, he has suffered significant epidermal trauma. What is our first concern? How do we respond?"

The oldest boy, brown-haired, with Rebecca's eyes and jaw, said, "By cleaning the necrotic tissue from the wound, then sterilizing, and finally applying an antibiotic ointment before either dressing or leaving the wound open, depending upon severity."

"Very good. Now. Step forward and observe as Dya begins the process on the first wound."

Talbot gritted his teeth as those childish and fascinated eyes all crowded around to watch.

Unlike in Rebecca's scenario, he didn't scream. No, he kept his jaws clamped, held his breath, and yes, a couple of times, tears slipped down his cheeks. But he didn't scream.

Not in front of kids.

Sucking snot, why couldn't they be like normal kids back in Solar System and watch holo vids about space pirates, heroic Corporate officers, and lost puppies?

19

In the curious way that Dan Wirth categorized his universe, fury came off more as an entity, being possessed of its own shape, essence, and form. At that particular moment, Dan bathed in its red-raged glow. Let it run up and down his bones, and felt it surge along his muscles, tensing them, drawing them tight. Like a pulsating knot, it burned in his belly.

Walking down the avenue toward The Jewel, however, he maintained his iron control, kept the mask in place that had served so well to keep the swells, the gawking marks, and the smugly superior investigators completely clueless.

"Never give the bastards a hint as to what you're really feeling, boy." His father's words echoed down deep.

This evening, as never before, he fought the battle. Hot as the fury burned inside him, he kept his expression beneficent, an amicable smile on his lips, a lightness in his stride as he passed the few pedestrians on the street who hadn't been in the inquest.

Not that they might yet know of his drubbing during the proceedings, or how he'd been forced to climb up on that table and make that toilet-water-sucking speech. Offering fucking consolation? A bonus? Those three cretins had put him in the position of looking like a thumb-fingered fool. Him. Dan Wirth!

Top that off with the fact that no sooner had he been contemplating just how he'd get revenge on his wayward indentures than that Corporate slit, Aguila, stepped up front and chopped him off at the knees. The silly bitch couldn't have humiliated him more if she'd slapped him in the face in front of the whole damn place.

Her and her starch-assed marines.

"Well, I don't have to eat your shit, you twitch-legged, Corporate slick." The fury burned as Dan nodded politely to one of the school teachers who herded a batch of fifteen little kids toward the education dome. He even managed some mindless platitude about the weather, cheery as could be.

Yeah, bull-goddamn-shit.

He waved, glanced at the setting sun, opened the door, and stamped into The Jewel. The rest of his people would be coming posthaste to open. After the depth of his defeat, no doubt there'd be a flood of curious people rolling through the casino in an attempt to suss out just what kind of response Wirth would give. Hoping they'd see the great man sulking, plotting, or better yet, exploding in anger and vowing vengeance.

"Oh, what a woeful price to pay for a profitable evening." He stopped short, glancing around the now-quiet room. The tables waited, the stocked bar ready. All the wood polished. The door leading back to the cribs was open and awaiting customers. The cage, too, seemed to be holding its breath. The bars and counter reminding him of a curious face awaiting his response to this day's humiliation.

"Assholes," he muttered, considering the soon-to-arrive crowd. "Tonight the house gets fifty percent." Wouldn't take but a moment to reset the machines.

That'd be a start anyway. Just a slight psychological edge for tonight. Hopefully the marks would take away the notion that he was still a winner, that the odds forever favored him. Even though Howe, Valerie, and Kung waited in shackles aboard the Supervisor's shuttle.

She goddammed swiped them right out from under me!

He hadn't known a rage like this in years. Not even when Nandi threw him naked out of her personal quarters aboard *Turalon.*

He stopped dead still in the middle of the room, closed his eyes. Let the fury explode within him. Felt it hot in his blood as he clenched his fists and flexed every muscle until his entire body shook.

"Nobody does this to me." He laughed at the depth of the rage. "Valerie, Kung, Howe, you pieces of sucking snot, you've got to be made an example of. You get away with this, others will try. Nobody chaps my ass like that.

"And as to you, Supervisor? You think you're delightfully safe down there in your little mine? Happily protected and insulated? Think you've got nothing to fear from an operator like me? This isn't Solar System, you skinny slit. You don't have a clue of what I can do to you."

Even as he said it, the door burst open, Art Maniken at the head of his crew. As they filed in, all eyes fixed on Dan, as if anxious, fearing the extent of the explosion.

Instantly Dan's façade fell in place, the easy smile and dimples lighting his features.

"All right, people. Let's get ready for a busy night. I want you all on your toes. Marching orders are to make this a party night. Art, spike the drinks. Just enough mash to give the marks the merest hint of a high. Not enough that they know they've been dosed. We want laughter tonight."

"Yes, boss." Maniken flipped him a salute.

"The rest of you. Joyous. I'll be adjusting the odds as the evening progresses. We want the sounds of revelry floating out into the community, so the doors stay wide open."

"Right," Schemenski called back.

Finally he turned his attention on Allison, tall and regal, dressed in form-fitting finery. Her dark blue eyes fixed speculatively on his, an anxious twist, half smile, half worry, hovered on her full lips.

By all that was holy, she was a beautiful woman.

And all his.

His, damn it! To do with as he liked. No contracts. No strings.

That sense of authority redirected the fury, sent it tingling into his pelvis.

"Allison, my love." He spread his arms wide. "You and I have business in the back."

He took her hand in his, seeing the widening of her dark pupils, the slight parting of her lips. The faintest red flush appeared at the base of her neck.

"Come, my love," he told her as he led her toward her room in the back.

He could feel the tension in her body. She knew it would be rough. And, knowing that, he wondered if she'd drug herself, or just play along, ride the tiger he was about to unleash on her. Sometimes she did that, as if she were punishing herself, meeting his violence and savagery with her own.

Those nights, the sex was the best.

Absently he wondered if he was going to get the dress off of her in one piece, or if he'd have to find her a new one.

20

Talbot sat propped against the arm on the big couch and stared out through the window at the sunset bathing the distant trees that covered Rondo Peak. Curious, that. He was wearing Rondo's robe, looking at the summit where the man had been killed. And here Talbot was, belly full, his wounds treated, a cup of warm tea in his hands.

After the medical, they'd started quizzing him. Listening in detail as he told them about *Turalon*. Port Authority. Supervisor Aguila coming to Donovan. How the triumvirate was tried for treason and acquitted. The arrival of *Freelander*.

And finally his flight south with Garcia and Shintzu.

Then came time for chores, and they all vanished, the kids scurrying for their work clothes and the elevator. That had been an hour ago.

The lift clicked into place, the cage opening. He glanced back to see Dya emerge from the foyer, some sort of greenery in a homemade wheelbarrow that she rolled into the kitchen area.

"Need anything?" she called from the kitchen.

"No. I'm fine. Made a cup of tea like you showed me."

She came striding across the room, slipping work gloves into the belt on her overalls. "Any pain?"

"No. Remarkable salve you've got."

"I'm proud of it. Distilled from blue nasty. That's a rather rare shrub this far south. Since I already knew it had narcotic qualities, I hypothesized that it could be manufactured into an anesthetic." She glanced back at the kitchen. "Be right back."

He watched her pad across the room and turned his attention to the last of the golden light bathing the side of Rondo Peak.

Perhaps ten minutes later she emerged from the door that supposedly led to the personal quarters, this time

wearing a casual one-piece synthetic. Not that the garment
was sexy, but the way it hung from her broad shoulders and
curved around her waist in folds bespoke of something el-
ementally female.

Maybe I'm feeling better.

She pulled a container of something from the refrigeration unit, walked over, and seated herself just down from
him. She raised a knee, leaned back, and sipped from the
drink. "It's been eight years since we've had any contact
with the outside. And today Kylee finds you fighting with
the old nightmare. Talk about ultimate improbabilities."

"Hard for you to believe? Put yourselves in my boots."

"That was really dumb, you three flying out here."

"I'm well aware, Mrs. Simonov."

At that she started. Smiled. "Long time since I've been
called that. Everyone here is first name. Last names sort of
died along the way. You're going to be Mark. Like it or
not."

"Works for me." He paused. "That daughter of yours.
Kylee. I mean, what's with letting her just wander around
out there? Alone. Not even a weapon. Even with armor, I
came so close to dying so many times . . ."

He shrugged to emphasize his lack of understanding.

"She wasn't alone. Rocket was with her."

"You trust your little girl to the care of an alien alpha
predator?"

She fixed hard blue eyes on him. "I trust Rocket more
than I'd even trust Rebecca. Kylee and Rocket are bonded.
As to what that means, we're still working it out. Something biochemical. They're growing together. Maturing
together. I'm not sure if it is a sort of symbiosis, but Kylee
remains Kylee, and Rocket remains Rocket. She understands quetzal behavior and instincts, but doesn't manifest
them herself. Rocket understands what it means to be human, but doesn't present himself as human. Call it a work
in progress."

"Your daughter is a science experiment?"

"Oh, God, Mark. We're all experiments on Donovan.
Even you. Tell me that you haven't absorbed an incredible
amount of data about this planet, what lives on it, and how
your technology could be better equipped to deal with it."

"Sounds a little cold, don't you think?"

Her brow pinched slightly. "Forty of us came here. The first twenty, of which only Rebecca remains, were fourth ship. I came with my parents on the fifth ship. We were to ultimately build three southern research bases that would give us a broad understanding of the forest region south of Port Authority. Sort of a leapfrog on the way to the equator.

"By the time my folks and I arrived, the first twenty were down to three. Five potential locations had been abandoned as hopeless, and everything was relocated here as a last resort. The design that would become Mundo Base had been substantially redrawn into what you now see.

"Su arrived with the last complement of six to be assigned here. That was nine years ago. Just before we cut contact with Port Authority. Since then, we've learned. Figured out how to survive here and adapt to Donovan's rules. Many of our most important lessons came at a terrible price."

She waved around. "Three women, eight kids. Rondo was our last husband. So, until some of the children mature, we're it."

"Last husband? Singular?"

"He was a good man, charming. Monogamy in the wild is an unnatural state for most species, even *Homo sapiens* when you actually dig into the anthropological literature. Our first concern was survival; antiquated cultural baggage like one man, one woman, was a leisure we couldn't afford. It's bad enough that we're down to such a limited gene pool."

"What about Port Authority?"

She shrugged. "We originally stopped communicating with them because we had trouble with Clemenceau. How do we know that these new people, or this Supervisor of yours, wouldn't try to come in and take this away from us?"

At the no-give question in her eyes, he could only shake his head. "I don't know how to answer that."

Her blonde eyebrow raised. "You do understand the dilemma you now pose for us? Granted, none of the aircars work, so you couldn't fly out if you wanted. The radio has been disconnected for eight years now. Our last message was that we were abandoning the base and flying straight north to Port Authority. Obviously we never arrived. So, hopefully, we're long lost, dead, and forgotten."

"And if I showed up, it would lead to uncomfortable questions." He nodded, an eerie sense of premonition stirring down inside.

"You can stay here. Learn. Become part of the experiment. We have specific uses for a man. Uses for which you would be most adept. But you do understand, we can't help you get back."

"So, you're saying I'd better stay. And like it?"

She nodded, a coldness behind her eyes.

"And the alternative?" he asked.

"Let's just say that you wouldn't like it."

21

A little after midday, Shig led the way into The Jewel. Talina, out of second nature, fought to keep from resting her hand on the butt of her holstered pistol. The room was sparsely occupied; a couple of prospectors at a table over against the wall played a card game as Shin Wang dealt out from a deck. In the back, Angelina—dressed in a gauzy white see-through dress—sat on a man's lap. When he wasn't fondling her left breast, he was placing coins on the faro table while Wirth's man, Schemenski, laid out the cards.

"So this is a casino?" Shig mused, stopping short, staring around with wide eyes. "I expected more, well, pizzazz. Lights, bells, flashing signs. I read a treatise on how two centuries of psychosocial research has gone into determining just the right amount of stimulation, subliminal suggestion, and arousal to cause the majority of people to bet without inhibition. Did you know that in the middle of the twenty-first century, some casinos actually pumped intoxicants into the air and used hypnotic suggestion to bilk their victims?"

"If Wirth could figure out how, he would," Talina growled.

Shig, meanwhile, had wandered over to the craps table, then to the roulette wheel.

"Bless my lucky stars!" Wirth's baritone bellowed from the cage in the rear. The man appeared in the doorway, leaning out. "Can it be? Or do my eyes deceive me? Could that really be Shig Mosadek? Our beloved and noble leader, come to my unworthy establishment?"

Wirth started forward, dressed in a fine black suit, quetzal-hide vest visible beneath his long-tailed coat. "We are humbled and honored, sir. And, yes, even the ever-competent Officer Perez, stalwart protector of the weak and servant of the people, is at your side."

Wirth paused, throwing up his arms. "Which I suppose

would suggest that instead of a pursuit of salubrious relaxation, your fine presence is the harbinger of town business."

Shig was still staring at the roulette wheel, apparently unaware of Wirth's bombastic approach. The richer and more powerful the man got, the more irritating and overblown his speech became.

"Knock it off, Dan," Talina told him. "I still remember the Skull who stepped off the shuttle the day you arrived. What's with the sudden pomposity?"

Wirth ignored her, stepping up beside Shig. "You a fan of roulette?"

"Never seen a roulette wheel before," Shig said. "Could you spin it?"

"Want to take your chances? One turn of the wheel? Toss a coin down. Best odds are red or black, odd or even. After that, well, it becomes the will and grace of the gods."

Shig tossed a silver ten SDR onto red.

"The bet is placed!" Wirth added, and with a showman's flourish, spun the wheel. Then he snapped the ball in the opposite direction.

Shig watched, a smile on his lips, as if absolutely fascinated and enchanted.

The ball spiraled down, clicked and bounced, landing on red 12.

"And the man is a winner!" Wirth cried. From a pocket, Wirth produced another ten, setting it atop Shig's coin. "Would you care to try again, Shig? I'm betting you'll double."

Instead Shig—still grinning like a star-struck child—retrieved the coins. "No. But thank you. I have always wanted to do that. I saw it in a VR holo years ago. Sometimes just a simple fulfillment of a fleeting aspiration can provide a sense of sattva."

"A sense of what?" Wirth asked blankly.

"Forget it," Talina told him. "It's Buddhist."

"Hindu," Shig rejoined.

"Right," Talina snapped, grabbed Shig by the arm, and pulled him away from where he'd bent over to peer more closely at the wheel with its numbers.

"We've got a problem," Talina told Wirth, trying to keep her voice even.

"I'm hoping it's Shig, and that he's ready to explore the fascinations of games of chance." Wirth then made a tsking sound. "But I'm betting it's not. Otherwise you'd have beaten him bloody to keep him out of my nefarious clutches."

"Don't push it." Tal narrowed an eye. "I'm not in the mood."

"Have a seat." Wirth gestured to the nearest table. "Can I offer a refreshment? Beer, wine, something stronger?"

"No seat," Tal shot back. "We're not even close to those kind of terms here."

"Then what, pray tell, good officer, can I do for you?" Wirth's eyes had turned a deadly shade of brown.

"We have brokered a deal with Supervisor Aguila," Shig told him, a bemused expression still on his round face. "Her people, locked away on that compound down south, are finding their leisure sorely limited. Hofer has just sold his warehouse to Aguila, who is turning it into a dormitory. As soon as it is finished, the Supervisor is going to shuttle her people, in rotation, to Port Authority for rest and relaxation. A change of scenery, if you will."

"They have assets? Plunder?" Wirth asked.

"They will be paid in Port Authority SDRs," Talina told him.

"Why do I like this already?" Wirth asked, as if to himself.

"Because, you two-legged piece of shit, you're going to make a stinking fortune, assuming we can come to a deal." Talina tugged on Shig's arm as he looked longingly back at the roulette table.

Missing none of it, Wirth barely bit off a smile. "What kind of a deal?"

"The kind that results in no trouble for anyone," Shig said with a sigh. "A request tantamount to asking Capella to rise in the west, but one that we nevertheless have to find a way to ensure. I am aware that you have your differences with the Supervisor."

"The slit stole three of my contract indentures. What's to keep her from coming after the others?" Wirth pointed a finger. "That, my friends, is bad for business."

"Nice try," Talina told him, once again tugging on Shig's arm to get his attention away from the roulette table and back to the subject at hand. "So you've got what, ten, maybe fifteen *Turalon* deserters working on the outlying farms and mines? What's that compared to a couple hundred of Aguila's people a month rolling through here, dropping coin on your crooked games and girls?"

"You do make a point, Officer Perez."

"We can make another point," Shig said, surreptitiously running his finger along the polished wood of the roulette table. "Granted, Tosi Damitiri is the exception, and a vile one at that, but honestly, some of the other indentures aren't exactly living in what we would call humane circumstances, are they?"

"Hey, when I took them on, I had no idea that the Corporate witch was going to stay." Wirth raised his eyebrows, as if in dismay. "My plan was to bring them back to town, train them for the tables. Put them in better circumstances that were going to make me more profit than picking cabbages or hauling rocks. But as long as Aguila's flying in without a moment's notice, what's my choice?"

"She's offered an amnesty." Talina struggled to keep from spitting on the guy. "So, maybe the indenture turned out to be a bad bet. Like if Shig had bet on black a moment ago. Not every bet wins, right?"

"You play in a different casino than I do, Officer."

She narrowed her eyes, pictured his face filling the pistol sights. "So, here's the deal: You and your goons can work with us to ensure that Aguila's people don't end up with their throats slit, their heads broken, shot through the heart, or with their guts hanging out."

"And if they go out of their way to start it?"

"We'll have a ten-marine security force working with my people. You're an operator, and as slick as they come. You know damned well how to monitor a situation. Especially when it pays."

Shig added, "Our concern is making sure that Aguila's people get back on their shuttle with their bodies in one piece and ready to go back to work. As long as they stumble aboard alive, fit, and physically unharmed, you're free to use your games, drink, and entertainments to fleece every last cent you can from them."

Shig paused, then added, "Which you won't, because

I'm told that's bad for business. Thirty-five percent. Isn't that the percentage of your take?"

Wirth considered, thoughts racing behind his now-calculating eyes. "I think we can come to an accommodation. But here's the thing: I can run my establishments just fine, thank you. But I won't be held responsible once they're out my door. Say a mark wins big. I'm not having my people walk him home. If some local decides to help the poor bastard back to this dormitory the Corporate slit's building, and somehow misleads the clod into a dark alley . . . ?"

"We'll work it out," Talina told him. "Some sort of signal whereby we can have security on a mark like that."

"Then, Officer Perez, I think we can do business."

"Why did I figure that would be the case?" Talina asked darkly.

God, what I'd give to shoot you dead for the slug-sucking maggot that you are.

The quetzal inside made its presence known by sharpening her senses, sending the thrill of combat through her muscles.

"Yeah," she whispered to the beast, "too bad we can't."

Grabbing Shig's arm, she jerked him away from where he was looking too fondly at the roulette wheel.

22

For once Mark Talbot had a name for the chirring, whining pulsations of sound. Kylee had told him in no uncertain terms that it was called the chime, and it was made by the little creatures called invertebrates.

"Not that we're even close to understanding Donovanian evolution," Dya had explained. "Naming them 'invertebrates' was the first frame of reference the initial researchers had to fall back on. Their evolution and adaptive strategies are turning out to be a great deal more complex."

"Who'd have thought?" Talbot asked himself as he wiped sweat from his face and winced at the ache in his back. "I'm actually learning something that doesn't have to do with regulations, rank-and-file weapons drill, or crowd control."

He tilted his head where he bent over the bean plant and stared up past the hat brim at Capella; the alien star burned an actinic and blinding white from high in the sky. Out in the midday sun, the temperature had to be close to forty Celsius. He'd already drained his water bottle.

Across the field, heat waves rose in silvery patterns, making the fruit trees, pines, and forest beyond dance and sway. He'd been hotter, though. In Sudan. Desert training back when he was just out of boot.

Bending back to his work, he continued to pluck bean pods from the plant, taking all the ripe ones as Damien had showed him, leaving the ones that continued to mature.

Talbot shifted his basket slightly so he could pull a big, thick squash from the next plant. The field here was a hodgepodge of beans, corn, squash, cabbage, carrots, and broccoli. According to Rebecca, they shared nutrients, and the corn provided just enough shade to ameliorate the harsh sun until the afternoon showers came rolling in from the west.

One thing he could say, the dark red soil certainly seemed fertile, for the crop was substantial. Additionally, the original seed stocks had come from hydroponics applications and had been modified to produce endlessly.

He snapped off another ripe-looking squash, shuffled over, and stripped five ears of corn from several of the tall plants, all of which topped off his basket.

He paused, arched his back, and pulled off his floppy hat. Woven from strips of leaf, it was light, airy, and the wide brim provided shade from the brutal sun.

A flock of scarlet fliers went wheeling and diving overhead, their calls raucous. The chime shifted, swelling on the hot, still air, and then altered its tremolo before subsiding.

"What the hell are they saying to each other?" he wondered. "Hey, look at the stupid human standing out in the hot sun picking plant parts."

He grinned, bent, and hoisted his basket, fitted his arms into the shoulder straps, and shrugged the load onto his back. Turning, he plodded his way back down the row toward the high mushroom tower of Mundo Base.

In the forty days since Kylee had found him in the forest, he'd settled in, recovered his strength, and fallen into the routine they had established for him.

In a lot of ways, he felt like that old children's story he'd watched as a kid: *Alicia through the Wormhole*. The one where the young station girl falls past the event horizon and drops into a distorted and off-kilter universe that reeks of the insane.

He smacked his tongue in his dry mouth, enjoying the strain on his body as he almost trotted back, and made his way past the shops and outbuildings to the tower base. Inside, he hung his hat on the hook they'd given him, kicked off the slightly oversized quetzal-hide boots, and padded barefoot to the lift.

Engaging it, he watched the tower's skeleton swish past as he rose to the main level.

Passing through the foyer, he carried his basket into the kitchen and placed it on the counter. Damien, the twelve-year-old boy, and Shantaya, nine, both Rebecca's offspring, were already at work on the week's menu. They were slicing crest meat into thin strips which would be rinsed, soaked, and finally stewed in cactus pad mucilage to cut the meat's heavy metal content.

Where he came from, the idea of kids cooking a week's worth of food on their own, without supervision, would have defied credulity.

"There's enough food out there to feed a small army," he observed.

"The original farm was designed to feed five hundred," Damien told him as he pulled a ceramic blade through beet-red crest flesh. "Population has been in decline since."

Talbot studied the kid; even at his tender age, he had Rebecca's bones, the same dark brown eyes and wavy brown hair. Dya had told him that Rebecca's ancestry was something called Ainu, from northern Japan.

Shantaya, Damien's little sister, had the same resemblance, though the wider nose must have come from Rondo, the father.

"We will attend to the vegetables," Shantaya now told him. "Rebecca would like to see you in the lab."

Talbot took a moment to wash his hands and scrub the sweat from his head and neck. Then he crossed the foyer to the east lab. Originally, this space had been dedicated to dormitory cubicles, but as Donovan whittled away at the population, more and more lab functions had been transferred from the surface to the dome. Rebecca and Dya had divided the space, each filling their sections with microscopes, centrifuges, FTIR machines, and spectrographs. As to the rest of the jumbled and exotic equipment, Talbot had no clue.

His combat armor—recovered from the forest three days after his arrival—now rested on an elevated table, looking for all the world like a defunct robot. The kids had helped him clean it, oohing and aahing over the various scars left by quetzals and death fliers. The power pack was up to seven percent, but would go no higher.

He found Rebecca at her desk where it faced the window with its view of the eastern horizon. Looking out at the vista was to see an endless ocean of bumpy, rounded treetops that faded into the distance. Like a rumpled carpet of the various greens and blues.

"Have a seat," Rebecca told him as she checked a data sheet by her right hand and added a notation to the holographic display projected by her notebook.

Talbot dropped into the chair, studying the tall woman as she concentrated. Nothing about her could be called particularly attractive, but she exuded a kind of presence and command. Sometimes, given his background, it was all he could do to keep from saluting and calling her "Colonel."

Rebecca terminated the display on her notebook, then reached for another of the data sheets, handing it to Talbot.

He stared down at row upon row of what seemed code. Four or five letters and numbers in orders that made no sense to him.

"I don't understand. What is this?"

"Your genome," she told him. "Or, at least, the part of it which is of interest to us. We took the sample the day you arrived. We just haven't had time to run it until yesterday."

"Okay, and why is this important?"

She turned her thoughtful dark eyes on his. "You've been here for some time now. Worked in quite nicely, actually. Initially you were a little reticent in the company of the children, but you seem to have come to an understanding."

"Yeah, well, they're not like any children I ever knew. Kids are supposed to be laughing, teasing each other, watching holo-VR, and being, well, kids. When your kids are not in class with you, Su, or Dya, they're working. Half the time I think they're some kind of midget adults."

Rebecca smiled, a faraway look in her eyes. "I remember the kind of childhood you are talking about. Seems like a fantasy. Long time ago, different universe. Here we don't have the luxury to let children be children." A pause. "I'm curious. What do you think of us, of Mundo Base?"

"It bothers me that I'm locked in my room every night. Sort of feels like I'm a convict. Some sort of parolee. Not to be trusted. Hell, Rebecca, even if you had any family silver or jewelry to be stolen, where would I fence it?"

"Pending our conversation here, perhaps we can change that. When you arrived, we didn't know you, or what you represented. We took that precaution for your protection. And ours."

"Afraid I was going to mug you in your sleep?"

"No. Actually, we were afraid you'd do something stupid, like try and sneak out some night, hotwire an aircar, or screw something up, create some sort of mess."

"Hey, I get it. It's just that I 'effing don't like being treated like a child. I'm a combat vet who's been up to my ass in the shit, so you have no idea how humiliating it is to be told that I can't set foot past a certain line unless I'm accompanied by *a child* to keep me safe."

"But the fact is—"

"Yeah, yeah. They know a fricking lot more about Donovan's dangers than I do." He softened his reaction with an amused grin. "Hey, I was out there."

He jerked a thumb over his shoulder. "But for that armor, I'd have died the day we first set down. So, here's the thing: I don't have to like it, but I'm smart enough to know when to swallow my lumps, shut up, and listen. Especially when it's Kylee, Damien, or Shantaya trying to keep me alive."

Her thoughtful eyes continued to assess him. "Tell me the rest. Be honest."

He shrugged. "Just because I feel like I'm out of my league most of the time doesn't mean that I'm not glad to be here. But honestly, if I thought my squad was still on-planet, I'd rather be back with them. That longing, however, is more than balanced by the fact that I'd be brought up on charges for absence without leave, tossed in the brig, or maybe even shot. So, Rebecca, it is what it is."

"You seem to be particularly taken with Kylee."

"Her and Rocket? I never thought I'd feel this way about a kid and an alien."

"Special place in the heart, huh?"

"That's a pretty good way to put it."

She nodded. "And how do you feel about me, Dya, and Su?"

"A little distant. As if you see me as something more than a lab specimen, but less than a man."

She stared off past the horizon. "Of course you'd think

that. It's just been the family for so long. So few of us. Then just us three. I think we began to assume there were no other human beings. Your arrival was . . . unexpected."

"Intrusive, you mean? Actually, I get that. I came from a big family myself. I'm an outsider. You're the C.O., the leader. You have the right to distance yourself. Dya? I think she makes the effort, but just can't quite trust herself to lower that last barrier. Su? I think I make her nervous at a fundamental level."

"You do. Some personalities just grate. You do not exhibit the skill sets Su expects in a man, but she is station-born, where the men she enculturated with acted differently."

"How so?"

"In her world, your companion, Shintzu, would have been the one to survive. Males are more, let us say, decorative where she comes from."

"Shin was plenty tough." He shook his head. "That a slug got her? That was just luck of the draw. Literally. We tossed a token to see who'd bathe first that day."

"And Mundo Base?"

"It's falling apart around your ears, Rebecca. I've been making a list of things that need maintenance. Half the light panels are burned out. That soft rattle in the lift motor? I'd bet the bearings are starting to wear. I found some rubber gasket material in the big shed and stuffed it into the crack where the window was leaking by Taung and Ng-yap's bunks. But it needs to be sealed from the outside, because there's no telling where the water is going between the walls. And that's just the start of the list."

"Which means?"

"Eventually, maybe in the next couple of years, you're going to have to give up the dome."

"No."

Talbot spread his hands. "Rebecca, look at my armor back there. In this humid environment, even the best voltaics eventually will end up compromised. Seals crack, moisture and biological material infiltrate, and electrical circuits short out. Power packs have a life span, as you know. When the original refrigeration units went bad, Rondo wired in the power pack from one of the aircars. The second one is running the base atmosphere plant.

Technology, even the best, wears out. Entropy is part and parcel of whatever universe we're in here."

"And then?"

"Like Dya says: Move, adapt, or die." He paused. "Or contact Port Authority and see if we can barter for replacement parts from either *Turalon* or *Freelander.*"

She flinched. "There is a reason we cut the ties last time."

"Talina Perez shot Clemenceau years ago. They declared independence, granted deeds and titles. What they call a 'libertarian' society."

"Talina Perez was Clemenceau's ruthless hired gun."

"Might have been. Now there's a council. Shig Mosadek, Yvette Dushane, and her."

"Shig?" She fingered her chin. "Inoffensive Shig? The teacher? That's a surprise. Dushane, now she was a tough one."

"You guys decide what you want to do. I'm just telling you, you've got problems coming. There's a reason the floor slopes under the kids' bedrooms. The floor joists are rusted through. You know as well as I do that things are falling apart. Eventually, however, it's going to be something big. You might want to start planning for that unfortunate reality, because it's coming."

"What part do you see yourself playing in that future, Mark?"

"You tell me. This is your home. Your family. For the time being, I'm here on sufferance. I'm willing to haul my weight, shoulder my share of the burden, but like the kids constantly tell me, I've still got a lot to learn."

"Actually your door has been unlocked for more than a week now. That you haven't tried it indicates that you're content with your life here. Now that you know, we will trust you not to do anything stupid—like go for an evening stroll outside under the moonlight and get eaten. Or open a vial of some poisonous substance Dya has concocted from one of the deadly plants."

"Thank you. I'll do my best to stay alive." Then Talbot lifted the data sheet. "What's this all about?"

Rebecca didn't even hesitate when she said, "We want your contribution to the future."

"I said I'd shoulder my share."

"Thank you." She fixed him with her curious brown eyes. "Dya has compared your genome with each of ours. The genetic load isn't prohibitive in any combination. Dya will ovulate sometime in the coming week. We'd like to try and impregnate her if you don't have any objection."

Talbot started. Mouth open.

Rebecca lifted an eyebrow, as if to hint that it was his turn to answer.

"I, uh . . . Well, just how would this . . ." He felt an odd constriction at the base of his throat.

"The usual way. Unless you'd be more comfortable simply ejaculating into a cup, in which case we can use a syringe to inseminate her."

At a total loss, he just stared.

23

Dan Wirth never ceased to amaze. Talina tucked her thumbs in her belt where she stood outside in the darkness and stared into The Jewel's gaudily lit interior. Through the door, she could see most of the gaming tables, all crowded with men and women.

Liquor was flowing freely; Wirth's waitstaff navigated their way through the crowd with drinks. Laughter rose and fell along with the excited calls of "Place your bets, ladies and gentlemen!"

Most surprising, though, was the band playing on a raised platform in the back. Wirth had sprung for the musicians. Not just recordings or synth, but the real thing. The last time she'd heard them, she and Cap . . .

No, let it go.

To her surprise, she found herself tapping her foot to the catchy tune. *Old Orion*, wasn't it?

The night around her felt oddly warm for this time of year, and, in the dark of the moon, the sky above appeared as a black mat dusted with a billion stars. If she looked up in the northwest, she could see the dot of reflective light that was *Freelander* following its high orbit. The ghost ship with its legendary temple of human bones constructed from the ship's dead, both murdered and naturally deceased.

"Number eight wins!" came the call from the craps table, followed by hollers of delight.

Talina shifted to see the back of the room where Wirth himself manned the cage, exchanging SDRs for chips to use at the tables. Allison's absence meant that someone had managed to pony up the exorbitant price Wirth charged for her "special" sexual services.

Hard to believe she was the same woman Talina had once known. But then, she'd always been delicate of mind and spirit. Trish had called her a "china doll" once. That was the thing about dolls, they existed for others to play with, dress as they would, and use as they would.

"Another reason to put a bullet in Wirth's head," she whispered under her breath so that the marine standing in the shadows just beyond the door couldn't hear.

In The Jewel someone whistled in surprised delight. Yells and clapping ensued.

"Everything look all right to you?" Abu Sassi asked as he emerged from the night and saluted the marine standing at the door.

"Looks fine, Corporal."

"Threes over kings," Step Allenovich whooped as he slapped cards on one of the poker tables. "Read 'em and weep, boys."

To Talina's practiced eye, Step looked to be moderately sober. But then, he knew the stakes. If any of this got out of hand, Kalico would shut it down in an instant.

"Corporal, keep an eye on that big guy in the back. That's Art Maniken. He's Dan Wirth's doer of evil deeds, head-breaker, and arm-twister. He's the one who will most likely give you a high sign if anyone starts to get out of hand."

"Think that's likely?"

"To my complete surprise, I don't. My guess is that for the time being, all parties are going to be on their best behavior. Wirth's making money, your people are hell and away from Corporate Mine, the rest of Port Authority is seeing new faces again. If there's a maggot in the fruit, it's going to be a loner. Maybe a Wild One come to town who doesn't know the rules and thinks he's still in the bush."

"How will my people know?"

"Anyone you don't recognize that starts trouble? Stun him or her, give us a call, and we'll pick them up and handle it."

"Thanks, Talina. Gotta tell you, I think we were all getting a bit stir crazy down there."

"Stay frosty, Corporal." She tapped him on the armor, took one last look, and walked the half block to Betty Able's brothel.

Stepping in the door, Talina found the couches in the waiting room occupied by no less than six men and three women, all waiting for an opening with whichever man or woman they desired. Betty stood behind her bar, dispensing glasses of whatever libation a waiting customer might desire.

In one corner, Shin Wong played poker with a blond-haired man, a short stack of SDRs before him on the table.

Talina shot an inquiring look at Betty when the madam met her gaze. The buxom, middle-aged blonde gave her a slight shrug, and the flat-handed, "level sailing" gesture that indicated no problems.

Talina backed out and sighed.

Accessing com, she asked, "How we doing, Trish?"

"Nothing to report, Tal. Perimeter's tight. No one has tried passing the gates. Not to say it isn't early yet."

"Yeah. I'll drop by Inga's."

"Stay frosty."

"You, too."

Talina, wary from experience, kept her steps to the middle of the streets. Here and there—where the right design of light panels had been included either in *Turalon* or *Freelander*'s cargo—pools of light illuminated what had once been darkness. At least until they started to burn out in another five or ten years.

Didn't matter, she'd take what she could get.

The quetzal inside snuggled warmly around her spleen.

"Bet you'd like a good fight, wouldn't you?"

Yes, the soft voice in her mind said.

"Asshole."

The quetzal didn't reply.

She wondered if there was ever any way she could make peace with the beast.

Talina exchanged greetings with the occasional people she passed, some locals, others transportees. Not surprisingly, even Kalico's people knew who she was and treated her with respect.

At Inga's, the benches out front were filled, people enjoying the warm and sultry night. She acknowledged the greetings, nodded to the marine at the door, and stepped inside.

Here, too, the tables were mostly full, and a knot had formed on the south side of the bar where Inga and her helpers were filling cups and mugs.

A single figure sat in Talina's chair on the north end, surrounded only by emptiness.

Talina trotted down the steps, acknowledging waves, nodding to people who called greetings.

Walking up beside the lone woman, she said, "You're in my chair."

"Thought you were working."

"I am."

"The nice thing about your chair," Kalico Aguila said, half turning to meet Talina's eyes, "is that no one bothers anyone sitting in it. It's like sacred private space."

"I've broken a lot of heads over the years to keep it that way." Talina tapped the wood with a hard finger. "You know, you're the only person who'd dare to put her butt on my chair. Not sure what I ought to do about that."

"If you decide to break my head"—Kalico seemed to stumble over the words—"Private Michegan will shoot you dead before my body hits the floor."

The Supervisor lacked coordination when she tilted her head to indicate the combat-armored marine standing no more than ten paces away. Back to the wall, rifle in her hands, she was keeping track of every move Talina made.

Kalico blinked, eyes dull in a drunken stare. "You still irritated that I wanted to shoot you, Shig, and Yvette? Is that what's always eating at you?"

Talina noticed that Kalico wasn't drinking wine this evening, but had a glass of Inga's whiskey on the bar before her.

"While that didn't exactly endear you to me, I'd let it pass as reaction mass through the tubes."

"Then what?" she snapped. Blinked. And her head wobbled. "What is with you, Talina? It's like you're always ready to fight. And what's this hatred for Spiro? Granted, she's a . . . well . . ."

"Sour, angry, constipated bitch in need of a smack to the side of the head and general psychological counseling?"

Kalico frowned, cocked her head. "Well, yes. That's just what she is. Constipated in the soul. Angry. But she's *my* angry bitch, understand?"

"Just between us, Supervisor, did you have your angry, constipated bitch kill Cap Taggart?" Talina asked mildly.

Kalico, drunk or not, flashed quick blue eyes Talina's way. "Ah, I see."

"See what? Cap's killer popping into your mind? Was it you? Spiro? One of the other marines?"

Kalico stared at her as if trying to focus. "You had to be there. On *Turalon*. I was watching everything falling into chaos. And then *Freelander* appears like a fucking ghost. Cap was my strong right arm. I *needed* him. But when I needed him the most what's he do? He strolls in from the dead and hands me his resignation to run off and be a Donovanian." She smiled wistfully. "That was like having my guts pulled out."

"So you ordered Spiro to kill him?"

Kalico shook her head. Blinked hard, as if to clear her vision. "I might have said, 'I want that man dead,' or something to the effect, but I never gave that specific order."

Kalico squinted her eyes, as if looking back in time. "No. It wouldn't have been because of me. If that were the case, Spiro would have saluted, said, 'Yes, ma'am.' and marched off to do it. Even Deb Spiro, as lacking in imagination as she is, and hating Cap as much as she did, would have made sure she was acting under a direct order."

Talina watched carefully; Kalico struggled to form her words. "Spiro would have immediately implemented such an order. Cap would have been dead. That very day. And very publicly shot."

"He had trouble with her down at the shuttle field fence. Maybe she waited until later, bided her time?"

Kalico lifted her whiskey, sipped it. "She's cold enough to do it that way. Angry. Angry woman. But she worshipped that man. I say worshipped. Thought he walked on vacuum. When he left, well, as hard as I took it, that was nothing compared to Spiro. Like the universe betrayed her."

"So, you didn't order Cap's death?"

"I did not. I'm a Supervisor. You know?" She blinked, struggling to focus. "I didn't understand, you know? It's this damned planet. What it does to a person. How it changes them. Like it pulls who you are out of you, and puts a new you back inside that you never expected yourself to be. Does that make sense?"

"Supervisor, you're drunk."

"No. I've only had . . . what? Four of these? Or is it five?"

As Kalico squinted at her glass, Talina stepped over to Michegan and quietly said, "Dina, I need your help."

"Sorry, ma'am, but I don't take—"

"Shut up. Kalico's about to fall off that stool. Give Private Miso the high sign to come help you. I need you to quickly, efficiently, get the Supervisor off that stool. Tell her that something's come up, whisk her through the door into Inga's back room, and get her to her quarters."

"Uh, quarters?"

"Isn't she staying at the dormitory she built back of the assay office?"

"No. I, uh, assumed we'd take her back to the shuttle."

"Gate's locked."

"Shit."

"What's wrong with the dormitory? Boot one of the hired hands and—"

"You don't understand. That's the Supervisor. It'd be my ass if she woke up in a bunk bed surrounded by eight other people."

Talina gestured to Katsuro Miso across the room. The private came slowly, trying to act casual, as if a combat-armored marine could.

"What's up?" He glanced uneasily between Michegan and Talina.

"You know where my dome is?"

"Yeah. I was there that night you killed the quetzal."

"Put Kalico in my bed. Sheets are even mostly clean. But you two stay with her. Remember, I've got a plastic-covered hole in my wall."

"You got it, Tal," Miso said, snapping off a salute, much to Michegan's horror.

"And not a fucking word about this on the com. Just get her there, keep her safe, and keep your clap-trapping mouths *shut,* you hear me?"

"Yes, ma'am."

As they started for Kalico, Talina called, "And be damned sure you lock Inga's back door on the way out!"

The last thing she needed was to have Inga land on her because the supply room was left open and half the town found its way in to drink for free.

24

Kylee and Rocket led the way at a trot; the blonde girl's hair bounced in silky yellow waves with each stride. Matching her pace, the quetzal shimmered in patterns of green, the colors seeming to flow through the beast as it passed various shades of surrounding vegetation.

Overhead, the mighty forest stretched up into a green, aqua, and blue infinity of thick triangular branches that faded into a sea of viridian, turquoise, and teal leaves. The chime rose and fell; hoppers flitted across dizzying heights in the air high above.

Talbot shifted the rifle as he followed along behind. It wasn't his military-issue weapon—for which he only had one round remaining—but an old bolt gun he'd found in the armory with nine rounds of ammunition. The women had told him they didn't like the rifle's heavy recoil and preferred their spring-fired tubes that shot poisoned darts. The venom was something concocted by Dya from the crushed bodies of one of the more colorful invertebrates that crawled around the place.

As they proceeded, Talbot kept his eyes peeled, desperate to identify the next danger before the girl or the quetzal could. So far, he hadn't even come close.

"You made Dya happy," Kylee remarked as if offhandedly.

Talbot's lips bent. Dya wasn't the only one. He'd been nervous the night she'd come to his bed, unsure what to expect. Of the three women, he'd liked her the best, had even entertained erotic thoughts about her.

What started out as a friendly conversation, as she tried to put him at ease, had turned into a rather remarkable night. The best he'd ever had with a woman. In those hours, he'd gone from a mere source of precious genetic material to a lover, and by morning light, to a friend, as he and Dya had watched Capella rise over the eastern forest horizon, holding each other and laughing.

Figuring that Kylee had something else on her mind besides his sexual relationship with her mother, he picked the most probable cause, and said, "It wasn't that big a deal. I just reset the hinges on her lab door and rewired the grow light in her botanical cabinet. She's lucky no one got electrocuted the way those wires were hanging out."

Kylee tossed her familiar "you're an idiot" look over her shoulder. "I was referring to the sex, Mark. Since then, we've all been a little worried about you."

"Whoa. Hold it. Both of you." He pulled to a stop.

In unison, girl and quetzal spun around in the trail. As he'd noticed so many times, something about the way they walked didn't disturb the roots beneath their feet.

"Worried how?" he asked. "And more to the point, why am I discussing these things with a nine-year-old girl?"

She gave him her most innocent blue-eyed stare; Rocket fixed him with all three eyes, mouth slightly agape in what passed for a quetzal's mimicry of a smile.

"Mark, you're my best friend. Don't best friends discuss things that are important to them?"

"Well, yeah, they do. But a man and a woman's relationship in bed—especially with the woman's daughter—isn't a common topic of conversation where I come from."

"Here he goes again," she told Rocket. "God, I have to explain *everything* to him." She turned back to Talbot. "You have become a husband. In a family. That means . . ."

She frowned, as if suddenly struck by something important. "Wait a minute. I forgot about how it's done in Solar System. I can be as dense as a rock sometimes."

"How's that?" Talbot asked nervously.

She looked at Rocket, then they both looked quizzically up at Mark. "Do you need a wedding ceremony? Would that make you feel more married than just a consummation?"

A consummation? Where did she get these words? Mark shifted the rifle to his shoulder, unable to keep from laughing at the absurdity of it. "Kylee, I . . ."

"Well, would you? I want you to feel more at ease. You

worry me. Sometimes it's like you're just holding on. Bewildered."

"*I* worry *you*?" He arched an eyebrow, looking out at the forest that had killed so many of her people and his. "You're nine, for God's sake!"

Her smooth face went serious. "Well, but for Rocket, you're my best friend. You don't always demand that Rocket and me be better than we are."

"Rocket and I. If Su heard you say Rocket and me, she'd have you figuring calculus problems all night."

"See? That's just it." She grinned shyly. "You didn't hammer me with it. You and Rocket just let me be me."

He started walking along beside them, the trees being open enough here. "Yeah, well, maybe I let you slide too much. What do you think, Rocket? Should we make her do calculus problems while you and I scout for chokeya plants?"

Rocket swiveled two eyes his direction and uttered a musical trilling that Talbot knew meant yes.

"You two." Kylee shook her head; nevertheless she was searching the forest around them. "I mean, calculus is fun, but . . . Wait. There. Chokeya."

Talbot followed her pointing finger, seeing the plant where it blended in between two smaller tree trunks.

"Do you want me to do this?" she asked, holding a hand out.

"I think I can cut a plant," Talbot told her. "Consider it a test, a rite of passage on the way to manhood."

"What's a rite of passage?"

"Something that men do on the way to becoming worthy and ranked individuals in their society." He winced. "Like consummation."

She nodded, as if this made perfect sense.

Talbot slipped the machete from where it rode in his pack, eased back behind the smaller bole. Leaping out, he swung the long blade, neatly severing the inch-thick stem a couple of inches above where it emerged from the ground. He jumped back out of the way.

The chokeya whipped back and forth like a severed snake as its higher branches clung to the tree above; droplets of fluid gleamed as they were flung this way and that.

The three of them backed away, out of range, and waited.

"You like Dya, don't you?" Kylee asked.

"I do. More than I thought I would. Once she relaxed . . . I don't know. It's weird. What people used to call a marriage of convenience, but the more I get to know her . . ." He ended in a shrug.

"Do you think you could love her?"

"Sure."

"What about Rebecca?"

He glanced at her. "That's a tougher call. She's . . ."

"Coming to your bed eventually."

"Kylee!"

"Think it through." Kylee reached up, putting a hand on his arm. "What do you think Rebecca and Su are going to do? If you're married to one, you're married to all. That's what husbands do. And if you say no? What's Rebecca to think? Dya's good enough, but she's not? She's running out of time, you know. It won't be long before she stops ovulating."

Talbot stared down into Kylee's erstwhile blue eyes. "You really are a dwarf, you know. A much older being hiding out in a little girl's body."

"I just don't want you getting into trouble." Kylee looked away as she draped one arm over Rocket's shoulders. The quetzal's skin reflected pearlescent reds and alternating waves of white which signaled contentment.

"I know," he said with a sigh. "It's just hard sometimes. And then I look around and see that it's just us."

She nodded. "Got to be pragmatic."

"What do you think about that? Damien's going to be a man soon; is he going to be your husband? I don't see a lot of choice, gene pools being what they are."

She frowned again. "I used to think so. Assuming he and I live that long. But since you showed up?" She raised a finger. "If I tell you something, you can't tell anyone else. No one."

"Okay, it will be our secret."

"Only Rocket and I know. It's just that, well, I've been thinking about the other people on Donovan. The ones in places like Port Authority. I think Damien would like a different wife than me. Not that he's said, but, I kind of know. We're family, but somehow it's already uninspiring to think of Damien and myself. Granted, I'm only nine. I'm told it will be different after I sexually mature. But, Damien and I, we're family. The few times we've talked about it, we both thought that we'd opt for artificial insemination."

Talbot laughed. "Am I actually hearing this? Yep. You're nine, all right. Nine going on twenty-nine."

"You showing up has changed things." She ran her fingers over Rocket's sides, flares of color erupting under her fingers. "We're wondering if maybe other people would show up and bring us new possibilities."

Talbot sighed, his eyes on the dying chokeya plant where it twisted back and forth in ever decreasing gyrations. Turned out there was more than one way to die on Donovan.

"They might," he told her softly. "The cargos from *Turalon* and *Freelander* have given the people on Donovan another lease on life. I've looked at the radio. It just needs to be plugged into a power source. We could call Port Authority again, but that's a decision to be made by Rebecca, Dya, and Su."

Kylee shocked him when she said, "There's an aircar power pack in the back of the refrigeration room. I remember when Rondo put it in there. He said it would keep longer in the cold, and it's wired into the photovoltaics to keep it charged just right."

Holy shit.

"Why are you telling me this?"

"Because I know that Su and Dya are worried. And, now that you're becoming a husband and father, you are part of the family. If there's ever an emergency, you need to know."

"I see."

"And the other thing is that, like Rocket, you're my only other special friend. So I'm trusting you." She gave him her best ravishing smile, "And since I've come to realize that you're not a pedophile, I can trust you not to betray us. I can, can't I? You wouldn't, would you?"

The intensity with which she said it hit him like a thrown stone. "Not on your life, Kylee."

She pointed. "Plant's no longer dangerous. Let's go cut it down and get it back to the lab. Dya wants the liquids. She thinks they expand and contract given electrical charges. If she's right, it might mean a way to power things."

"How would that work?"

Kylee glanced up at him and shrugged, saying, "How would I know? I'm only nine."

Talbot threw his head back and laughed in a way he hadn't for years.

25

At the first tickle in her gut, Kalico Aguila scrambled off the bed, slipped, and almost fell. She barely registered her surroundings. Caught a glimpse of a toilet through an open door, and charged headlong into the small bathroom. For the moment, misery dominated her universe, and she barely reached the toilet before her stomach pumped. And pumped. And pumped.

Finally, gasping, sweat beading on her face, neck, and back, she slumped down next to the bowl and ran fingers through her hair in an attempt to claw it out of her face.

She'd barely focused on the small room—duraplast everywhere—before the dry heaves wracked her body. For what seemed an infinity she tried to puke herself inside out.

As she again fought for breath, she squinted through eyes half-blinded by a stabbing headache.

"Dear God," she whispered. "What the hell is wrong with me? Just let me die."

"It's called a hangover," a not-so-sympathetic voice said from the door.

Kalico flinched, rubbed her mouth, and shot a sidelong glance to where Talina Perez, dressed in a coarse fabric robe, leaned against the frame. The woman had her head cocked, dark eyes knowing.

"A hangover?"

"The old-fashioned kind. In the world you come from, you just take a pill, and it directs your body to oxidize the alcohol molecules, moderates the headache, and stimulates your neural reflexes to the point you never have to feel the pain." Talina gave an innocent flip of the hand. "Welcome to Donovan. No pills. Here, we do it the hard way."

"Shit on a shoe, Perez, but you're fucking depressing." Kalico fought the sudden watering of her mouth, one hand to her stomach as she sat half-naked and sprawled on the bathroom floor. "Where in hell am I?"

"My place. I had Michegan and Miso haul your drunken ass over here where no one could see the spectacle. Figured you'd want to deal with the aftereffects in privacy."

Kalico glanced down at her skimpy underwear. "Where are my clothes?"

"All folded neatly on the back of my chair where they'll stay clean and presentable. I figured my sheets would just have to take their chances. Thanks for making it to the flushing god instead of spewing all over my floor and bed."

"What next?" Kalico whispered, wishing her brain would stop hammering her skull into pieces.

"My suggestion?" Talina pointed at the cramped stall. "Take a long shower. It helps. Then get dressed, and I'll have breakfast made for you."

"Why are you doing this?"

"Because, much to my disgust, Supervisor, I think you were telling me the truth last night."

"About what?"

"You don't remember?"

Kalico squinted, realized it hurt to think. "Last I remember, I was sitting at the bar. Wait. You were bitching at me about being in your chair."

"Why did you order Cap's murder?"

"Cap's . . . ? What? I never ordered . . . Why would you think I had Cap killed?"

"Yeah." Talina sighed. "That's what you said last night, too. It pains me to admit, but I actually believe you. Which is why you woke up alive this morning, and why I'll make your breakfast. Meanwhile, you can suffer like the rest of us do after too much of Inga's whiskey."

"Wait. If I tell you I killed Cap, will you just shoot me? Put me out of this misery?"

Talina paused in the doorway, a dark eyebrow lifted. "Nice try, but you'll be back to normal in a day or two." And then she was gone.

Kalico closed her eyes, floated in the dark misery. "A day or two? Clap-trapping hell. Maybe I'll shoot myself."

When she finished her shower, toweled off, and stepped out of the bathroom in a weak-kneed wobble, it was to find her natty black pantsuit laid out at the foot of Perez's bed.

She glanced around the small and Spartan bedroom, cramped as it was where the side of the dome curved down along the outside wall. The bed, a dresser and wardrobe, a chair, and a large trunk were the only furnishings. On the partitioning wall hung a series of holos, images that had to be Perez's family back on Earth. A couple showed Perez and a muscular man dressed in quetzal hide. That must have been Mitch. In another, a younger Talina Perez smiled where she was holding a rifle in front of a dead quetzal; the admin dome could be seen in the background. A crowd was gathered around, all of them looking remarkably clean in freshly issued coveralls.

Other than that, the room was as basic as the woman who lived in it.

Kalico dressed and ambled wearily out to the breakfast bar where a big glass of water and a steaming cup of coffee waited. The place smelled of beans, peppers, and corn. Perez stood over the small kitchen stove, a spatula in her hand, her black hair pulled back in a ponytail.

"Drink the water first. See if it stays down," Talina told her. "Water's cheap. You don't want the precious coffee coming back up. I'd consider that a crime."

"Where are my people?" Kalico sipped the water tentatively.

"Finnegan and Tompzen are outside. One at my door, the other keeping an eye on my plastic."

Kalico glanced at the transparent patch on Perez's wall. "That quetzal did that?"

"Batted my couch right through the wall. Tough beasts, quetzals."

"I heard it broke Cap up pretty badly."

Perez filled two plates with her concoction and brought them over to the counter. Setting Kalico's before her, she slipped onto the next stool and stared thoughtfully at the breakfast. "Yeah. Crippled him. He didn't have a chance when his murderer opened that valve."

Kalico picked up a fork. "Something's coming back. You said last night you thought it was Lieutenant Spiro?"

Talina gave her a sidelong glance. "She hated Cap and me. That's no secret."

"You ever think that whoever killed Cap might have actually done you and him a favor?"

"I do." She paused, making a face. "But only when I'm really in the mood to hate myself for being a selfish and self-absorbed shithead."

Kalico cut off a bite of the wonderful-smelling mix on her plate, tried it, and almost sighed at the flavors. Then the tang of the peppers set her mouth on fire.

"You think this is a remedy for hangover?" she asked hoarsely as she chugged water.

"You'll have to trust me on this. Among my mother's people, your malady is called *la cruda*. The Maya have been treating hangover like this for the last seven hundred years. It's the vitamins, the heat. You won't believe it, but you'll feel better, quicker."

"Yeah? Blessed vacuum." Despite the burn, she savored another bite. "I used to handle spicy food well. Maybe it's because I've been eating ration for so long. Fire and ice, what's that wonderful taste?"

"It impressed me that you people eat rations over there."

"What have I got that I can trade for these ingredients? I mean, seriously? What's in this? This might be the single best meal I've eaten since spacing from Transluna."

"Ground corn, a mix of refried pinto and Anasazi beans, a spice called achiote from one of the annatto plants in the greenhouse, bits of diced chamois meat, and my crushed chili rojo from ripe poblanos."

"Seriously, what do you want in trade? I've got a lot of gold."

"Gold is everywhere. How about a shuttle?"

Kalico stopped short. "A shuttle?"

"You have ten of them mothballed up on *Freelander*."

"As you Donovanians say, damned straight I do." Kalico might have been hungover, but all of her senses flashed onto high alert. "What would you do with a shuttle? That's like handing you a key to *Freelander*."

"*Freelander*? What would we do with it?"

"Strip it? Set up an orbiting colony? A lot of manufacturing and fabricating can be done in vacuum and freefall that's impossible in atmosphere and gravity."

"That's where you're planning on manufacturing your carbon-fiber cable, isn't it?"

"It is." The heat from the peppers had Kalico's nose running, sweat dampening her lips and cheeks. It might have been illusion but she could feel the alcohol seeping from her pores.

Then Kalico added, "Assuming I can get anyone to set foot on that bucket for long enough to put together a factory. *Freelander*'s a death ship. You, um . . ."

"Go on."

Kalico shot her an evaluative glance. "Listen. People see things up there. Flickers of movement. Shapes. Shimmers. Images at the edge of vision. Weird feelings, as if something unseen, out of sync in time, just passed through your body."

"Ghosts?"

"Maybe. For the simple-minded. More like anomalies that defy our understanding of physics. At least in the kind of universe we're familiar with. Hell, what can any of us know about the infinite variations in the multiverse? Wherever *Freelander* went it took one hundred and twenty-nine years to get here. It was damn spooky. Especially when the ship was only missing for three years in our universe and timeline."

Talina chewed, swallowed, and gestured with her fork. "You don't strike me as the superstitious kind. So, the ship's really haunted?"

"You ask me, parts of it are still out of sync with time. Like it brought with it part of whatever universe it was in."

"All right, that should put your mind at ease about us claiming your ship and putting a colony on it."

"Then, why do you want a shuttle?"

"For the same reason you do. For its heavy-lift capabilities. Pete Morgan's got an oil well out the other side of the Wind Mountains. We're transporting two drums of oil per trip by aircar. A shuttle would haul the big twenty-thousand-gallon tank in one trip."

"I could lease you mine."

"You could." Talina pointed with her fork again. "But, speaking of simple-mindedness, what happens if your shuttle suffers a mishap? Core malfunction? Some of the trees uproot one of their less desirable neighbors and toss it on top of your shuttle? Some computer glitch? Sabotage by an unhappy worker?"

Kalico stiffened, slitting an eye. "Is that a threat, Officer Perez?"

Talina started, her mouth puckering. "No. Pus and ions, where do you come up with this nonsense? The point I was making is that you've got one toilet-sucking shuttle on the planet, and you're using it for a lot of chores it wasn't designed for, like recharging cores for your smelter. Meanwhile, you've got ten up in orbit. If your shuttle breaks—no matter what the cause—how the hell are you going to get up and retrieve another shuttle?"

Kalico blinked, seeing it all unfold in her mind. "Holy shit." She took a deep breath, feeling even more queasy in her stomach. "Am I really that stupid?"

"I don't know," Talina answered. "But I have an active imagination. Seriously, what happens if you lose your one shuttle?"

"At the mine I've only got space to park one. The service life for my A-7 is fifteen years. My people are scrupulous in their maintenance. To think of the shuttle failing . . ."

Talina sipped from her cup of tea. "Welcome to Donovan. It's a whole new way of thinking about the unlikely . . . and knowing it's probably going to take place."

She paused. "Supervisor, this isn't Solar System. More to the point, this *really* isn't The Corporation. You, Shig, me, Yvette, we're not—and we don't have to be—friends. What we are is on our own. Abandoned. You have shuttles, a freaking haunted space ship, and a smelter. We have food, spices, talent, and a Donovan-trained population. Just like your people coming here to Port Authority for rest and relaxation, you have things we need. Between Port Authority and Corporate Mine, they're the only two legs we have to stand on. Cut one off? How do we walk our way into the future?"

"Yeah, I think I was already coming to that conclusion."

"The old way of thinking. For you. For us. Is going to have to change."

Kalico scooped up the last of her breakfast, wishing it

went on forever. Damn it, her farm was already failing, making her that much more reliant on Port Authority.

"We either figure out a way to work together, or in the end, none of us are going to make it."

"What about Lieutenant Spiro?"

Talina didn't bat an eye. "I withdraw my statement. Some of the old way of thinking isn't going to change. Before too long either I'm going to kill her, or she's going to kill me. No other way around it."

26

W hen Talina Perez hurried into the hospital dome, it was to find Raya Turnienko in conference with her nurse and assistant, Felicity Strazinsky. They were standing over a bed where Terry Mishka—who had a farm out at the edge of the bush just west of the aircar field—had had a too-close encounter with a slug.

When Talina glanced into the room, it was to see Terry, flat in bed, leg elevated. A long white bandage ran from the inside of his ankle up about halfway to the knee, marking the site of Raya's incision where she'd dug out the slug.

Terry had been lucky: he'd caught a ride on a wagon within moments after he'd felt the thing pierce his foot.

"How's it look?" Talina asked.

"Got it before it divided," Raya told her, looking up from the notes she was jotting and then handing them to Felicity.

"Terry," Talina called, "you getting careless, or what?"

Mishka made a face. "Careless. Sasha warned me about having a hole in my boot. It's been so long since I've seen a slug out there, and I knew better than to be standing in one place down in the bog. Thing is, I just wasn't paying attention."

"Yeah, well, at least you're not ending up a one-legged farmer," Felicity told him with a smile.

Sasha Mishka, Terry's wife, burst through the hospital's front doors, a grim set to her wide, sun-browned face. Her worn clothing still muddy from the field, she came pounding down the hall.

"How's Terry?" she called, urgency in her voice.

"Fine," Raya said, stepping out. "By the time I got to it, I think the slug had figured out it had made a mistake. After chewing on flesh as tough and gamy as Terry's, it practically jumped out of the incision on its own."

Raya gave Sasha a wink, adding, "Felicity can fill you in." To Tal, she said, "Got a minute?"

"Yeah. I got your message. What's up?"

Raya beckoned with a finger, leading Talina to her office. "Have a seat."

Talina dropped into the chair across from Raya's. The tall Siberian cocked her head, dark eyes pensive as she settled behind her desk. "Since finding the TriNA in your system, I've been going back. Been running tests on blood samples I've been taking over the last couple of years. The results are interesting."

She slipped a data sheet across to Talina.

Tal ran her eyes down the names, most of them locals from Port Authority, but interspersed were Wild Ones. About twenty of them. Behind each name either a + or - sign had been written. Most of the plus signs were listed behind Wild Ones. For example, she noted that the entire Briggs family were pluses.

At the end was her own name, with a prominent plus behind it.

"What am I looking at?"

"The number of people who have TriNA in their blood or tissues," Raya told her thoughtfully. "Incidentally, I checked your old samples from a couple of years back. You were negative. I think we can conclusively say that the day you killed the quetzal in the canyon is when you were infected."

"Mostly Wild Ones," Talina noted, going down the list again.

"Notice something else?" Raya asked. "Briggs, Shu Wans, Philos, the Andanis, and the rest? The really successful and self-sufficient families that have carved out farmsteads and outlying claims?"

"They're all positive." Talina tapped her chin with an index finger.

"And, with a few exceptions, people from town are negatives. Including folks like Tosi Damitiri. People who might work outside the fence—even have a place within an easy travel radius—but who don't spend that much time in the bush."

"So people who live the life, so to speak, are going to be infected?"

Raya nodded. "That's the hypothesis. I've had Mgumbe

running tests on the specific markers, the discrete sections of TriNA that mark its origin. It's time-consuming, delicate work, and we're doing it during the off hours, but it appears that most of the local TriNA infections around Port Authority come from chamois or crest. Not a big surprise given that they are most often food animals."

"And the Wild Ones? Like the Briggs boy, Flip?" She pointed at one of the larger plus signs.

"Quetzal."

"Maybe the one that French-kissed me that day?" Talina remembered her encounter with the quetzal outside the Briggs farmstead. The one that Flip had told her "just hangs around sometimes."

In answer to her question, Raya just shrugged.

"But you haven't seen any sign that having Donovanian TriNA in a person's system is detrimental?"

"Not so far, but, Talina, we're at the beginning of this. If not for you, we wouldn't even have recognized it. Who knows what the long-term effects are going to be?"

Talina felt the quetzal wiggle around behind her liver. The thing always seemed to know when it was the topic of conversation.

"You figured out how it talks to me yet?"

"Haven't a clue beyond the fact that it's some sort of molecular stimulus that triggers synapses, which trigger neural microcircuits, that activate the right dendritic trees, and fire the right neurons in the speech centers of your brain. But what makes that so fascinating is that your quetzal TriNA is utilizing what neurologists call your prior knowledge.

"What boggles Mgumbe, Cheng, and me is that somehow the quetzal TriNA molecules know their agenda, are organized to learn your neurology, can figure out how to manipulate it, and can achieve the desired end. By that, I mean they employ an input signal to gain a desired response through the language center of your brain. Do you realize how sophisticated that is?"

"I realize how creepy it is."

Raya didn't take the bait. Instead she leaned forward. "Talina, how often does the quetzal stimulate the wrong word from your language center? By that, I mean, make a mistake? For example, it means to communicate the word 'fear' but instead you hear 'feat.' A very similar word phonetically and structurally."

"It's always been on the money." That Raya was taking this so seriously made her feel unsettled. "You want to cut down to the bones of the matter?"

"Think of it this way—" Raya clasped her hands together as she leaned across the desk. "You are an alien creature. From a completely different biology and cultural system, using a completely foreign neurology, anatomy, and vocabulary, and somehow mere molecules have mastered the difficult task of interfacing with some of your most complicated mental and emotional functions. It has done this associatively and with reinforcement and demonstrates a knowledge and goal, learning strategy, and evaluation of performance. In short, your quetzal molecules are what we'd call intelligent actors."

"You're looking really grim about this, Raya."

"Yeah. I'm thinking we've completely misread Donovanian life. We've always thought of the quetzal in terrestrial terms. An organism. Like a shark or man-eating tiger." She paused. "I'm wondering now if a quetzal isn't just the vehicle—the packaging. What if the TriNA is the actual heart, soul, and essence of the creature?"

"I don't get it."

"You ever heard the old axiom that a human being is just a DNA molecule's way of propagating and disseminating more DNA? What if a quetzal is just TriNA's way of getting around, experiencing its world, and expanding its horizons?"

"And now you think it's moving into humans?" Talina swallowed hard. "Into me?"

Raya once again gave her one of those enigmatic shrugs. "Hey, like I said, we're just at the beginning here. The takeaway is that your quetzal shouldn't be able to talk to you. Shouldn't be able to stimulate physical pain, fear, and all those other emotions. You shouldn't be able to 'feel' it. And most of all, you said you can frighten it in return? That's a two-way feedback. Your ability to trigger neurons, which in turn send a signal that affects an emotional reaction in the quetzal molecules, shouldn't be possible either."

"So, what does that mean?"

"If you really think about it? It means true first contact with an alien intelligence."

"Intelligence? Isn't that a bit far out?"

"Tal, I don't know what to think at this stage of the game. One of the problems is that your quetzal didn't meet Donovan at the landing site and say 'Take me to your leader.' This is *alien* life. *Alien* intelligence. Trying to fit it into any kind of a human framework for the understanding of intelligence? That might pan out to be an absolutely ludicrous exercise in futility."

"Holy shit," Talina whispered, aware of Raya's dark-eyed stare.

"Yeah, whole new world, isn't it?" Raya said uncertainly.

And a lot more threatening. The sudden queasy feeling didn't make Talina feel any better.

27

If there were any feeling that absolutely annoyed Kalico Aguila, it was the sensation of being trapped. She'd felt that way on *Turalon*. Now she felt it again as she tramped down the main avenue. As if there were no options but capitulation.

Behind her, Privates Finnegan and Tompzen followed along through the morning, nodding at the locals they passed, returning greetings.

Kalico kept her frosty gaze ahead, not that she needed to keep her expression severe. The damned hangover saw to that.

She shot an evil, narrow-eyed glance at Inga's as she passed, asking herself, *What the hell was I thinking last night?*

But she knew full well why she'd done it. She'd gone and taken Perez's stool, knowing that no one would bother her there. That she could just sit and listen to people being happy, sharing fellowship. From her isolated stool, she could imagine herself part of the crowd, share the companionship, if only vicariously through the whiskey.

"My God, I can be a blinking idiot on occasion, can't I?" she growled under her breath.

What if Perez hadn't shown up? What if she'd climbed down off that stool, done something really stupid? Tried to make herself one with the rabble? Stumbled, slurred her words. Thrown up on herself or someone else?

"You are a Supervisor, you stupid bitch," she muttered under her breath.

Worse, she owed Perez now. Bad as that was, the woman had saved Kalico from herself. That could not be allowed to happen again. One more mistake, and Kalico could lose it all.

As could happen with the shuttle at any instant.

What the hell had she been thinking?

She pushed open the door to the admin dome and started down the hall. Finnegan and Tompzen tromped along behind her, looking tough in their dress uniforms, combat rifles slung over their shoulders.

At Yvette's office, she found the woman in conversation with two farmers. The man and woman couldn't have been more obvious if they'd had signs across their chests, given their chamois shirts, pants, and wide floppy sun hats.

"I need to see you and Shig," Kalico called in the door. "Five minutes, conference room. Have coffee sent."

Without waiting for confirmation, Kalico let herself into the conference room, ordering Tompzen and Finnegan. "I only want Shig and Yvette in there. No one else is to disturb us."

Both of her marines snapped out perfect salutes, taking position on either side of the door, grounding their rifles as they stood at attention.

Kalico walked back to the farthest chair and pulled it out. An unwelcome tickle in her gut made her pull a trash can close. Not that she'd need it—but better to be safe than hurl her breakfast all over the floor.

For long moments she sat, her headache down to a dull throb after the aspirin Perez had given her.

She went over her proposal. Trying to work through the fading whiskey fog to the most advantageous terms.

What am I missing?

Or, should she try and blast out more mountain to create a bigger landing field and keep the second shuttle there?

On the verge of making that decision, Shig and Yvette entered, each smiling.

"Good morning, Supervisor," Shig greeted, that eternal and enigmatic smile plastered across his face. "How can we be of service this morning?" He seated himself across from her.

Yvette had a sardonic look on her face as she dropped into a chair, saying, "Oh, no problem at all, Supervisor. You didn't interrupt a thing. In fact, Ollie was just saying, 'Wouldn't it be nice if the Supervisor ducked in this morning and disrupted our meeting? That would be uncommonly kind of her.'"

Kalico blinked. "Excuse me? Who is Ollie? And why on Earth would he be—"

"They call that sarcasm, Supervisor," Yvette told her. "Never mind. It's not important. Now that we're here, and coffee is ordered, what can we do for you?"

As Yvette spoke, Shig's bushy black eyebrow had lifted in subtle amusement. He now sat with this hands steepled, fingertips pressed together.

"I have a proposition." Kalico ordered her thoughts. "To date, our relationship has proven fruitful for both sides. I have been pleased with the cooperation that you've shown me and my people. I would like to expand on that relationship."

"Very well," Shig said mildly. "What did you have in mind?"

"You will remember that we came to an agreement over the *Turalon* food rations. It has come to my attention that my people are finding the rations somewhat, shall we say, monotonous."

"Not to mention about to run out," Yvette said dryly.

"I would like to expand the choices available to my cafeteria. I am also aware that a good many transportees, finding their contracts untenable, have allowed you to expand your agricultural production. Rather than make demands that would be upsetting to your agriculturalists, I will be happy to leave the transportees to labor for your farmers. In return I would like the ability to purchase their produce at fair market value."

"Done," Shig said easily.

Kalico saw Yvette's slight smile. Ignored it. Plunged on. "Recently it has become apparent that my medical facilities, not to mention my med tech at Corporate Mine, are not up to the challenge of caring for my people. Our original agreement has been that Felicity Strazinsky has flown down to Corporate Mine to work in my clinic three times a week. Instead, I would like to initiate an air ambulance to immediately lift my sick and injured to the Port Authority hospital."

"Of course," Yvette told her. "You can call in the nature of the emergency while you're in the air. Raya will have everything prepared upon arrival."

Kalico shifted, the first fingers of suspicion slipping past her fuzzy brain. Not a single dissent?

"In our initial agreement, we laid out lines of separation between your people and mine."

"We did," Shig agreed.

"I would like the ability to offer employment to your people on a case-by-case basis."

Shig smiled and nodded. "Granted."

"Why aren't you at least counteroffering?"

"We are libertarians, Kalico," Yvette said softly. "In our original contract, we stated that your people would stick to Corporate Mine. That if they came to Port Authority without authorization, we'd send your people back. If you go back to the paperwork, the only stipulation you made was that you would deny entry to any of our people at your discretion. Our people are welcome to do anything, make any deal they wish. It is not our responsibility to tell them they can't."

"So I can hire anyone I want?"

Shig spread his hands. "Hire away."

What the hell else had she misread about Port Authority? Damn it, there had to be a trap here somewhere.

"So you will grant me free rein in Port Authority to do as I wish?"

"Within reason," Yvette told her. "If you come in and start impressing people, seizing their belongings, infringing on their private property rights and denying them free will . . . Well, unless of course, it is their free will and choice to deny themselves such freedoms. We really don't care."

"What else did you want to discuss?" Shig asked amiably.

"I have only one shuttle on the planet, but ten berthed aboard *Freelander*."

"That is correct," Shig told her as coffee was brought in. Conversation stopped while cups were dispensed and filled.

Over a steaming cup of black coffee, Kalico said, "I need space to park another. I don't have room at Corporate Mine. You have a shuttle field. If something happens to my A7, I'd be planet-bound. Unable to ascend to orbit to recover a replacement."

"That would indeed be the case." Yvette's lips quirked slightly.

"If you would allow me to park my spare shuttle in your landing field, I would allow you to use it on occasion, with my approval."

"That would be very kind of you," Shig told her. "Of course you may park as many shuttles as you would like at Port Authority. In return for the use of one at our discretion, we will accept the responsibility for its maintenance and upkeep."

Still feeling as if she were missing something, Kalico said, "Well then . . . I guess we have a deal."

Shig and Yvette locked eyes, some silent communication passing between them as Yvette said, "Yes, I guess we do."

28

Talbot was working atop the dome roof with Damien and Kylee, scrubbing out one of the rainwater collectors where a slimy green algae of terrestrial origin—if that meant anything—had taken root in the tanks and piping.

For two weeks now, he had been grappling with the fact that Dya was pregnant. And then, that morning, came the startling revelation that Su had conceived. Apparently as a result of their first coupling.

He was still trying to get his head around the implications. Coming, as he did, from a rural section of England, he'd been raised in a rather traditional family, in a culture where a woman who wanted to have a baby had to first pass certain genetics tests, obtain a license, and then undergo a strictly observed Corporate-monitored pregnancy. The entire process was managed and controlled by The Corporation.

Until he'd walked out of the forest, nothing in his mental template could have entertained the notion of "pragmatic copulation," as Dya phrased it.

Hell, he was still stumbling over the complexities of polygamy. It wasn't anything like he'd imagined. But then, dealing with his three wives was challenging enough. Each had her own little peculiarities, and essentially he was the newcomer in their house, their territory. But ultimately, the looming reality that there was only the four of them—literally the only adults in their world—acted as the final arbitrator in their relationship. That knowledge tempered all of their interactions.

As Talbot puzzled over his curious new life, he stopped short, frozen in midscrub.

The distant, high roar of the shuttle couldn't be mistaken. The sound rose shrilly, a distant booming.

"It's a shuttle!" Damien cried, turning from where he ran a swab through one of the pipes.

Talbot jerked himself up straight, staring off to the northwest. "Coming in from orbit. There's a ship up there!"

For long moments they listened as the sound grew in the north and faded.

"They've crossed the threshold," Talbot said. "Hear the way the sound dropped off? They just slowed enough to drop below the sonic barrier. If we were closer to Port Authority, we'd hear the thrusters."

"Tell me about Port Authority," Damien said. The lanky kid reached up to flip curly dark-brown hair out of his eyes. He had his mother's angular face, was going to be tall and thick-framed like she was.

As he told Damien about the shuttle landing field, the fences, the cafeteria, Inga's, and various domes, he watched the young man's eyes gleam with excitement.

"Rebecca would never allow us to go there." Damien was thoughtful. "There would be other people my age, wouldn't there? Males and females?"

"There are."

"I would like to meet them." Damien stared off to the north, a wistful look in his eyes.

And no, Rebecca would never allow them to go there. In so many ways she remained an enigma. Of Talbot's three wives, she only rarely came to his bed. He wasn't sure how his wives worked it out. Nothing was ever said to him. When he retired it was usually Dya who crawled under the covers with him, not always for sex, but often just to sleep with him. A couple of nights a week it would be Su. And every so often, after the lights were out, he would feel Rebecca slip under his covers. She was always gone by morning, fading away in the night as quietly as she had come.

And somehow over the weeks, the awkwardness of it had evaporated.

"The thing we forget," Dya once told him, "is that prior to the industrial age, more than sixty percent of human cultures were polygamous, matrilineal, or both. Usually because of a surplus of females. In many ways, we're just like those early horticultural societies. Donovan is hard on men."

As he considered that, a second roar built in the northwest.

"Two of them," Kylee said softly, her blue eyes, like Damien's, filled with wonder.

And what does that mean for me?

Talbot took a deep breath. Glanced down at the two kids. His kids. He hadn't recognized the precise moment that eight strange children had become wards, let alone precious to him. It just happened.

Kylee? Well, of course. He had a special relationship with her and Rocket. But more and more, he'd been spending time with Damien, answering questions about Solar System, the Marines, combat, what it was like to space when symmetry inverted, and especially about what the great ships were like.

The women had even tasked Talbot with lessons, teaching Earth and Solar System history, The Corporation, the history of war, and economics.

And now two shuttles had Kylee and Damien's eyes aglow with possibilities.

"It's not all wonderful," he told them. "Here at Mundo Base you have family. People you know and can rely on. Once you get out into the rest of space? Things get a bit trickier."

"How so?" Damien asked.

"You don't know the rules out there. Here everyone is honest. The only people who tell lies here are Shine and Ngyap. Shine's three. Ngyap's four. Like the other day when the lamp got knocked over. Ngyap said he didn't do it. At four, he's not smart enough to know that he was the only kid in the room. Tuska and Taung, at six and seven, have both figured out that a facile lie doesn't work anymore. They'll still try it when the situation is more complex, but not often."

Talbot waved off to the north. "But once you get into the real world? You've got to know the rules, understand that it's all a series of complicated, often contradictory expectations, opportunities, and challenges."

Kylee asked, "Like the fact that you broke the rules flying south?"

"Just like that. They consider me a deserter. Even though we didn't mean to do anything wrong or malicious when we broke the rules, it doesn't matter. Not to Supervisor Aguila."

"Do you ever want to go back?" Damien asked. "Would you, if you could?"

"Yes. There are parts of that life that I miss. Sometimes so much that it hurts. And I don't know how long we can hang on here. We're going to have trouble. Eventually something important is going to wear out that we can't fix. Sometime in the coming years we're going to have to move out of the dome when the power fails. Or the lift is going to break. Something structural will fail. We don't have the parts to repair things."

"Living on thc ground's not so bad," Kylee told him as she stared out at the forest. "Quetzals do it all the time. We'll be okay."

"What if you just went for a look?" Damien asked, his gaze still fixed on the distant north. "Just like a scouting trip? Would you do that?"

"Not without a really, really good reason," Talbot told him. "First, I promised I'd stay here. And even if Rebecca, Su, and Dya asked me to go, I've got a lot to lose by doing so."

"Like what?" Kylee asked.

"Like all of you." He waved around. "I've become part of this place, part of the family. On Earth I was part of a big family. When I was a marine, I was part of the Corps. Now I belong here. I wouldn't want to be away from you."

"Even Rebecca?" Kylee asked with false innocence.

"Even Rebecca." He gave her a wink, then followed Damien's gaze to the north.

At that moment, Dya and Su climbed up out of the hatch and onto the roof.

"Was that a shuttle?" Dya asked, shading her eyes with a slim hand. The wind teased her blondc hair.

"Two of them. Approaching from the west." Talbot experienced a curious sense of warmth as Dya stepped under his right arm, while Su took his left hand in hers. She stared north, concern in her dark brown eyes.

Su, too, was something of a mystery. More than even with Rebecca he took pains to be eternally polite, respectful, and considerate. In return, Su had begun to respond in kind with little gestures like she did now, taking his hand.

"Another ship?" Su asked. "What does it mean, Mark?"

"We won't know for a couple of days. Meanwhile, I think it'll be a good night to set up the telescope. We know where *Freelander*'s orbit is. Let's scan for another ship."

"There's a quicker way," Dya said.

"What's that?"

"The radio," Su told him, giving him a sidelong glance. "Just how broken do you think it is?"

"Not very," he admitted. "Just needs plugging into the power."

"If there's a ship," Damien said, "Two Spots at Port Authority will be talking about it a lot."

He glanced suspiciously back and forth between his wives. "Thought the radio was strictly off limits?"

"We just wanted to see what you'd do," Dya told him with a smile. "You never even tried to hook it up."

"Another test?"

"All of life is tests," Kylee told him with a toothy grin. "Sometimes you just have to figure out what the test is on a given day."

"If it's another ship," Su said darkly, "it means more supplies, more aircars. Better transportation."

"And that means that eventually someone is going to come looking for us," Dya said softly, eyes searching the horizon.

"And that," Talbot finished, "would be bad for all of us."

He could see everything he'd built here being taken away as someone Corporate—who thought like Kalico Aguila and her marines—stepped down from an aircar.

29

S hig stood with his thumbs thrust into his belt as he considered the sleek delta-shaped shuttle. It rested on the far edge of the landing field against a backdrop of shipping containers. Graceful and otherworldly, it looked totally out of place. An angel fallen from its realm.

It amazed him that Aguila thought she had driven a hard bargain.

But in the end, what were any of them going to do? Perched atop her high ridge where the Corporate Mine was situated, she barely had space for the one shuttle, the aircars, haulers, mucking machines, and other equipment. Down at the farm and smelter she could park a shuttle short term, but the march of the trees onto cleared land remained relentless.

The shuttle landing field at Port Authority was the perfect place for the new arrival from *Freelander*.

"How does it feel to see that beauty sitting there?" Trish asked as she stepped up beside Shig and rested the butt of her rifle on the ground.

"Like we have a fighting chance again," Shig told her. "Oh, not that we wouldn't have made it otherwise, but with heavy-lift capability, life will be easier. And this way we have access to the entire planet."

"Heard she had a whole string of demands, but that most of her terms involved food."

Shig nodded. "I think Talina's cooking convinced her. You've had Talina's breakfast?"

"Trust me, the only thing the woman knows how to cook is corn, beans, chilies, annatto seeds, and tomatoes. She has Ruben Miranda growing a special plot out on his farm. Keeps it just for her."

"She saved his life once, years ago, didn't she?" Shig mused.

"Ruben and the two kids." Trish stared thoughtfully at

the shuttle. "I heard that you and Yvette said yes to everything Aguila asked."

"We did." Shig tilted his head back to enjoy the warm rays of the sun. "Medical, research, the whole ball of wax, as the ancient saying goes. We got everything we wanted."

"I thought it was her terms or nothing?"

Shig shot a sidelong glance at the young woman. "With the addition of the *Turalon* deserters and those additional transportees who didn't have critical skills, we're expanding our farms. Reclaiming land that we didn't have enough people to work. We're creating a surplus, so what better place to send it than to Corporate Mine?"

"But she gets access to all of our research? We have to treat all of her people in our hospital? Use our drugs? Take up our beds? And she can conscript our key people like Cheng at a moment's notice?"

"Hire. For a wage. That's different. The irony is that Kalico might have intellectually understood that our people are free to hire themselves out to anyone they like. But she still can't get past the deep-seated belief that Yvette and I had to give permission. So she walked away satisfied that she'd scored a victory, when she could have hired anyone she wanted, whenever she wanted."

Trish fumed. "I don't like. I don't trust that woman. Come on, why'd you really agree? Especially when it comes to medical, research, and the rest?"

"Because the Supervisor's interests are our interests. You are blinded by the moment: We are all feeling rather flush and optimistic. New expansion, piles of equipment." He gestured. "A shuttle. And of course, an influx of new people."

"Yeah, so?"

"Look beyond the moment. Put our circumstances in perspective. Think of the processual history of human activity on Donovan. Chances are that Corporate Mine will fail," Shig said softly. "And when it does, what then? Aguila's people will retreat here. But by then our own attrition will be evident. Equipment will be wearing out, power packs failing. We depend upon our technology for survival here, but technology is finite."

"So we're just prolonging the inevitable?"

"I said chances are. There are ways to increase the probability for success. One way is to do anything in our power to see that Corporate Mine succeeds. Especially that smelter."

"And you trust Aguila?"

"Aguila isn't the concern. Oh, she's still clinging to her self-identity as a high and lordly Corporate Supervisor. Such illusions of status and prestige are hard to shed, after all. Now that she's face-to-face with bitter reality down at Corporate Mine, she's showing remarkable progress in her evolution as a human being."

Shig pointed. "But that shuttle sitting there? The fact that she asked all of the right things as compensation, means that she's learning who the real opponent is, and how dangerous an adversary it will be in the end."

"What opponent?" Trish shot him a wary green-eyed look from the corner of her eyes.

"Oh, come. What opponent is there? Donovan, of course."

"Hey, we're still here. We've got a whole new shot with all of this equipment. With that shuttle sitting out there."

Shig arched a brow. "Talina has a quetzal inside her. Since discovering that surprising fact, Raya's been rerunning some of the blood samples from the Wild Ones. She's finding different amounts of TriNA in most of them. But what's particularly significant about the findings? Ah, it's the successful ones, like Chaco and Madison Briggs. The Philos. The Shu Wans. The Wild Ones who are best adapting to the bush. The most successful are all infected."

Trish scowled out in the direction of the distant trees. "I've been playing cop, Shig. Haven't had time to keep up on the latest research. Want to tell me why you're so worried about this?"

"Because Raya thinks TriNA is more than an analog to our DNA. DNA carries information vertically, down through time and generations, replicating, recombining through successive offspring. For the most part—barring viruses, some bacteria, and RNAs—DNA is pretty much confined to the individual organism. By that, I mean that I can't incorporate your DNA into my body. If Raya is right, TriNA not only carries information down through time, passing down from generation to generation, but it also moves laterally, carrying information from organism to organism, and perhaps even across species boundaries."

"Which means?"

"I think it means that Donovan has been as busy investigating us as we have been investigating it. We are alien and new and, for the most part, not that much of a threat. But look at the history, Trish. See the patterns. Of the eighteen original outposts and research bases we established, only three are left: Jade, Three Falls, and Ytterbium. From a maximum of thirty-five hundred people at Port Authority alone, we're down to four hundred and some. Counting Aguila's people, there might be just over twelve hundred humans on the planet."

"Our pregnancy rate is up."

"Yes," Shig nodded, his eyes on the shuttle. "But it's still not keeping pace with attrition. The thing that really frightens me is that Donovan will strike back one of these days. When it does, it will be at the Corporate Mine. That's the most threatening intrusion. Deep in the forest, where Aguila is waging a war on the trees."

Trish took a deep breath. "And if we lose the smelter, we lose the future." A pause. "I don't know. Donovanian life communicating, acting in concert? That's pretty wild, Shig."

"Tell that to Talina."

"You think Donovan's going to hit back?"

Shig nodded. "It's just a matter of time."

30

Talbot shut the radio down and unplugged the power. He'd made a habit of disconnecting it in a way that Damien couldn't figure out.

Not that the boy would go out of his way to disobey, but, hell, Talbot had to be honest. It was one thing for a kid to keep his mitts off if the act of hooking up the radio was a complicated and potentially dangerous process. It was something else if the forbidden world was just a flip of the switch away. No harm, no foul if no one figured it out, right?

Or at least, that's how Talbot would have thought of it when he was Damien's age.

Talbot stepped out of the radio room door and closed it. The hallway was quiet, the last of the children gone to bed a half hour ago.

He padded into the main room, finding his wives all sitting at the dinner table, cups of tea steaming as they talked.

Walking to the pot, he took down a cup and poured one himself before seating himself across from Rebecca.

"Anything new?" she asked.

"Supervisor Aguila is having trouble with her mine and smelter. They can't keep the trees out of their agricultural ground. She's desperately trying to get some kind of poison from Cheng up at Port Authority."

"Won't work," Dya told him.

"God, no." Rebecca thoughtfully rubbed her long shins, then straightened. "We stumbled upon the timber belt by accident."

"Think we should tell them?" Dya asked, gaze distant. "Maybe a random radio call? Just a short announcement? Then shut the set down?"

"No!" Su and Rebecca snapped in unison.

Dya smiled, as if amused by herself. "It's not like they'd know where it came from. Not if it was quick."

"They'd know someone had a radio," Rebecca countered. "Just them asking the question: 'Who was that?' That might be all it takes for them to start thinking back. Counting off all the bases. Wondering which of them called in. Now that they've got these shuttles, it's more than just aircars that we have to worry about. They're not going to risk an aircar on a long-distance trip to check out the old bases, but they might with a shuttle."

"It's a whole new capability," Su agreed as she pulled her legs up and clasped her arms around her knees. She glanced at Talbot. "You're sure they're not going to use *Freelander* as an orbital platform?"

"I doubt it. For one thing, I don't think Aguila has the people to spare. Not if she's trying to make this mine of hers a success. Second, she'd have to put a gun to someone's head to get them to stay on that bucket." He rubbed the back of his neck. "I've never been so freaking scared in all my life as I was when I was aboard. I'm not kidding. I don't buy the notion of ghosts and heebie-jeebies, but there's something unnatural on that ship. Something that sends a chill through your very soul."

"Well, at least there's that," Rebecca said thoughtfully. "Still, it's unnerving that your Supervisor Aguila is only a little more than two hundred kilometers north of us."

"Someday," Dya said, "they will figure out that we're here."

"Not necessarily," Su countered. "The colony is at a high-water mark. This is as good as it gets for Port Authority and this Corporate Mine. From here on out, Donovan is going to start doing what it always does. It's going to start whittling the numbers down. Day by day those people are going to be finding themselves more and more concerned with just staying alive. The technology is going to slowly fail. They won't have time to look for us."

"Speaking of which," Talbot said, "I put the last fuse in the main pump. Note the key word: last. If it goes, well, I'm not sure I've got the electrical chops to concoct a substitute that will allow the pump to work without frying the whole thing in the event we have another lightning strike."

Su glanced at Rebecca. "I know the dribble of water kept you in the bathroom this morning. If the pump goes, the rest of us will have to take the lift and go outside in the morning."

Rebecca arched a canny eyebrow, glanced at Dya. "Won't be a problem for long. If the past is any indication, the morning sickness will pass in a couple of months."

Dya's smile consisted of a smug quirk of the lips. Su and Talbot stared at each other, then at Rebecca.

"You're pregnant?" Talbot asked, apparently the last to know.

"You're quite the guy, Mark. Three for three." Rebecca made a dismissive gesture. "If this little girl goes to term, she'll most likely be my last. But in the meantime, we had better give the coming months some serious thought."

Talbot took a sip from his cup of tea to still the flutter in his stomach. Crap. How did a fellow come to terms with the notion that he had three women pregnant with his children at once? The thought of it left him shocked and stunned.

"How's that?" Su asked.

Dya said, "Three women, coming to term within a couple of months of each other. We're going to be waddling around like zeppelins during that last trimester. All of our activities are going to be significantly curtailed. Mark and the kids are going to have a lot to shoulder."

"More so after the babies are born," Rebecca mused. "Remember how pressed we were when Shine was a neonatal?"

"Sure, we had two newborns to deal with," Dya said. "But there were still seven adults here. Things are different now."

Talbot chewed his lips as he tried to anticipate what was coming. Back home, his mother had been part of a community, and, of course, The Corporation with its clinics and obstetricians took care of everything. Mum's pregnancies had almost been a nonissue, almost a remote phenomenon.

"We can start preparing," Talbot said. "The farm pretty much takes care of itself. Between me, Damien, and Kylee, we can keep the food production up and do most of the maintenance. But anything that needs your strenuous physical attention should be addressed between now and then."

Su was watching Rebecca. "You are in your forties. What if there's a complication?"

"Dya will know what to do."

Dya lifted an eyebrow. "Up to a point."

"What do you mean? Complications?" Talbot asked.

Dya fixed her cool blue stare on him. "Mark, it's probably nothing. We've all carried to term before. But we're out here on our own."

"Used to be that more women died of childbirth than any other cause," Su said absently. "But that was back before modern medicine."

Which was when it sank in that if anything did happen, it was going to be up to just the four of them to somehow deal with it. That there was no clinic to call. No hospital.

They'd done it before, right?

But if something goes wrong, how the hell am I going to keep them alive?

31

The mine shook as the charge went off. Instantaneously the blast thundered, muffled by the surrounding rock. Kalico hunched at the concussion, then glanced around at the miners waiting in the hollowed-out area they called a stope.

Little more than a thirty-meter chamber, it was an area where the threads of pure gold and lanthanum had been woven through the rock like a spiderweb. In the harsh white light she could see the gleam of it in the walls all around her.

But the big prize now was a finger-thick band of almost pure cerium that ran like a ribbon into the depths. Even better, around it could be found nugget-rich pockets of lanthanides, scandium, and yttrium. And still better yet, the deeper the vein ran, the more they were protected from contaminating ground water with its oxides and sulphates.

Some concentrations were so pure they could be plucked from the ore, many without needing any further refinement.

As the last of the echoes died away, the miners nodded to each other, most of them perched on various flat surfaces on the mucking machine. The mucking machine, dominating the center of the stope, looked like some grotesque mechanical insect with its wide, multiconveyor mouth that could switch this way and that like weird mandibles.

Kalico turned to Talovich; in the gleam of the overhead lights his face looked thin and smudged with rock dust. "You said you wanted to show me the section that has you concerned?"

He nodded. "Just a little way down here."

Talovich led the way over the uneven footing. Crushed rock turned under Kalico's boots where it had been laid as base fill over the cracked and shattered tunnel floor.

Talovich stopped, shining a thin beam at the ceiling. "See where that fracture line runs up into the overhead rock? See the angle it takes? There's another down here a ways. Gamble tells me that those are faults. He can tell by something called slickenside where the rock's been rubbed in one direction."

"And why should that concern me?" To Kalico, it all looked like rock.

"Because of all these cracks running up between the faults. The faults act sort of like the top two sides of a triangle, and the tunnel roof is the bottom. That triangle of rock had already been fractured before we blasted the tunnel through it, which just broke it up more."

"So you're telling me the bottom of the triangle could fall out and bring the whole thing with it."

"You're learning, Supervisor."

"What do you need to shore it up?"

"Two days. It's your decision, but I wouldn't set the crew to mucking this latest shot until I had that shored, ma'am. If that came down at the wrong time, you could lose the whole crew and the mucking machine."

Staring up at the cracked rock sent a shiver through Kalico's stomach. She looked back at the miners, the men and women just visible up the tunnel. Her men and women. People she knew. People she ate her meals with.

What a different world.

Back in Solar System, The Corporation utilized people like replaceable parts. People were cheap. Workers were always breeding more workers by the millions. Production quotas were all that mattered.

She herself had operated under that philosophy. Had sustained significant losses in several asteroid-mining operations she'd administered from her office in Solar System.

She glanced again at the miners. She *knew* these people. Here she depended upon them, and they depended upon her.

"Damn straight. Do what you need to do," she told Talovich. "Make it safe. And don't take any risks yourself while you do it, understand me?"

"Yes, ma'am." He gave her a salute, and added a little nod of respect and appreciation that wasn't required.

Not because of her position, but because of her concern.

As she made her way past the mucking machine and

drills, she gave a nod to the miners, who nodded back, some of them even smiling.

She rode one of the skip cars back to the surface, oddly touched by Talovich's nod and the miners' greetings. The realization triggered an awkward feeling—as if their shared fates and mutual dependence were both a vulnerability and an asset at the same time.

She stepped out of the tunnel entrance where Capella's light burned down hot, clear, and liberating after the confines of the mine.

The grading crew was waiting for ore. She stopped short, inspecting the two men and three women, all dressed in dusty overalls, hair pulled back, faces smudged, helmets on their heads.

"We've got a potential for cave-in," she told them. "Nothing's coming out until Talovich gets it shored up. I'm sending the shuttle down for timbers. If any of you'd like to ride along and lend a hand, tell them I said it was all right."

"Thank you, ma'am," one of the older women said. "We'd enjoy the change in routine. And there's always use for an extra set of hands."

Kalico gave them an encouraging smile, patching into her com and ordering the shuttle to power up.

They all knew the drill now. Attitudes had changed since first she'd given Talovich free rein to make the mine safe. Following that she'd brokered the rotations to Port Authority. Where once her people had felt hopeless, they now laughed, shared a newfound camaraderie. Actually got more accomplished. Had a sense of spirit they hadn't had even in the beginning.

She hadn't had a desertion in months.

The first shipments of fresh produce from Port Authority had come in. The kitchen staff—not the sharpest of her personnel—had made a mess of the first meals, burning the greens and stews. The beans had tasted like charcoal.

Kalico took her helmet off, staring out across the ocean of trees spreading to the east. Maybe she could hire Millie and a couple of the cafeteria kitchen staff from Port Authority to come down here and teach her kitchen crew how to cook? Shit on a shoe, it couldn't be that hard to make a stew.

She was halfway to the dome when it happened. The first flock consisted of forty or fifty of the creatures, multi-colored, about the size of flying cats with two wings in front and two in the rear along with a fluffy-looking tail. At the bend of the wings the beasts had curving claws: thin scimitars no longer than her hand that glistened in Capella's hard light.

The colorful creatures came whisking up from the lowlands and over the fence. Chittering in a way that reminded Kalico of bats, the column of them twisted, curling through the morning like animated smoke.

Kalico had never seen the like before. And still they came until maybe a hundred, and then more, poured over the fence, fluttering, wheeling, and darting down into the yard. The beating rhythms of all those wings had an almost disorienting effect; it blocked sound, stifled thought, juddered at the ears in a most unpleasant way.

Where he worked on one of the aircars, Bennie Saenz straightened, staring with fascinated eyes as the column of flying creatures dropped down and surrounded him.

Kalico barely had time to take in the sight before Saenz was engulfed. His hideous scream was drowned by the thrumming beat of the wings.

Accessing com, Kalico cried, "Spiro! Alert! We're under attack."

Then, out of impulse, she ran to help Saenz. It wasn't more than fifty yards, but in the time it took her to make half the distance, part of the flock rose up into the air, wheeled, and immediately fixed on her.

Kalico pulled to a stop, saw them coming, and dove for a packing crate. She wasn't entirely inside when she pulled the door closed, trapping five or six of the closest attackers inside with her.

Immediately they were on her, biting, slashing, chittering.

In the crate's darkness, Kalico flailed with her arms. Kicked. Screamed.

She was being flayed alive with razor blades. The stinging cuts just kept coming. In the darkness, the flapping creatures battered into the crate walls, thumped against her sides, legs, arms, and head. They tangled in her hair, cutting, biting.

She managed to grab one. Got a hand on its warm body, another on one of the wings, and twisted.

Her com was filled with a cacophony of shouts, questions, all coming in on top of each other.

Kalico ignored it. Shut it out of her mind.

The creature she grasped screeched and flopped. Kalico twisted harder, adding her panicked screams to the fluttering beast's. She felt its body break, heard the muffled snap of its bones.

She dropped it, stomped on it, heard it crunch beneath her boot. Clawing at the air, she captured another, whimpered as it sank teeth in the web between her thumb and forefinger. She got hold of its head from behind. Tore it loose from her hand. Again she twisted, felt the snapping of bones. Dropped it, clawed for another.

The cuts kept coming. The pain in her side resolved into realization that one was chewing on her, eating into her side.

Reaching down, she grasped it, bellowed her agony as she tore it loose, and slammed it into the crate wall. Then she twisted, hearing its insides pop.

She dropped it, stomping in the darkness, crushing the writhing bodies under her feet.

Got another one, throat straining as she roared her fear and pain. All of her strength went into the savage act of trying to rip the thing in two.

Desperately, she clawed through the air, finding nothing but the smooth crate walls.

And then silence. Just the chaos coming through her com. She ignored it. Terror. Just sheer terror. She couldn't think. Could only whimper.

Nothing moved in the blackness. The only sound that of her panicked breath puffing in and out of her frantic lungs. She could feel blood running down her skin, wiped it from her eyes. Felt it hot and sticky on her stinging hands. Smelled it, thick and musky in the close air.

Something chattered weakly on the floor, and she stomped. And kept stomping, feeling the rubbery bodies crunching on the duraplast. And stomped and stomped.

She wanted to sink down. Couldn't. Not when the floor was covered by those things.

Her whole body stung, pain building from the cuts and bites.

For long moments she stood half-hunched in the darkness, heart hammering, struggling to catch her breath. Her nostrils clogged with the cloying and coppery odor of blood—and something else, pungent, alien, and sour. Had to be the broken bodies of the creatures she'd killed and crushed.

She fought the urge to vomit.

Got to get out of here.

But did she dare? Were the flying things still out there, waiting for her to crack the crate's door?

She swallowed against the urge to hurl, felt for the door, and put her ear against it.

She could hear shouts, the occasional report of a rifle. But nothing close.

Unlatching the door, she slipped it open a crack. Through the sliver, she stared out at the yard, seeing it vacant. No swarm of four-winged terrors could be seen. Nor did she hear the ominous fluttering sound of their wings.

Opening the door wider, she fought to still the trembling in her bloody and stinging hands. Saw nothing, and stepped out into the light, ready to leap back into the safety of her crate.

"I need help over here," someone called. "For God's sake, bring me a litter. Something to carry a person!"

Accessing her com, Kalico asked, "Spiro? Report?"

"We've got people down all over."

"Where are those things?"

"Headed back for the trees to the south. Where are you?"

She looked around, spotted the aircar where Saenz had been working. Stared in disbelief. His bloody skeleton lay atop the vehicle's hood.

"In the yard," she whispered, staggering forward, gaping in horror at the bloody bones.

That was a living, breathing man mere minutes ago. The flesh had been stripped away as if by knives. The man's clothing lay strewn about in ripped tatters. The rib cage had been emptied, as had his pelvis. The crimson-streaked skull had no eyes, just bloody sockets that seemed to gaze vacantly at the now-empty sky. Even Saenz's tongue had been eaten out, the cartilage of the nose chewed away. Blood continued to dribble slowly from the severed arteries and veins that had once served the man's brain—apparently the only organ the flying terror hadn't been able to reach.

Kalico blinked, went weak as nausea spun the world around her. She braced a bloody hand on the aircar, looked down to find her coveralls ripped, torn, and soaked in crimson. Blood coursed down her face to drip from her chin. Her hands reminded her of chunks of freshly butchered stew meat.

She might have been gutted the way she sank to the ground, thankful for its solid support.

Spiro came pounding across the yard, her rifle at the ready. She pulled up, shot a horrified glance at Saenz's skeleton, then frowned as she stared down at Kalico.

"Ma'am? Is that you?"

"Where are those things, Lieutenant? If they come back . . ."

Kalico winced as she tried to wipe the blood from her face again.

"Miso!" Spiro bellowed. "We need the shuttle now! The Supervisor's wounded!"

"How many others?" Kalico asked.

"Four dead that we know of, ma'am. Another two wounded, one maybe worse than you."

"Make sure all the wounded are on the shuttle. Don't miss anyone, Lieutenant. I'm not setting foot aboard until all of my people are safe and accounted for. You understand?"

"Yes, ma'am. But, ma'am, you're bleeding and—"

"Not until we have everyone who needs aid."

"Yes, ma'am."

Four dead?

Kalico tried to blink the blood out of her eyes, felt the world slide sideways. Then the ground seemed to tilt. The light slowly faded to gray, and she sank into a deep, soft, and cushioning fog.

32

All it took was the mere sight of the specimen on the table. Talina had barely had time to recognize the mobber: colorful, four wings, the hooking claws, the triangular head with its deadly jaws. A dead cousin to the one that had hovered but a hand's length from her nose that day in the forest.

Talina suffered a violent jolt of pain—as if a spear of it exploded in her gut. Bent her over and caused her to gasp. Taken by complete surprise, she clutched at her stomach; an almost mind-numbing fear burned electric through her nerves.

"Run!" The quetzal's word hissed through her brain.

"Talina?" Raya and Step cried in unison, both reaching out to stabilize her.

"It's the quetzal," she said through gritted teeth, willing the pain to subside. "Yeah, you piece of shit," she told it. "I know what it is."

"Talina?" Raya demanded. "What's wrong? How is the quetzal doing this?"

"Triggers the limbic system," Talina said. "It's not an attack. It's afraid. Afraid of what's on the table. Even if we all know it's dead."

"You know what it is? Good," Step said, his thick arm still out to support her if she needed it. "Now you can tell the rest of us."

Talina willed herself to stand straight, shoving the quetzal's fear into the back of her mind. "Cap and I ran into them in the forest. We called them mobbers. Saw them chase after a bunch of leapers and finally kill a quetzal."

"I remember you mentioning that," Stepan told her, nodding thoughtfully as he studied the crimson, green, and blue creature on the table.

The last time Talina had seen one up close, it was staring into her eyes, hovering not more than a foot in front of her face. Even then the quetzal had her paralyzed with fear. For good reason.

Now she leaned down, using a stiff wire to poke and prod at the four-winged beast. The body was about the size of a housecat's—but diamond-shaped through the torso. Each corner of the creature's body sported a wing with ventral and dorsal prominences to anchor the musculature to flap them. What looked like colorful feathers were not, having a similar shape but entirely different physiology from the terrestrial feather. The claw that protruded from the joint midway down each wing reminded her of a sickle: thin, curving, and seemingly glass-sharp. The head sported three eyes, had wicked, razor-sharp, serrated jaws. The tail, not quite as long as the animal, had a downy pelage.

"Doesn't look so bad up close," Talina said as she laid the probe down and backed away from the table. Around her the lab hummed, its refrigerator rocking slightly on mismatched legs. Only two of the four light panels still worked.

"Five people are dead," Step reminded. "And I mean, wow. The swarm was only over the mine for ten minutes or so. In that time they stripped three people down to the bones, and finished off half of another. One, a woman, died of exsanguination on the way here, and the Supervisor and one of her marines look like walking hamburger."

"Until you see a flock of these things"—Talina kept a hand to her belly where the quetzal was twitching nervously—"you can't believe it. That young quetzal the mobbers killed? The thing didn't have a chance."

She bent down again, looking at the three eyes, now half-lidded and gray in death. "They're visual. They key on movement. They depend on frightening their prey into flight, then they're on it. My quetzal told me they're not very smart."

"Five of Aguila's people wouldn't agree with you," Stepan muttered.

"I didn't say they weren't effective," Talina told him. "Crocodiles aren't smart either, but they're the most deadly predator of humans on Earth. We're in the middle of the twenty-second century, and they still kill more people than all the lions, leopards, and other big beasts combined in the rewilded areas."

"Why haven't we run into these things before?" Raya asked thoughtfully.

"I think they're just a deep forest species," Step answered. "If they are the apex predator, there won't be many of them. Probably numbering less than two percent of the population of their key prey species. I'd guess they don't like open areas like the bush around Port Authority."

Step indicated the wings. "These guys evolved for mobility, not speed."

"I've never seen anything fly the way they do," Talina agreed. "Not even the most agile insects back on Earth."

"What about defense against them?" Raya asked. "We've got a couple of hundred people on virtual lockdown at Corporate Mine. They're terrified to leave the dome."

"Cap and I escaped by lying still. I mean, like not moving a muscle. The mobbers looked us over, couldn't figure out what we were."

"I'll have Two Spots radio that tidbit to the mine." Step smiled grimly. "'Just hold still.' That ought to go over real big."

"They might be visual hunters, but I'm not sure that just lying still will work anymore."

"Why not?" Raya asked.

"Because this particular swarm has figured out that humans are food. Kalico told me that the swarm only left after it was full. Once they digest their kill, why the hell wouldn't they be coming back for another meal?"

33

Talbot hunched in the midday sun, wrenching on the ramada roof that protected the all-important giant prickly pear cactus plants, kept them from receiving too much rain. A brief wind had torn up one side, lifting the transparency that shed rain into the collectors but still allowed Capella's hot light through to the great, green cactus pads. Occasionally harvested, the pads were ground up into a slimy mixture called mucilage, through which water was filtered to remove toxins.

More than once Talbot had wondered just who, exactly, had first figured out that cactus goo could be turned into a water filter for heavy metals. Whoever it was must have had a whole lot of empty time on his hands: "Hey, Mom! Guess what I figured out today while I was playing with the heavy metals and cactus pads!"

He smiled at the notion and threaded a fastener through a homemade washer he'd cut from old tin. With a wrench he tightened the fastener to the right torque and checked his work.

Not quite as good as new. The transparency had yellowed, and cracks showed where the plastic was eventually going to fail. Brace the roofing as he would for the moment, wind and weather were eventually going to have their way.

He turned at the sound of the bang.

Muffled, it came from somewhere around the tower, or perhaps from one of the shops. Sort of metallic sounding; he wondered if something had been knocked over. Perhaps a sheet of metal? Some container?

No doubt it would be waiting for him to set right when he got back.

He moved his ladder, climbed up, and began retorquing the next fastener.

Minutes later he heard someone desperately calling,

"Mark!" and looked up to see Damien running hell bent down between the rows of pepper plants.

"What's up?" Talbot called, aware that Damien wasn't slowing.

"The lift broke! It's Kylee! She's hurt. Bad."

For a long second, Talbot stared, his heart dropping in his chest. *Dear God, not Kylee.*

He leaped down the ladder, calling, "Where is she? How bad?"

"In the cage!" Damien cried. "At the bottom of the lift. I think the cable broke."

Talbot threw the wrench toward his tool box, extending, running full-out for the towering base of the dome. Damien, always fit, didn't have a chance of keeping up.

As he ran, a cold fear drove Talbot to run like he hadn't in years. Kylee . . . Sweet, smiling, too-old-for-her-years Kylee.

Gasping for breath, he shot past the storage sheds, scattering roos in all directions. To his surprise, Rocket was already at the door, making his worried clicking sounds and scratching to get in.

How could he know?

"Hey, buddy," Talbot called past heaving lungs. "Let's see, huh?"

He flung the door open; he and the quetzal crowded through.

At the bottom of the lift Rebecca and Su were frantically trying to lever the cage door open with a pry bar.

"What happened?" Talbot called, hurrying across the duraplast floor. But he could see. The cage had hit hard, cable piled around it where it had fallen from above.

"Door's wedged!" Rebecca cried, as frantic as Talbot had ever heard her.

He didn't hesitate, but wrenched the bar from her hands. At first sight, the blood seemed to freeze in his veins. Kylee was down, on her side, her blonde hair in disarray. She lay slightly curled, left leg out straight but at an awkward angle. The image of a broken bird flickered in his imagination.

Fitting the end of the bar in the bent door frame, he took a moment to study where it was warped, got his purchase, and threw his weight behind it.

Metal screeched, and with a bang, the door flipped open.

Then Talbot and Rocket were inside. As he bent down over the girl, Rocket's tongue was flickering over Kylee's lips in that weird quetzal way that had once so creep-freaked Talbot.

"Easy," Talbot told the whimpering girl. "We're here. You're going to be all right."

Kylee answered with a mewing sound, her jaws quivering, eyes closed and tear-streaked. Rocket kept making a purring sound, his colors juddering through yellow, black, and bursts of worried blue.

Kylee reached out with a tenuous hand, her fingers tracing the quetzal's muzzle.

"Where's she hurt?" Rebecca demanded.

"Looks like her left leg." Then, bending close, he said, "Kylee. Focus now. Where does it hurt?"

"Everywhere," she said weakly. "Left side. Oh . . . please . . . Make it stop."

Talbot swallowed hard. Waved Rebecca back where she and Su were trying to crowd into the lift. "I need something to use for a stretcher. Go! Find it now."

"But what if she—"

"I've got her. Go!"

As the women hurried away, Talbot began feeling along Kylee's right leg, finding the bone intact.

"Hey, kid. Look at me." He lifted her head, checking her pain-wracked eyes, her respiration, and heart rate. "I'm going to press on your stomach and sides. It might hurt."

To his relief, though she winced, he didn't find the hardness associated with internal hemorrhage. When he carefully straightened her, the scream that tore from her throat was that of a dying animal.

She screamed again when he palpated her left hip.

Trained in combat EMT, he knew what he was feeling; the extent of her fractured hip and upper femur left him reeling.

Rocket continued to flick his tongue along Kylee's lips, then focused his three-eyed stare at Talbot.

"Broken hip and upper leg," he told the quetzal. Took a breath, fought to still his own racing heart, and added, "Not good."

Rocket's collar flashed out in a sudden band of cold blue, a clicking sounded deep in the creature's body, and it blew air from the vents behind its back legs and tail.

Rebecca and Su crowded through the door with a large plastic board they used to transport equipment. Yeah, that would do.

"Find me straps," Talbot called. "She's got a fractured hip and upper femur. I've got to strap her on to get her up the stairs."

Tie-down straps solved the problem.

Rocket moved back as Rebecca and Su helped Talbot shift Kylee onto the board—the way she shrieked, gasped, and panted broke his heart. Carefully, they secured her. The girl seemed to be drifting from hazy consciousness to inert. Again Talbot checked her pulse, finding it oddly slow.

"You do that?" he asked Rocket, who flashed an orange yes answer through his collar.

"Don't know how you did, but thanks," Talbot told the young quetzal. Then he propped the board over his shoulders and lifted. Carefully, he eased his burden out of the bent cage. Damien stood to one side among the crates, his large brown eyes panicked.

Kylee whimpered, air catching in her throat.

"Damien," Rebecca called. "Go find Dya. Tell her what's happened. But just because it's an emergency, I want you to take extra care out there, hear me?"

Damien nodded, and like a shot he was through the door.

"Rebecca, take the litter's bottom. Help me on the way up the stairs," he told the woman. "I don't want to jar her against the sides or railing on the way up."

"We've got her," Su told him as Rebecca steadied the back of the board.

Talbot looked up the stairway where it curled its way upward around the dark inside of the tower.

"Just like boot camp," he told himself, and started up the stairs.

By the time he made the top, Talbot had come to the conclusion he wasn't the same man he'd been ten years ago. But, stagger and pant as he might, he'd made it.

Legs like fire, he humped his load into the solarium where Su leaped to pull the plants off that same table they'd laid him on that first day.

With tender care, Talbot laid Kylee onto the tabletop, shrugged out of the straps, and once again, waited to catch his breath.

Kylee looked unearthly pale, her eyes flickering behind delicate lids. Rocket, perched high on his back legs, had his claws set in the tabletop, his three eyes fixed with worry.

"We need a CT," Rebecca told him. "Su, you and Mark, get her pants off."

As Rebecca hurried off to her lab, Talbot used the scissors to cut away the homespun fabric. The bulge in Kylee's left hip made him grit his teeth. He could see blood beginning to darken beneath the delicate skin of her buttocks.

Just pray that her colon, intestines, and bladder aren't ruptured as well.

Then Rebecca was back with the handheld CT. Dialing the resolution down to fine, she extended it. Slapped it hard to get the screen to work, and made a slow survey of Kylee's left side.

Looking over Rebecca's shoulder, Talbot bit his lip as the image displayed a dislocated femur, the ball and neck snapped off. Kylee's hip had broken through the socket leaving the bone in three distinct pieces.

"Oh, dear God," Su whispered, dropping to one of the chairs and shaking her head.

"That's . . . bad," Rebecca said softly, her eyes losing focus.

On the table, Kylee tried to shift and cried out. The agonized sound she made literally made Talbot's bones ache.

"What have you got for pain?"

Rebecca's mouth worked. She swallowed. "A potion made from blue nasty."

"The narcotic?"

She nodded.

"Get it."

Talbot laid a hand on Rocket's quivering shoulder, saying, "We're going to get her something for the pain. It'll knock her out for a couple of hours. But you'd better know, it's serious."

Rocket flashed an orange yes, never taking his eyes from Kylee's.

Rebecca was back. From a jar, she used a thin rod to take a dab of the paste-like contents. Working it past Kylee's lips, she placed it on the girl's tongue, then carefully resealed the jar and washed the rod.

Within moments, Kylee's breathing deepened and her expression went slack.

"What's next?" Talbot asked.

Rebecca just stared, eyes seemingly fixed on an impossible distance. "I . . . don't know."

"That kind of a break? She's going to need surgery. This is way beyond stitching up cuts."

Rebecca's expression pinched. "I don't think the injury is fatal."

"Fatal?" Talbot snapped. "Here. Look at me. Focus."

He took her head, swiveling it to stare into her stunned brown eyes. "Even if it's not fatal, Kylee—our Kylee—will never walk again. Do you understand?"

Rebecca, holding his stare, nodded slightly. "But what can we do?"

"There's a surgeon in Port Authority," Talbot said. "Dr. Turnienko."

"We can't do that." Su dropped her head into her hands where she sat in the chair. "They'll know about us. They'll come here."

Talbot took a calming breath. "What if we go to them? I mean, what if I go. Take her there. We'd just be another two Wild Ones."

"How would you get there?" Rebecca asked, a brittleness behind her eyes.

"Take one of the aircars. I heard about the spare power pack in the refrigeration room. I looked the cars over, the Beta unit looks to be in the best shape."

"You can fly an aircar?" Rebecca asked. "You know how?"

"I'm a marine. Before that I trained on one when I was a teenager."

Rebecca, expression lined, had her gaze fixed on Kylee. "This is a big decision. We all have to discuss this. It will change everything."

Talbot pointed. "That's Kylee! Damn it! If she survives, she'll never walk again. Spend the rest of her life in horrendous pain. Unless you plan on drugging her."

"But to take her to Port Authority? To The Corporation?" Su was shaking her head. "They *killed* my husband! I *swore* they'd never find me again."

"Port Authority isn't The Corporation anymore. Clemenceau is long dead." Talbot spread his hands, pleading.

Su lifted her tear-filled dark eyes to meet his. "You said Talina Perez is one of the rulers there."

"Yeah. So?"

"Who do you think executed my Paolo?"

"And won't they arrest you as a deserter?" Rebecca asked in wooden tones.

Talbot rubbed his forehead. "Hell, they may not even recognize me. And so what? You see that little girl? She's mine. You all made me part of the family. Made me a husband, right? If I have to sacrifice myself to save Kylee, I'll do it. Just like I'd do it for Damien, Tuska, Taung, or any of the kids."

He glared hard into Rebecca's stony eyes.

"The answer is no," Su declared. "You talk about sacrifices? Maybe it's Kylee who has to sacrifice for the rest of us. Rebecca, Kylee knows as well as you do that sometimes one of us has to give up something to keep the rest of us safe."

"Safe?" Talbot countered. "Mundo Base is falling apart around your ears. Kylee's here because the lift cable broke. Where the hell was the safety brake?"

"Rondo took it off. Used it to clamp two broken trusses together under the dome floor. The weld broke in a high wind a while back. He was going to weld it, but was killed before he could get to it." Rebecca winced. "We just sort of forgot about it."

Talbot nodded. Hell, he spent his days trying to keep the place in repair. "It's time to face facts. From here on out, everything we eat, study, or work on up here has to be carried up the stairway. That's a huge inconvenience. Now you tell me that some of the structural framework for the dome is damaged? How long since anyone has inspected it?"

Rebecca shrugged.

The sound of pounding feet preceded Dya's arrival. Panting, she burst into the room, grabbing up Kylee's hand, asking, "Baby? Dear God, what happened?"

Talbot stepped over, reading the terror in her eyes. "She's sedated. It's bad, Dya. Broken pelvis and femur. Maybe more."

She glanced at him, tears welling. "Can we cast it? Put her in traction of some sort?"

"She needs surgery. To have the bones pinned," Rebecca said, walking up to put her arm around Dya's shoulders.

"Talbot wants to take her to Port Authority," Su said bitterly. "I say no."

Dya reached down, running her fingers over Rocket's head as tears leaked down her cheeks. "Port Authority? Take her to those monsters?"

"They have a surgeon, Dya."

"You took a CT, right? Let me see the image."

When Rebecca handed it to her, Dya bit off a cry—and her desperate gaze turned to Kylee.

Rebecca said, "Better to kill her now than to let her live like this."

34

The endless forest passed below as Talbot flew Kylee, Dya, and the terrified Rocket north. Below the speeding Beta aircar, the tops of the great trees created rounded and irregular mounds of various greens, turquoises, and teals. They had left the deep forest behind, and since they'd crossed the southern arc of the Wind Mountains, the country had turned more to a scrubby forest. What Dya called the bush. Occasional patches of brush and grasslike vegetation could be seen in the openings.

Talbot couldn't help but flash back to the first time he'd flown over this same terrain. He, Garcia, and Shin, marveling at the endless carpet of green over which they passed, never having a clue about the world that lay beneath, or its dangers.

The Beta skimmed effortlessly northward, clipping along at two hundred kph. Talbot had had his doubts getting the machine prepped, charged, and airworthy. He'd prayed it would fly, that it wouldn't drop them somewhere in the trackless forest.

From the chronometer, they had less than a half hour's flight time to Port Authority. At this altitude he could just see the faint blue line of the Gulf off to the east. The Wind Mountains had faded into a hazy smudge in the distant west.

Dya crouched at the bench seat in the back and made her latest check on Kylee. Rising, she stepped around Rocket and up beside Talbot, her attention fixed on the northern horizon. "She's still stable."

Talbot glanced back where Kylee rested under blankets and atop the padded litter they'd fashioned. Rocket, ever faithful, had curled himself on the floor next to her seat. The little guy was nearly comatose. Flying terrified him; the entire trip, a dazzling display of color had played across his hide. Mostly he kept his head down, eyes clamped tightly closed.

It hadn't crossed Talbot's mind that they'd have to take Rocket. But then, without him, there was no telling what the impact of separation would be. On either the quetzal or Kylee.

And then there was Port Authority to think of. As Talbot recalled, they didn't exactly like quetzals there.

Dya, gaze crystalline blue, mouth set, looked as if she were at the end of her endurance. "I hope this isn't a mistake."

"Makes two of us." Talbot reached out an arm and laid it across her shoulders to give her a reassuring hug. "I've taken the serial number plate off the frame. There's nothing to link the aircar back to Mundo Base. You and I, we're just farmers from a holding out to the west. There's nothing to link us to the south. Even if I'm recognized and arrested, I'll tell them Garcia, Shin, and I went west. Just like Cap did. When Kylee's well, you can fly back south. No one will be the wiser."

She shot him a sidelong, worried look. "You know I can't fly this, don't you?"

"What?"

"None of us can. We never learned."

"Now you tell me?"

No wonder they mothballed the aircars; but then, if they hadn't, that last power pack would have been worn out years ago.

Lashed on the trunk were two cases, each filled with jars of Dya's various salves, pastes, poisons, laxatives, painkillers, and medicines. The results of her years of study as she distilled and experimented with the various forest plants.

The most valuable trade they had to offer in return for Kylee's care.

"There," he pointed, recognizing the scar from the clay pit, having seen it on the numerous times he'd ridden down on *Turalon*'s shuttle.

He turned the wheel, correcting course, and heading for the distant domes.

"I never thought I'd be back here." Dya ran nervous hands over the backs of her arms. "Pak and Paolo must be weeping in their graves."

She'd told him about Pak, her first husband. Kylee's father. How he'd given Clemenceau an ultimatum. How he'd been shot down in the street when Paolo pulled a gun in a bid to keep them from being arrested for desertion. How it had broken her heart. Even considered suicide rather than live without him.

Her second husband, Torrey, had been a geologist. The most she'd say about him was that he was Tuska's father, and a good man. He'd vanished in the forest, went prospecting along the rim where it sloped off to the south of Mundo Base and never returned. Damien had found his pack beneath a rock outcrop a couple of years later.

Talbot studied Dya from the corner of his eye. The wind was ruffling her yellow-blonde hair; the set of her firm jaw indicated a steely resolution. The way she gripped the hand rail, the tension in her broad shoulders and stiff back, spoke volumes about what this was costing her.

From behind, suffering sounds could be heard deep in Kylee's throat.

Talbot ground his teeth and wondered how he'd come to love her so completely that he'd have traded places with her in an instant.

Dropping altitude, he circled, coming in from the west. They passed over the last of the bush, farmland now beneath them. Here and there, people working the crops and tending to the farmbots looked up and waved.

Ahead, Port Authority lay behind its ditch and high fence, the lines of domes ivory-colored in Capella's hard light. The clutter of wood-and-stone buildings packed in among them like some medieval hodgepodge.

Talbot flew over the aircar field, then the fence, setting his sights on the hospital dome where it stood next to admin, the shuttle field fence behind it.

"You ready?" he asked. "This is it."

Dya's jaws were knotted. She gave him a short nod of the head.

Talbot set the Beta down in the street before the hospital's double doors. His heart beat anxiously in his chest, muscles charged, adrenaline pumping. Felt like combat.

Out of second nature he grabbed up his rifle, slung it over his shoulder. If he was recognized, there was no telling which way this could go.

Talbot killed the power, then jumped over the seat, barely missed stepping on Rocket, and lifted the back of Kylee's litter.

Dya had clambered over the side, helping to brace the litter on the aircar's frame as Talbot climbed out and took the back. "Come on, Rocket."

The quetzal, on unsteady legs, leapt out onto the street, a rainbow of colors rippling along his sides. Rocket's tongue flicked this way and that as it quested along the side of Kylee's litter.

Talbot led the way, barely aware that people had stopped short to stare. Then he flung the doors open with one hand, charging into the hallway, calling, "We need a doctor! Now!"

A woman, dressed in a white apron, stepped out of an office a couple of doors down past the waiting area, a clipboard in her hands.

"We've got a nine-year-old girl," Talbot thundered. "Broken hip and femur. We need a doctor. We have trade. We'll pay."

The woman started forward. "Bring her this way . . ."

She stopped short, eyes going wide. "Good God! That's a *quetzal*!"

"His name is Rocket," Dya called. "He's Kylee's pet. He won't hurt you!"

The clipboard fell, hitting the floor with a clatter. The woman was backing away, face gone white. She seemed paralyzed.

"Where's Dr. Turnienko?" Talbot asked. "Get her! Kylee's hurt."

The nurse's gaze remained fixed on Rocket, as if mesmerized by his splashes of color.

"Where's the surgery?" Dya almost screamed. "Now!"

"D-down the hall. Second right." The nurse backed into the room from which she'd come, slamming her door behind her.

"Shit!" Talbot bellowed. "Come on."

At the second door to the right, Talbot backed through, carried Kylee to the raised table beneath a thick cluster of overhead lights. Yep. It looked like an operating room:

cabinets filled with medical supplies; surgical tools under glass in an ultraviolet sterile case; all the monitors, hoses, and electrical gizmos.

A siren began to wail, loud, offensive.

Rocket hissed, as if the noise frightened him.

"Let's get her up on the table," Dya told him, and together they shifted Kylee's fragile and broken form onto the padded table.

"Stay with her," Talbot said. "I'm going for the doctor."

He stepped out into the hallway, found it vacant. The siren continued to wail.

Not knowing what else to do, he opened the door across from the surgery. A woman, partially swathed in bandages, and obviously a patient, was just getting out of bed. Talbot caught her in the act of pulling a coat around her shoulders.

"Where's the doctor?" Talbot demanded. "Which room?"

"Should be in her office, but with the alert, she'll be headed to the front."

"What alert?"

The woman, her thick black hair pulled back, stopped short and studied Talbot with remarkably blue eyes. Even with the bandages on her cheeks, he was looking at a beautiful . . .

"You're Supervisor Aguila," Talbot said, realizing why she looked so familiar. "What happened to you?"

"Mobbers," she snapped. "Who are you? And more to the point, what are you doing in my room?"

"I need the doctor."

"Well, good luck. A quetzal in the compound outweighs whatever's wrong with you."

"A quetzal in the . . . Shit! That *stupid* woman."

He wheeled around, blocking the Supervisor's door, and looked down the hall. Here they came. At the entrance, armed men and women were forming up.

"Can this get any worse?" Talbot wondered.

Looking the other way down the corridor, he could see additional people looking in the rear entrance windows, rifle barrels silhouetted through the glass.

"Port Authority shuts down over a quetzal alert," the

Supervisor said from behind. "Nothing's going to happen until the whole town is searched and either the quetzal's destroyed or the town's determined to be clean."

Talbot clenched his fists, ground his jaws, and cursed himself for a fucking fool.

"The quetzal's here, damn it," he gritted. "He came with me. His name's Rocket, and he's not going to hurt anyone."

"Are you out of your mind?" she demanded.

"Yeah, I probably am." Talbot laughed, hearing the maniacal tones behind it.

At the front entrance, the doors opened; two women and a large man entered at a crouch, rifles shouldered. Competent, capable, they started forward, sweeping for a target. Stopping at the front lobby, they showed perfect form as they cleared the room.

Talbot eased out into the hallway, heart thudding at the base of his throat. "Hey! Down here!"

He watched as they stopped short, the woman out front calling, "Get to cover. There's a quetzal in the building!"

"He's with me. His name is Rocket. He's in the surgery with my daughter Kylee. She has a broken hip and femur. All we want is a doctor. We have trade."

"Who the hell are you?"

"We're Wild Ones. From a farmstead out west. My daughter was injured in a fall. We have trade. Just fix my little girl, and charge our power pack, and we're out of here."

Some sixth sense made him glance behind. They were coming in from the rear, as well. Talbot slipped his rifle from his shoulder, calling, "That's far enough! Not another step."

"We kill quetzals here, mister," one of the men behind him called.

"You'll have to kill me first," Talbot called.

"Not a problem," the lead man called, raising his rifle.

Talbot stepped back into the protection of the Supervisor's room, leveling his rifle. "Put the gun down! Bunched up like you are? A full-auto burst will leave your blood and guts all over the hall!"

Shifting, it was to see that the group coming from the front had split up, diving into rooms.

"Hey!" Talbot called. "Before you idiots start something you can't handle, I'm standing in the Supervisor's room. You go to shooting in here, we're going to have a real mess."

He shot a glance back over his shoulder, saying, "Can you believe this shit? All I want is to get medical aid for my daughter? Are these people nuts?"

"That seems to be a common theme around here. But then I didn't bring a quetzal into a hospital, either." Supervisor Aguila had backed up to her bed, adding, "You know they're going to kill you, don't you?"

35

*A*quetzal in the hospital? When the alarm sounded, Talina had felt a rush of cold blood run through her veins. She had leaped out of Shig's office, slammed open the weapons locker door, and stripped a rifle out of the rack. Even as she went sprinting down the admin building hallway the siren began to blare its deadly warning.

"Make a hole, people!" she had hollered at the knot of folks waiting outside of Yvette's office to file paperwork.

"What have you got, Two Spots?" she had demanded, accessing her com system as people scrambled to get out of her way.

"Felicity says that a man and woman burst into the hospital carrying a child on a plank. And she insists that they had a quetzal with them. She just turned and bolted her door before she called me."

"A man, woman, and child. With a quetzal?"

"You know as much as I do."

That had been before she, Trish, and Step Allenovich had carefully stepped through the entrance to the hospital. She'd seen the dusty Beta parked in the street outside.

Now she stood, her body protected by Raya's office doorway, her rifle at the ready as she scanned the hallway. She could just see the Wild One's rifle barrel. A military weapon, capable of full-auto fire.

The guy wasn't kidding when he said he could fill the hallway with blood and body parts. And worse, the fool had the Supervisor hostage?

"Listen, no one has to get hurt," Talina called. "What's this about a quetzal?"

"His name is Rocket!" the guy hiding in Kalico's room bellowed back. "He's not going to hurt anyone!"

"Iji here," the botanist announced in her ear bud. *"We're in through the rear. Spiro might be able to shoot the guy through the Supervisor's window."*

"Roger that." Talina peeked around the door jamb. To the gunman, she shouted, "What on Earth possessed you to bring a quetzal here?"

"He's bonded with my daughter," the guy shouted back. "Just get the damned doctor down here to check Kylee out! She's badly injured. Maybe dying. And leave Rocket alone. He's not going to hurt anyone. You get it?"

"Hey, take it easy."

"Easy?" he bellowed back. "We just came to get a child medical attention, and now I'm up to my ass in the shit! You hurt my kid, or her quetzal, and you'd better be ready for hot rounds."

Hot rounds? The way he talked? Talina frowned.

"Stand down, Marine. No reason to get into the shit. Not here. If I come out, can we talk? No tricks?"

"Best news I've heard all day. But where's the doctor?"

"Two Spots? Where's Raya?"

"Locked down at the cafeteria."

"Escort her to the hospital."

To the marine, she called, "She's on the way. Coming out!"

"You sure that's a good idea?" Trish called from where she sat ready on the other side of the hall, gun braced on Felicity's door frame.

"Hey, who knows more about quetzals than me?"

To her com, she said, "Everybody hold. Let me see if I can figure this out."

Taking a deep breath, Talina set her rifle butt-down against the wall and stepped out into the corridor, hands up. "No tricks," she reminded as she walked slowly forward. She had that eerie, queasy feeling as the military rifle's muzzle centered on her gut.

She stopped no more than three paces from Kalico's door and stared into the marine's eyes. He might have been thirty, tanned, with a clear-eyed stare, the rock-solid type who'd been down-range, seen it all. She thought he looked vaguely familiar. One of Cap's guys. His dress was unusual, textile rather than chamois or quetzal hide. But clearly handwoven.

"Supervisor?" Talina called. "You all right?"

"Hell no. These damn cuts aren't healing. But if you mean has this guy hurt me? No."

"Talina Perez, right?" the marine asked.

"You?"

"Mark." The gun didn't waver. "Don't hurt my daughter or her quetzal."

At that moment, a shadow played over the window on the opposite side of the room.

Talina accessed her com, ordering, "I said, everyone was to . . ."

The glass shattered as Lieutenant Spiro thrust a rifle barrel in, barely aiming as she fired past Kalico. The round tore through the marine's arm, spattering blood and tissue. Cracked through the surgery door across the hall.

Talina jerked at the spatter.

The rifle fell with a clatter as the marine half spun. Talina was staring into his wide eyes, light brown. Clear. And watched as he slowly sank to the floor.

"He's down," Spiro said into her com. "Supervisor's secure."

Talina bit off a curse, dropping down as she bellowed, "Spiro, you stupid, fucking cow!" she snapped. "I had this under control!"

"Yeah, some control," Spiro said, breaking out the last of the glass before levering herself through the window. "A guy with a gun was in the Supervisor's room. Turns out it was a deserter, Mark Talbot. My only regret is that I took a snap shot and winged him instead of center-punching the piece of shit. Now, let's kill this quetzal and get things back to normal."

Talina ripped a zip tie from her belt, grabbed a bandage pack from the emergency tray beside the door, and pulled the pad tight to stanch the blood from the marine's wound. Fortunately the bone wasn't broken, but he had a hell of divot through the triceps.

Talbot, huh? She barely had time to wonder where the other two were. How they'd ended up as Wild Ones.

Talbot was gasping, trying to sit up.

"Stay down," Talina growled.

"Not the quetzal. It'll kill Kylee. Kill me."

"What the fuck?" Spiro muttered, pushing past Kalico.

Talina beat her to the surgery door, eased it open and peered around the jamb to see a blonde woman crouched down in the corner, her arms around a young quetzal that was shooting patterned flashes of yellow and black, its collar fully expanded, tongue flicking.

And there, on the surgery, lay a blonde girl. Maybe ten. Covered with a blanket.

Spiro pushed past, raising her rifle. To the woman, she said, "Step back. Now!"

The blonde woman had tears in her eyes, was fighting sobs. "You kill me first," she said hesitantly. "Go on. Get it over. You murdering *bastards*!"

"Suit yourself," Spiro told her emotionlessly, sighting down her rifle.

"Save them," the quetzal whispered in Talina's mind.

Talina suffered that palpitation of the heart as she shucked her pistol and jammed the muzzle against the back of Spiro's head. The lieutenant froze.

"You press that trigger, you're dead, bitch," Talina crooned in Spiro's ear. "Now, lower the rifle. You step back. Easy. And you walk your ass out of this hospital. And if I so much as see you here again today, I'll consider it proof that you and I are going to settle this once and for all."

From behind Talina, Kalico Aguila's weary voice said, "Lieutenant, you are dismissed."

"Ma'am! There's a deadly animal right here! You can't expect me—"

"Dismissed, Lieutenant!"

Talina stepped back, pistol up, finger hovering over the trigger. Every nerve in her body tingled as it jazzed on the adrenaline high of combat. In her gut, the quetzal was hissing and clawing.

As Spiro's raging gaze met hers, Talina felt her mouth flood with saliva. For once, she was as ready as her quetzal to kill the woman.

"Later." Spiro mouthed the word.

Talina nodded, flinty eyes meeting Spiro's, fully aware that they'd passed far beyond the point of no return.

As Spiro left the room, Talina took a breath, seeing where Spiro's bullet had shattered one of Raya's surgical cabinets. A bottle of priceless antibiotic was exploded all over the inside of the cabinet, and daylight could be seen through the resultant hole in the wall.

Talina holstered her pistol, stepped over to the little girl, and lifted the blanket. They weren't kidding about her leg and hip. "Ah, shit."

"Don't hurt Kylee," the crouching blonde said. "Please. We'll do anything. Pay anything. Just help her."

Talina stepped over, crouching down where the woman and quetzal huddled in the corner. She thought something was familiar about the blonde. But the quetzal took her full attention. A juvenile, its three frightened eyes fixed on hers. From the colors shooting over its body, the creature was terrified.

On the table, the little girl was moaning in time to the quetzal's deep-throated chittering. Damn, how closely linked were they?

The quetzal inside her was purring in reassurance. Like she'd done the right thing.

"It's all right," Talina told the panicked juvenile. Felt her mouth water as the little quetzal's tongue flicked out, played softly across her lips. She forced some of her saliva past her lips, let the juvenile lick it, having no idea what she might be communicating.

Aloud, she said, "You're safe now." The quetzal's colors shaded subtly into milder yellows and blacks.

"Tal?" Trish called from the hallway.

"Yeah. We're cool. Get Raya in here. Now!"

Where she stood inside the door, Kalico had braced herself against the emergency tray, her gaze fixed on Talina, the woman, and the quetzal.

"How is my husband?" the blonde woman asked, still shaken.

"Shot in the arm," Talina told her. "How in the hell could this have gone so bad?"

"Because, Perez," the blonde woman said through gritted teeth, "you're all murderers here. But your doctor is the only hope my daughter has."

36

Kalico Aguila had never heard a gun fired up close. The sharp sound had been physically painful—like a dagger driven through her ears and into her head. Her hearing had rung for almost two hours. The wall of her room, the hallway, and even Talina Perez had been spattered with bits of blood and tissue.

That, more than anything else, had soured her on Spiro.

Clusterfuck. It was an old term, and one that had her emotionally on edge. Pile that on top of already feeling vulnerable from the unending torture of her wounds.

Would they never heal?

Turnienko—who had tried everything—remained perplexed that any kind of tissue healing was progressing so slowly.

Under it all, Kalico was just plain tired of pain—of not daring to move too fast for fear of tearing her stitches.

And most of all, she was desperate to know what was happening at Corporate Mine where her people were slogging along, barely meeting quota, and forever scurrying around close to cover.

The damnable mobbers had been back once already, but this time everyone had managed to find cover. How could people produce when they were afraid to get more than two steps from a safe hiding place?

She eased her way across her room, hating the fact that her window was now only a plastic sheet. Hardly the kind of security that would allow her to sleep in peace. Especially after a quetzal alert. The memory of Talina Perez's broken wall notwithstanding, that fragile film of plastic wouldn't slow a single mobber.

"Different room tonight," she told herself.

She stepped out past where Private Miso had washed the blood speckles off her wall, and glanced down the corridor. A marine now stood outside her door, dressed in combat armor, rifle at parade rest. Spiro's order, given that a quetzal was just across the hall in the surgery.

Kalico slowly walked down to peer into Wan Xi Gow's room. Gow, like her, had been rudely cut up by the mobbers but managed to escape. Similar to hers, the marine's wounds were healing so slowly as to be barely perceptible.

He lay on his bed, eyes closed, chest slowly rising and falling.

Across the hall from Wan, Mark Talbot, one of her missing marines, lay drugged after surgery to debride his wound, stitch the muscle back together, and stretch the skin of his arm tightly enough to suture.

She studied the marine's sun-bronzed face and wondered where in hell he'd been. Let alone where his two companions had ended up.

Hard to believe he'd showed up here, all these months later, claiming he had a wife, child, and pet quetzal.

She was halfway back to her room when the door to the surgery opened and the blonde stepped out. The woman stopped short; her blue gaze had a bruised look, her mouth set hard. Something about the strong lines, the strength in her gaze, drew the eye.

"How is it going?" Kalico inclined her head toward the surgery.

"Dr. Turnienko is doing a remarkable job. She's gluing the bones together piece by piece with an osteoblastic adhesive. She did the hip first; now she's working on the femur, closing up as she works her way out." She lifted an eyebrow. "How's Mark?"

"Sleeping. I just checked on him."

The woman's lips pursed. "You're really a Supervisor?"

Kalico chuckled humorlessly. "Unfortunately, every time I ask myself that same question, the answer always remains a yes." She started to offer her hand, then thought better of it. "I'm Kalico Aguila. I'd shake, but I'm just held together by sutures."

"Dya." She hesitated, then added, "Dya Simonov."

"Don't let me keep you. If you need to get back to your little girl . . ."

"No. I mean, a person can only take so much. And Kylee's going to make it. I could tell by Rocket's colors.

He's starting to relax, which means Kylee's past the danger point."

"The quetzal knows?" Kalico asked. "How?"

"The bond is partly chemical, partly body language, maybe smell."

"Fascinating." Kalico added, "You look beat."

"So do you." Dya gestured. "Your wounds. It was death fliers, wasn't it? They're not healing because the creatures have a gland at the base of each claw. It secretes a molecular compound that acts as a poison. While it's deadly to Donovanian life, it blocks the RNA receptors that trigger wound response in human cells. Makes them feel all warm and rosy. I've got a salve that will allow you to heal."

Kalico felt her heart leap. "How much do you want for it? All of it?"

"It will depend on what they ask in return for Mark's and Kylee's surgery. But, since I don't know that yet, just wait here."

She turned, striding down the hall with a purpose, and out the door. Moments later she was back with a crate. Kalico could hear the rattle of glass jars.

"My room's here," Kalico told her, leading the way.

Inside, Dya set the crate down, rolled up her sleeves, and shut the door behind her. "Take your clothes off. I'll need to remove your bandages."

As Kalico complied, she asked, "What is this stuff?"

"A mixture I distill from stonewood sap, cutthroat flower, and gotcha vine. Donovanian chemistry tends to be complex. The stonewood sap holds the two digestive enzymes from gotcha and cutthroat flower in suspension. Once in the wound, the sap triggers an immune response. As your body begins to break down the sap, the enzymes are released and begin to denature the death flier's poison. Essentially it attacks the molecule at the hydrogen bonds breaking it into the terrestrial equivalent of polypeptide chains that—"

"Right. Whatever you said, in whatever language that was."

Dya actually smiled slightly as she peeled back one of Kalico's bandages and started on her right hand.

"Itches," Kalico said as the first of the salve eased into her cuts.

"Good." Dya concentrated as she worked from wound to wound, dipping out a milky-looking paste.

"Private Talbot said you were his wife and that Kylee's his daughter?"

"That's right."

"Last I knew he was an AWOL marine."

Dya shot her an evaluative look and stopped her ministrations. "I plan on taking my husband, daughter, and Rocket home with me. If you're going to hinder that in any way, I'll pack up my salves and go. Right now."

"Maybe you'd better tell me the story. And how he ended up out at your farmstead. The other two, Shintzu and Garcia? They out there, too?"

Dya shook her head. "Dead. Long before Mark made it to us. Listen, Supervisor, those three made a mistake. They flew out to see something of Donovan. They set down, and the forest took over. A nightmare got Garcia, a slug got Shin, and the roots got their aircar. Took Mark months to make it to our place. Call it a miracle."

"And in the months since?"

"He's become one of us. Married into the family. I'm pregnant with his child. He would have given his life for Kylee. I'd give mine for his. Simple as that."

As bluntly as the woman spoke, it had to be the truth. The salve had continued to itch, but with a cool feeling that soothed her wounds.

Kalico considered the woman, read the resolution in her eyes. She had crossed her arms, holding the ointment in one hand. Kalico could see no give as the woman awaited her decision. As the old saying went, Donovan taught hard lessons. Kalico wondered if she had learned any of them.

"If your salve really works on these cuts, I'll make sure that you, your daughter, and her quetzal are safely delivered back to your farmstead in a new aircar. Your daughter's care here will be completely compensated. I offer you that in return for those boxes of salves and ointments you've brought."

"And Mark?"

"He's still under contract. Marines are treated differently than contract labor. While officers can resign a commission after having served the requisite number of years, privates don't have that luxury. For the moment, given his new circumstances, I'm willing to keep an open mind. But first, I'd like to hear his version of the story. How he, Garcia, and Shintzu happened to end up out there."

"Mark goes home with me." Dya crossed her arms.

"You've got spunk, but don't push me too far. Mark's future remains mine to determine." Kalico raised a hand to stop Dya's outburst. "That doesn't mean that we can't find a workable solution before this is all said and done. I don't know if I'm being played for a fool. If his story pans out, let's just say that I might be persuaded to send him back with you. Assuming, that is, that your salve actually works."

Dya studied her, hard calculation behind the woman's eyes.

"Best I'm willing to do for the moment," Kalico added. "Which is a whole lot better than just ordering Spiro to pack Talbot up at gunpoint and ship him off to Corporate Mine. I'd rather not employ that option."

Dya began dipping from the salve again. "You seem to be cast from a different mold than Clemenceau."

"Clemenceau sought to succeed by force. My strategy, slowly learned, is to create mutually beneficial alliances rather than festering resentment. But don't think I won't resort to the harshest measures if no more salubrious solution presents itself."

"Is Talina Perez your assassin, too?" Dya asked bitterly.

"No. I have Spiro for that." Kalico made a face. "When it comes to Perez and me? That gets a bit complicated. My original plan was to put her up against a wall and shoot her for murdering Clemenceau. She outflanked me."

"Too bad."

"No love lost for Perez, huh? You're not alone in that regard." Kalico paused for a beat. "Don't forget that if it hadn't been for Perez, Spiro would have shot your quetzal."

Dya jerked her head toward the surgery. "Perez is sitting in there with a rifle across her hips, ready to shoot Rocket."

"It was the only way Turnienko and Strazinsky would agree to do the surgery. What did Perez ever do to you?"

"Killed my first husband and a friend of mine. Shot them down in cold blood on Clemenceau's order."

"She after you, too? That why you ran?"

Dya flared, cheeks reddening. "Wanting to be left alone wasn't any crime. All Pak and Paolo did was tell that maggot Clemenceau that if he ever threatened us again, ever came after us . . ." The woman blanched. Swallowed hard. "Like you say: Donovan teaches hard lessons."

"But you've learned them," Kalico mused, glancing at the crate with its glass jars, all full of who knew what kinds of miracles like the ones being rubbed on her perplexing wounds.

"Not entirely." Dya glanced up. "No telling what this is going to cost us. Mark's already got a hole in his arm, and you've just threatened to have him arrested. The hospital's surrounded by townies just waiting for the opportunity to kill Rocket. Somehow I have to keep my family alive and manage to get my power pack recharged."

"What else you got in that box?"

"Salves, poisons, narcotics, antibiotics, anesthetics, emetics, a lot of things."

"And Rocket's really a pet?" Kalico mused, glancing at the surgery door. "Do you know how difficult that is to believe here?"

"More than a pet. They're linked. Do everything together. Maybe it's even symbiotic. God alone knows what would happen if you separated them."

"Fascinating," Kalico mused as Dya rubbed more ointment onto the cuts on her shoulders. "Which direction from Port Authority is your farmstead?"

"West."

And that, Kalico suspected through sheer gut instinct, was the first lie the woman had told.

37

Talina yawned, stretched, and ambled down the hospital hall toward the main entrance. The fact that Rocket hadn't eaten anyone to date had gone a long way toward decreasing tensions. At least inside the hospital. Just outside the hospital's doors, a collection of locals waited, all of them itching to plug the beast. One thing was sure: Talina wasn't leaving the hospital for a while.

Not fifteen minutes ago, Felicity had given Talina a smile and said, "I have to stop by home and make sure that Shan and the kids are all right. Then I'll drop by your place and pick up some extra clothes for you. It's no problem."

"Know my door code?" Talina had asked.

"Five. Five. Four. Two," Felicity had told her with a wink. "Or just climb through the plastic like those *Turalon* crew did."

Good woman, Felicity. She was even getting over her bone-deep fear of Rocket, having worked in proximity to the predator for most of the day without so much as a bite taken out of her. Additionally, Talina suspected that Felicity felt guilty about her role in getting Talbot shot, and the overreaction to Rocket's arrival.

She shouldn't. We've never had a "pet" quetzal inside the compound before.

Just inside the main entrance, Private Tompzen stood at attention, dressed in combat armor, his rifle at his side.

"How's the little girl?" he asked.

"Raya's monitoring her. She thinks the surgery is a success. The bones are all back where they belong. Now it's just a matter of seeing if there are any complications from infection. After that it's a slow transition to physical therapy, electrostim, and giving the cartilage in the hip socket time to heal."

Talina glanced out at the night beyond the window. In the hospital lights a collection of armed men and a couple of women bearing rifles loitered about, all nervous as hell about the quetzal in their hospital. God help the little creature if it set so much as a foot outside.

The aircar remained where it had landed that afternoon. Trish had already gone over it, trying to figure where it had come from. Someone had removed all markings and vehicle ID. And done it recently, as the sialon where the ID strip had been was remarkably clean in comparison to the rest of the car.

Dya had carried the two crates in, and they now lived in Mark Talbot's room. Kylee—and her quetzal—were in the post-op, the little girl hooked up to every kind of monitor.

"What a day, huh?" Tal remarked.

"That really is Talbot down there?" Tompzen asked.

"In the flesh."

"He say where Garcia and Shin are?"

"Not to me. Simonov and the Supervisor have been pretty chummy all afternoon, though. She might know."

"Thought her name was Dya."

Talina gave one last look through the window; the collection of locals loitering around the peripheries seemed wary but not panicked. Others were coming and going. Everyone in town was curious about the little girl and her alleged "pet." Half the town had already tried to get in to see it, shoot it, or take a holo.

"Dya Simonov. Took me a while to recognize her."

"She a friend of yours?"

"I shot her husband," Talina replied, feeling a dead spot inside where her heart should have been.

During the long hours of surgery, the hatred behind Dya's eyes had hung between them like a poisonous mist.

Talina turned, strolling back down the hall, wishing for a cup of coffee. Truth be told, her entire day had been miserable, and she was in a foul mood.

She nodded to the guard at Kalico's door and crossed the hall to the post-op. In the low glow of the room lights, the quetzal was curled beside the bed, its three eyes immediately fixed on Talina as she entered and walked over.

Kylee's eyes were open, and she looked worried, asking, "Where's Dya?"

"Your mother's with Talbot. How are you feeling?"

"Funny." The little girl's face screwed up. "It's all new. So many people. I miss Rebecca, Su, Shantaya, everybody. Who are you?"

"Talina Perez." She gave the little girl a smile. "Must be a shock. All these new faces."

Kylee blinked. "Rocket and I are both scared. Strange place. Strange people."

"How long have you and Rocket been together?"

"Four years."

"And he never tried to hurt you?"

"What? Why would he?" Kylee looked up at her like she was crazy. "He's my best friend. You people don't understand."

Talina felt her own quetzal stir inside her, the beast slightly agitated by Rocket's presence. As if the juvenile could sense it, too, it was staring at Talina as though she were some sort of monster.

"I'm asking because I have a quetzal inside me. Unlike your Rocket, it wants me dead. Has tried to kill me."

Kylee's drugged blue eyes widened, studied Talina thoughtfully. "How incredibly lonely and abandoned you both must feel."

Talina smiled weakly, remembering that she'd killed this girl's father. "Yeah, well, there's an old saying that life's just shit stew and every day's another spoonful."

"If it wasn't for Rocket, Dya, Mark, and my family . . ." The girl's eyes lost focus. Then cleared again. "You could come live with us. We could make it better for you."

A part of Talina's heart melted.

Kid, if you only knew.

"Hey, Raya says your surgery went well. I just wanted to come and check on you and Rocket. You sleep now."

"He's hungry," Kylee said.

"I'll see what I can do." Talina glanced at the quetzal, aware of the worried shine in the beast's eyes. "Might be some chamois over at the cafeteria."

She accessed her com, asking, "Two Spots? Can you see if you can find some raw chamois or crest meat? Maybe a kilo. Check with Millie. If not, see if Trish can run some down from one of the hunters. We need to feed this quetzal. Make it a priority."

"Feed the quetzal? Are you out of your ever-loving . . . ? Yeah, yeah, I get it. Roger that."

Talina winked at Rocket, stumped by this new twist. The creature really did seem maudlin when it came to Kylee.

The beast in her gut shifted, and she could imagine all the TriNA in her blood and tissues squirting molecules back and forth.

Yeah, we're all a little baffled, you piece of shit.

"I'll make sure Rocket's fed. If you need anything, you page me."

"Thank you." As if she were trying out the syllables, Kylee added, "Ta Li Na. Nice name."

"So's Kylee."

Talina let herself out into the hall, coming face-to-face with Dya Simonov.

The woman didn't even hesitate, asking, "What were you doing in there?"

"Went in to check on your daughter and Rocket. I've got the cafeteria hunting down meat for Rocket. Kylee told me he's hungry. Should have thought of it before. Shouldn't be more than ten or fifteen minutes before it gets here. It would help if you were there when Mellie brings it. Our relationship with quetzals being what it is here."

"Yeah, shoot them all down on sight, right?" Dya's gaze had gone diamond hard.

"Listen, what happened back then—"

"Don't." Dya raised a hand, lips quivering. "Just leave it alone."

Talina nodded, started down the hall, and turned. "Just for the record, what I did that day made me sick. It was the final straw."

"Whole lot of comfort there, Perez." Dya didn't look back as she closed the door behind her.

"Shit."

With nothing else to do, Talina wandered down and knocked on Turnienko's door.

"Yes?"

Talina stepped in, found the MD seated, staring at data projected in green columns above her desk. Additionally, the remote patient monitors were glowing off to the left where they were projected against the wall.

"What are you still doing here?" Turnienko asked, shooting Talina a sidelong glance.

"Hey, we've got a deserter, a little girl, a hungry quetzal, and Kalico Aguila just down the hall, not to mention an uncertain and nervous crowd with loaded weapons outside the front door. We've had one shooting in here today, and, but for a hair's breadth, almost two. You really think I'm going down for a nightcap at Inga's before I trundle off to spend the night in my own comfy bed?"

"No, I suppose not." Turnienko frowned at the data. "This is fascinating."

"What are you looking at?"

"Kylee's bloodwork. She's loaded with TriNA. Her brain is remarkably active, extraordinarily integrated. Some of the brain matter that we associate with cognition, however, has anomalies. It's thicker, has more blood flow, and is organized differently."

"Meaning?"

"My guess? Those are the pathways through which she and the quetzal communicate. I'd bet if I set the scan, I'd see the beginnings of something similar in your brain. The difference being that Kylee's been linked to the creature for four years, and her brain is still developing. You were just recently infected. You aren't sharing quetzal molecules back and forth every day either."

"So Rocket's screwing with her brain?"

"Yes. And no." Turnienko gave Talina another of those pensive looks. "It's highly selective. It's leaving the areas of Kylee's personality centers untouched. As if it wants Kylee to stay Kylee." She gestured her frustration. "The closest analogy I can give you is that it's some sort of quetzal implant that functions like our cyberimplants do. Kylee and Rocket are clearly symbiotic. They augment each other. She's got the same sensory improvements you do: enhanced vision, hearing, energy, scent, and endurance. Better, actually, because they're integrated."

"Supergirl?"

Turnienko shook her head. "More like nine-year-old-Donovan-quetzal-girl. She's a kid. A very well-educated, courageous, and physically traumatized kid. But if we don't have a post-op infection, and if she'll follow the physical therapy, she should come out of this walking, and have a normal life."

Talina sucked her lips, frowning at the floor.

"What?" Turnienko asked.

"Must feel good. To go home, I mean, and crawl in bed, and know that today you saved a little girl from a living hell of pain and immobility."

Turnienko pushed back from her desk. "And it's balanced by the fact that after all this time, Aguila's wounds haven't healed a lick. No matter what I tried. And then, Dya Simonov walks in, smears Aguila's wounds with a home-cooked paste, and within hours, the lacerations are closing." She shook her head. "Am I missing something? Just totally incompetent? Or what?"

"The woman's a botanical chemist, Raya. It's sacrilege, I know, but within the bounds of her specialty, she's probably way smarter than Cheng. And she has had the time to concentrate on her research down there."

"Down there?" Raya lifted an eyebrow. "Thought she was from out west somewhere. But then, they've been really evasive about exactly where their farmstead is."

"Don't blame 'em. Clemenceau gave them good reason to vanish." A beat. "So did I."

"Is that guilt I hear, Tal?"

"Yeah. Unlike you, I'm in a different line of business from saving lives."

"So, where's Dya from?"

"Let's say I'll keep their confidence for now." Even as she said it, Talina wondered what possessed her. Some deep-seated guilt about Pak and Paolo? Or the knowledge that Talbot and Dya been desperate to bring Kylee and her quetzal here, enough so that they'd even removed the ID plate on their aircar.

"How many kids out in the bush have bonded with quetzals?" Turnienko wondered. "And what does it mean?"

"How the hell should I know?"

"If anyone should, it would be you." Turnienko tapped her long fingers on her chin as she stared at the projected data. "Rocket and Kylee bonded for a reason. It didn't just happen like a random attraction of atoms. That quetzal you killed out in the canyon that day sneaked into Port Authority for a specific purpose. It ate Allison's infant, and fled. Stupid us, we've always attributed these attacks to hunger. But there was plenty of easier prey for your quetzal.

"Then, when you ran it down, it went out of its way as it was dying to infect you, helped to keep you alive out in the bush until its mate could cleverly sneak in and try to kill you. Why?"

"*Yes,*" Talina's beast whispered.

Talina frowned. "Every time Allison's baby is mentioned, my quetzal tells me 'empty' as if that means something."

"Empty," Turnienko repeated thoughtfully. Then her gaze sharpened as she stared at a projected holo of Kylee's brain. "And maybe it was. It was newborn."

"Yeah, couple of months."

"Given what we think we know about TriNA, it can carry information between organisms, right? Maybe eating that baby was an attempt to learn. To absorb its knowledge. And all the quetzal got was a primitive little animal dominated by a desperate need for food, comfort, and security."

"That's what babies are. Little self-centered, demanding creatures."

"But, Tal, think about how perplexing that would be to an organism that doesn't have to start its life as a blank slate. Doesn't have to completely learn its culture, language, history, and which behaviors are acceptable as norms change with each generation. Instead, all that knowledge is contained in molecules. Molecules that it can share with others."

"So you're saying it's a whole new order of intelligence?"

"Could be."

"Better than ours? Smarter?"

Turnienko shook her head. "Not necessarily better. Different. We're not seeing quetzals suddenly building aircars, hospitals, or factories. They don't modify their environment the way we do. Don't make tools that we know of, and certainly don't make tools that are used to make other tools."

Turnienko pointed an index finger at Talina. "And before you start going all environmentalist and creepy on me, keep in mind that the first interaction—the first contact, if you will—was when a quetzal ate Donovan the day he first put foot on the planet."

Talina crossed her arms. "Raya, we don't have a clue about what the long-term impact of our presence is going to be on Donovan. We've essentially infected the planet with our microbes, fungi, and plants. Not to mention us, and our mines, houses, and technology."

Turnienko narrowed a questioning eye. "Guess we shouldn't be surprised or shocked when Donovanian life infects us in return." She paused. "I wonder how many of the one hundred and sixty people who shipped back to Solar System were infected with TriNA? What the long-term effects of that are going to be on humanity back home?"

"Either way the genie is out of the bottle."

Talina felt her quetzal shift inside her, somehow smug.

"Keep in mind, Tal"—Turnienko returned her gaze to her data holo—"we're just exploring the initial hypotheses. If they turn out to be correct, we still don't know what they mean. We may be tinkering with the tip of the iceberg here. But whatever the ultimate outcome, we're committed. It's just a matter of paying the price when we finally figure out the consequences."

"Tal!" Two Spots' voice announced in her earbud. *"We've got a report of a small explosion in the domestic area. Trish told me not to bother you while she checked it out. Turns out it was at your dome. Was Felicity Strazinsky supposed to be in your bedroom?"*

"Affirmative. She was going to pick up a change of clothes."

"Yeah, well, Trish say's she's lying in your living room. And she's dead."

38

Growing up on Donovan as she had, Trish had had more than her share of grisly experiences. Seen some pretty awful things. The bombing of Talina's bedroom, however, sent a sick shiver through her. This wasn't a normal act of violence. Sure, Donovan was a tough place with its stabbings, shootings, and the occasional fistfight. But there was an understood code. People here just didn't act with such senseless and impersonal violence.

The electrical in Talina's dome had been blown by the explosion, leaving the whole house dark. Trish had resorted to hauling in lights to illuminate the scene. In the actinic glare, the damage to the bedroom was sobering.

While going over the room on hands and knees, Trish noticed the ravaged bit of threadlike, almost transparent, string. Out of place, it had been tied to Talina's bed leg. At first she didn't think anything of it.

Call it sheer dumb luck, but from her angle the glint of a reflection caught her eye. Trish crawled closer to the bed where it had been crushed into the wall. By chance the small proximity detector had somehow been blown into Talina's bedding and still clung to the spread. Given the velocity with which it hit, it had broken a couple of threads, and now dangled there, one jagged edge caught in the fabric.

"Tal?" Trish sat back on the ruins of the bedroom floor and accessed com. "Did you have a proximity charge stored in your bedroom?"

"Negative, Trish. All I had were twenty rounds of ammunition in the drawer beneath the gun rack out front. Other than that, the only thing explosive in the house was my temper."

"Shit." Trish made a face, took a set of tweezers from her "crime kit" and removed the proximity fuse. She carefully bagged it for Cheng's analysis. Looked like military issue. Had it slammed into the wall instead of the soft cushions, it would have shattered into such small fragments she would have probably missed them.

Shifting around, she searched along the bottom of Talina's splintered chest of drawers, used the tweezers, and pulled out another frayed length of string. No more than six inches of it. Tied off to the closest leg.

Then she looked back at the doorframe—at the bloody spot where Felicity's body had been blown into the front room. Raya Turnienko would have the final say at the autopsy, but from what Trish figured—given the direction of the wounds—the blast had been low. Centered right where the duraplast floor was buckled, cracked, and depressed. In a direct line between where a string would have been run across the floor, maybe ankle-height between the chest of drawers and the bed leg.

"Definitely murder."

She stood, taking a hard look at the wreckage. The side of the dome had been blown open to the night; the dividing wall was bowed and popped loose from the curving ceiling. Shrapnel scars pocked every surface; bits of the jagged metal were visible here and there where they had bounced around the room.

On the opposite side of the house, the plastic sheeting had been blown entirely away from the quetzal hole.

Shig and Yvette—escorted by Step Allenovich—arrived out of the night. Given that it was Talina's house, she had been asked to stay away and guard the hospital from any potential rampage by the quetzal. The idea was that this would be an independent investigation—as if Talina could have possibly had a motive to blow up Port Authority's only nurse. Let alone a woman Tal considered a good friend.

"What have you got?" Yvette asked, glancing around at the wreckage.

"My call is that someone tied a string between Tal's bed and her dresser. It was attached to an explosive triggered by a proximity charge. The string probably held the charge at just the right height and angle so that whoever stepped into the room would catch the full blast.

She held up the transparent baggie with the recovered proximity detector. "Cheng can confirm it through the chemistry, but I think it was military issue. Not that we're short of explosives anywhere in Port Authority, given the mining around here, but this was small. Think antipersonnel small. And you can see the shrapnel scars for yourselves. Felicity was peppered with them. Lots of random lacerations, as indicated by the amount of her blood on the floor."

Trish pointed her lights at the pooled crimson on Tal's living room floor.

"Any idea when the bomb would have been placed?" Shig asked, his round face thoughtful.

"Nope."

"Was Tal's door locked?" Yvette asked, her grim eyes on the drying blood.

"Open when I got here, but Felicity was here to pick up a change of clothes for Tal. Like so many of us, she knew Talina's door code. Not that it was necessary." Trish pointed at the gaping hole in the wall where tatters of plastic remained. "Lately that patch has kind of been like a freeway for anyone trying to get into Talina's house."

Shig fingered his chin, eyes fixed on the blasted bedroom where bits of torn fabric ruffled in time to the breeze blowing through the blast-ventilated house. "Anything missing?"

"Not that I can tell, but we'll need Talina to look everything over."

"Who'd want Talina dead?" Yvette asked.

"Dan Wirth?" Trish happily brought up her prime suspect for every possible crime. "Tal's the only person in Port Authority he really and truly fears. And then there's Spiro, maybe the Supervisor, and I can list a whole host of people whose heads Talina has cracked in the past."

Yvette narrowed her eyes. "You know that it was Dya Simonov's daughter who was brought in today. Dya has no reason to love Talina. Maybe on the way up, she brought an old military-issue antipersonnel mine along, just as a reminder to settle old scores?"

"Can't rule it out." Trish took a deep breath, smelling the blood and aftertaint from the explosive. "And didn't Talina and Spiro have a set-to earlier?"

"They did. Tal stopped Spiro from shooting the quetzal." Yvette exhaled bitterly. "Why Felicity? She never harmed so much as a bug. Half the people in this town owe their lives to her."

"A lot of people loved her," Shig mused. "They're going to be wanting blood over this."

"Yeah." Trish felt her anger brewing. "So do I. You been to see the family?"

"Just came from there," Yvette answered, looking back out through the door where a crowd had gathered in the glow of hand lanterns to await word on what had happened. "Shan and the kids are still in the 'I can't believe it' stage. But the realization is going to sink in. I don't envy them."

"How do you want to handle this?" Trish asked.

Shig raised his eyebrows in a look of futility. "Let me make the announcement. Tell people the investigation is ongoing, but the preliminary results indicate it was an assassination attempt on Talina. We agree on that, right?"

"We do," Trish told him. "But let's rope this off, put a guard on it. Come morning, I want Cheng to go over this room with the proverbial fine-toothed comb, make sure I didn't miss anything. That, and Talina might see something that will give her a clue when we're done."

Shig continued to finger his chin, looking around at the ruins of the home. "You know, we've never had a murder quite like this. Not even back when Clemenceau was at the height of his reign of terror."

"A bomb isn't the Donovanian style of murder," Yvette agreed. "I'd say this was a newcomer."

Yeah, Trish agreed silently, *and I'm going to find out who.*

39

"A bomb? Officer Monagan, are you out of your mind? If I were going to murder Talina Perez, it would not be through a means as messy and indiscriminate as a bomb. For the same reasons that Felicity Strazinsky's unfortunate death so perfectly illustrates. I may be many things, but messy and gross aren't among them."

Dan Wirth's words echoed in Trish's thoughts as she stalked down the main avenue and away from The Jewel. Of course she'd gone there first thing. Hoped to catch the slimy cretin off guard, before he had time to devise a lie.

And the problem was, coupled with the man's brown-eyed look of irritated disgust, she'd actually believed him for once in their miserable relationship.

Trish ran that knowledge through her head as she walked into the cafeteria, glanced around the big room. Not more than a quarter of the long tables were occupied even at peak hours, given the size of the place and how few people lived in Port Authority these days. Most of the families cooked at home.

But there, next to the dispensing line, sat the target of Trish's quest.

As she walked across the room, all eyes followed her, the conversation this morning considerably quieter than usual. People were discussing Felicity's murder, hard eyes fixing on Trish as she passed between the tables. By the time she arrived at Spiro's, a tomb would have sounded cacophonous in comparison.

Lieutenant Spiro sat across from two of her marines, Anderssoni and Abu Sassi. A plate of corn, chili, beans, and tomatoes, bristling with chunks of chamois meat, sat on the table, half-eaten before her.

Spiro looked up, her black eyes hardening, a grim smile bending her lips. "Well, well, here comes Officer Monagan. Would have figured they'd send Talina. If what I hear is correct, it'd be her opportunity to shoot me in the back and blame me for that poor nurse's death. What did Tal do? Leave a seismic charge lying around? That's criminal negligence, even here in lawless Port Authority, isn't it?"

Trish bit the inside of her lip until she had control of her emotions. Then she politely asked Abu Sassi and Anderssoni. "Could you two give us a moment?"

"Nope. They stay," Spiro said in clipped terms. "Anything you've got to say? Questions you want to ask? Go for it. I was with both of these men last night at Inga's. In fact, that's why Abu Sassi, here, looks a bit peaked. This is one of those mornings he's wishing he'd stayed a Muslim and didn't succumb to the evils of alcohol."

"You were in Inga's all night?" Trish raised a skeptical eyebrow.

Spiro glanced at her privates. "What time did we first get to the tavern?"

"Five or six?" Anderssoni said warily, glancing sidelong at Trish and then Spiro.

"What time did we leave?" Spiro continued, her black eyes fixed smugly on Trish's.

Abu Sassi's expression was strained and slightly green. He glanced up. "It was after everyone heard the bomb."

"So," Spiro concluded, "if I were the culprit, I would have had to go to Perez's before I went to Inga's. Like early afternoon. Except I was with people the whole time. Different marines, the shuttle crew. Someone should have seen me entering Perez's house, since it would have still been bright daylight. After that, I was at the tavern the whole night."

"And you never left?"

"Nope. Ask around, Officer. And tell Perez that if I so much as catch a glimpse of her sneaking up to shoot me in the back, I'm taking her out first."

"What makes you think Talina would shoot you in the back?" Trish asked.

"That's how she did it yesterday. From behind. Put a pistol to my head." She reached around with a finger and tapped the back of her scalp. "Just here."

"Heard you were going to endanger a woman's life."

"I was going to shoot a *quetzal*!" Spiro's voice boomed.

"And anyone who says that those damn beasts can be tamed is a toilet-sucking fool!"

Mutters of agreement broke out around the cafeteria.

"And you never stepped out last night? Like just to get a breath of fresh air?" Trish prodded, aware that the privates were both sitting stone-face-forward, as if at uneasy attention.

"Went to the head a couple of times. You know the story: Inga just rents beer. You drink it at the table, and piss it out in the head."

Spiro waved an irritated hand. "So there you go, Officer Monagan. Sorry. I wasn't your mad bomber, so buzz off like the noxious little fly you are and go bother some other poor fool."

Spiro lowered her eyes and went back to forking up corn and beans.

For a long moment Trish stood there, long enough to start looking foolish. "Yeah, later, huh?"

She turned and headed for the door, the room still silent. She nodded to people as she passed, seeing downright anger in their eyes mixing with the worry and uncertainty. Felicity was a beloved fixture in the community. She'd sewn up their wounds, dispensed the medicines that eased their aches and hurts, delivered their babies.

Now a quetzal was in their hospital, and someone had tried to assassinate Talina, but killed Felicity.

This could get really ugly, really fast.

Sure, you were at Inga's all night. Why don't I believe it?

At the door, Trish looked back. Spiro's black eyes were like lasers, a mocking and victorious smile on her lips.

40

Talbot scooped up the latest of Rocket's feces, which the young quetzal kindly deposited on a sheet of paper in the men's room. Rocket watched him as he dropped the globular excrement into the toilet. Just like with humans, what went in had to come out. And Perez had been explicit: "The quetzal doesn't set foot outside the hospital. Too many people here have lost loved ones to quetzals. I can't guarantee Rocket's safety."

"We okay?" Talbot asked.

Rocket flashed orange, chittering softly.

Talbot held the door, followed Rocket out into the hall, past Abu Sassi, who watched him with slitted and hard eyes where he stood guard at the Supervisor's door.

Yeah, yeah, I know. I'm a scum-sucking deserter.

Then they were back in post-op where Kylee lay elevated on the bed, talking to Dya.

"Rocket!" Kylee called gleefully. She reached out to run her fingers over the quetzal's mouth when it climbed up on the bed. So far Rocket had been remarkably careful to stay away from Kylee's incision.

Talbot leaned down, checking the long cut, now purple with one of Dya's antibiotics. Dr. Turnienko had been skeptical, but after the Supervisor's sudden turn toward recovery, had allowed it.

"Any word on who put the bomb in Perez's house?" Dya asked.

"Didn't talk to anyone. Still can't believe someone blew up Felicity. Tough place, this Port Authority."

"Yeah. Sooner we're out of here, the better," Dya told him.

Talbot bent over to kiss Kylee on the head. "How you doing, buttercup?"

"What's a buttercup?"

"A flower back on Earth. It's a term of affection, kid. You do affection, don't you?"

She grinned and winked at him.

At that moment the door opened. Supervisor Aguila leaned in. "Private Talbot, might I have a moment?"

Dya gave him a worried glance and nodded. "We'll be all right."

Talbot followed Aguila out into the hallway, past Abu Sassi, and into her room. Somehow he was relieved that she was no longer in the same room he'd been shot in.

"How's the arm?" she asked, retreating to her bed and seating herself.

"Itches and aches. I'm told some muscle was damaged, but it should heal up and be completely functional in a month or so."

"Things shouldn't have gotten that far out of hand. Spiro's been keeping a noticeably low profile over the last couple of days."

"She's always been . . ." He shrugged, knowing when he was over the line.

"Intense?" Aguila finished for him, her keen blue gaze seeing through his reluctance.

"If you wouldn't mind, ma'am, how can I be of service?"

"I'm trying to decide what to do with you. I'll be more likely to be lenient if you'll just tell me the truth. Why did you three fly out into the bush? Were you deserting?"

"No, ma'am. We just wanted to see it. Donovan, I mean. We were looking at the next two years locked up in *Turalon*. Hell, maybe even ending up like those poor bastards on *Freelander*. Sure, it was ill-advised. Stupid. Call it what you want, but we wanted to be able to go back and say, 'Yeah, we went out in the bush. Nothing to it.'"

"What went wrong?"

"Garcia didn't even make the loop back to the aircar. Shin and I didn't identify the thing that got him as a nightmare until later. And when we got back to the aircar, it—along with the coms—was already crushed. You'd have to see it to believe it. What the roots do, I mean. How quickly they can completely engulf an aircar."

"I've got my own problem with trees and roots," she told him. "Would you be willing to narrate all the steps you took? Tell me everything you learned on that trip? Explain how you survived and why Shin didn't? Sort of like a manual on what to do if a person goes down in the forest?"

"Yes, ma'am. But I can tell you now, the only reason I made it was the armor. And the reason Private Shintzu died was because she thought taking a bath was safe. She wasn't out of her armor for ten minutes before the slug got her. And, if I'd known what to do, I might have been able to save her."

"What did you find out there with Dya and Kylee and that quetzal?"

"A family. A place to belong. Love. A reason for my life."

"These medicines Dya manufactures, can she make more?"

"She can." Talbot's eyes went to the cases that now rested on the floor beside Aguila's bed. "Looks like you've become a convert. I heard that Dr. Turnienko is desperate to get her hands on those."

"The good doctor and I are dickering." Aguila smiled grimly. "And don't worry, I've made arrangements with Turnienko to cover any and all of your medical care here. Dya, I've learned, drives a hard bargain."

"I see."

"No, you don't. You could have bargained with that narrative of yours. Knowledge on Donovan is power, Private. It's wealth. You might want to learn that lesson."

"Yes, ma'am."

Aguila placed a finger to the corner of her lips where a hint of a mocking smile lingered. "Question: Had you not run into disaster in the forest, would you have returned to service without issue?"

"Yes, ma'am. The three of us, we backed Spiro. Thought that Cap had betrayed his oath and loyalty." He shot her a wary look. "Since then, I have come to other conclusions and discovered other priorities."

"She's a remarkable woman, this Dya of yours. And I can understand your dedication to the little girl. However, you have obligations to The Corporation and the Corps. Obligations I'm unwilling to set aside just because you've found a family."

"But Dya said—"

"I told her I would consider your situation. Put yourself

in my position. I have a marine who demonstrated poor judgment. No matter that your motives were not desertion, your actions contributed to the death of two marines. The loss of an aircar and three combat-capable suits of armor." She paused. "Had Dya not bargained for your life, I would have had you shot."

Talbot's stomach dropped, lead-heavy, a sick feeling at the base of his throat.

God, I'm going to lose it all.

"I am in a precarious position here, Private. All that stands between me and disaster are the people who serve me. My marines, my engineers and technicians. I am not in a position to just let trained personnel wander off to their own ends—no matter how enticing they might suddenly find their personal lives. Or how remarkable their spouses may be."

Talbot closed his eyes, the sick feeling expanding.

"To allow such behavior would be corrosive to discipline and maintaining order. If I let you wander off into the bush with your new family, why shouldn't I let Spiro? Or perhaps my chief engineer? Why you, and not them?"

Talbot took a deep breath. "I understand, ma'am. If I could, however, you need to know that if I don't go back, they're going to lose it all. The place is falling apart as it is. Kylee's here because a cable broke on the lift. They've carved that farm out of the forest, figured out how to adapt. If you assign me to Corporate Mine, it's a death sentence. Might as well evacuate them, give the whole place back to Donovan."

She was looking at him as if he were a fool. "You don't learn anything, do you?"

"Ma'am?"

She chuckled in self-amusement. "Your words were, 'They've carved that place out of the forest. Learned how to adapt.' All right, since you're impoverished in the skills necessary to save yourself and your people, I'm dictating the terms."

She leveled a finger. "Your wife has already bargained for your life. In return for the medicines, my deal with her is that you will not be officially charged with desertion or dereliction of duty. I have agreed to ensure your family's safe return home. You, however, are still in service to The Corporation. My terms are the following: You may go back to your farmstead, but only if we establish a mutually beneficial relationship. You say they have equipment wearing out? That the place is falling apart? I will provide replacement parts. Have my people fix this cable that broke. In return, I want the opportunity to send my people to learn what your people have learned. I want to see how they've adapted, and if there are lessons there that I can implement at Corporate Mine."

Aguila paused, eyes narrowed. "It's more than just you and your wife, isn't it? Just how many people are living at this mysterious farmstead of yours?"

Talbot swallowed hard. "A few."

"Uh-huh." Aguila read his expression like a master. "Your job description will be as advance reconnaissance and training. Among your duties will be survival training for the rest of my marines. Show them what you learned in the forest."

Talbot felt a chill run up his spine. Rebecca and Su would go apeshit. "And if I can't agree to that?"

"I will have your butt loaded onto the shuttle and shipped to Corporate Mine to serve out your term of enlistment. You can teach survival there as well as at your farmstead."

"Supervisor, you don't underst—"

"You are a Corporate marine, mister. Now, you think it through. In anyone's book, I just gave you every break. Call it above and beyond fair. Take it, or leave it."

Talbot could imagine Rebecca's burning gaze, see the anger in Su's eyes. And Dya? God, this just went from bad to worse.

"That will be all for today, Private," Aguila told him with a grim certainty. "You are dismissed."

41

Talina stood in her blasted bedroom, hands on her hips. Her bed—the one she'd shared with Mitch and then Cap—was smashed against the far wall. Her dresser now consisted of crushed plastic. The splintered end table would make passable firewood. The back wall, of course, looked beyond repair where it had been blown apart. The rest of the room showed pits and gouges from shrapnel.

No one had bothered to clean up the dried blood where Felicity had died. An unjust end for the woman who had selflessly dedicated her time to binding up people's wounds, treating their fevers, and sometimes spending entire nights holding their hands to keep them from dying alone and in terror.

Talina closed her eyes. Tried to let the rage and sorrow wane before she did something stupid.

Her quetzal, too, was stewing.

The beast made no sense. Half the time it was rooting for her ruin, and at other times, like this, shared her rage and wanted to initiate combat at the least provocation.

"Piece of shit," she growled at it.

"*Fight now.*"

"Not yet. Have to figure out who did this first."

"*You know.*"

"Yeah. I know. But it's not that easy. At least not among humans."

She made a face, turned, and had a last look around. Trish had taken Talina's few possessions, packed them after Cheng and Mgumbe had gone through them looking for evidence. Not that Talina had much, just her rifles, some changes of clothes, and a few knickknacks and mementos that she'd picked up over the years. Those few belongings had been moved a few domes down to a vacant house.

All that remained were a couple of chairs and the kitchen table, along with her pots, pans, plates, and silverware.

She turned, stepped out the door, and left it gaping wide behind her. Anyone who wanted in could step through the holes in the walls.

With Trish minding Rocket and keeping tabs on the hospital, Talina walked cautiously toward Inga's. The quetzal's disquiet and her own awareness that someone was trying to kill her sent that eerie jitter through her bones, and she turned her ever-more-acute quetzal senses to her surroundings. She carefully inspected the rooftops, the gaps between buildings, whether a door was ajar or a window open from which a sniper could take a shot.

She had never been hunted like this before. Over the years before *Turalon*'s arrival, Donovan had become a straightforward kind of place. Face to face, person to person.

So this is what it feels like to be on the other side.

The depths of her hypocrisy gave her a sour sense of amusement. Made her wonder at the lengths to which she'd go to mislead herself.

As she once had with Pak Simonov and Paolo Su.

Back then she'd convinced herself she was just doing her job. How much misery would she have saved people from if she'd just turned and shot Clemenceau down instead of following orders?

The quetzal squirmed around inside, a shiver running along her muscles as it did.

"You're not the only monster living in my skin," she told the beast.

At Inga's, she glanced around, nodding to passersby, aware of the looks they were giving her. Hell, the whole town knew that someone had tried to kill her. She could see the difference in their eyes as they called their greetings, as if to say, "See, it isn't me."

And then there were the darker looks that said, "Why Felicity? It should have been you."

Talina opened the door, stepped inside, and took a moment at the head of the stairs. With her quetzal sense, she placed faces, noted where people were sitting, made a hasty assessment of which could be possible assassins. The uncomfortable conclusion was that over the years, she'd had occasion to piss a lot of people off.

"I guess no one lives forever," she soliloquized, and started down the stairs. All eyes turned her way. Brazenly she walked down the central aisle between the long tables, and nodded in response to the occasional call and tip of a hat.

At the bar she climbed into her chair, calling to Inga: "Got a mug of that stout?"

"Coming up, Tal. Cash or credit?"

"Cash." Then she added, "But to offer me credit? It's nice to know that someone thinks I'll be around long enough to pay my bills. Thanks for the vote of confidence."

Inga chuckled in time to the somewhat-forced laughter from those close enough to have overhead.

Talina rotated her chair, bracing her elbows behind her on the bar to look over the room. As Inga set her mug on the counter, Talina asked, "So what are people saying?"

Inga lounged on the bar, her thick arms crossed. "There's a whole lot of mad out there. First over the quetzal and why it's still alive. Let alone in the damn hospital of all places. And then there's Felicity. People loved that woman, and they're ready to gut whoever did it, string the culprit's intestines around like bunting, and flay the son of a bitch's ever-loving hide off with dull knives."

"I don't blame 'em. First for Felicity, and second, she went there on my account. Doesn't matter that I couldn't have known. I'm partly responsible. Not to mention the bomb was meant for me."

"Don't you go torturing yourself, Tal. Got any idea who's behind it?"

"Trish thinks Spiro. I hear she's got an ironclad alibi. That she was drinking in here all night with her marines."

"Maybe."

Talina shot a sidelong glance at the big blonde woman. "Maybe?"

"You know how it is in here at night. And that night the place was packed. It's not every day that a little girl flies in with her pet quetzal. Or that a murdering monster is locked away in the hospital while the little girl's undergoing surgery. Most of the town was either here, the cafeteria, or standing around watching the hospital, waiting for carnage to ensue."

"And Spiro?"

"Oh, she was here all right. You heard about the scene she made?"

"I've been locked in the hospital since Rocket arrived. Haven't heard a thing."

"Spiro sat just over there. Talking pretty loud and free, too. All about how you were a back-shooting bitch who wouldn't dare to meet her face-to-face."

"I see."

"Well, you might want to know that a lot of people groused about it. Muttering among themselves that the Talina Perez they knew never belly-crawled from a fight. But given that Spiro was armed, backed by two of her marines toting automatic rifles, no one pushed it. And everyone knows that with Aguila's people, you, Shig, and Yvette want them to keep their noses clean."

"Smart of them."

"So Spiro was here." Inga paused. "Off and on."

Talina straightened. "Off and on? You want to elaborate on that?"

"I wasn't paying any more attention than normal, but I can tell you that a couple of times that night, she was gone for a while."

"How long a while?"

"Sometimes to use the bathroom. And once for maybe a half hour or so. Long enough for me to wonder if she was going to stiff me on her tab. That was just after dark. Then, I look up, and she's back. Acting up. Ordering drinks and making sure those two marines were draining them down. By the end of the night, they had to carry Abu Sassi out between the two of them."

"And everyone else is talking about the quetzal," Talina mused.

"And lots of people coming and going," Inga reminded. "Like I say, it wasn't the same as a normal night when everyone was minding everyone else's business like they usually do."

"You remember what Spiro was wearing? She have her pistol with her?"

"Sure. Had her whole utility belt. The one with all the pouches, equipment, and such. Generally they only wear those when they're wearing armor. Sort of bulky, you know?"

"Yeah, Inga. I know."

And a cold certainty settled in Talina's bones.

From here on out, the course had been set.

Talina placed a two-SDR piece on the bar. "Keep the change. And until this is finally over between Spiro and me, you'd better insist on cash up front. I wouldn't want to see you getting stiffed if you give that woman credit."

42

Talbot sat in the visitor's chair with his head in his hands; the heavy feeling in the pit of his stomach could have been a cold stone. His arm ached and burned where the bullet had torn through. To keep a clear head, he'd stopped taking Dya's painkiller paste. Around him the hospital room whined and hummed.

"I went out and checked the aircar," he told Dya. "It's still down below twenty percent. I was 'escorted' by Tompzen. Told that it wouldn't be recharged until the Supervisor approved it. Clever choice that. Tompzen and I never really got along. She's making sure that we don't slip away in the night."

Dya dropped into the chair beside him, reached out, ran her hand over the curve of his back. "We'll figure something out."

"Dya, think this through. Kalico Aguila is a calculating Corporate bitch. She's like an implacable spider, and we're stuck full in her web."

"Why the hell would she care about us? I thought I had a deal with her. That she wouldn't charge you with desertion. That we could go."

"You did. She's not charging me with desertion. And you and Kylee can go. She'll even escort you. Personally. She's just made the point that the only way I get to go back to Mundo Base is as her agent. She's no one's fool. She knows we have a successful farm in the forest. That we've somehow found a way to keep the trees from overrunning the fields. And better yet, you show up with all these marvelous medicines. Things even Dr. Turnienko can't conceive of. Add to that that I survived for months in the forest. She wants what's in my head. Wants me to teach it to her people. Wants to know the secret of Mundo Base and all that it's achieved."

"We can't let her, Mark."

He shook his head. "I'd say you and Kylee go as soon as she's well, but damn it, Dya, I'm trapped." He looked at her. "You know the problems. Mundo Base is falling apart. Not so long from now, the three of you are going to be in the third trimester. And then what?"

"We deal with it. Just like we always have."

"Sure. But back then the lift worked. By now it's really sinking in down there. Rebecca, Su, and the kids are finding out what a chore it is to climb that rickety stairway every time they have to go out. And up until now, you had more than a single fuse for the pump. And it wasn't all three of you having babies at once."

"We've all carried to term without issues in the past."

"But with all the extra work and stress, what happens if something goes wrong? Especially if when it happens, you're down on the ground? None of you can fly the damned aircar, even if it has a charge."

She had no answer, just stared woodenly at the floor between her feet.

"I mean, God, I lay awake all last night worrying about what might have broken since we flew north. What if something critical failed? One of those trusses under the floor broke? What if Damien or Shantaya or one of the other kids got hurt?"

Dya raised her gaze to the bed where Kylee slept, the monitors projecting holographic data in green, orange, and blue on the wall behind the girl's head. "Living is risk, Mark. We have no guarantees. Just gotta be tough and tackle whatever life throws our way."

"The Supervisor said she'd fix what was broken at Mundo." Mark winced as he shifted his wounded arm.

"Isn't that price too high to pay?" Dya rubbed her palms back and forth. "Once she gets her claws into Mundo, it's all over. We lose our home."

"Yeah, I know." He glanced sidelong at her. "But I'm not seeing a way out of this. The lift was the first major failure. Eventually the pump is going, and when it does, that's the end of the dome's water system. Or maybe it's an electrical short and the power goes out. You said there's structural damage under the dome floor? What happens if it all gives way?"

"Hadn't thought that far ahead. We're lucky enough if we can fix something the day before it breaks. In the past, every time we ran out of a spare we just cobbled things together or retired the piece of equipment."

"You do know that eventually there's an end to that. The dome is going to be uninhabitable. Maybe in the next year or so. When that happens, what's the plan? What have the three of you decided?"

Dya continued to stare hollowly at Kylee's sleeping form. Rocket shifted where he curled on the floor on the opposite side of the bed. "Honestly, we figured another ten years at least. By that time, Damien, Kylee, Shantaya, and Taung would be young adults. Having grown up at Mundo, they'd be the ones to pick the new direction. See the way to our future because they weren't raised in our old cultural paradigm."

Talbot inclined his head toward Kylee. "As you can see right there, sometimes things go wrong with long-term plans." He smiled humorlessly. "Like I said, I don't think you've got a year before the dome has to be abandoned for good. And about the time that happens—if it even takes that long—the three of you are going to be tending three infants."

Her eyes slitted as she gave him a curious appraisal. "You almost make it sound like it's our problem. Not yours."

"Good. Because I'm afraid that I'm going to lose all of you. That I'm the price we have to pay for the family's continued freedom. I mean, scared down to my bones."

"Why?"

"Because, if it turns out that the only way to keep Mundo safe is for me to go to Corporate Mine, I'll go. At least you, Kylee, and Rocket get home."

She sat silently, brow pinched in thought.

Talbot added, "I never understood love. Not really. Not deep, total love. Not until I walked out of the forest that day. And since that time, all of you, even Rebecca, have become my entire world. I'd do anything for you."

He stared sadly at Kylee, wondering what it would be like to never see her smile again. "If I thought that surrendering everything that I am to Aguila was the answer, I'd do it in a heartbeat."

"Let's see if we can keep it from coming to that. If you don't fly us home, how are we supposed to get there? You've got to take us, because we sure can't have anyone else fly us down there. Especially Aguila. It would give the whole thing away."

She paused. "And Mark? I couldn't stand to lose you. It would break my heart. Kylee and the children have come to love you. Even Su, in her own way."

He forced himself to concentrate. "Tell me, Dya. Think it through and be honest. Say the pump goes, or the floor breaks, and you have to move down to the ground. What do you think the chances are of all eleven of you—not to mention the infants—being alive this time next year?"

"All of us?" She shook her head sadly. "If it wasn't for you, Kylee would be a cripple. Maybe even dead. Mark, I'll be honest: Unless the lift is repaired, and we can come up with spare parts, we don't have a chance without you. Not long term."

"Yeah," he said softly. "That's my thought, too."

And just behind that door, across the hall, Kalico Aguila must have known she held all the cards.

43

Desch Ituri nodded respectfully as he entered the hospital lobby. Behind him came Aurobindo Ghosh and Igor Stryski. Though Kalico could barely place him, she vaguely remembered that Stryski was a mechanic who worked on the equipment.

She had chosen the waiting room since it was the only place that offered even a hint of formality. She had summoned them here today since, for the first time, with her wounds healing, she dared to actually wear clothes.

"We're so delighted to see that you're improving, Supervisor," Ituri greeted, standing uncertainly in the middle of the room, hands laced before him. The others nodded in agreement, eyes respectfully lowered.

"It's taken longer than anticipated. Raya may actually remove some of the stitches from the smaller wounds tomorrow. I should be back to the mine in a couple more days. Meanwhile, I need to hear what's been happening. How is production?"

Ituri carefully arched an eyebrow. "We're running at about sixty-five percent, Supervisor. I think, within a week, we'll be up to one hundred. I've had people on another project."

"What project?" she almost snapped.

"Building the shot tower, ma'am."

Kalico glanced irritably around the small waiting room, feeling cramped and frustrated. "And what, pray tell, is a shot tower?"

Ituri glanced over his shoulder at Stryski. The mechanic swallowed hard, obviously intimidated. "Well, uh, ma'am, it's a tower. About twenty-five meters tall. Hollow on the inside. With a furnace at the top. Structurally it's designed to withstand the weight—"

"Mister Stryski, I could give a good goddamn. What's it for?"

"For creating shot, ma'am," Ghosh interjected when Stryski froze in terror.

"What in hell is shot?"

"Lead pellets, ma'am," Ituri told her. "At the top of the tower we melt lead. It's poured out, molten, over a screen. The liquid lead then dribbles through the screen before falling the twenty-five meters. As it falls, the molten droplets cool and harden before landing in the soft material at the bottom. We end up with round pellets of shot. Round pellets have a ballistic property that allows a predictable dispersion of shot."

"What are we shooting?"

"The cannons, ma'am." Ghosh swallowed hard. His eyes wary in his full-moon face.

Kalico took a deep breath. "Cannons?"

Ituri, Ghosh, and Stryski glanced uneasily at each other before Ituri nerved himself enough to ask, "Didn't Lieutenant Spiro tell you?"

"Apparently not." Spiro again. What the hell was wrong with the woman? She hadn't seen Spiro since Felicity was killed. Kalico was already prepared to rip a new patch off the sulking lieutenant's ass; now it appeared she'd rip two.

"We radioed," Ghosh quickly interjected. "Explained the whole process."

"Well, I didn't get the message. What cannons?"

"Smooth bores," Ituri continued. "Made from three-meter lengths of that sialon piping. We're reinforcing the breech area. Fenn Bogarten is manufacturing a slow-burning nitro-based gun powder. Something that should work to give us about three hundred meters a second at the muzzle."

"Wait. Back up." Kalico raised her hands in frustration. "Who authorized the building of these things?"

Ituri winced. "Uh, I did, ma'am. It's the only solution."

"Solution to what?"

"The mobbers, ma'am."

"Cannons?"

Ituri and Ghosh both nodded anxiously. Stryski looked like he was about to throw up.

Ituri shrugged expressively. "Think of them as oversized shotguns, ma'am. Shotguns with ten centimeter bores on pintle mounts that we can swivel, aim, and shoot into the mobbers. Given our shot patterning experiments, with the discharge of all four guns, we should be able to decimate an entire flock. A quick reload, and with the next round, our sky should essentially be clear."

Kalico closed her eyes, seeing it unfold in her head. "Why didn't you just say so?"

"Um, we did, ma'am. Two Spots said he'd relay it to Spiro. Thought she was keeping track of things while you were, uh . . ."

"The mobbers have been back?"

"Every two days," Ghosh told her. "It's like we're now part of their rounds. They're regular enough that we're ready for their arrival. Keep everyone under cover while they prowl around. Takes about a half an hour before they lose interest. We stay under cover for another half hour, just in case."

"How soon before these cannons of yours are ready?"

Ituri glanced at Ghosh and Stryski. "Three or four days? We need to pressure test the barrels, make sure Bogarten's powder is safe. Figure out what our operating pressures are so we don't blow ourselves up."

She gave them a slow smile. "I want to be there. I want to see those vile little bastards blown out of the sky."

"We've got the lead, ma'am," Ghosh told her. "It's just making the shot and testing that still stand in our way. Then it's just a matter of getting the flock in the right position where we can concentrate our fire, and, well, they're in for a hell of a surprise."

Kalico lifted an eyebrow. "What about production? Sixty percent, you say? Surely not everyone has been working on the cannons."

"Smelter's been running at about thirty percent, ma'am." Ituri shifted uneasily. "We've been concentrating on lead production. Lead's easy. Low melting point. You know that one upper-level vein in Number Two that was rich with lead? We're mining that as fast as we can. We kind of made that decision on our own. Figured the mobbers were problem number one."

She nodded her approval. "Good work. What about the farm?"

"Lost another acre or so," Ghosh growled. "We tried hooking an improvised ripper bar on the back of a hauler in hopes we could sever the roots, drive the trees back. Damn near lost the truck when the trees grabbed the ripper and pulled back."

"At this rate, how long before the forest reclaims the whole farm and smelter?" she asked woodenly.

"Maybe a couple of months?" Ghosh hazarded. "But that's just a guess. I'm not a biological science kind of guy."

"Remember how you laid out a line of that toxic smelter waste?" Ituri gave her a sidelong glance. "I don't know what to say except this is Donovan. The trees never even hesitated. Radioactive or not, they just rootched their way across."

"Rootched?"

"That's what we've been calling it. Sort of a mix between roots and ruts and wiggling through the ground."

"How's morale?"

Again the three looked at each other. Ituri, to his credit, bravely said, "Supervisor, I'll be honest. It's like we're under siege. I mean, sure, the cannons will probably deal with the mobbers. Shooting those freaking shits out of the sky will be a definite up for our folks. But then what? People are wondering what's coming next. Down at the smelter, it's the trees. Right there before your nose. They're closing in. Sure, we can blast them out again. But the forest is endless, and it's going to eventually overrun the smelter."

"And up at the mines," Ghosh added. "Sure, we're working, piling ore. But what's the point? Where does this lead us? Who knows if a ship is ever coming back to Donovan? People are starting to wonder if this is the rest of their lives. If they're going to be making hole until they die. Especially after what happened to you."

Ghosh hesitated. "Supervisor, for the moment, the only thing they have to live for is a chance to rotate back to Port Authority for a little relaxation. They're starting to lose hope."

Ituri spread his hands. "Somewhere soon, ma'am, they're just going to quit. Figure it's better to be shot by Spiro's marines than keep living this shit."

To Kalico's surprise, Stryski chimed in. "Worst part was

seeing you go down, ma'am. You're like the rock under our feet. There every day. Until the mobbers got you, we all thought you were invincible. And if you were, we were. But seeing you go down?" He shook his head. "It's like, what if you die? Then what do we do?" He raised his hands in palms-up surrender.

Kalico took a deep breath. "So help me God, I will *not* lose what we've built. Even if I have to blast that damn forest back with a nuclear device." She smiled wryly. "Assuming we can build one in time."

Ituri shot Ghosh a relieved glance. "Well, ma'am, most of your bosses and crew chiefs are behind you. I mean, a lot of us were skeptical at the beginning. Working with you, having you there, sharing with us every step of the way, we want this to work just as badly as you do. One of the reasons we three came was to see if your heart was still in it, or if you'd given up after what the mobbers did to you."

"I *do not* give up."

"That will make a lot of people happy, ma'am." Ghosh actually smiled his relief. "But what about the forest? It's going to win in the end. It will either overrun the smelter, or we'll have to disassemble it and move it somewhere closer to Port Authority."

Kalico stared out the window at the avenue where Mark and Dya's aircar still sat. She'd long ago grown used to the small knot of men and women who hung around with rifles to keep an eye on the hospital in hopes the quetzal would step out so they could shoot it.

Damn, these people hated quetzals. After all this time, worry about Rocket hadn't abated in the least.

But the aircar . . . was there some clue?

"Any of you gentlemen know anything about that model of aircar?" She pointed.

As they crowded close to look, it was Stryski who said, "Sure. It's a Beta. Dad had one when I was a kid. Mostly modular construction, but the performance parameters could be remapped for increased acceleration. I used to race Dad's. Nothing formal. Just for beer money."

Kalico considered. "So, could you tell how far that one ran to get here?"

Stryski said, "Sure. All it takes is a teslaometer to read

the elon ratios on battery performance. The system's algorithms are designed to maximize charge based on travel history. It won't take me but a couple of minutes. I can tell you how far it flew and at what speed."

"Can you tell which direction it came from?" she asked.

"Not on Donovan."

"Then, Mr. Stryski, why don't you go unravel that aircar while Ituri, Ghosh, and I enjoy a cup of coffee."

As she watched Stryski step out into the warm sunshine, Kalico smiled happily. So her people were on the verge of despair? Maybe a deserter, a wounded little girl, a juvenile quetzal, and a local herbalist had just handed her a whole new lease on Corporate Mine.

44

The dice tumbled across the craps table's green velvet with a lively patter, bounced off the far wall, and settled with the one and six showing.

"Natural seven!" Art Maniken called. "Up pops the Devil."

Where he stood off to the side, Dan Wirth kept his expression blank, allowing no trace of the gloating smile that bloomed from the roots of his soul. A single word echoed in his mind: Fruition.

Private Tompzen stood with his feet braced, both hands on the rim of the craps table, his features ashen. The good private had needed a six. High odds for either an easy or hard six or eight. But not with those dice. And the marine, tough and ready as he considered himself, wasn't up to discerning the tiny magnets that had sealed his doom.

"Oh, baby," Angelina cooed where she stood at Kalen Tompzen's side, one hand on his shoulder. "I just knew you had it."

Tompzen's lips quivered as Art raked in the chips, calling, "New shooter. Is there a new shooter?"

But the thirteen other patrons in The Jewel that afternoon were buried in their poker, keno, and an odd game of pinochle in the back corner.

"Hey, babe," Angelina told Tompzen. "Come on. Let me buy you a drink. That was a hell of a game you just rolled."

"Fuck!" Tompzen growled through gritted teeth, disbelieving gaze fixed on the dice that had so suddenly betrayed him.

Art's eyes were half-lidded, the bouncer standing easily, having palmed a small taser into his left hand just in case.

"C'mon, baby," Angelina said, tugging at Tompzen's hand. "Luck always changes. After so many wins, I thought . . . Well, luck just stinks sometimes."

She artfully pried him away from the craps table, leading him back to a table in the rear next to the cage.

Art nodded in relief, a slight grin on his face. Tompzen wouldn't be a problem. Art didn't really like any of the marines, but he understood his job and tolerated Tompzen and his holier-than-thou, "I'm a marine" attitude. They needed Tompzen, He was the only one who'd dared to disobey orders. Aguila—the canny slit—had insisted in no uncertain terms that her marines consider The Jewel off limits, and especially the tables.

It had taken weeks to get Tompzen primed, allowing him to infringe ever so slightly. Take a throw or two on the house. Nothing said as he was paid out the occasional ten, twenty, or hundred.

Almost a month had been invested to get the marine set up for today's game. The manipulation had been perfectly orchestrated. Just the right advances of chips. Everything jotted down in the book.

The swelling of pride in Dan's chest left him feeling like a master. Perfectly played.

Now the poor sap sat at the back table, Angelina pouring him a healthy two fingers of whiskey before she sat down to commiserate with her "dear" friend.

Dan checked the time. Ambled by the other tables, making his friendly rounds and calculating his winnings. Slow afternoon. And it would be slow tonight, but then they generally were when the Corporate people were out of town.

And he couldn't play Tompzen when there was a chance that any of Aguila's people might see the Supervisor's wayward private at the tables.

Dan waited until Tompzen had downed his first whiskey and was halfway through his second. Waited until the marine was laughing, fingering Angelina's body suggestively. Maybe having forgotten he'd just lost more than seven thousand at the table.

Placing his finger to his earlobe, Dan gave Art the signal. Art ran a finger along the line of his jaw in reply and walked back to the cage where Allison sat behind the window waiting to cash out chips.

Art leaned close to the grill, talking low.

Allison's voice sounded slightly alarmed.

That's when Art stepped over to Tompzen's table, pulled out a chair, leaned close, and asked the marine something.

Angelina kept smiling, saying just loud enough, "Of course Kalen can cover his marks." She gave the private a sparkling look. "You can, can't you, baby?"

Tompzen went stiff, which was Allison's cue as she stepped out of the cage, bending down to whisper something in Art's ear.

"Yeah, yeah," Tompzen growled. "Of course I can cover my marks."

Allison shot Dan a look. His cue as he ambled over, smile wide on his face. "So what's happening here? I find half my crew at your table, Private. Whatever story you're telling, it must be a doozy to lure my people away from work. No way I want to miss out on the punch line."

Tompzen looked up, a half-dazed, half-angry look on his face.

"Honey," Allison said, slipping her arm into Dan's. "Kalen here has good credit, doesn't he? I mean, advancing him five thousand was all right."

Dan stopped short. Let his smile freeze the appropriate amount to indicate shock. He narrowed his eyes just the slightest as the marine watched. "What's his ledger say?"

"He's behind a little more than seventeen thousand, boss," Art said quietly. "I thought Allison knew."

"I'll pay it," Tompzen insisted stubbornly.

Dan gave them his bland smile this time, extending his arm toward the door in the back. "Ladies, gentlemen, let's retire to my office. Angelina, darling, why don't you keep an eye on things out here. Surely this is just a misunderstanding. Allison, would you get the books? Come on, Kalen. Let's go figure this out. I'll even stand you for another whiskey in the back."

And, thus reassured, the marine stood, letting Art escort him back down the hallway, past the cribs, to Dan's office.

Like leading a lamb to slaughter. After closing the office door behind him, Dan poured the man another drink. Handed it to him, and gestured. "Have a seat. This is probably just a math error. It's not like Allison to miss one of these things. How's the Supervisor, by the way? I hear that some medicine woman from out in the bush has the most magical ointment. That it's healing up the mobber cuts like a miracle."

"She's coming along," Tompzen said, looking more than a little rattled now. He was clutching his tumbler of whiskey as if it were a talisman.

"And miracle of miracles, that fucking little quetzal hasn't eaten anyone in the hospital yet? Go figure. Of course, half the town's packing loaded weapons itching to see the little terror step out onto the street."

Allison entered with the book, settling behind Dan's desk. Art had taken a position slightly behind and to Tompzen's left. Art was right-handed. Perfect position if he had to sap the marine in the back of the head.

Tompzen now sat bolt upright as Allison opened a page and ran her finger down a column. "Oh," she said softly.

"Oh?" Dan asked.

Allison raised her eyes. "Kalen's total is seventeen thousand, seven hundred and fifty. I mean, it just built up slowly. Four hundred, five-fifty. A couple of thousand. Another couple of thousand. Then five thousand today."

"Allison?" Dan said testily.

"Your call," she told him coolly. "You said to mark his account good. Who was I to deny an account that you said was good, Dan?"

"I am good!" Tompzen cried irritably. "I mean, I just didn't know how much it was. Like Allison said, a little here, a little there."

"Yeah, it adds up," Art growled. "So, okay, we're in the shit. How do we work this out? I mean, boss, do we take it up with Spiro? Or go straight to the Supervisor? This is a pretty big hole to fill."

Dan enjoyed the sight of quick-rising sweat; it now left a sheen on Tompzen's cheeks. The marine swallowed hard, realizing just how deep in he was.

"Now, now, Art, back down. The last thing we want to do is take it up with Spiro. Not until some damn fool puts a gun to our heads. No, no."

Dan stepped around, bottle in hand, and poured another splash into Tompzen's glass. Meeting the panicked marine's eyes, he kindly asked, "You can't cover any seventeen thousand SDRs, am I right?"

"I'll figure it out, Dan. I swear. I mean, damn. If Aguila ever finds out?" He winced. "Shit, they'd shoot me. I mean, I've been watching that woman. She's already pissed about the mine being off schedule and the fucking trees taking over. And then she gets cut up by mobbers. Now's not the time to get in her shit. And she was dead serious about The Jewel being off limits."

"So, we work around it," Dan told him, a reassuring tone in his voice.

"Boss, we can't afford to be stiffed," Art muttered. "Not for seventeen thousand! Hey, I like Kalen, too. But word gets out that you let him walk owing seventeen k, and we might as well close the fucking doors and call ourselves suckers."

"Then what, Art? Take it out on poor Tompzen, here?" Dan asked.

The marine turned another shade of pale.

"People who short us have a habit of . . ." Art didn't finish the sentence. Didn't need to. Tompzen had gone spring-wire tense as the cold realization ran through him.

"No!" Dan barked. "Look, Art, Kalen's not one of those shitty little pricks." Dan fixed on the marine's nervous eyes. "Kalen, you say you're good for it. I say you're good for it."

"But, boss!" Art cried.

"There's other things than money," Dan insisted patiently. "I mean, okay. Kalen, you don't have the seventeen k, right? How about we work this off in other ways?"

"What other ways?" The man swallowed hard.

"Easy stuff. Favors. I mean, you don't really *like* that Supervisor of yours, do you? You've never really come out and said it—a point in your favor by the way—but you think Aguila's a snappy, spoiled Corporate cunt, right? She's running that mine down there like she's a tin god. And a couple of days back, didn't I hear you say you wished the damn mobbers had finished the job?"

Tompzen, scared stiff, jerked the faintest of nods.

"Yeah." Dan settled a haunch on his desk and gave the marine a knowing smile. "Hey, you're among friends. We're all on the same side here. Me, I've had more than my share of problems with Aguila. Given half a chance, the slit would cut my throat in a second. Good thing I got out from under her contract."

Dan paused to let the words sink in, then added, "You could, too. There's a way out of this for a really smart man. Let's face facts: Aguila can't make it. Not if what I hear is true. The forest is going to win. It's overrunning her farm. And now the wildlife is whittling away the people down there. Even came within a *pendejo*'s width of killing Aguila, high and mighty Supervisor that she is. They're going to have to move the smelter, or watch the trees take it. It's just a matter of time, right?"

Tompzen frowned slightly, nodded. "She's losing."

Dan set the bottle on the desk and crossed his arms. "Of course she is. She might have been 'God and Thunder' back in Solar System, a Corporate Supervisor with all the delusions of invincibility. But Donovan doesn't take Corporate orders. So, the question remains: What happens when she fails? What does a man like you—a man who plans ahead—look forward to after Aguila's plans go to shit?"

"I'm still a marine. Have to take whatever orders Spiro gives."

"Kalen, think larger. Me? I stepped off *Turalon* expecting to herd cattle. What kind of future is that? But, as in all things, Donovan had already attended to the damn cows. Yet here I am. Outside of Aguila, I'm the richest man on this planet. Master of my own empire. People live and die at my command. What could you do if you had the opportunity? What heights could you rise to if you were on the right team?"

Tompzen winced, smart enough to sense the trap. "What do you want me to do?"

"Well, I sure as hell don't want you shot for breaking Aguila's rules! And you do owe me seventeen grand. But, if you have the balls, if you're smart enough, you could come out of this in a year or so with everything you've ever dreamed." A beat. "Assuming you can dream large enough, and that you can use your head."

Tompzen worked his lips. Shot a glance at Allison, who sat with her finger on his column in the ledger book. The poor sap knew that Art was behind him for a reason, and it wasn't good. Knew that Dan held his life cupped in the palm of a hand. Yeah, he was smart enough to know when his neck was fully in the noose.

"Okay, I guess I'm in."

"That's the ticket!" Dan clapped his hands. Reached for the bottle, and poured another splash into Tompzen's glass. "Welcome to the winning team. Now, why don't you go out and collect Angelina. We're slow. Take her back to her room for a couple of hours. Drop a little mash, and let her turn you every which way but loose. I mean, the lady has some serious talent when she's allowed the time to use it."

Tompzen was smiling in anticipation as he stood and hurried for the door.

"Bingo!" Dan said softly as the man closed the door behind him.

45

"*Trish! Trouble at the hospital!*" Two Spots' voice announced in Trish's ear as she left the main gate checkpoint on her appointed rounds. Up until now the twilight evening had been quiet. All of the posts were manned, the gates secured, everyone on the security rotation in their places.

She immediately broke into a run, weaving a path around the warehouses, dodging old and broken equipment, vaulting over the occasional box or crate.

She hammered her way around the curve of Inga's and onto the avenue. Ran full-out for the hospital where a crowd had gathered out front.

Even as she pulled up, Talina stepped out of the double front doors, her slick-action automatic rifle held crossways before her.

"What the hell is going on here?" Talina demanded, bracing herself before the door, feet positioned for combat.

The crowd growled back at her. Maybe fifteen men, a handful of women, and a couple of male teens. The people shifted, all bearing rifles of various makes and calibers.

Bernie Monson stepped forward, his arm hanging in a sling. Beside him, Wye Vanveer, another of the miners from the clay pit, thrust a finger in Talina's direction.

"It's like this," Vanveer began. "Bernie's got a broken arm. Broke it yesterday, and he ain't going in no building with a fucking quetzal in it."

Vanveer glanced around at the crowd that was muttering in assent. "None of us are. So, we've been discussing it. It's our damned hospital. Doesn't belong to no Wild One. Let alone some abomination of a girl who's mated up with a quetzal. You ask me, that's just freaking unnatural. So, here's the thing: You charge that aircar of theirs, load these damned Wild Ones up, and ship their asses back to where they came from."

"Damn straight!" Bernie bellowed, wobbling slightly on his feet. He cradled his broken arm, adding, "What the hell, Tal? I been in agony for the last damn day 'cause I ain't going in no place with a stinking quetzal lurking around."

"And it's not just them," Sian Hmong cried as she stepped forward. The delicate-boned woman added a whole new level of complexity to the equation. Miners? Tal could just crack their heads. Mothers and teachers? That was a whole new ballgame.

Hmong knotted a dainty fist in emphasis. "At the school, we're half-petrified. I've been talking to the other parents. Our kids aren't sleeping. We're spending nights up with the guns ready. It's like having a predator constantly lurking in your shadow. The quetzal goes. That's final."

"Ever since these people came here, it's gone to shit," Bernie muttered, blinking his eyes hard. "Like a cascade of events. I mean, would Felicity have died if they hadn't shown up with that beast? Heard you and Spiro got into it over the murdering little bastard. That's why she tried to blow you up, right? Over the quetzal? So you actually put a gun in her back to stop her from doing what's right?"

Trish slowly eased around to one side, figuring just where the best angle was going to be to make a difference when this all came apart.

Talina, however, smiled, shifting her rifle to brace it on her hip. "Listen, I've been keeping an eye on the quetzal. He hasn't so much as flickered an angry color. If you'd just all relax and give Rocket a break—"

"*Rocket?* You've *named* it?" Bernie demanded, weaving more on his feet.

From Bernie's flushed expression and glassy eyes, Trish figured he'd been down at Inga's slugging down "pain-killer" for most of the day.

"Yeah, it's named." Talina took another step forward, hot glare settling on Bernie's. "What of it? You want two broken arms? Just push me."

Sian Hmong, backed by Amal Oshanti and Friga Dushku—women who essentially ran the school—stepped forward, arms crossed defiantly. The teens followed along uncertainly behind them.

"You going to break our arms?" Sian asked. "We want our

families safe. We demand that you, Shig, Yvette, and whoever else, get that *thing* out of Port Authority, or by God in heaven, I'm going in there and shooting it dead myself."

"No one is going in to shoot the quetzal," Talina said.

"Or what?" Sian demanded. "You going to shoot me down, Tal? To protect that thing?"

"Or me?" Amal Dushku almost spit out the question. "Because I'm coming right behind Sian."

"And you're going to have to kill me, too," Friga added, her square jaw set, her green eyes slitted. "I lost two of my boys to quetzals. I've got two girls left. And as God is my witness, no filthy quetzal is going to get them. Not while I'm alive. So here's how it goes: You either get that damn monster out of our hospital, or we're doing it. Period. Decision's made."

Talina again shifted her rifle, dark eyes darting from person to person. Then she shot a look Trish's way.

"We're held hostage here," Vanveer cried. "I'm with Bernie. I'd rather live with a broken arm than go in there with that thing."

"And what if it's one of the kids who gets hurt? You going to put a child in there next door to that thing?" Amal Oshanti asked.

"Not while I'm drawing a breath," Sian followed up fervently.

"You're on that thing's side, aren't you?" Bernie asked, slurring the words. "That's the story, ain't it? That you got a quetzal inside you? That what this is all about? You're on that little girl's side. You're . . . you're *infected* with that thing's blood and stuff."

Trish watched the others nod, shuffle their feet with new resolution.

Talina's lips twitched, her eyes narrowed.

Uh-oh. Bad sign.

"Hey, people!" Trish bellowed, bulling her way forward before Talina came unglued. "That's damned well enough! First point. Talina's killed more quetzals than anyone in Port Authority. Second point. Most of you wouldn't be here today if she hadn't covered your mangy asses sometime in the past. So whichever one of you wants to pick at scabs? You come to me, and we'll see how it ends."

Trish turned. "Tal, you've been on the inside keeping Raya and everybody else safe. You don't know what's festering out here. Half the town's stewing. Especially after what happened to Felicity. And yeah, it's not the little girl's fault, but facts are facts. If that quetzal hadn't been here, you and Spiro wouldn't have gotten into it."

"The lieutenant was going to shoot Dya Simonov to get to the quetzal. Don't fucking pin this on me, Trish." Talina's eyes had taken on that stone-dead quality.

A shiver ran down Trish's spine. Shit. She'd never thought she'd see Talina look at her that way.

"Tal, all I'm saying is that there's more to this than just that little girl. It's no one's damn fault, but one way or another it's tearing this community apart. It's time to fix it."

Talina's jaw muscles knotted.

Trish stepped forward, heart pounding. Stopping just short of Talina's rifle, she added, "The hospital belongs to the community. You know I'm right."

Talina took a deep breath. "Yeah."

"Work with me?"

Talina sidestepped to face the crowd. "Quetzal's gone tomorrow." A pause. "But if that little girl develops complications? Dies out there in the bush? That'll be on your shoulders, and I sure as hell won't forget."

She turned, started for the door, then called over her shoulder, "Bernie. I'm sending Raya out to fix that arm of yours."

And Trish barely heard Talina's muttered, "Piece of shit that you are."

Then she was inside, the doors swinging shut behind her.

46

The fact that it was Trish, of all people, who'd sided with them. That burned deep down inside.

Talina strode angrily down the hallway; didn't bother to knock on Raya's door, but burst in, asking, "Tell me about Kylee. If she has to go home, what are her chances?"

Raya jumped, eyes gone wide. "Jesus." She took a breath, collecting herself. "I mean, well, as long as there's no post-operative infection, as long as she doesn't reinjure the bones, she'd probably be fine. Why? What's happened?"

"Bernie fucking Monson, clay miner extraordinaire, is standing outside the front door with an armed posse. He's got a broken arm, he's drunker than a lord, and he's scared to set foot inside the hospital because he just knows Rocket is going to eat him."

"An armed posse?"

"Hey, they've been waiting out there for days. People are getting tired of it." Talina slapped a hand to the wall. "Damn it, if Rocket hasn't caused trouble so far, why would they think he's going to go berserk now?"

"Because Spiro is stirring things up. There were gunshots in the hospital. Someone blew up your house and murdered Felicity. Aguila's operation is failing down south, and she's in here, too. We've just learned what mobbers are, and what they can do. Folks are eventually wondering if they're going to come here now that they've had a taste of human flesh. And, finally, there's a quetzal in their hospital. It's supposed to be a place of sanctuary. Work it out, Tal."

Talina took a breath, feeling her own quetzal stirring. "And they're blaming me. Say I'm infected with quetzal. That that's why I'm protecting Rocket. The implication is that I can't be trusted anymore."

Raya's knowing brown eyes softened. "Stressful times, huh? What do you want to do?"

"I said Rocket would be out of here tomorrow. I could deal with the hotheads like Monson and Vanveer. I can't fight the families when it's Sian, Amal, Friga, and their like worrying about the safety of their kids and the rest of the children."

Raya nodded. "My advice? Go tonight. Tomorrow would be like a circus show. Everyone's going to want to watch Rocket the pet quetzal fly off in an aircar. No telling who might demonstrate an error in judgment that could turn catastrophic."

"Yeah." Talina accessed her com. "Two Spots? Patch me through to Trish."

"Roger that."

A second later. *"Trish here. What's up, Tal?"*

"How's the crowd out front?"

"Congratulating themselves. The women have left. My bet is that once Bernie's arm's set, most of them will go to Inga's."

"Okay, I'm sending Raya out to set that asshole's arm." Talina took a deep breath. "Look, it's getting dark out there. I know it's an imposition, but I need you to take an escort past the gate to the aircar field. My outfit, the one with the night vision gear, should be charged up. Drop it off at the hospital back door."

"Tal, are you out of your mind? You're flying that damn quetzal out tonight? Didn't we decide night flying was a bad idea?"

"Hey, Trish. I just had my legs chopped out from under me. And you helped them do it. Remember? Since I'm on my own here, I'll run it my way. Now, can you get my aircar to the back door, or should I go get it myself?" She regretted her tone of voice the moment she said it: bitter, pissed, and resentful.

"Go fuck yourself, Tal. I'll have your damn aircar at the back door in fifteen minutes."

47

Talbot sat on the edge of Kylee's bed, arm around Dya's shoulders. The monitors were glowing, the room feeling warm and snug. Rocket lay curled on the floor making curious purring sounds.

"So, if we can't think of a way to escape this place, if Aguila's going to make it us or Mundo Base, what does this mean for Rebecca and Su and the rest of us?" Kylee asked.

"It means we have a choice," Dya told her. "We can try and escape. Get away from here before you're well. It means we'll have to find a way to get you out of the hospital, somehow sneak you to the airfield, and steal an aircar. Then we have to make sure we're not followed on the way home."

"But they'll come looking for us," Mark said wearily. "They know we exist. Your wonderful salves are curing Aguila. She's practically quivering with curiosity about how you've managed to adapt to the forest. And, Dya, that woman is desperate. She'll stop at nothing."

"The base is falling apart, Mark," Dya told him. "Are we just fooling ourselves? Especially if within a year we're living on the ground?"

"Other people live on the ground. I've heard of the Briggs, the Philos, and Andanis. Can't be that hard. We've got standing structures that can be defended. Locally there's stone. Lots of timber. We can build something more suited for habitation and defense than the shops and sheds."

"Rocket and I," Kylee added, "we'll help. Keep guard. Like Dr. Turnienko says, we've got quetzal sense."

Dya shook her head, shoulders slumping. "You said Aguila would deal? Fix what's broken? Maybe it's worth it."

"Not your decision to make by yourself," Mark reminded. "That should be up to the others. We can't decide for them. Rebecca and Su would take that as a betrayal."

"The only other choice is not to go back," Dya told him.

"Aguila can't follow what was essentially a one-way trip. Knowing Rebecca and Su like I do, I'm not sure they wouldn't prefer that we abandon them down there rather than bring the whole world crashing into Mundo Base."

"Dya," Kylee reminded, "they're pregnant. How long can they climb the stairs with the lift broken?"

"The move to the ground is inevitable," Dya countered. "The old dormitory is being used for storage. It'll be easily converted back to living quarters. It has running water from the cistern. It's a short walk to the fields. Damien and Shantaya can work the fields. The science will have to be put off, that's all. They can get back to it when the babies are older."

"And we'll just surrender ourselves to Aguila?" Mark asked.

Dya shrugged. "We have skills that she desperately needs. We can trade. Contract for a time. Start at a year. She'll push hard for more. In the end, it's Donovan. She'll meet our terms."

Talbot reminded, "I'm the weak link, the leverage she can use against you."

"Maybe. But she's smart enough to know that if she pushes too hard, she'll piss me off to the point that I refuse to give her so much as the shit off my shoe. She's got my medicines, but she doesn't have the formulae to manufacture them." Dya tapped her head. "That's up here. Makes me wonder what Shig and Yvette would pay for what I know. Maybe enough to buy you free of Aguila."

"But that still leaves Rebecca, Su, and the kids abandoned at Mundo." Talbot fingered his chin. "That's family. People we love and who depend on us."

"Mark, more than anything, we need to buy time. Let Kylee heal." Dya squinted uncomfortably. "A couple of months. Wait until they relax. Somehow, along the way, someone's got to recharge the aircar. We slip away some morning just before dawn."

"Not the way they guard the gates here." Mark rubbed the back of his neck with his good arm. "If we could just talk to Rebecca and Su. What do you think my chances are of sneaking into the admin dome and getting to the radio room? If we just had a little luck on our side and someone down at Mundo was monitoring the radio . . . ?"

"Won't do you any good," a voice said from behind.

Mark's stomach dropped as he turned to see Talina Perez standing in the doorway. He asked, "How long have you been there?"

Dya went pale, loathing and despair in her fallen expression.

"Long enough." Talina closed the door softly behind her. Stepping around the bed, she looked down at Kylee. "How you doing, kid?"

"Fine. Dr. Turnienko says I'm healing real fast. Says I've got quetzal power."

"Yeah, I've got a little of that myself."

"Son of a bitch." Dya, hopeless, shook her head in defeat. "Talina Perez, once again fucking up my life."

Talbot tightened his arm around her shoulders. "One day at a time, wife."

To Talina, he said, "So, there it is. Now that you know we're ready to run, what are you going to do? Turn us over to Aguila?"

Talina pursed her lips. "Sorry. Change of plans. You know the Frankenstein story? About the monster? It's a classic, right? Remember the townspeople? The pitchforks and burning torches?"

"Get to the point, damn you," Dya said through gritted teeth.

"The point is, the locals are going berserk. I just had a standoff with a group of the good citizens at the front door."

Perez bent down, staring into Rocket's three eyes. "Sorry, buddy. But you have to go. And since you can't go without Kylee, she's in the same fix. But somehow, given what I just heard, I don't think Mark and Dya want to stay here either."

Dya, still seething, asked, "What are you talking about? Supervisor Aguila's got a watch on our aircar."

"And last I checked," Talbot told her, "the power pack was still at twenty percent."

"Yeah," Talina said, standing. "And it's going to stay that way." She fixed her eyes on Dya. "Last time you and I had dealings, I did you and yours dirt. Now, I don't really give a rat's ass what you think of me. You're a hell of a lot more right about me than you know. But I owe you and whoever's left down at Mundo. So you're going home tonight."

"What about Kylee?" Dya asked. "She can't travel yet."

Talina smiled down at the little girl. "Sorry, kiddo, but you're going to have to. Now, I've talked to Raya. She's put together an emergency kit in case there're complications. And we're working out some alternative scenarios if you take a turn for the worse."

Mark disengaged from Dya and stood, skeptical eyes on Talina. "We can't take you there. It's not our call. We *won't* take you to our home."

"She knows," Dya whispered. "She's been there."

"But I thought . . ." Then he put it together. "Right. They never came looking because they thought you were all dead. Abandoned the place. Whatever."

"My aircar's out the back door," Talina told him. "Raya's getting a stretcher for Kylee. Pack your stuff. Once we're in the hall, not a word. Aguila's in a meeting in her room with that shithead Spiro and a couple of her engineers. We need to go fast, quietly, and without a fuss. You all got that?"

"So you take us back, and then what?" Dya demanded. "It means you've got your claws sunk into us again."

"Your trouble is with Aguila. I represent Port Authority. Shig, me, Yvette? We haven't missed you since you've been gone. Won't miss you once you're back at whatever's left of Mundo. Call if you need medical or supplies. We'll deal. Either SDRs or trade. So far as we're concerned, go live your lives. Mundo's yours."

"Hard to believe." Dya seemed unconvinced.

"Yeah. Call it lessons painfully learned. Now, come on. We've got to get you the hell out of Dodge before either the pitchfork-carrying locals or the high and mighty Supervisor gets it into their heads to make my life more difficult."

Talbot took a deep breath. "Why should we trust you?"

"Given who I am, and what I've done? Sucks, doesn't it? Let's just say I'm doing it for Kylee and Rocket. That way there's no weird awkwardness about debt and forgiveness, okay?"

Raya Turnienko stepped into the room bearing a pack and collapsible stretcher. Her Siberian features bespoke a tense unease.

Within moments, Mark had helped pack their few belongings. With Dya and Perez bearing the stretcher, they eased out of the room. But for the whisper of their shoes on the floor, and the clicking of Rocket's claws, they moved silently.

Passing Aguila's room, Talbot heard voices. Aguila's strident, declaring, "Lieutenant, I'm at the end of my rope with you! We lose the smelter, we lose Donovan. Do you understand? If wc can't beat back this damned forest, all of humanity's . . ."

And then they were past. Out the back. Into the darkness where Trish Monagan's shadowy form waited by an aircar.

"Tal," the security officer asked, "you sure you know what you're doing here?"

"Nothing more than I have to, Trish." Talina's voice dripped bitterness.

And then they were loaded, Kylee carefully placed on the back seat, her form wrapped in blankets. Rocket immediately curled on the floor, his hide a kaleidoscope of riotous colors muted by darkness. Yeah, he really was terrified of flying.

"See you, Raya," Perez called as she donned night vision, spun up the fans, and lifted into the darkness.

Talbot settled on a seat next to Dya, taking her hand. "Hope this works out," he murmured into her ear.

"I don't know that we've bought ourselves anything but a little time," she replied. "When Aguila finds out, she's going to be pissed. Eventually, she's going to come looking for us. You know that."

He did. And when that day came, it would mean he'd have to go up against his old team. He wondered if the armor would be up to it.

48

Setting her aircar down onto the damp ground in an opening between the outbuildings, Talina spooled the fans down. Capella's first yellow rays were sending spears of light across the treetops; they illuminated the great, white mushroom shape of the Mundo Base dome. Gave it a golden hue. The sheds and shops among which she'd landed still remained in the tall forest's retreating shadow.

As the aircar went silent, its whine was replaced by the rising and falling of the chime as invertebrates greeted the morning. A flock of scarlet fliers descended from the forest on the south to land among the corn, beans, and squash plants in the field. Spots of brilliant red, they commenced their morning hunt for invertebrates.

Taking a last check, Talina noted that she was down to a thirty percent charge in the power pack.

Rocket, first to react, leaped bodily over the gunwale, chirring, whistling, and squeaking happily. His mouth open, he pumped air through his body, testing scent, exhaling through the vents at the root of his tail. Colors of white, pink, and orange flowed in splotched patterns of joy across his hide.

"How are you doing, buttercup?" Talbot asked as he checked Kylee's blankets.

"We home?"

"Just landed," Dya told her daughter with a smile. "Bet they're not even up in the dome yet."

Talina retrieved her pack and rifle, asking, "How do you want to do this? You want to go wake them up, and I can fly Kylee to the roof?"

Dya said, "Don't know that the roof can take the weight. First floor in the tower for now. At least get her under cover for the time being. Make breakfast. Once we're all fed and talk to Rebecca and Su, we'll figure out what the next step is."

Talbot swiveled off the side rail, landing on the firm soil with both feet. "My God, it's good to be home."

Talina noted the look of relief in the man's face. "So, you're married to all three?"

"That a problem for you, officer?"

"No. Just proves you're a better person than I am. I never thought I was smart enough to manage even a single marriage. Let alone three at once."

"Different here," he said, as if it explained it all.

Yeah, welcome to Donovan.

She helped Dya maneuver the stretcher handles to Talbot, who winced at the pain in his wounded arm as Talina crawled out and took the stretcher handles from him.

The walk to the tower base lasted no more than seconds, and Talina took in the changes since the last time she'd been here. Lots of mothballed equipment. Some of it tarped. Some of it cannibalized. But then, that was Donovan, too.

Nevertheless the place had a neat look. Cared for. Signs of industry could be seen in the dried vegetables hanging from vines inside open-sided sheds. The shops had been all tightly closed against the night. She trod on beaten earth, marked as it was by feet and tires.

What really sank in was that Mundo was huge. All those acres in cultivation behind the tree line. More food growing than the people here could possibly eat. Most of it growing wild, from the looks of it.

"Hard to believe it's just been you, Rebecca, and Su," she told Dya. "I don't know how you did it."

"Hard work. But we're losing. Not enough of us."

At the dome, Talbot cycled the lock, opening the door wide. Rocket was the first through, turning expectant eyes on Kylee as she was carried in and placed on a table.

Talina looked around, took in the stacked crates and boxes, the few remaining light panels that flickered just enough to leave the room gloomy. She walked over to the bent lift cage, stooped, and felt the frayed cable where it had spilled across the floor.

"I think we have cable similar to this from the *Turalon* cargo. Tyrell Lawson and a couple of his hands could have this whole thing back up and running in a couple of days."

"That'd be a godsend," Mark told her before bending down and kissing Kylee's head. He added, "Welcome home, precious."

"Good to be here." Kylee waved a hand. "Go on. They're going to want to know that you're here. Rocket and I, we'll be fine."

"Yeah, not bad for a pedophile, huh?" Talbot gave the little girl a wink. She giggled in return.

"Pedophile?" Talina asked as she followed Talbot and Dya up the stairs.

Talbot said over his shoulder, "It was a boogeyman yarn they told the kids about the kinds of men who lived in Solar System."

"Good. Otherwise I'd be forced to shoot you in the back."

"Naw," Dya called back. "We'd have already shot him ourselves. Thought of it on occasion. Not because of pedophilia, but just because he's a pain in the butt sometimes. Turns out he had a saving grace. He was too good at chores and sex to waste."

Talina lifted an eyebrow; Dya's entire demeanor had changed, sharpened, as if since landing she'd once again grown comfortable in her own skin.

Damn, what a climb. By the time she'd reached the top, Talina could feel her wind.

At the landing, Dya opened the door to a foyer, calling, "Hello! Rebecca? Su? You here?"

"Dya?" came the call. "When'd you get back?"

"Just now."

A scrambling could be heard, feet pounding, the excited cries of children.

Talina followed Dya and Talbot into the main room, seeing that the furniture looked a little more shabby; the great curving window that allowed views of the rugged country to the north had yellowed.

A lot of potted plants were growing in the room. Gave the place a tropical sort of feel.

Rebecca, older, harder and thinner, came first, a flimsy and worn robe doing little to cover her lean body. The tall woman's hair was now cut short. Lines had carved themselves in the corners of her dark brown eyes and full jaw. A toughness lay in the set of her lips, smiling though they were.

Su Wang Ho followed, now a mature woman with long, gleaming black hair. A look of sheer joy illuminated her features; white teeth shone behind her petite lips as she threw her arms around Dya.

And then came the flock of children: a boy teetering on the start of his teen years; a host of smaller ones of all sizes, not that Talina was any judge of ages.

They all clustered around, hugging Talbot and Dya, clinging to their legs, calling questions. After hugging his women, Talbot was on his knees, laughing like a lunatic, gathering children into his good arm. The man looked positively radiant.

"How's Kylee?" Rebecca demanded, brooking no more interruption.

"Alive. Healing." Dya disengaged from a little three-year-old that had to be hers, and stood. "She's downstairs with Rocket. Dr. Turnienko did the surgery. If she heals without incident, she'll walk again. Live a normal life."

"Thank God," Su cried, throwing her arms around Dya and hugging her again, a look of relief flooding her face.

At which moment Rebecca first logged Talina's presence. Shock. The faint frown followed by recognition. Rebecca stiffened, asking, "What the *hell* is she doing here?"

If hatred could thrive in words, Rebecca's were acid with loathing.

Everything stopped. All eyes turned.

"Hello, Rebecca. Su. Sorry to intrude."

Su's eyes flashed recognition, alarm, and then brittle hatred: the woman wheeled, running for the rear.

"You better have a damn good reason for being here." Rebecca's chin was quivering with rage.

"She does," Dya interjected herself between Rebecca and Tal. "Things got a lot more complicated than we thought. We've done the best we can. Hear us out before—"

Su emerged from the rear, some sort of tube thing in her hands. The look in her eyes had gone wild as she slid to a stop on bare feet beside Rebecca. The tube rose in her hands, the woman's hair flying around her head.

In the last instant before it could come level with Talina's chest, Dya slapped the thing up. Something shot from the end, the sound of rebounding springs loud in the room.

Nothing wrong with Tal's instincts. She'd barely ducked out of the way as the black dart streaked by her ear.

"Why'd you interfere?" Su screamed in Dya's face. "She murdered Paolo! Shot Pak down in the street!" A look of absolute disbelief crossed Su's face. "And you brought her *here*? You, of all people?"

Talbot stepped forward, calming. "Stop it! All of you! Damn it, we're in trouble. Real trouble. And right now, Perez is the only person keeping us from disaster. I mean it, stand down."

He stared intently into Su's hot eyes, easing the tube from her hands, saying, "But for her, neither Dya nor I might have ever made it back. Rocket would have been killed. It didn't work like we'd hoped it would. Too much went wrong up there."

Rebecca, almost trembling with rage, knotted her fists. "We should have tried to fix Kylee ourselves. I knew it was a mistake."

"We couldn't have," Dya told her, walking up and hugging Rebecca. "I was there for the surgery. Watched what Turnienko had to do to save Kylee's leg and hip. That was the price."

Su was still glaring, seething venom in Talina's direction. "I never thought our home would be profaned by that bitch, but here she stands. Makes me want to vomit."

Talina kept her features stiff, feeling her heart thumping dismally in her chest. Hard to see that much hatred concentrated behind another human being's eyes. To know that it was all centered on her.

The children were watching with wide, solemn eyes, having backed away to safety behind the adults. Given their new terror, Talina wondered if they were silently telling themselves, she's a *pedophile!*

The quetzal in Talina's gut chattered in amusement.

Talina raised her hands in surrender. "Hey, I'm not here to cause any trouble. All I need is a charge, and I am out of here."

"A charge?" Rebecca asked.

"I've got thirty percent in the power pack. That gets

me halfway back to Port Authority. Just tell me where to plug in."

Rebecca glanced sidelong at Dya and Talbot. "We'll have to pull voltaics from the condensers, use some of the solar collectors from the refrigeration in the ground lab."

Talbot sighed and rubbed the back of his neck. He glanced at Talina. "It'll take a couple of days."

"What?" Talina snapped.

"This isn't Port Authority," Rebecca shot back. "Recharging aircars isn't an everyday occurrence. We had far better uses for the charging equipment. Think basic utilities: Light. Heat. Power."

Talina nodded. "I understand. But you need to know. Time's critical. If I'm not back, don't check in, people are going to come looking for me. Won't take them long to look up Mundo Base's coordinates and plot a straight line here. I better go down and call in."

"Use the radio here," Mark told her. "Something short. Quick. That Aguila can't put a directional locator on."

"Yeah, well, hopefully, and with a little luck, she still doesn't know you're missing. Won't for another couple of hours."

"The new Supervisor?" Rebecca asked. "We're afoul of her? How'd that happen?"

"She was in the same hospital. It was one of her people who shot Mark." Dya made a face. "Would have shot Rocket. Might have shot me if Perez hadn't stopped her."

"Shot?" Su cried. "That's what happened to your arm?" She rushed forward, hatred dissolving into concern as she took Mark's hand and inspected the bandage on his upper arm. "How bad is it?"

"It'll heal," Talbot told her with a smile. "And the only way they could get me was from behind."

Rebecca put her hands up. "Wait! Stop! We all need to hear this from the beginning."

"And there's Kylee to think about," Su added hotly. "We need to get her up the stairs."

"Dya?" Talina asked, "Do you want me to fly her up, or do you think the two of us can manage that stretcher?"

"Carry her," Dya responded. "Save as much charge as you can in your aircar's power pack. We want you out of here. Might have to rest a couple of times on the way, but more than that, I guess we have to."

Talina met Rebecca's and then Su's hard gazes. "While I'm down there, I'll call in. Tell Two Spots I'm taking a couple of days. That people aren't to worry."

"That's brazen of you," Su almost spit. "If it were up to me, you'd be dead and buried days before they thought to come looking for you."

Talina smiled grimly. "Yeah, well, given general sentiment, you're far from alone in feeling that way."

"Go with her," Rebecca told Dya. "Monitor her call. Keep an eye on her."

Talina turned, led the way back to the foyer.

"My apologies," Dya said as they stepped out on the dark landing. The steel mesh wiggled under their feet. "You helped us. Kylee, Rocket, Mark, and me. But some things just can't be forgiven."

"I know. Maybe better than you and Su. It's not like I could forgive the person who murdered Cap. Can't forgive Spiro for what she did to Felicity. Some things are just too far gone to end any way but in blood."

The stairs rattled under their feet as they descended in the dark gloom.

"I know you acted under Clemenceau's orders."

"That's not an excuse, Dya. I just have to live with the consequences." Talina hesitated. "That tube thing? Su was trying to kill me, wasn't she?"

"If that dart had hit you . . . Suffice it to say it wouldn't have been a pleasant way to die."

"Any way to hurry the charge on my aircar? Might be safer for all parties concerned if I slept somewhere out in the forest."

"Mark and I will talk to Su and Rebecca. You can bunk in my room tonight along with me and Kylee. I imagine Su and Rebecca are going to want their time with Mark after being away."

"I'm beginning to see what you're so desperate to protect. I'll do what I can for you."

"Why? What's it to you?"

"Maybe I'm a sucker for dying dreams."

"How are Rebecca and Su and Damien?" Kylee called from her stretcher as Tal descended the last of the stairs.

"Fine, fine. Looking forward to seeing you, buttercup," Dya called. "Talina and I are going to haul you up to the top as soon as we attend to the aircar."

Talina shot the little girl a wink. Rocket was prowling around anxiously and bolted from the door as they opened it. Like a shot he was onto the beast Dya had called a "roo" before the herbivore could react.

Through the quetzal in her belly, she felt his thrill at the chase and kill, could almost feel the creature's blood swell with the taste of fresh meat and blood.

Su came within a whisker of killing me up there.

She'd call Two Spots, all right. "Dya. As soon as I make that call, we need to start charging my power pack."

"No sense in tempting fate, huh?"

"What do you think?"

49

Gone! In the middle of the night? Kalico Aguila sat at the window as her shuttle banked right along the spine of the mountain and backed air as it settled over Corporate Mine.

"Damn you, Perez," she muttered under her breath, still fuming over the revelation that Talbot, his wife, kid, and quetzal had flown away into the wilderness.

She glanced to the rear where Spiro sat buckled in with the rest of the marines. The lieutenant had a smug and victorious look in her dark eyes.

The bitch shouldn't be gloating. She'd killed a nurse. A woman who had ministered to Kalico's wounds with a reassuring smile and kindness. And who left a family behind. A most valuable human being given Donovan's necessities.

Spiro might not have meant to kill Felicity, but that didn't excuse the fact that the woman was dead. Worse, Spiro had done it in a clumsy way. From the moment she shot Mark Talbot through the hospital window, Spiro's judgment had gone from bad to worse.

What am I going to do with her?

Not that Kalico cared one way or another about Spiro's feud with Talina Perez. The security officer had been a constant irritant from the moment Kalico had set foot on Donovan. She might respect Talina, even enjoy her company on occasion, but the woman's interests were too often at odds with her own.

In a sense, Perez and Spiro were alike in that they were the only two people on the planet who essentially held life and death in their hands without the worry of consequences for their actions.

The shuttle touched down easily, and Kalico unbuckled her seat belt. She eased to her feet, careful of her still-healing wounds where the fabric of her suit rubbed.

To the pilot, she called, "Ensign Makarov. I need to see you in my office as soon as you get the shuttle secured."

"Aye, ma'am."

Stepping to the hatch as it was opened, she descended the ramp to find a crowd waiting. Even as her feet hit dirt, the people were clapping. Their cheers caught her by surprise.

For a moment she stopped, her five marines packing the ramp behind her.

Capella's bright rays shot beams off the windshields and metal of the parked equipment. The ground beneath her reflected warmly, and the high perimeter fence glittered against the tree-green backdrop of the mountain. In the forest beyond, the chime rose and fell in a musical harmony.

"Must be a holiday," she called as her people pressed close. Her quip spawned laughter.

Aurobindo Ghosh, standing in the forefront, called back, "We're glad to see you upright and walking, Supervisor. A lot of us were worried. But having you back, well, we know that we're going to make it now."

A couple of "That's right," and "Here, here," calls came from the crowd.

My God. They really do care.

She lifted her chin, pasted the wry smile on her lips, and walked up to them. "Not only are we going to make it," she told them. "I've got a lead on some new information that's going to give us the edge. Lieutenant Spiro?"

"Ma'am." Spiro stepped up beside her.

"Get those medicines to the clinic. Each of the salves and ointments has Simonov's instructions for their use. From here on out, if we have mobber-caused injuries, we don't need to rely on Port Authority."

"Yes, ma'am."

Kalico turned back to her people. "That's right. New medicines. That's just the start. There's also, apparently, some way to keep the trees back. Something the Wild Ones have figured out but are guarding somewhere in the back country. For us, it's just a matter of running it down, learning how they did it, and applying it to our needs here. That, my friends, is the break-even point."

Whistles and applause greeted her words.

"Now, while I've been indisposed, you've been holding the fort. How are the cannons coming along?"

"Tested this morning," Desch Ituri called, stepping to the front. "We can throw enough pellets to saturate a hundred-square-meter circle at optimum range. We're there, ma'am."

"And when are those flying maggots due back?"

"Tomorrow morning, unless there's a deviation," Ghosh told her.

"I cannot wait to see this unfold." She clapped her hands in delight. "Maybe, like the Wild Ones, we'll make adornments out of those colorful tails and jewelry out of their claws."

That brought more whistles and clapping.

"Now, for the rest of you. Take a good look at the person next to you. And the one behind. All of you. You've stood together. Kept us going while I was locked away in the hospital. Starting tomorrow, after the mobbers are blown out of our sky, we're back to taking normal R&R rotations to Port Authority."

More hoots and calls. The joy in their faces warmed her heart.

"Don't get me wrong, people. We're still hanging in the wind. Hanging *way* out in the wind. We could still lose this. In fact, we will if we don't find those Wild Ones. But I've got some information on where they are. I figure it's only a matter of time before we run them down and learn their secrets."

Again the shouts of approval.

Careful of her healing wounds, she raised her hands high. "I want to thank all of you for your forbearance over the last weeks. We've taken our licks. Now, it's time to take back our mine, our skies, and our fields. All of us. Together. Because it's for our people, those same men and women who stand with you today. That's who we're really working for."

She paused for effect.

"Each. Other." She emphasized the words, gave them a last cheery wave, and added, "Now, folks, I'm weary, and still healing. Anyone with needs, see Lieutenant Spiro for an appointment. Meanwhile, stay safe, and keep an eye on the skies."

They continued to cheer as they followed her to her dome.

"Ituri, Ghosh," she called over her shoulder. "You're with me."

Hurt and ache as she might, she'd been too long from the mine. Too much needed her immediate attention.

Once inside the cool recesses of the dome, she found her office and sank carefully into the seat. The damn cuts, many still sutured, protested painfully. Closing her eyes, she took a couple of deep breaths, and looked up.

Ghosh and Ituri stood at ease before her desk. "Desch, bring me the map. You had Stryski plot Dya and Talbot's aircar range from Port Authority?"

"Be right back," Ituri said, ducking out of the room.

Even before he could return, Juri Makarov, the ensign who piloted her shuttle, appeared in the doorway, entered, and saluted.

"At ease, Juri. I've got a job for you."

"Yes, ma'am."

Ituri hustled back into the room with the map and spread it over her desk. The familiar features of her section of Donovan were instantly recognizable: the coast, the mountain ranges, the major rivers. Onto this had been plotted Port Authority's location. And from that center an arc had been drawn from the southern coastline around to the west of the Wind Mountains.

From the Corporate Mines, she noticed that the southern curve of the arc was still more than two hundred kilometers farther into the wilds.

"Take a look, people. Somewhere along that radius is a farmstead. A hidden little cluster of humans who hold the secret to our success here. I suspect it's going to be small, camouflaged, effectively rendered invisible from the air.

"Juri, you have sensors that can penetrate the trees. Just to cover all contingencies, I want you to start fifty kilometers south of what Stryski plotted as their maximum range. They might have had a hard tailwind the day they flew in."

Ensign Makarov fingered his chin as he stared at the long arc. "Lot of territory to cover, ma'am. Couple million square hectares."

"They flew in on an aircar," Kalico mused. "They've got to have electrical power down there. How else could they keep a charge in the power pack?"

"Hell, ma'am, why didn't you say so," Makarov told her. "With the lateral sensors, I could ping them all the way from orbit. Throw in the thermal sensors and LiDAR, and I'll have them no later than the second pass."

She spared him a mocking lift of her eyebrow. "Don't get too cocky. Like I say, they're probably camouflaged down there."

"Yes, ma'am." The ensign was hiding a smile.

A knock at the door announced Lieutenant Spiro. She had an even more dour expression—as if being back at the mine was proving to be a real imposition. No doubt taking up her duties here had a lot less appeal than strutting around Port Authority, drinking at Inga's, and slurping down the comparatively extravagant meals in the cafeteria.

"Yes, Lieutenant?"

"Want to know if I can stand down the Port Authority detail, ma'am."

"You may, Lieutenant." Kalico hesitated. "And what's gnawing at Private Tompzen? For the last day he's been sullen and staring off at nothing like he's wrestling with demons. Almost as if he's not himself."

"Way ahead of you, ma'am. Noticed it myself. When I asked, he said he had some 'personal issues' to work through. Said it had nothing to do with me or the other marines. Maybe he got jilted by some woman."

"Yeah, well, keep an eye on him. I don't need him disappearing into the forest and doing a Talbot on us." She paused, letting her anger rise. "Talbot. This is twice now that he's run out on me."

"Yes, ma'am."

Kalico was far from done with her wayward marine. Talbot was out there. She let her gaze trace that long arc. Somewhere along that curve . . .

Hope you're ready, because we're coming for you.

50

The best course, Talina figured, was to leave the Mundo women alone. Not impose herself or be a reminder of the bitter past. Just being at Mundo had already pulled the scab off a long-festering wound.

Damien, the twelve-year-old boy, had helped her disconnect a couple of nonessential pieces of electrical equipment. Then they'd wheeled a series of solar panels and a charging unit from the scavenged equipment over to her aircar. It was a fricking make-do contraption of wires, voltaics, and regulators, but charge was slowly flowing into her aircar's power pack.

"Thanks," she told the boy. "Listen, there's no sense for me to tie up your whole day. Go on back to whatever you need to do. Me, I'm just going to lay low and keep from pissing anybody off."

The kid just eyed her with those dark orbs that looked so much like his mother's. The entire time the boy had barely spoken a word. He'd treated her as if she were a deadly, venomous beast who might lash out at any moment.

Now he swallowed hard, finally asking, "Is Port Authority as bad as they say it is?"

"Bad? No, Damien. It's just people trying to get along and survive. It's a whole lot better than it was in the days when your people left. That was partly my fault. I served a very bad man. But he's long gone. We've tried to make things better."

"There are people my age? Males and females?"

Odd that he'd use those terms to describe other kids. But then, what should she expect, being raised as he was by a bunch of scientists? "Sure. A couple of dozen."

"What are they like?"

"A lot like you. Smart. Tough. Learning what they need to know to survive Donovan."

"Maybe someday I could go there. I'd like to know

those people. Find out what they are like." He glanced sidelong at her. "But I wouldn't want to be shot, either."

"You won't be shot." Talina chuckled in ironic amusement. "Hell, boy, I was the shooter back then. You want to come to Port Authority, you'll come under my protection. I'll give you a guided tour of the place. Introduce you to all the young people your age, and see that you get home without issue to boot."

His expression pinched as if he were wondering if he could trust her.

"I may have my faults, Damien, but no one doubts my word. Not even your mother, Dya, or Su."

She made another check on the charge trickling ever so slowly into the aircar. "Now, go on with you. I'm going to take a walk down through the fields. Keep out of everyone's way."

"Don't go past the tree line," Damien told her as he picked up his tools.

"I've been in deep forest before. I'm not the kind to tempt fate." She shot him a wink and watched as he walked away.

Taking a deep breath, she looked up at the dome, thought she saw someone peering down at her from the curving transparency of the main window, though it could have been a reflection.

She slung her rifle, laid a palm on the butt of her pistol, and strolled leisurely past the sheds, shops, and stacked equipment to the closest of the fields.

Taking it in, she saw cabbages, lettuce, corn, beans, varieties of squash, huge cactuses growing under an awning, an herb garden, pepper plants, giant sunflowers, peas, and a host of plants she couldn't name. Things they most definitely didn't grow at Port Authority.

Dang, if we could just talk them into trading.

As she walked down the elevated causeway, the tended part of the field gave way to a riotous chaos of intergrown plants. An agricultural profusion gone completely wild once past the last of the corn stalks.

The chaos of green just kept going until it stopped at the line of brush: mostly terrestrial fruit, berry, and nut bushes.

A line of fruit trees followed, and finally the pine belt just this side of the forest.

"My God," she whispered. "We could feed every man, woman, and child on Donovan from this one field and still have food left over."

As she said it, the chime rose and fell in its incomprehensible musical patterns. She could see the occasional hopper, and sometimes a roo as it wiggled through the profusion in search of invertebrates to munch.

She caught movement from the corner of her eye and turned to see Rebecca, expression stern, eating the distance between them with long strides.

Talina kept a hand on her pistol, waiting. At least Rebecca wasn't carrying one of those tube guns.

"What are you doing, Perez?" Rebecca asked as she stopped a couple of paces away.

"Figured I'd go for a walk." She waved at the fields. "This is amazing. I've never seen anything like it. I mean, in pictures of farms back on Earth, the crops are laid out in rows. Here everything's growing on top of everything else. Like a humping jungle."

"It's Capella's energy, the rains, and most of all the nutrients in the soil," Rebecca told her. "And none of the deleterious fungi, viruses, or microbiota that have evolved to parasitically effect plants back on Earth. When the first seeds were brought here, they were accompanied only by beneficial microbes. Think of it as a perfect world for a terrestrial plant. No diseases. The only predation comes from what we harvest."

"Rebecca, you're sitting on a clap-trapping fortune here."

"Are we?" The woman's mouth tightened. "We're a bit conflicted, Perez. You got Dya, Mark, Kylee, and Rocket out. Kept this new Supervisor from taking our husband. But that doesn't make us friends. And now what? Do we let you fly off and tell all of Port Authority what you've seen here? Or is that just inviting disaster?"

"Disaster's coming either way, I fear." Tal stared up at the thickly needled pine trees. "What species are those?"

"A mixture of loblolly and Southern pitch pine. Both

species that literally drip sap. Works pretty well to keep our species in and Donovan's out. As part of our long-term research on our impact to the planet we closely monitor what's growing out in the forest. We've only recorded a couple of volunteer terrestrial plants whose seeds somehow made it out past our containment. So far the boundaries are remarkably efficient."

"So you can keep our stuff in and Donovan out?"

"Pretty much. But why don't you tell me about this coming disaster?"

"Rebecca, we need each other. Our people would love to trade for some of the foods you grow here. For Dya's medicines. In return, we have supplies. Like cable. And the kind of people who could fix your lift. Maybe get some of your equipment working again."

"Sounds like the kind of beginning that could end in dependency." Rebecca's expression went flinty.

"Not just no, but *hell* no! We don't want dependents. Means they have to be taken care of. Subsidies. Wasted time. Take it up with Shig. He'll talk your ear off when he's not spouting all that Taoist Buddha Hindu crap." Talina pointed. "What kind of berry bushes are those?"

"Blueberries, raspberries, blackberries, and some wild plum mixed in."

"Holy shit," Talina whispered. "Didn't know such things had ever been tried on Donovan. Let alone were growing."

"Our original mandate was as an agricultural research station."

"Cherries?"

"Along the western tree belt."

"Dear God." Talina shook her head. "If we fix your lift, put in a new cable, repair your dome floor and pump, how many loads of fruits and vegetables would you trade?"

"Maybe you didn't understand when I said we're not interested."

Talina arched an eyebrow. "Oh, I picked up on that without any problem at all. But Port Authority isn't the disaster you're facing. It's Kalico Aguila, her shuttle, her marines, and the fact that she *will* find you. I figure you've got a week before she's setting down in your front yard. I can promise you, the good Supervisor doesn't ascribe to a single libertarian value. She's made a bit of progress, but she's still fundamentally Corporate in her mindset."

"Dya told me that she told Aguila that we were somewhere off to the west."

"So I heard. Like I said: end of the week at the latest. Less if she figured out how far Dya and Talbot actually flew to get to Port Authority."

"We disabled the locator beacons in the aircars years ago."

"Your problem is the shuttle. If it even passes anywhere close, you're going to be the big electrical blip detected by the lateral sensor array."

As Talina spoke, Rebecca's face went ashen. "Hadn't thought of that. We can't shut the place down. The refrigeration, the lights, the pumps, the lab equipment, the coms."

"So, you figured out how . . . ?" Talina stopped short and cocked her head. It came from the south, the distant roar just discernible to her quetzal-augmented hearing. "Screw me with a skewer. How wrong could I be?"

"What?" Rebecca, too, had cocked her head, listening hard. An instant later, as the sound grew, the woman shifted her gaze to the southern sky above the treetops.

It came in high, a slim silver delta that left a thin white contrail through the humid air and patchy bits of cloud.

Talina and Rebecca watched as it made a slow, leisurely circle of Mundo Base, banking wide, then dropping down for a closer look.

"Game's up," Talina noted dryly.

Rebecca might have turned to stone.

Then, to Talina's surprise, the shuttle didn't land, but headed directly in the direction of the Corporate Mine.

"Why didn't they set down?" Rebecca asked.

"My guess? Aguila's not on board. She wouldn't waste her time riding around while they searched. I'd say you've got a reprieve. Maybe hours, maybe a day or two, before they're back."

"Oh, God. I just want to be sick."

"So, how about we go back, sit down with the others, and figure out just what we can do?"

Rebecca's eyes betrayed panic; her hands were trembling. "It's over, isn't it?"

"Yeah. I guess it is."

51

Talbot sat on the sofa in the main room, his wounded arm aching. Dya had dropped into the chair across from him. Su and Rebecca huddled defensively on the cushions to his right and left. The children, all but Kylee and the littlest, Shine and Ngyap, sat cross-legged on the floor, thoughtful faces fixed on the adults.

Talina Perez, looking dangerous with her holstered pistol, leaned against the wall next to the great, curving expanse of window. She had her hip cocked, arms crossed, listening.

"The only place they can land something as big as the shuttle is on the fields," Talbot told his wives. "No telling how many crops they'll destroy."

"It's not like a nonrenewable resource," Su said bitterly.

"What do we expect?" Rebecca wondered. "Surely they're not just going to arrest us all at gunpoint, are they? I finished out my contract years ago."

"I haven't," Su said miserably. "I've got three years. She can order me arrested."

"She won't," Perez stated. "It's Talbot she's after. He's the key to your cooperation."

Talbot winced. "Yeah. Listen, what if I'm not here? I can hide out at one of the research stations in the forest. Lay low until—"

"What?" Rebecca demanded. "You're eaten by a bem, or sidewinder gets you? And what if she leaves a garrison here? You've got to come in sometime."

"No," Dya said emphatically, her eyes pinning Talbot's. "We're family. We face this together. What they do to one of us, they do to all of us. Either that, or we've learned nothing from what happened to Paolo and Pak. As a family unit we have a little more leverage than just Mark by himself."

Su asked, "What's to stop them from shooting us all

down? Even the children? This is just another Corporate Supervisor after all. What value do our lives have compared to the wealth of Mundo Base, let alone the symbolic power of destroying renegades who once dared and defied Clemenceau?"

"She won't shoot us all down," Talbot declared, placing a reassuring hand on Su's knee and giving it a squeeze. "We're worth way more to her alive than dead. She's a smart woman, competent, and determined to succeed. From what I learned in Port Authority, her mine and smelter are doomed unless she can figure a way to keep the forest back. She's desperate. And we're the key to her ultimate success."

Dya said, "Mark's right. The woman I met will stop at nothing to get what we have. Back in Port Authority, the only leverage she had was over Mark. I, however, had something she wanted, so she bargained. But now that they've found us? Hey, we're on our own out here. She can do anything she wants. No witnesses."

Rebecca asked, "Do you think she'd occupy Mundo? Keep us captive? Make us work at gunpoint?"

"It's not beyond her," Talbot agreed, a sinking in his gut. "Like Dya said: Way out here, who's going to know?"

"So, we're screwed one way or another?" Rebecca noted. "Whatever's coming, are we better off to just surrender, hope for the best terms we can get?" She glanced at Dya. "You dealt with her. What do you think?"

Dya shook her head in a hard no. "That woman will take all she can get. If we just offer ourselves up, she'll snap us up like a scarlet flier does an invertebrate and ask for even more. Our only hope is to figure an angle, how we can negotiate from strength."

"How do we do that?" Rebecca asked. "I mean, once she's landed, she's going to figure out that the secret's the pine belt. That the wealth is the produce. All she has to do is remind us that this is Corporate property, that Su and Mark are under contract. That the rest of us have been living here for years without contract. Essentially mooching room and board. That what's in our heads is only fair compensation for what we owe The Corporation."

"Yeah," Talbot said with a weary sigh. "That's pretty

much how it's going to go. That's the card she played when she landed at Port Authority. The difference here is that we don't have a whole town behind us. It's just the four of us. And no witnesses."

Talbot reached out with his wounded arm and laid his hand on Rebecca's shoulder as she closed her eyes and fought despair.

"Fuck them!" Su cried, the first tears leaking down her face. "We're going to lose it all anyway, right? I say fight them. Tell that Corporate slit that if she wants Mundo, she'll do it over our dead bodies!"

"And the children?" Talbot asked quietly. "You'd do that to little Taung, Ngyap, Shine? Or are you thinking about a Masada-style mass suicide?"

"It would make a statement," Dya mused. "Eventually it would get out that three pregnant women and all these kids died rather than submit to The Corporation. Perez would tell everyone in Port Authority." She paused. "But I'm against it."

"Me, too," Talbot and Rebecca said in unison.

"Damn it," Su said between sniffles.

"Corporate's got us by the balls," Dya admitted, an emptiness forming behind her eyes. "She's got the law, the marines, the shuttle, and we've got nothing."

"We could leave," Rebecca mused. "Move farther back into the forest, start from scratch."

"It would be hard, dangerous," Su agreed. "But no one on this planet knows the forest like we do."

"Be reasonable," Talbot said. "How would we carry the basic tech? We don't even have a functioning aircar. The only one that works is back in Port Authority. Trust me, but for my armor, I wouldn't be here. And sure, we're all forest-wise, but you know the odds. We might lose half of us in the first six months."

"What's the status of your armor, Mark?" Perez asked from where she'd been listening.

"Last I looked, it's at around seven percent."

Rebecca added, "I've been fiddling with it in my spare time. The power pack's been so long without a servicing it won't hold a charge. There's maybe an hour's worth of power if it's not used strenuously. Way less if you push it."

"As if we could fight our way out of this," Talbot whispered miserably. "Listen, the best plan is the first plan. Aguila lands, I walk out and surrender. I go back to Corporate Mine as her hostage with the understanding that you all will cooperate and teach her people everything you know about agriculture and dealing with Donovan's forest. Dya trades her formulae for the ability to stay here and continue her research."

"Give Aguila everything?" Su protested. "Even you?"

"I'm the weak link," Mark told them.

"If she keeps to the deal," Rebecca reminded. "Seeing Mundo, why should she? It's hers for the taking. Legally."

"This is all my fault," Talbot declared.

"The lift would have broken with or without you." Dya arched an eyebrow. "We're together in this. However it works out. Family."

"Family," Rebecca and Su declared. Then Rebecca added, "I vote that we attempt to hold her to the original deal."

Talbot said, "As long as she thought it was just Dya, Kylee, and me on a remote farmstead, we had a chance. Once she really sees Mundo, we're screwed. Completely, totally, and thoroughly screwed."

"We lose it all?" Rebecca asked in misery, as if she couldn't believe it.

Perez had been staring out the window at the grounds below. Now she asked, "Rebecca? Do you have a piece of scientific equipment that would project focused heat across a distance of, say, fifty meters? Maybe like an infrared projector?"

"What part of the words 'agricultural research base' did you not get, Perez? Of course we do. And, in case you haven't been paying attention, our lives are falling apart here. We're about to lose our home and our integrity. So, do you mind?"

Perez turned, expression thoughtful. "Actually, I do mind. And on a whole lot of different levels. Dya and Mark are right about Aguila. As it sits right now, you don't have a leg to stand on." She smiled, emphatically repeating, "As it sits right now."

Talbot saw a sudden hope flicker to life in Dya's face as

she shifted her attention to Perez and asked, "What are you thinking, Talina?"

"Depends on a lot of variables at this point, but I need to know, if it meant a chance to save yourselves, would you tear down those drying sheds that you've built on the old landing pad?"

"Tear them down?" Rebecca asked.

"Yeah, to create a space where the shuttle would land right here, next to the shops and storage buildings. Might need to move some of that mothballed equipment, too."

Talbot shot to his feet, walking over to stare into Perez's eyes. "Why?"

The woman gave him a catlike smile. "We've got at least twenty-four hours, worn-out combat armor, an IR projector, two combat-capable rifles, and tactical position. The unknown is if Aguila will have her marines fully suited up. Still, we start from strength."

"Didn't you hear? My armor's shot. Less than an hour before it seizes up. When it does, I'm essentially paralyzed. Locked solid. And another thing. I've got one round of explosive left for the rifle. One. As in *uno*."

"Should do the trick," Perez said airily, and turned to Rebecca, Su, and Dya. "Of course, I'm assuming you won't mind participating in a little white lie? Falsifying some records, perjuring yourselves in the name of the common good?"

"What the hell are you talking about?" Su asked, scrambling to her feet. "And why the hell should we trust a piece of walking shit like you?"

Rebecca rose, placed a restraining hand on Su's shoulder, and said, "Easy, Su. Talina, assume we're at your mercy. What do you need?"

"We'll need a clean sheet of paper. Can your radio room still receive scanned data? Print it?"

"Of course."

Perez glanced from face to face, and then down at the children where they waited on the floor, looking frightened and stunned. "Okay, folks. Let's get to work."

To Talbot she said, "You and Dya, get the armor down to ground level. Then figure out how quickly and cleanly you can knock those sheds down and get the debris clear of the shuttle landing field."

To Rebecca and Su, she said, "You two, you're with me. We've got paperwork to do."

"How will this save us?" Su demanded hostilely.

"Not sure it will," Perez told her. "But even a toilet-sucking chance is better than no chance at all. Either this works, or we're all dead."

52

When it came to the scales of personal vendetta, Kalico Aguila kept very good score. Since the shuttle's return yesterday afternoon, she'd been stewing not only over the photos that betrayed the extent of Mark Talbot and Dya Simonov's deception, but when and how to act against them.

The mobbers, however, ranked at the very top.

And they were due again sometime around midday.

Kalico meant to be present when they came. Meant to play a role in the extermination of the whole accursed flock if she could. But then people had been telling her that she was a vindictive bitch since she'd been in her teens.

That didn't mean that she couldn't concentrate on finalizing her plans for Talbot and his complicitous wife. "Farmstead out west, my unholy ass," Kalico muttered as she studied the images taken by the shuttle as it had flown over Mundo Base the day before.

Across the table from her, Lieutenant Spiro bent over the enlarged image, arms braced, expression thoughtful. She shifted, pointing with her right forefinger. "There's another person. Two women down at the southern end of the field. Another two children going into this shop-looking structure. Then this woman here by this shed and this man picking vegetables in the field."

"That's Talbot." Kalico indicated the white speck on his upper arm. "That's the bandage where you shot him."

"And none of the women are Dya Simonov. She's blonde. These are all brunette or black-haired. How many people do you think are living there?"

"A lot more than we thought." Kalico smiled. "Mundo Research Base. Makarov wasn't even twenty minutes into his search before he had them. Oh, how cunning Simonov and Talbot were. Just a small farmstead hacked out of the forest? In a rat's ass! The dome by itself is stunning."

Spiro grinned in satisfaction. "I am so going to love busting that guy."

"Lieutenant, I do *not* want him hurt. He's important to Simonov, and that woman's important to me. Very important. Do you understand?"

"Yes, ma'am."

"Repeat it so that we're clear."

"You do not want him hurt."

"Correct. Your mission is to fly down there, land, and apprehend Mark Talbot. Once you have him in custody, you are to bring him back here to me. You are not to harm anyone else. You don't break anything, shoot anything, or act in a manner that will in any way alienate Dya Simonov or any of the other inhabitants."

"And if they resist, ma'am? I can go in with the best of intentions, but in any conflict, the other side has a say in how it's going to go down."

"Are you telling me, Lieutenant, that you can't figure out how to conduct an apprehension without precipitating a shootout? Is this your way of saying that I'd better do this myself because you're incapable of following orders?"

Spiro stiffened, lips twitching, eyes hot. "No, ma'am!"

"Good. Because you've stretched your rope remarkably thin, Lieutenant. You and I both know that you meant that grenade for Perez, but you got a nurse. A nurse who'd been treating me, for God's sake! So if you can't get Talbot out without poisoning the well at Mundo, I need to know. And the reason's pretty clear: We're all going to have to be drinking from that water."

"It's a Corporate property," Spiro countered. "It's *yours*. Those people down there are yours. Who gives a damn what they think?"

Kalico sighed, fingered her chin as she studied her lieutenant. "They've been independent for six years. Clemenceau had two of their men shot. By Perez, no less, which is a stroke of luck for me."

"She flew them out of Port Authority."

"To keep from having to face her own people over that little girl's damned quetzal. No. I have to play this very carefully. If I go in there slamming my fist, giving orders, telling them their meat is in my frying pan, there's no telling what they'll do. Fanatics are crazy. They might burn the place down around their ears just to keep me from getting my fingers on it."

"So I apprehend Talbot. What then?"

"Leave them for a couple of days. Let them stew about his fate. Let them integrate the knowledge that Corporate Marines took one of theirs before I show up and give them a human face, a more personal approach."

Kalico was thinking of her people, the ones now firmly in her corner as they fought to save Corporate Mine. Her job was to convince Dya that while yes, Mundo Base was Corporate property, there was a way that she and the others could stay. Could continue their lives at the price of a few staples and the loss of a little control.

"And who knows? Some of those people down there might still be under contract." To Spiro she added, "You remind Talbot that he's a marine and under orders. That contracts will be fulfilled. Agreements must be upheld. Tell him specifically while in the presence of others, that I am willing to consider his absence as official leave rather than desertion and dereliction of duty." Kalico smiled, adding, "We want to look as reasonable as we can."

"Yes, ma'am."

Kalico checked the time. "Take a small detail. No more than five. I don't want to panic those people or make them think they're invaded."

"Yes, ma'am."

Kalico studied her lieutenant. "Deb, I mean it. If you botch this, don't come back."

Spiro's lips were twitching again. She snapped a perfect salute, barked, "Yes, ma'am," and wheeled on her heel. Back erect, she strode from the room.

After she was gone, Kalico stared down at the image. The place was a perfect rectangle. The forest crowding a thick line of terrestrial trees. Mature trees that had been there for years. Could the answer be as simple as that? No burning, explosives, walls of fire, poisons, or trenching? Just trees?

She chewed her lips as she studied the place. The lift broke and Kylee was injured. What else was falling apart at Mundo?

She whispered, "Mundo is Corporate property. But it is your home. As The Corporation's Supervisor on Donovan, I have an obligation to my Boardmembers to maintain the property. In return, we are willing to pay those of you who aren't under contract to continue your fine work."

Give consideration to their sense of independence. Let them maintain the illusion that they still have it.

Yes, that should do it.

53

Exhausted, Talina walked down the hall toward the bedrooms. She had just finished a superbly cooked breakfast—one filled with freshly baked dark rye bread, cereal made of chia, teff, and assorted berries. Tastes that her mouth had forgotten even existed.

They'd finished with preparations late the night before; it had been well after midnight when she, Talbot, Rebecca, and Dya had struggled wearily up the poorly lit stairs. Damned long climb that. Just a couple of trips had turned her into a "fix the lift" convert.

Talina had actually managed to catch four hours of sleep last night. They'd put her in Dya's bed, sharing the room along with Kylee and Rocket. She'd felt a bit awkward, having killed Dya's husband. That somehow, taking the woman's bed played out as a form of ultimate betrayal. Her discomfort had been short, however; she'd been out within moments of her head hitting the pillow.

It wasn't Talina's business to speculate on where the others slept, or how they'd occupied the hours. Maybe they'd all shared the same bed, realizing this might well be the last night they spent as a family.

What did you do when you faced the end of your world? Talina suspected it was a lot more about holding each other, taking comfort from that primate need to hug loved ones close in times of trial.

As Talina stepped into Dya's room, it was to find Talbot already there, butt propped on the edge of Kylee's bed. He was holding the crutches he'd made. Had figured they would give the girl a boost, a chance to look forward to walking.

Rocket perched at the window, staring out at the morning. His head swiveled, his three eyes fixing on Talina. A chirped greeting issued from the beast's throat. Rocket had already made his way down to the ground, enjoyed his morning hunt, and carefully climbed his way back up the stairs. He had to go slowly to keep his claws from catching in the grating on the steps.

No doubt the young quetzal missed the lift, too.

Talina's own quetzal curled tighter inside her, as if irritated at the youngster's presence.

Walking in on the conversation, Talina said, "I'm just here to collect my rifle and pack. Be gone in a second."

"No, stay," Kylee pleaded.

Talbot told her, "Kylee thinks you're a hero."

"Kid, I'm a lot of things. Hero isn't one of them."

"You got Rocket and me out of Port Authority when people were going to kill him." The girl looked up at Talina with solemn blue eyes.

Rocket chirped in agreement.

The more Talina got to know the young quetzal, the more she suspected that the creature's understanding of human speech was a lot more sophisticated than anyone knew.

"Not the preferred alternative. We wanted you in the hospital where Raya could keep an eye on you. How you feeling? Any pain?"

Kylee grimaced. "It's like a throbbing ache from the top of my hip down to my knee. Rebecca was in this morning, checking temperatures. Nothing in the deep tissue to indicate infection. Dya says that her research indicates accelerated vascularization, especially around the incisions. When the shuttle showed up yesterday she had tissue samples under the scope. She says there are unusual protein sequences. Probably quetzal mixed in with normal human scarring fibers in the dermis."

"Are you really nine?" Talina asked skeptically.

"Why do people keep asking that?" Kylee wondered. "I'm just telling you that we think my healing is remarkably advanced given the extent of the trauma."

Talina glanced at Talbot. "I tell you, Kylee's the result of an experiment to put a thirty-year-old scientist into a nine-year-old girl's body."

Talina winked when Kylee stuck out her tongue in a very nine-year-old's petulant riposte.

"I thought the same thing the day she found me." Talbot reached out, ruffling her silky blonde locks.

"So, do you think they're coming today?" Kylee asked. "Did you get everything ready?"

Talina walked over and picked up her rifle. "Rebecca was still assembling the IR projector when I came up to grab a quick breakfast. At least they weren't waiting for us at first light. That would have screwed us royally."

"What Talina's saying is that I have to go, too," Talbot told Kylee, standing, and placing the crutches against the wall. He took the little girl's hand, giving it one last squeeze. "No matter what, you know that I love you. So you just concentrate on getting well."

"It's serious, isn't it?" Kylee asked. "You sure Rocket and I shouldn't be there?"

"You kidding?" Talbot cried. "If you hadn't gotten yourself hurt, we'd sic you and Rocket on Supervisor Aguila. The rest of us could just stand back and watch as you took her apart."

"Think I'm scary, huh, Mark?" Kylee asked.

"I sure as hell wouldn't cross you, kid," Talina told her. "If I were Aguila, I'd be shaking in my boots."

Rocket chirped again.

"And you, you little twerp"—Talina pointed at the quetzal—"you do everything she tells you."

Rocket replied with a rapid clacking of his jaws, bands of white and iridescent red rippling in waves along his collar.

Kylee's expression darkened. "What you're doing, it could all go wrong, couldn't it?"

Talbot nodded. "We're playing one hell of a bluff down there. Speaking of which, I've got to get ready. See you, buttercup. You know how much I love you."

"See you, too," Kylee said. "You be careful, Dad."

Talbot bent down and kissed her forehead, then hesitated on his way to the door, looking back one last time.

"Talina?" Kylee asked. "Could you stay a minute?"

Talina shot a mystified glance at Talbot before he walked away, then turned back, asking, "What do you need, kid?"

Kylee studied her as if choosing her words. "Thank you

for what you did for us in Port Authority. Especially for keeping Rocket safe."

The quetzal studied her, chittering, bands of blue and pink running down its sides.

"Just doing my job. You and Rocket, you're in a different place than the rest of Donovan. Maybe way ahead of the rest of us. My people don't know what that means yet. Hell, I've got a quetzal inside me, and I'm terrified."

"I'm sorry for you," Kylee said softly. "So's Rocket."

The young quetzal uttered a deep-throated warbling, its three eyes fixed on Talina.

"Don't be sorry. Maybe it's that karma that Shig's always rattling on about."

"Because you killed my father and Paolo?"

Talina's gut tightened, her quetzal hissing in derision. "Some things can't be forgiven. They can only be atoned for."

"I've got a bad feeling about this. So does Rocket. We've talked about you. A lot. We think you're a good woman who was in a bad circumstance, and Pak was at the wrong place at the wrong time. If it were up to me, I'd ask you to come live with us. I'd like it if you were part of our family. Rocket and me, we think you're worthy."

Talina stopped short as the words sank in. She swallowed hard. Struggled for words. Couldn't find anything but guilt.

"You keep Mark and Rebecca safe down there," Kylee told her. "Make sure we win."

"Yeah," Talina said through a tight throat and fled the room. Damned kid, why the hell did she have go and say a thing like that?

54

The mobbers were late. Again Kalico checked the time, then turned her eyes to the sky. What if they didn't come today? What if they came by surprise, say, tomorrow afternoon? When shifts were changing? When her people weren't prepared?

As she had all morning, she carefully scanned the strategically parked vehicles and the large open space they'd created where the shuttle usually sat. A circle of packed clay, fifty meters in diameter. She, Ghosh, and Ituri stood right in the center of it. Three crates, hatches open, had been dug into the ground. Surrounding her, Privates Finnegan, Miso, Anderssoni, and Michegan stood in their gleaming combat armor. Each carried a quickly fabricated eight-gauge shotgun. The twenty-pound pieces boasted rotary magazines filled with hastily constructed shot shells.

The cannons waited on elevated platforms around the compound peripheries; armored marines serviced each piece. The fields of fire had been carefully chosen to disperse the maximum amount of shot with the minimum potential of damage to vehicles and equipment.

But it all hinged on getting the entire flock in close. Concentrated in that open circle. The kill had to be fast, clean, with as little chance as possible for any of the flying fiends to escape.

"Come on." Kalico took a deep breath.

"They haven't made a kill since the first attack," Ghosh reminded. "Maybe they've lost interest?"

"Think we should have sacrificed a victim? Oh, say, maybe Tom Dalway?"

"The young man who sweeps up the cafeteria and empties the trash?" Kalico asked.

"The guy's about as lazy as they come." Ituri frowned up at the sky. "You ask me, he's a complete waste of skin."

"This is patrol two," her implant told her. *"We've spot-*

ted them. They just took a dive into the forest about three thousand meters to the south. We're backing off. We'll try and maintain visual. Hope to spot them when they emerge from the trees again."

"Roger that," the radio room responded. *"On your toes, people!"*

As per signal, Bill Jones detonated a blasting cap, the bang loud enough to alert everyone that the mobbers were coming. Normally they sounded the siren, but had decided not to, lest—thinking the humans alerted—the beasts might not press their attack.

"You ready?" Ghosh asked, dropping to a knee to once again test the door to his subterranean crate.

Kalico experienced an unsettling squirmy feeling in the pit of her stomach. "Bit nerve-wracking, isn't it?" she asked, and couldn't stem the nervous laughter that followed.

Ituri, too, stooped to check his crate. That plastic door would be all that stood between him and the flying terror.

"Sure do envy those marines in their armor." Ghosh had straightened and slapped Miso's impervious carapace.

"Hey, we gotcha covered, Doc," Miso told him, his servo-augmented arm swinging the shotgun as if it were a straw. "We clean up anything the cannons miss."

"Yeah, don't worry about us," Michegan added. "Even if we catch part of the blast, at this distance lead pellets will just spatter on the armor. Biggest danger we face is from lead exposure when we clean the stuff off later."

"Got them," Kalico heard in her implant. *"Two hundred fifty degrees, about a thousand meters and closing."*

"Shit," Kalico whispered, dropping down to make sure her own door swung freely.

It did.

She stood, heart beginning to pound. Nervous energy pumped its jitters through every muscle.

"Rethinking this plan?" Ghosh asked dryly. "I sure am."

"We've got to have bait," Kalico told him. "Who else could we ask to do this?"

"Don't dismiss our people so readily," Ituri added, his gaze pinned on the southeast. "You didn't have to do this, Supervisor."

"Yeah"—she licked her suddenly dry lips—"I did."

Images of the flapping horror lingered just behind her conscious mind. Memories of the pain and sickening terror of those slashing claws, the jaws ripping at her flesh. Something deep in her psyche shrieked in terror.

"They're on the ascent. Seconds away, people. This is it."

"Fuck," Kalico whispered under her breath. Aloud, she said, "Make it good. We can't go to ground too soon. Wait for my order."

"Don't wait too long." Ghosh swallowed hard. The man's face had blanched to an uncommon white.

The first of the mobbers appeared so quickly they might have squirted into the sky. Then came the rest, shooting in behind the first. A living column of intermingling hunters. Thousands of beating wings—the sound of them triggered a panic that froze Kalico in place.

In that instant she was back, in the darkness, flooded with fear, pain, and horror. She could feel the beasts as they beat against her body, fluttered off the insides of the crate. A crawling anticipation ran across her skin: tender, quivering in anticipation of the cuts and tearing jaws.

She blinked, couldn't breathe. Conflicting images flashed in her vision: Here and now mixing with then and there. Confusion. The sure knowledge that she was about to die.

"Kalico!" Ghosh screamed as the column of flapping death—a silhouetted writhing and pulsing mass—filled the sky.

"What do we do?" Ituri almost squealed as the swarm began to split in two, as though to search in different directions.

Got to get them here.

Here.

"Here!" She put words to her terrified thoughts. "Here, damn you!"

Move. Got to move.

"Hey, you motherfuckers! Here!" She leaped, waving her arms, frantically, charging forward. "Come on, you pieces of shit! Come get me!"

Kalico's desperately charged muscles lent her strength as she jumped high, screamed her fear and rage. She leaped up, leaped again, shrieking, cursing, kicking and darting, anything to draw their attention.

The splitting flock slowed, hesitated, and she could sense the sudden attention she'd drawn.

"You bastards!" she bellowed at them, voice tearing. "I'm going to kill you all! Shoot your carcasses from the sky! Come and get me, you flying shits! Come try your luck!"

She leaped again, flailing her arms about, ran to one side, stopped, and ran back.

And, oh, yes, here they came. The tone of the chattering calls deepened, became a hollow hooting. She'd heard that sound before; knew what it meant. Like ice water dumped in her veins, she froze. Fought for breath, and watched the oncoming mass of screeching, flapping terrors. Colors were flashing in vibrant, almost glowing reds, blues, and yellows across their bodies.

"*Kalico!*" Ghosh's screamed warning barely penetrated the magnitude of what she was seeing. The flock blotted Capella's light. A vast movement of death. Centered on her. Devouring the very sky.

Run!

She might have been made of wood, so slowly did she turn. In her panic, she fixed on Ghosh and Ituri. It struck her that she'd never seen them look so horrified. How odd that their faces could contort so, that their eyes could express such soul-rending terror?

Her feet barely touched the earth, her arms pounding with each stride. She seemed stuck in time and space. A mote unnoticed by the universe.

The sensation lasted but an instant, and she flickered back to reality. The world snapped into sudden focus. Details clarified: the texture of the beaten clay beneath her feet; the glinting of light on the marines' armor; the black muzzles of the raised shotguns; the distant forest greens beyond the perimeter fence; even the rush of air past her ears and through her hair as she sprinted with all her might toward her buried crate and the protection it provided.

She was still a couple of meters away when Ghosh and Ituri dove for their boxes.

Bastards didn't wait for my orders!

She barely had time to consider the implications when Miso, the closest marine, fired his shotgun.

She heard the shot ripping air past her right ear, was slapped by the gun's report, and half stumbled.

Not a heartbeat later, Michegan's weapon discharged. Something flapped immediately behind her head. She felt her hair jerk as it was grabbed.

Oh, God no!

There, in the ground. Right before her!

Kalico threw herself headlong into the sunken crate. Hit hard. Yellow streaks of light flashed through her head at the impact. She couldn't breathe, could only gasp.

I'm going to die.

She managed to turn her head, to stare up at the beating wings. Saw the sunlight glinting on those deadly claws. Met the eyes of the nearest three-eyed beast dropping from the sky . . .

And jerked as the lid was slammed shut from the outside.

An instant later, she heard and felt the impact as tens of bodies slammed against the duraplast. She clapped hands to her ears, whimpered as a hundred mobbers clawed at the thin sheet of graphite and plastic that separated her from death.

She flinched again when the first cannon fired. Air hissed as the shot ripped through it. Pellets tore through flesh: a surprising, wet, snapping sound.

Then came a series of concussions as the other cannons fired. The snappier bangs of the marines' shotguns followed in short order. Bodies were whacking into the ground, thumping hollowly off the crate door above her. Death literally falling from the sky as a fury of shot tore into the swarm.

Petrified, Kalico huddled against the smooth sides of her crate. Inexorably, her whimpers faded, and she began to sob.

She couldn't stop the shaking, or the nausea that came rushing up from her gut.

I can't stand this. God, just let it be over.

55

"**K**alico?" came Ghosh's call. "You all right?"

In the darkness of her protective crate, Kalico Aguila shivered, blinked, and slowly lowered her hands from her ears. It took three tries before she could manage a feeble, "Yeah, I'm all right."

Her heart continued to pound, and she was trying to nerve herself to open the door when the lid was pulled back. Capella's harsh light blinded her, and she threw an arm up. From its protective shadow, she squinted up at the two shadowed silhouettes looming above.

An arm was extended, and she somehow summoned the energy to reach up. Let them pull her up from her would-be coffin. Curious, wasn't it, that she could consider the crate in such terms?

She took a deep breath of the fresh air, found it mingled with an odd scent—a fatty, coppery, and sour smell.

Unwilling to trust her legs to support her, she compromised by sitting on the edge of the crate where it lay flush with the ground. As her eyes adjusted, they had to absorb the sight: hundreds of torn, bleeding, and ruptured bodies lay in all directions. Spots of fierce color—blues, yellows, and greens intermingled with the iridescent and striking scarlet that made mobbers so visually stunning.

This time, when she met the beasts' three-eyed stare, it was to look into death's dull gaze. Mouths that had once snapped with vicious intent now gaped; tongues lolled onto the clay. The laser-bright wings with their curious non-feathers flopped out, extended or broken. The claws, which had once terrorized Donovan's skies, glinted impotently. Even as she stared, the blood and fluids that had once powered the creatures leaked from their torn bodies, pooled atop the impermeable clays of the landing field.

"Kalico?" Ghosh asked again. "You sure you're all right?"

"Ma'am," Private Finnegan said, "you're bleeding? Did they cut you?"

She looked down, seeing the spots of crimson spreading on her clothing. "No. Just tore some of the stitches when I landed hard in the crate."

Private Michegan, shotgun at port arms, bent down on one knee. She raised her visor to expose concerned features. "You cut that damn close. I thought for a second they had you."

"Did we . . ." Kalico swallowed against the urge to throw up. "Did we get them? All of them?"

"Think so, ma'am. We'll have to run the video to be sure. But damn, I mean was that an incredible sight or what? You should have seen it. I mean, you will. On the video. But watching those cannon shots blasting through that flock. You'll see. Blew the damn mobbers into pieces in midair. Chunks and bodies falling everywhere.

"And between cannon rounds, we were trying to pick up concentrations, blasting any bunch that clustered. The fool things kept attacking us. As if they could so much as scratch our armor. They just wouldn't give up. It was crazy. They just kept at us until we shot the last of them out of the sky."

Kalico stared at the splotches of goo on Michegan's armor, realized it was mobber guts that literally dripped from the smooth surface.

"Wouldn't have worked without you, ma'am." Private Finnegan had secured his shotgun and came forward, kicking the corpses of dead mobbers out of the way. "They were splitting apart. Would have been two flocks in another couple of seconds. I thought you'd lost your mind when you went running out there, screaming. But, by damn, Supervisor, you sure knew your shit. You brought 'em right to the killing ground. You saved what was about to be a disaster, turned it into a success."

"Damn straight," Michegan added. "Ma'am, you can be on my fire team anytime."

Kalico took a deep breath, heavy as it was with the stench of new death. She thought her wits had recovered, so she stood, discovered her legs would hold her. That the shakes had gone.

She climbed the rest of the way out of her box, stepped

around a pile of broken and torn mobber bodies. "We're going to have to get this cleaned up. I say toss them into one of the skips, fly them out over the forest and pull the drop cord."

"Yes, ma'am." Finnegan gave her a crisp salute.

Ghosh and Ituri followed as she started picking her way through the mess of blasted bodies, then realized the hopelessness. Screw it, she wasn't going to reach the admin dome without fouling her shoes, so she took the straightest path treading on the corpses.

"You played that way too close for my taste," Ituri muttered. "I know you wanted them all, but what if they'd caught you?"

She was able to jump one last pile of corpses. The few outliers could now be easily avoided. From the dome, the mine, and various pieces of equipment, people were now flooding out, exclaiming as they tried to absorb the scene.

"I didn't realize how close that was," she told them. "I was going to yell at you for not awaiting my order."

"By the time I reached out and slammed my lid shut, I didn't have it latched before they were clawing at the duraplast," Ituri confessed. "I have no idea how you got yours closed without trapping a bunch of those things inside with you."

"I didn't. Had to be one of the marines." But which one? She needed to find out.

She exhaled with weary relief as she stepped into the safety and cleaner air of the admin dome. Her muscles felt like rubber, barely managing the simple task of walking.

All she wanted to do was pour herself a stiff drink of Inga's whiskey before throwing herself on her bed to vegetate for a couple of hours. Wanted to tend her reopened wounds. For the most part, they'd ceased to bleed. But no. Damn it, her people needed to see her now.

Coffee. Today's success justified a cup of their dwindling supply of coffee.

Thus heartened, she actually smiled at Igor Stryski where he waited just outside her office door. "We got 'em."

Stryski's expression, however, didn't brighten. "Ma'am. I was in charge of checking stations before the mobber attack. I, uh, found something. You'd better come see."

"Where?"

"Barracks, ma'am. Male showers."

"Do you need us?" Ghosh asked, indicating Ituri and himself.

"Might be best if you came along," Stryski told them.

The mechanic led the way back out the front, along the path that led to the barracks where they backed against the perimeter fence. Inside, the building was quiet. Normal shifts had been dispensed with in anticipation of the mobber attack. She passed the ranks of cubicles with their four-tiered bunks.

The men's bathroom was in the rear right, the women's on the left. Strysky pushed the door open, leading Kalico into the room. The place was a prefab, like everything at Corporate Mine. Standard layout with six toilets, four urinals, seven sinks, and in the rear an open shower with four heads and a central drain.

The woman, naked, hung from a thick wire that had been pulled through a truss in the ceiling and tied off on the post that supported the closest toilet stall.

Kalico caught her breath, disturbed by the odd angle of the woman's neck, by the way her bruise-black tongue protruded between her lips, and how the wire had cut so deeply into her neck behind the angle of the jaw.

Lividity had purpled her feet and lower legs. The woman's gut sagged where the muscles now stretched, and a pool of urine had mostly dried around a single feces where her sphincter had relaxed. Letters that Kalico couldn't quite make out from this angle were scrawled over her chest and breasts.

"Know her?" Stryski asked.

"Red hair." Kalico rubbed the back of her neck. "Yeah, I know her. Rita Valerie. What's the writing?"

She stepped around, reading aloud, "I ratted out." She frowned. "What's that mean?"

"I don't know," Stryski said. "I didn't touch anything. Thought you'd want this taken care of carefully. I mean, I don't know what effect this will have on everybody."

"Why'd she kill herself?" Ghosh asked. "Last I heard she and the rest were relieved to be out of that man Wirth's hands."

"She didn't kill herself," Stryski replied. "There's no chair, nothing to stand on. She was hoisted." He pointed to where the wire was knotted on the post. "Whoever did it was strong enough to lift her weight and hold it while he tied her off."

"Or there was more than one," Kalico countered.

Stryski fingered his jaw. "No cameras in here. Couldn't pick a better place for a murder."

Kalico said, "Aurobindo, check with Petre Howe and Ashanti Kung's supervisors. Find out when they went on shift today, what their duties were, and if they were ever out of sight."

"Yes, ma'am. What do you want us to do with Valerie's body?"

Kalico considered. "Everyone's out front dealing with the mobbers. We've got a small window of opportunity here. I want her taken down. Tarp the body to disguise it, then fly it down to the farm field and bury her. Can you do that without being seen, Igor?"

"Yes, ma'am." He was giving her an uncertain look.

"Let's see who asks about her first. If her supervisors are the first, or if it's her friends. And how they ask could be important. Her disappearance might be more unsettling to the murderer than if we made a major investigation of it. Meanwhile, I want round-the-clock surveillance on Kung and Howe. Microdrones, long-range microphones, night vision. Whatever it takes. If they killed her, they'll discuss it. Probably sooner rather than later, and we'll have them."

"What if it wasn't them?" Ituri asked.

"In that case, we're playing under a whole new set of rules."

I ratted out. What the hell does that mean?

But the hanging woman with her swollen tongue and bugged-out, dead eyes offered no answer.

56

Lieutenant Deb Spiro watched the ground swell as she peered over Ensign Makarov's shoulder. The impenetrable forest stretched endlessly in all directions, while below the rectangle of cleared land seemed impossibly small, a tiny pinprick of human intervention in an ocean of clumpy greens.

"Talbot, you're going to feel even smaller and more helpless," Spiro promised. "You worthless piece of shit, you're about to lose even this fruitless refuge."

"Where do you want me to set down?" Makarov asked. "On the old shuttle landing?"

Spiro considered the compound as they circled the dome atop its tower. By damn, the ensign was right. There it was. A shuttle port where there had been none before. She'd thoroughly studied the reconnaissance images. There had been buildings there, and she damned well knew it.

"Yeah. If that's their invite, we'll take it. If they're planning a trap, let's spring it. Can you scan for explosives in case they mined it?"

"Sure. I can hit it with ground penetrating radar when we're at thirty meters. Any recent excavation will show up as a hot spot, and an explosives packet will have a different signature entirely."

"Do it. What do your thermal sensors show? I want to know just how many people are down there. Where they're hiding."

"You got it, Lieutenant." At his command, the sensor projections switched to a thermal image of the compound. "I've got two people, both adults, on the ground. Down south, at the edge of the tree line, I've got another adult and a bunch of what appears to be children. Seven of them. Shooting my projector through the dome, I've got what looks like two children in an upper bedroom and another adult in the base of the dome."

"That's it?" Spiro asked, glancing back at her four marines.

"That's it." Makarov sounded sure of himself.

"Damn, and I thought this was going to be difficult. Take us down. Scan the shuttle field, and if it's clear, put us down. Right up close."

"Affirmative, Lieutenant."

Spiro kept glancing at the lateral sensors, reading the little blips that indicated electrically powered machines, thermal signatures from water lines, cisterns, and different pieces of equipment. She saw nothing that resembled a missile, artillery tube, or potential threat to the shuttle. But then, way out here, they'd have never thought they'd be found.

"No sign of buried explosives, Lieutenant." Makarov had his eyes fixed on his screens.

She watched through the forward transparency as they dropped down past the dome. Makarov neatly maneuvered them onto the pad, setting them down like a feather onto a pillow.

"All right, people," Spiro called over the turbines as she clipped her helmet to her belt and stood. "We're just here for Talbot. Ordering him back to duty. Smile. Be friendly. Supervisor Aguila doesn't want any trouble."

"Right, Lieutenant," Michegan called back. "We're all warm and cuddly."

"Weapons hot?" Chavez asked.

"Chambered, safeties on, and slung," she decided. "If by some chance we end up in the shit, we'll have it figured in plenty of time to unsling, pull 'em up, and start shooting."

"Helmets?" Private Nashala asked.

"Clipped to your belts. We want them to see people, not faceless warriors. Just being in armor sends all the message we need."

"Roger that, Lieutenant," Miso replied as she headed for the ramp.

The thrusters had spooled down and a curious silence filled the shuttle. Palm hovering over the hatch release, Spiro couldn't help but smile. "Talbot, you poor son of a bitch."

She slapped the button. Hydraulics whined, and the hatch lowered to the newly baked clay.

The fresh odors of forest, moisture, and flowering plants carried past the acrid smell from the thrusters.

Spiro led the way down the ramp, her right hand on her rifle sling. Damn Talbot, anyway. She'd ended up in the shit because the moron had deserted in the first place, then brought a fucking quetzal into the hospital in the second. And, pus-bucket-fuck-up that it had been, she'd seen him through the window: An armed deserter, holding a weapon in an engaged position, not more than a meter and a half from the Supervisor. Looked just like a hostage situation.

Of course, she'd shot him.

"Wish I'd taken a half second longer to aim," she muttered. If she'd killed his ass, she'd have had more time to go after the quetzal. And that slit, Perez, would never have snuck up behind her.

She stepped out on the Mundo landing pad, taking a slow scan of the weathered buildings, the parked and tarped equipment. "Ensign Makarov? What do your sensors tell you?"

Got two people moving in your direction. Neither is carrying anything resembling a weapon, Lieutenant. The closest is going to appear around that big white shop at your ten o'clock.

"Roger that."

Spiro started for the corner of the building. What looked like an old-fashioned water pump sat slightly to the right. A desolate tractor, missing wheels, rested on blocks to the left.

Right on schedule a woman wearing a smock dress woven of some brown material appeared around the corner of the shop. Spiro figured her at about one hundred ninety centimeters, definitely mature. Maybe in her late forties. The woman's thick dark-brown hair had started to gray, and her face was weathered.

"Can I help you?" she asked.

"I'm Lieutenant Spiro. I need to speak with Private Mark Talbot. Corporate business. Doesn't concern you."

"The Corporation has no business here, Lieutenant. You are on private property. Not only did you not request permission to land, but you did so without so much as announcing your arrival. That being the case, we ask that you turn right around and leave."

Spiro tensed, a quiver of annoyance triggering a nerve in her cheek. "And just who are you?"

"I'm Rebecca Smart. Call me the village elder. Head of the family. And you, Lieutenant Spiro, are trespassing."

Spiro fought down her rising anger. "Rebecca Smart? Maybe you've been taking your name too seriously. Bucking me and my marines is anything but smart. Actually, you're full of shit. This is Corporate property. That's the Supervisor's jurisdiction. And I'm here on her business. That being the case, we'll fly where we want. Land where we want. Additionally, we expect Corporate contractees to comply with orders. Private Talbot is under my command. I need to speak with him."

"You say you value contractual obligations? Is that correct?"

"Damn straight, as they say here."

The woman smiled slightly. From a pocket she produced a sheaf of papers. "This *was* Corporate property, Lieutenant. Right up until your Supervisor brokered a deal with Port Authority to recognize properly filed deeds and titles to land, improvements, and equipment. I assume that, as a commanding officer, you're familiar with what a properly filed deed looks like? That you recognize Yvette Dushane's signature?"

Spiro glared, shot a suspicious glance at the paper the woman flourished. "Why don't you hand that over so I can take a good look at it?"

"Of course. Keep in mind, Lieutenant, that is only a copy. We keep the originals in a safe place, and its duplicate is on file in Yvette's records in Port Authority."

Spiro took the papers, scanning the contents. Could have been space shit for all she knew. She handed the papers back, saying, "I know bullshit when I hear it. We're not here to start a ruckus. We just need Mark Talbot."

"Thought Dya and the Supervisor had a deal."

"The deal was that Talbot wouldn't be charged with desertion and dereliction of duty. Now, Supervisor Aguila has kindly agreed, in her own words, 'that due to the special circumstances, Private Talbot has been on extended leave.' That leave is hereby canceled, and Private Talbot is required to return to his duty."

The woman crossed her arms. "We do not give him permission to leave. We will, however, offer the Supervisor compensation, to be mutually agreed upon, for Talbot's contract. Included in that will be Mark's willing agreement to teach the Supervisor's people survival skills, and to share his observations on forest ecology."

Spiro blinked. "Lady, are you right in the head? This is not a fucking negotiation. I'm here for my marine, and I'm damned well going to get him."

"As one of the governors of Mundo Base, I am ordering you, and your people, to get back on that shuttle and fly your asses out of here."

"Or what?"

"We will file charges against you to be decided at an inquest. I would suggest Inga's in Port Authority as neutral ground. Shig and Yvette can act as—"

"Fuck that. Miso!"

"Yes, Lieutenant?"

"Line out. Search the grounds. Don't break anything. Don't hurt anyone. Just find Talbot wherever that coward toilet-sucker has gone to ground."

"Roger that," Miso called. "Squad. Fan out. Search the premises!"

Spiro reached out with an armored hand and effortlessly pushed the woman out of her way. Made sure she didn't fling her against the shop wall like a rag doll. See? Deb Spiro could control her reflexes when she . . .

"Belay that order!" came a shouted command, and from behind a shed at the edge of the shuttle pad, an armored marine stepped out, rifle shouldered and at the ready. "Stop where you are," Talbot's voice thundered through his helmet speakers.

"Talbot, you piece of shit," Spiro said, wheeling, pawing for her weapon.

"Stand down, Deb." Talbot's speaker voice boomed. "I mean it. You take one more move, and I'll discharge a full magazine of AP into the shuttle thrusters. It's just a couple of ounces on the trigger. That's all it will take."

Spiro stared in disbelief. Took in the angle of his stance, his shouldered weapon's aim. Damn him, he wouldn't!

"You shot me, Deb. From behind. When all I was trying to do was keep a little girl alive." She could hear the stress in Talbot's voice. "Now, the Supervisor made a deal with the Donovanians that she'd honor their contracts. We've got you on video and audio not only saying that you won't honor those contracts, but physically pushing Rebecca out of the way. An unarmed woman who offered to deal fairly with the Supervisor."

Spiro took a hard breath, felt the frustration as it burned through her breast.

"Lieutenant?" Miso asked softly from behind.

"Don't even think it, Katsuro." Talbot called. "You and I, we were on opposite sides when Cap left. You were right. I was wrong. The rest of you, do you understand? We're willing to broker a deal to buy out my contract. I have that right under Corporate law."

Spiro blinked. Felt herself reeling. This was going right to shit. Aguila had given her a simple order. Get Talbot. Bring him back without fucking things up. And here they were, already fucked up.

"Talbot," she said past gritted teeth, "you come back and tell her yourself. I'm giving you an order, Marine."

"I'm on private property, Deb. I resign. Now, load up and fly out of here. Give Kalico our offer."

"I'm not your fucking errand boy, Mark!"

"No. You're an officer serving the Supervisor. Do your damn job."

Spiro realized she was blinking, that the woman, Rebecca, was watching her with knowing eyes.

"Not one word, slit," Spiro growled at her, the rage furnace-hot inside her.

"Leave us," Rebecca said firmly. "Before this gets out of your control."

In Spiro's ear, Makarov's voice said, *"Lieutenant, that other woman off to the left just pulled a weapon from where it was hidden inside the piece of equipment she's behind. I'm reading a thermal source."*

"Squad, helmets on. Prepare to deploy . . ."

She felt the hot spot the minute it lit up her cheek. Almost burning. Took a half second to recognize—then she was back in training. Feeling it again for the first time.

Deb Spiro's heart flipped in her chest, a desperate fear running cold in guts that, but an instant ago, had been fiery in anger.

"That's right," Talina Perez called from behind the old pump off to the left. "You know that feeling, don't you? Self-guided heat-seeking round, and we both know it's locked."

"Perez, you back-shooting cunt!" Spiro swallowed hard. The frustration built, bringing tears to her eyes. "I'm going to cut your damned heart out!"

"Not today, Deb." Talina's voice had no give. "You heard Rebecca's reasonable offer. Talbot's, too. You're in violation of Kalico's agreement. Violating our agreement with her."

The hot spot on her cheek had shifted slightly to the bone just under Spiro's left eye.

"Deb," Talbot called. "We've been reasonable. You push this, and Talina blows your head off. That happens and I shoot the shit out of the shuttle. Then whatever's left of the marines takes me out, kills Perez and a bunch of women and children."

He paused, then added, "Your call."

"Lieutenant," Miso said softly. "Speaking for the rest of us, we don't want it going down that way. Right, guys?"

A series of muttered assents came from her squad.

"Talbot?" Dina Michegan called. "We're standing down. No tricks. We're backing to the ramp and back into the shuttle. Don't, for God's sake, shoot it full of holes!"

"Roger that, Dina." Talbot's voice sounded slightly weak, as if he'd lowered the suit volume. "I'll stand you all to a round in Inga's one of these days."

Spiro stood as if rooted, trembling, gut muscles pulled tight as she glared her hatred at where Talina Perez watched her through the sights of a rifle that she'd propped atop the old tractor body.

The bitch has a self-guided heat-seeking round? Imfuckingpossible!

The heat spot that now moved to her nose proved otherwise.

Spiro took a deep breath, managed to nod, to wave her defeat as she turned, started to plod toward the shuttle.

"I can't let it end this way. I just fucking can't." The feeling was as if someone else, a stranger, had suddenly taken control of her brain. Like nothing mattered anymore. Like she wasn't even Deb Spiro. That the life she'd thought hers had just turned into illusion. A disjointed dream.

She fought to control the muscles twitching in her face, felt the spot on her cheek cooling now that she was no longer facing that deadly round. Didn't matter if it was targeting on her armor. She could take the hit. But if it was her hair? Could she feel it? Was it even now burning there?

At the ramp, she slumped, unslung her rifle, and looked back. Talbot still stood, rock steady. His rifle unwavering where it targeted the shuttle engines. Shit. AP rounds would have shredded the delicate fans.

Deb took a step, hesitated.

There. Look at that. She squinted, seeing the fucking little quetzal that appeared from between the buildings. Had to be the same one that started the commotion back at hospital. The little beast that had ruined her. The one that started her down the road that led to this shit.

"If you fail, don't bother to come back."

Across the distance, no more than twenty yards, she stared into the creature's curious eyes.

"Fuck you," she growled, flipped her rifle up, and shot the beast through the body. She saw the thing flip up in the air, come down kicking.

Then she was inside, calling, "Makarov! Spool up! Get us the hell out of here!"

Slapping the ramp control, she slung her rifle to clatter its way across the bay, and stomped past her mutinous marines.

"Thanks for everything back there," she told them as she bulled her way forward past their seats.

Throwing herself into the commander's chair, she glared out the window at the dome looming above the shops. "Wish this was a military shuttle. We'd leave this whole shithole smoking."

"Back to Corporate Mine?" Makarov asked, voice toneless. He sat, eyes forward, hands on the controls as the thrusters began to spool up.

"Port Authority," she snapped. There wouldn't be any going back to Corporate Mine. Not for Deb Spiro, anyway.

57

The shuttle's thrusters blasted dirt, dust, and hot, toxic-smelling gases in a howling gale.

Talina ducked down behind the old tractor body, eyes closed against the storm of debris. Damn it! All she could do was cower when every instinct was telling her rise up, put a round through one of the turbines. Bring that damn thing down!

Her quetzal was screaming inside her, causing her mouth to salivate. Concentrated peppermint extract tasted bitter on her tongue. Quetzal rage flowed into Talina's limbic system.

She shot Rocket!

Talina ground her teeth, impotent as her hair whipped, grit blasted her face, and her body was buffeted by the tearing air. It seemed an eternity. Couldn't have been more than fifteen or twenty seconds.

The deafening howl changed; the hurricane wind suddenly shifted as the thrusters angled back, driving the shuttle forward.

Gasping relief, Talina blinked her gritty eyes and watched the delta-shaped craft as it veered wide around the dome and roared its way north.

She straightened, vision tearing from the grit. With a sleeve she rubbed at her eyes, managed to clear them. Rebecca—filthy and coated with dust—rose from behind the protective bulk of the old solar-powered pump.

A glance Talbot's way showed him blown flat on his back, rifle still shouldered, but the muzzle now pointed up at the cloud-blotched sky.

Rocket's body had been blown back a couple of meters. The young quetzal's legs and tail continued to twitch.

"God damn it," Talina cursed past clenched jaws as she ran to where the quetzal lay. Setting her rifle to the side, she bent down, laying hands on the creature. Looked for the wound.

"Rocket? You stay with me now."

There, she could see the red-brown that served as quetzal blood leaking from the bottom of the creature's throat. Where was the exit?

Talina shifted, lifting Rocket's head, staring hard into his three eyes, now rimmed with dirt and mire. "You hang in there. We've got you. You've got to live for Kylee. Live for us."

Rocket's mouth opened, tongue flicking out.

Talina's saliva began to flow. She let it leak out onto her lips. Rocket's tongue played softly through the moisture and slipped back between the serrated jaws. A clicking, oddly muted, as if underwater, sounded from within.

"Damn you, don't you die on me!" Talina shouted. "You live, damn it! Live, you hear?"

Rocket opened his mouth, tried to make a sound, but weakly vomited a gush of blood and bits of tissue onto Talina's hands and forearms.

"Don't you do this," Talina pleaded. "Please, don't do this."

Rocket's back legs twitched, kicked, and the tail made one last desperate slap at the ground. Blood and fluids were dribbling out of his dorsal vents.

Talina was staring into Rocket's eyes, willing her soul into his. She watched helplessly. Felt a tearing inside her as the young quetzal's gaze flickered and went dead.

A howling burst out deep within her as her own quetzal screamed.

"Rocket? Stay with me. Stay with . . . Stay . . ."

Too late.

Always too late.

She hadn't seen Rocket. Hadn't known he was close. Couldn't figure what Spiro had shot at. Not until she'd stood, seen Rocket's twitching body as it flickered black, yellow, and indigo patterns of fear and pain.

Fear and pain.

She'd seen those colors often enough when she'd killed quetzals.

"Damn it, why?" she cried, knotting her fists. Pounded them on the dirt next to the dead quetzal's head.

In that moment she let loose the grief, the frustrations

and guilt. Let every rotten thing inside her flow out as she bawled her impotence against the universe.

Someone knelt beside her. An arm slipped around her shoulders. Stilling the last of the sobs, she dragged a dirty sleeve across her face in an attempt to wipe up some of the mess.

"You did all you could," a soft voice told her. Rebecca's voice. The reassuring arm tightened across her shoulders. "Oh, God, this is going to destroy Kylee and Dya. The rest of us are just going to ache and grieve. But Kylee? What's going to happen to her?"

Talina sniffed, hawked, and swallowed hard. Stared down at Rocket. Blood and fluids still leaked from his parted jaws. The colors now frozen. His three eyes seemed fixed on Talina's. Vacant. Staring blankly.

"I don't know." A pause. "Why the hell was he here?"

"He should have been with Kylee."

Talina forced the howling quetzal in her gut into submission. The damn thing was shooting its own waves of rage, grief, and pain through her. Talina ordered herself to ignore them.

She reached up, patted Rebecca's hand, and felt the woman remove her arm before Talina struggled to her feet.

Sucking hell, Rocket looked so pathetic. Talina walked around, pulled his tail out straight, arranged his legs and head into a more dignified position. Nothing she could do about the blood and guts.

The tears threatened again. She beat them back.

"Better check on Mark," Rebecca said.

"Yeah."

Talina turned. Talbot hadn't moved. Still lay flat on his back, the rifle pointed at the sky. Frozen.

What the hell?

If he's dead, too, I'm flying straight to Corporate Mine and killing them all.

She hurried after Rebecca, kneeling down to peer into the transparent visor. Not only was Talbot alive, but he was hollering something barely audible through the confining helmet.

Talina got thumbs on either side of the release latches at

the collar and clicked them free. Twisting the helmet to the right released the seal and let her lift it free.

"Thanks," Talbot said between gasps for air. "Suit's completely dead. Thought I was going to suffocate. What took you so long?"

"Rocket's dead," Rebecca told him. "Didn't you see?"

"What do you mean, Rocket's dead?"

Talina—working on the man's gloves—said, "Spiro shot him as she was leaving."

Talina got the rifle free and unlocked the bayonet-style locks at the wrist before pulling the gloves off. Rebecca was working on the arms, freeing them.

"This is going to kill Kylee, you know that," Talbot said bitterly. "Why kill poor Rocket?"

"Because I kept her from killing him at the hospital that day." Talina ground her teeth, forcing herself to concentrate on something besides rage.

Talbot said, "You kept him alive all right. Maybe, Dya, too." Then, in a softer voice. "Me, too, I guess."

Talina blinked back the tears. "Yeah, Mark. We were all fond of the little twerp."

Finally pulling off the legs and releasing the carapace, they pulled Talbot to his feet. He wiped the sweat from his face, bit his lip, and walked slowly over to where Rocket lay.

Kneeling, Talbot ran his hands reverently over Rocket's head, speaking softly.

Talina turned away, walked to where she didn't have to hear. Instead she fixed her eyes on the horizon. North. Up there. Spiro would have headed straight back to Corporate Mine. Right to Aguila to report.

My next stop. And, Kalico, I doubt you're going to like how this turns out.

The quetzal inside her hissed in support.

"Yeah, you piece of shit? That thing we're feeling? That's called grief. You getting the idea now? Figuring out why we've been hunting your sorry asses down and killing you every time you eat a human?"

Her quetzal echoed the chittering and clicking sounds of assent she'd learned from Rocket.

"Tal?" Rebecca called.

Talina reluctantly peeled her gaze from the northern horizon and plodded back. She tried to make herself see Rocket as just another dead quetzal. Couldn't do it. Felt the tearing pain in her soul.

"How do you want to do this?" Talina asked.

"Get a stretcher," Talbot said. "Carry him back to the Dome."

Rebecca added, "Then we have a cemetery out back. He was one of us. He deserves to lie among our people."

Our people. That meant Pak and Paolo along with the rest.

She turned, figuring to head for the tower base for the stretcher. Surely, between the three of them, they could carry Rocket's corpse. He couldn't weigh more than seventy kilos.

Talina froze, swallowed hard, her heart beginning to pound.

"Dear God, no!" She placed a hand to her mouth.

Rebecca and Talbot looked up, both stunned.

Emerging from around the corner of the shop, hobbling on her crutches, came Kylee.

"Now, sweetie," Rebecca said, charging forward. "You shouldn't be up! Shouldn't be here! What are you doing?"

Kylee kept hobbling, seemed not to hear. Seemed not to see. As if she were in a trance. Possessed by something alien, something vacuous.

"Rocket?" the girl called, her voice eerie, almost a screech.

Rebecca stopped short, stepped out of the way as Kylee hitched along on her crutches.

Talina would remember the instant Kylee's gaze fixed on Rocket. She'd remember the glazing emptiness that filled the little girl's eyes, the hideous scream that tore from her throat.

58

Could this get any worse? It had been a simple assignment: Fly down to Mundo and collect Mark Talbot. How the hell could even Deb Spiro screw that up?

Kalico threw her arms up in despair as she paced across the shuttle field. Cursing like a marine, she gave voice to her displeasure. Her people, smart as they were, knew damn good and well that they'd better steer clear of her and her wrath.

As she pounded across the shuttle field, she kept glancing down south, toward Mundo Base, and tried to calculate the extent of the damage.

First had been the agonizing silence as she'd had the communications officer repeatedly call the shuttle. Nothing for a couple of hours.

And then a reply from Ensign Makarov: *"Ma'am, we're inbound. All I can tell you is that after Mundo, Lieutenant Spiro ordered me to maintain com silence, then ordered me to fly to Port Authority. She ordered me to set down outside the gate, at which time she, Chavez, and Nashala exited the shuttle. Soon as they were dirtside, I dusted off."*

Kalico had demanded, "What the hell happened at Mundo? Where's Talbot?"

"He's still there, ma'am. Threatened to shoot up my shuttle when Spiro wouldn't honor Mundo's deed."

Deed? What deed? But Makarov insisted he didn't have a clue.

"Spiro, you ignorant bitch!" she railed at nothing in particular. It felt good to stomp, to shake fists, and rage.

She'd been riding high after blowing the mobbers out of the sky. Then, like a roundhouse to the chin, she'd had to deal with Rita Valerie's gruesome, hanging corpse with its insane message.

And now this?

It had been such a simple assignment.

She saw the shuttle before she heard it. Just a flash of silver in the northern sky as Capella's setting rays reflected from the craft's side.

Retreating beyond the downwash zone, Kalico waited while the shuttle circled, slowed, and settled onto the fired, ceramic-hard surface of the pad.

The spool-down seemed to take forever, and then the ramp dropped. Katsuro Miso and Dina Michegan came striding wearily down the textured surface—a bitter, almost defeated set to their shoulders. Not that their expressions were any better.

"What the hell happened?" Kalico demanded as she stepped out to meet them.

"They were ready for us," Michegan growled, spreading her hands. "Talbot was in full armor, had his service weapon. Said he'd hose the shuttle turbines with AP. Uh, you know what armor piercing rounds would do to the thrusters, right?"

"Come on, Dina," Miso said. "Start at the beginning. Some woman named Rebecca came out. Spiro started well enough. Asked to speak to Talbot. This Rebecca said that we were trespassing on private property. That she had a deed. Asked Spiro if you, ma'am, didn't give your word that deeds would be honored."

"It went downhill from there." Michegan kept glancing away, as if to avoid Kalico's eyes. "Spiro ordered us to fan out and search the place. The woman objected. Spiro pushed her out of the way, and that's when Talbot popped up."

"And there was another shooter, too," Miso added. "Talina Perez with self-guided rounds in a service rifle. Spiro said she felt the IR on her cheek."

Dina Michegan said, "Spiro was losing it, ma'am. The four of us, Miso, Chavez, Nashala, and me, we tried to talk the lieutenant out of unleashing a shitstorm. Then we beat feet for the shuttle. I mean, they had us. Said it was all being recorded. If it had gone completely to shit . . . Well, we didn't want to be part of that mess afterward."

Kalico closed her eyes, her fists knotted at her sides. She forced herself to breathe deeply, to still the frantic beating of her heart.

"But you got out without shots being fired? No one killed?"

"Just the quetzal, ma'am. We didn't see it, but just before the ramp closed, Spiro fired a single shot. On the way to Port Authority she bragged that she'd center-punched, as she said, 'the little shit.'"

"She shot Rocket?" Kalico conjured an image of the young quetzal as it walked down the hospital hallway with Talbot. On the way to the men's room of all things.

The beast had looked at her, curiosity behind those three gleaming black eyes.

"That was a little girl's pet."

"Yes, ma'am." Michegan shifted uncomfortably. "Wouldn't have been our call, ma'am. You said no trouble. Nothing broken or killed. We were just trying to keep Spiro from—"

"You said she went straight to Port Authority?"

Miso extended a hand, fingers spread, as if to plead for compassion. "Don't blame Ensign Makarov, ma'am. He just followed the lieutenant's orders."

"And Chavez and Nashala?"

"They threw in with Spiro." Miso adopted a wounded expression. "Said that resigning from the Corps was now a well-established tradition. They shucked their armor, left it in the shuttle, and the three of them walked off at Port Authority. Said for us not to come looking for them. That we wouldn't like the reception."

"The little girl's quetzal is dead? You're sure of this?"

"Makarov, competent as he is, recorded the whole thing with the sensors and camera gear. It's all on tape."

Kalico knew it was bad.

Didn't know just how bad until an hour later when she reviewed the recordings.

So, how the hell did she get her hands on Mundo Base now?

With a murderer loose at Corporate Mine, Spiro gone rogue, and this woman Rebecca claiming she had a deed? And to cap it all, Spiro really had shot Rocket.

There's no friggin' way Dya will forgive this.

She desperately wished she were at Inga's drowning in a tall glass of whiskey. Just as she was imagining lifting a glass to her lips, her com interrupted the image.

"Ma'am? Petre Howe's been taken to the clinic. Said he's suffering from stomach pains. Just keeled over in the cafeteria."

"I don't understand."

"He's throwing up, foaming at the mouth. Uh . . . Just a moment. Word is he's gone into convulsions. They're going to check him for poison."

In just the short time it took her to get to the small clinic down the main hall and to the right, the poison had done its work and Petre Howe was dead.

59

Walking down Port Authority's main avenue, through the darkness and rain, Trish couldn't remember being in a worse mood. She was pissed off at the weather, it having started raining as she finished her last rounds. And then there was the festering gall of her spat with Talina. But most of all, she was irritated with herself.

From the moment Cap and Talina had walked out of the bush, things between Trish and Talina had been subtly different. Tal and Cap's relationship had changed everything. First the fact that he'd moved in with Talina, and then the ramifications of his injuries after the fight with the quetzal.

Growing up on Donovan as she had, given the deaths of her own parents, Trish had a very different perspective on life as a cripple. Had considered what it would have cost Port Authority to have Talina forever saddled with the care of an invalid. Most of all, Trish had feared what it would do to Talina.

She *loved* Talina. Worshipped her as a mentor and friend. Would do anything for her. Had done them, in fact.

And now I'm wondering if Tal is still on our side. Or if that thing *living inside her has turned her against us all.*

Trish made a face, shook the water off of her slicker, and stared up at the slivers of rain slashing down through the cones of light outside Inga's.

She took one last look around. Everyone had been at their posts for the night's watch. The gates had been locked.

But this was still a quetzal night: the sort of darkness in which they preferred to hunt.

She tried to shake off the mad along with the moisture as she opened Inga's door and stepped inside.

A raucous noise assaulted her ears. People having fun. Laughing. The banging and clinking of ceramic and glass mugs. The screech of wooden benches on stone cobbles.

She paused at the head of the stairs, taking in the room

below. About a third full, the place felt antsy, as though primed for trouble.

Or was that just her? A reflection of her own dark thoughts about Talina? Cap? And the way he'd died that day?

She pulled her slicker back, slung her rifle, and descended the damp steps, already wet from previous patrons coming in from the rain.

She made her way down the central aisle, nodding to old friends, acknowledging the occasional called greeting.

At the bar, Shig sat in the stool next to Talina's, his obligatory half glass of wine looking untouched before him.

A loud burst of laughter caused her to note Lieutenant Spiro and her two privates, Nashala and Chavez, where they sat with Pavel Tomashev and Boris Kashashvili. Sort of fringe Wild Ones, Tomashev and Kashashvili ran a sand pit that supplied the glass works, dug gravel when it was needed, did some hunting, and had a couple of claims that produced the occasional gemstone.

"Killed that little fucker dead!" Spiro announced to the world, lifting her glass high to the accompaniment of cheers from the two miners and Chavez. Private Nashala seemed more reserved, eyes wary as she fingered her half-full glass of ale and studied Spiro.

Something about the flush on Spiro's face, the glitter in the woman's eyes, triggered that sixth sense that warned Trish of trouble.

She pulled out Talina's chair, figuring what the hell, and plopped her butt into it.

At Shig's raised eyebrow, Trish said, "Tal's down south with her quetzal, right? What would she care?" To Inga, she called, "Pale ale."

"Coming up," Inga called back, looking harried. The woman's face shone with perspiration and a couple of locks had come loose from the bun at the back of her head.

"So, I saw the shuttle come in this afternoon." Trish indicated Spiro and her two privates. "What are they doing here?"

Shig thoughtfully ran his fingers down the sides of his wineglass. "Said they'd resigned from the Supervisor's service. Apparently they flew straight here from Mundo. My take is that something went wrong down there. Spiro's not talking about it beyond bragging that she and the two with her quit. Oh, and about killing that little quetzal."

Trish shot the lieutenant a glance as Inga placed a glass of golden ale on the bar. Inga hesitated, glanced uncertainly at Talina's chair, and asked, "Cash or credit?"

Trish tossed her a two-SDR coin. "Put it toward my account."

As Inga grabbed up the coin and headed to the other end of the bar where Step Allenovich was hollering for whiskey, Trish said, "Killed Rocket, huh? Bet that pissed Talina off."

"There will be trouble over this." Shig turned just enough to shoot a speculative glance Spiro's way. The woman was laughing too loudly as she slapped Chavez on the shoulder.

Tomashev and Kashashvili were sharing uneasy glances as they joined in.

"So, tell me, Shig. Is it just me, or is Talina different since she got infected by that damn quetzal? Why'd she back that beast against the rest of us?"

"I'm not sure that she did."

"Come on, Shig. She was ready to shoot the first person who stepped forward out there that night. I wasn't sure she wouldn't have shot one of the women. They were just worried about their kids. I mean, come on. I just made my rounds. Our gates are locked. We're scanning the night. And for what? Quetzals. We're at war with the things."

"History, Trish, is replete with stories about enemies becoming allies. Do all people believe the same things? Are all people fighting the same wars? Do we and Aguila see the world through the same eyes?"

"Of course not."

"Then, perhaps, neither do quetzals."

"They're fucking animals, Shig. And one of them has infected Talina. Hell, even Raya and Cheng don't have a clue."

"Fucking animals?" Shig gave her that maddening mild smile of his. "Are they? Had you said creatures, I would have agreed. But the term animal, that specifically applies to a biological kingdom of terrestrial life. Quetzals are Donovanian creatures. And, having neither penises nor vaginas, even your illusion to fucking seems completely unfounded."

Trish gripped her glass, tried to crush it, the tendons standing out on the backs of her hands. She was being petulant, and knew it. "Shig, there are times, I swear, when it's all I can do to keep from strangling you."

At that he chuckled, eyes alight. "Strangling me? Or strangling yourself? Anger is driven by either an infringement or injury from others, or by guilt. The two are often inextricable. In the end, Talina—by keeping the peace and buying time to remove the young quetzal—would seem to have acted properly and wisely. That leaves guilt as the source of your anger. Of what are you guilty, Trish?"

She closed her eyes, blocking out the growing shouts from Spiro's table behind her.

Shig. If you only knew.

"Ah," Shig said softly, almost drowned by the rising voices behind him. "Want to confess?"

"Not in this lifetime." She thought back to that long-ago day. Eyes, pleading. Just the thought of them left her heart like a rock in her chest.

"You taking her side?" Spiro demanded hotly, breaking into Trish's sudden misery.

"Not particularly," Kashashvili's voice rose. "Look, the lady's not my favorite, all right? She sticks her nose into too many people's business. Acts too damned high and mighty to suit me. Lot of people are scared of her. You should be, too, if you had any sense. But one thing Tal Perez is not, is a back shooter!"

"Bullshit!" Chavez burst out.

Trish turned just in time to see Chavez half rise, his face red, veins standing out from his neck as he glared hotly at Kashashvili.

The prospector, for his part, now rose to his full height, saying, "You damn Skulls come in here, think you're tough? You don't get it. Perez's been in the bush. She's a lot of things, but a coward isn't one."

"She's a coward!" Spiro insisted, standing beside Chavez before pushing him back down in his seat. Spiro shot a calculating glance around the room, then bellowed at the top of her lungs, "Talina Perez doesn't have the guts to face me. She wouldn't even face me this morning. Hid behind a tractor with a rifle. Before that, she snuck up behind me with a pistol. I call her a coward!"

The room had gone deadly quiet, all eyes turning to Spiro. The lieutenant was grinning, face flushed, a weird glaze to her eyes.

Shig reached out, placed a hand on Trish's arm as she slipped off the stool and reached for her pistol.

"And as for you?" Spiro told Kashashvili. "You couldn't lick a marine's ass if you were on your knees. And if you're one of Perez's sniveling backers, you're a cunt, too."

Spiro paused only long enough to knock Kashashvili's beer over before she stepped over the bench and started to leave.

"You don't call me that, you soft bitch!" Kashashvili grabbed for his pistol, pulled it.

Before Trish could break free of Shig's restraining hand, the man fired. A bottle popped and shattered on the back bar, liquor and fragments erupting in a haze.

Spiro had ducked as the bullet hissed past her. She was turning when Kashashvili shot again.

The second shot went wide, smacking the bar itself and splintering wood.

Spiro's hand moved in a blur. It might have been magic— as if the lieutenant's pistol appeared in her hand. Three deafening bangs. Like God's hammer cracking the world.

Kashashvili swayed, a stupid look on his face. His arm dropped. The man's pistol fell from loose fingers to clatter on the stone floor. He tried to form words, mouth working, lips oddly flaccid. Then he collapsed like a rag doll, head banging on the edge of the barroom table with a melon-hollow thud.

Spiro stood, feet braced, pistol out. A silly grin on her lips, the flush in her large-boned face turned a deeper red. Her glance went to the stunned people, rising slowly from their seats, as she called, "Any of the rest of you want a piece of me?"

Stunned, no one said a word.

"You saw that!" Spiro pointed to where Tomashev and Nashala were bent over Kashashvili's crumpled body. "That bastard shot first. At my back. At my *fucking* back!

Just like Talina Perez. And just like him, Talina Perez is going to get hers, too!"

"Trish?" someone called from a couple of tables back. "You going to deal with this?"

For an instant she froze, thoughts tumbling in her brain, confused.

Shig, however, stepped out, hands up, calling, "Nothing to deal with." He sent a glance Spiro's way, asking, "Might you perhaps reholster your weapon?"

Spiro—the idiotic grin still on her lips—fixed her unusually bright eyes on Shig, then back at the gawking people. As if against her will, she slipped the gun back into its holster, saying, "It can come out again. Just as fast."

"It needn't," Shig soothed. Then he raised his voice. "We all saw it. The lieutenant was walking away. Boris shot twice. From behind. Lieutenant Spiro acted in self-defense."

"You're going to let her go?" Trish asked incredulously.

Shig fixed concerned brown eyes on hers. "Did you see something I did not?"

"She called him a liar and a . . . a . . ."

"And?" Shig asked reasonably. "She was in the process of walking away."

"But what she said about Talina—"

"Is between her and Talina. Not *our* business. Not the community's."

Spiro, chuckling now, flicked her fingers at Trish, saying, "See you around."

Trish accessed her com. "Two Spots? We've got a legal shooting in the tavern. It's Boris Kashashvili. Send the cart around. We'll bury him in the morning."

"Roger that. Legal shooting. I've put it in the log."

Chavez rose and hurried off in Spiro's wake.

Trish stepped over to help extricate Kashashvili's mortal remains from where they'd fallen under the table and bench. As she got hold of the man's muscular arm and pulled, she asked Private Nashala, "You going with them?"

"Naw," Nashala told her. "We all quit today. She came in here looking for a fight. Me, I just want to do something where I'm not getting in other people's shit."

Trish could see the wounds now. Three holes weeping

blood into Kashashvili's shirt. Right through the sternum
and into the heart. No wonder there wasn't much blood.

"You all quit, huh?" Tomashev asked, his face stricken
as he helped to ease his partner's legs out from under the
table. He looked like he was searching frantically for something to talk about. Any distraction to lessen the shock.

"Spiro made it so that we can't go back to Aguila. You
been with him long?" Nashala asked Tomashev, empathetic enough to play along.

" 'Bout five years. He was . . . was my friend."

"Sorry," Nashala added. To Trish, she said, "It's all
right. I'll help get Kashashvili upstairs. From the looks of
the crowd, you might have your hands full down here."

Trish nodded, watched them as they carried Kashashvili's corpse down the aisle and up the stairs. Around her, the
talk was furtive, half angry, different people taking different sides as they periodically glanced her way. Obviously
wondering what came next. What she'd do.

"All right!" Trish bellowed. "It's over. Sit your asses
back down, or call it a night and go home. If there's a lesson
here, it's that you don't shoot your mouth off."

She swallowed hard, wishing her heart would finally settle down. Damn it, what had possessed Kashashvili? Sure,
Spiro was poison, but to try to shoot her in the back?

"Some men go to the wilderness because they know better than to try and live with others," Shig, reseated, told her
as he fingered his wine glass.

"Excuse me?" Trish climbed back onto her own stool
and sucked down a big draft of ale.

"Boris Kashashvili," Shig said. "People irritated him.
That's why he turned to the bush in the first place. He and
Pavel only came in today because they had to make a sand
delivery to the glass works. They had a couple of nice ru-
bies they wanted to convert to SDRs and buy parts for
their hauler, too. Figured they'd stock up parts and cache
them since it wasn't likely that replacements were coming
anytime soon."

"Did you see that?" Trish asked, still unsettled. "I mean
the way Spiro pulled that pistol and shot. Less than a blink
of an eye. And all the while she was being shot at." She
shook her head. "How do you stay that cool?"

"Her guilt is overwhelming."

Trish's heart had finally returned to its normal beat, despite the images of Kashashvili's shooting replaying over and over in her mind. "Guilt? Hey, I hate to break it to you, Shig, but that woman looked anything but guilty afterward."

"It's hard to hide an anger like hers. She doesn't care if she lives or dies, which implies an incredible amount of guilt. Enough that she hates herself for every breath she takes."

"Yeah, and what happens when Talina finally comes back to town?"

"Now is a very good time to get religion," Shig admitted. "The Western kind where you can pray in hopes it will affect the quantum nature of the universe and save someone you love."

And with that, Shig upended his glass and downed the whole thing.

60

As she piloted her aircar past the edge of the bush and over Port Authority's manicured farmland, Talina finally understood what it meant to be haunted. That look on Kylee's face: pain, disbelief, horror. Rocket's broken body. She couldn't shake the images that had been burned into her brain.

As they passed above, the farmers tending their crops waved. Talina shot them a salute back, but her heart wasn't in it.

Not with Kylee's scream still echoing inside her skull, or the mindless grief that had fixed in the little girl's expression.

But the worst had happened at the funeral. They'd dug a hole at the end of the line of graves just north of the tower. Not much, just a square pit more than a meter deep. Kylee had watched with vacuous blue eyes as Talina, Talbot, and Dya carefully lowered Rocket's limp corpse into the hole. As they did, waves of color rolled across his cold hide.

A knot had pulled tight in Talina's throat. She'd managed to hold back the tears, memories of the little quetzal and its obvious love for Kylee tearing at her the entire time.

Given her history with quetzals, how had she come to grow so fond of the little beast?

Talbot had climbed out, extending a hand to pull first Dya, and then Talina up and out of the grave.

"Rocket was family," Rebecca had stated tonelessly. "I remember our fear when he came among us. How he fearlessly came walking down the causeway at Kylee's side, chirping all the way.

"Stunned, we ran out, weapons in hand, and Kylee called, 'This is my new friend, Rocket. He's come to live with us.'"

Talina had glanced over. Kylee's face remained stricken, her lips quivering. Eyes unfocused. Was she even hearing?

"He brought wonder to our lives," Dya added. "He and

Kylee were inseparable. We will . . ." She swallowed hard, tears trickling down her face. "We will miss . . ." Her eyes closed, throat working, unable to finish.

Kylee caught them by surprise, dropping to her knees, crawling into the grave. Before anyone could react, she was down, curling herself around Rocket's body. And there she froze, whispering, "It's okay, Rocket. I'll die with you."

Su turned away, biting her knuckles, as she fled. The rest of the children watched in wide-eyed horror.

Dya kept whispering "Oh, my God" over and over.

Talbot, on the verge of breaking down, climbed back into the grave. As he laid hold of Kylee, the little girl burst out in shrieks and eerie, wavering screams.

Talbot had to tear her loose. Handed Kylee, kicking and screaming, up to Talina. It was all Tal could do to pull the girl up and out of the way. The miracle was that the child didn't rebreak a bone in the struggle.

Once clear of the grave, Kylee went limp. Soundless, barely breathing.

As Talina held her, she could sense the difference. Maybe it was the quetzal in her, but she knew the instant Kylee turned herself off. Like a switch had been thrown.

The girl didn't even look as dirt was shoveled into the grave. Made no move as she was carried back to the tower. Only her shallow breathing and periodic blink of the eyes hinted that she was even alive.

Kylee had gone catatonic. Her skin had taken on an ashen color. Nor did she respond when Dya made every heroic attempt to break through the girl's dissociative fixation on nothingness. To look into Kylee's eyes was to stare into desolation.

Eerie. Frightening.

Talina chewed her lip as she piloted her aircar toward the Port Authority landing field. She glanced at Rebecca. The woman sat stoically in the aircar's passenger seat. Getting Rebecca to return to Port Authority had been a major victory. Or perhaps, as the matriarch at Mundo, she'd just needed to escape the calamitous turn of events that had shattered her family.

Talina slowed her approach, hovered over the aircar

field, and settled onto her usual spot beside the perimeter fence.

Shutting down the system, she still had a twenty percent charge left in the power pack. Off to the left, four vehicles down, she could see Mundo's old Beta aircar. The one that had carried Talbot, Dya, Kylee, and Rocket to Port Authority in the first place. Someone had moved it from the street to the aircar field.

"We're here," Rebecca stated woodenly as she inspected the high fence. Then she turned her gaze to the buildings beyond the chain link. "I once swore I'd never be back. That I'd die before I set foot on this ground again."

"Times change, Rebecca. People change. Back then the only future was The Corporation. Now, for all we know, we may never see another of their ships for the rest of our lives. Who and what we are is who and what we decide to be. Just us. Maybe a couple of thousand people on the entire planet if you count some of us twice."

Rebecca collected her pack as Talina unloaded her own belongings. After plugging the aircar in to recharge, she found Rebecca staring anxiously at the gate where one of the guards stood, a bolt-action rifle conspicuous in his hands.

"Hey, Tal," the guard greeted. "Where you been? People been asking."

"Went south for the winter, Sam. Palm trees, coconuts, jerk chicken on the beach."

"Yeah, right."

She led the way, wondering what it felt like for Rebecca to pass through the gate. If Port Authority didn't come across as more of a prison than a town after Mundo Base. The entire time she'd been at Mundo, Talina hadn't seen a single fence.

But then, they'd had Rocket. Had brokered some sort of deal with Donovan that allowed cohabitation.

Made her wonder if perhaps, somehow, people had gotten it all wrong when Second Ship had founded Port Authority with its fences and security.

The quetzal inside her sent a hot flash of displeasure through her muscles. Damn, she hated it when the creature did that.

There was so much that they still didn't understand. Like how Kylee could walk that soon after surgery. Or what had happened to the little girl inside her skull when her best friend and symbiote was murdered.

"Lot's changed," Rebecca noted, almost cringing back from the people who called greetings as Talina led the way through the warehouse district. "Look at the new buildings."

Rounding the corner onto the main avenue, Rebecca asked suspiciously, "The Jewel?"

"Not everything here is an improvement. It's a gambling den started by a Skull that *Turalon* puked into our presence. The guy's named Dan Wirth. A real lowlife. Think rigged games, organized prostitution, racketeering, and just about anything unsavory."

"Why don't you shut him down?"

"Me, I'd do more than that. Shig and Yvette, however, are hung up about the role of government in a free society. They consider keeping a leash on my more tyrannical impulses as their role in life." Talina gave the woman a sidelong glance. "And, as you know from experience, that's not always such a bad idea."

"We're not part of Aguila's empire because of you. Even with what it cost us. It's got to be better than Corporate administration."

"Yeah, well, let's get those papers registered. Then it's for sure a done deal. One that Aguila can't lawyer her way around."

"Hey, Tal!" came a cry.

Talina arched an eyebrow as the auburn-haired woman came striding from Inga's front bench. "Trish."

How was this going to go?

"Who's your friend?" Trish asked, matching step, her expression guarded.

"Rebecca Smart, this is my second-in-command. Trish Monagan, meet Rebecca. She's here to represent the family that owns Mundo Base. Came a long way to see what we've done with Port Authority. Even survived a brush with Aguila's people to get here."

"You mean Spiro?" Trish asked, feigning nonchalance.

"You know anything about what happened down there?"

"She's quit the Supervisor." She hesitated. "Shot old Boris Kashashvili in Inga's last night after an argument. Legal shooting. Spiro and Chavez have taken up lodging in an abandoned dome down by the mine gate. Spiro's been making quite a show of herself." Again Trish hesitated, obviously not telling Tal everything. "She's been bragging about shooting that quetzal that was at the hospital."

Rebecca almost missed a step; her expression turned wooden.

"Yeah." Talina shot Trish a hard look. "I was there. I call it cold-blooded murder."

"Tal, for God's sake . . ." Trish bit off whatever she was going to say, the corners of her mouth going tight. After an awkward pause, Trish said, "Yeah, well, you've got business. I'll be off on my rounds."

"See you."

Talina watched Trish cut off to the right, as if escaping into the narrow gap between the foundry and the tannery walls.

"That sounded cold," Rebecca noted.

"We had a disagreement over Rocket. Some of our fine citizenry wanted to violently remove the little guy. Trish kind of cut me off at the knees the night I left."

Rebecca took a deep breath. "Idiots."

Talina led the way into the admin dome, finding it mostly empty as was usual at midday.

"Hey, Yvette," Talina called, leaning in the woman's door. "Got business for you."

The blonde woman looked up from her desk. Then past Tal's shoulder. "Good God! Rebecca? That you?"

"Been a long time," Rebecca acknowledged. "How's Hansen?"

"Skewer got him about five, no six years back."

"Sorry to hear that. He was a good man." Rebecca tried to smile. Couldn't.

Yvette stood and pushed her chair back. "Last we heard you'd abandoned Mundo Base. Vanished into the bush. Imagine our surprise when Talina radioed that you all were still kicking down there."

Talina said, "Yvette, we're here to register the deed for Mundo Base. That and a series of titles for the equipment down there." She lowered her voice. "Which, if you will recall, we did the day that Dya left."

Yvette's green eyes cooled. "The day that Dya left?"

"Could we step into the conference room?" Talina suggested, glancing up and down the hallway.

Yvette, mouth gone prim with unease, led the way.

Talina closed the door behind them, saying, "You've got to trust me on this. We need to backdate Mundo's deed. Blood's already been spilled. I've given my word."

Yvette, never one to shy from the blunt truth, asked, "This about you? About Pak and Paolo? Or is this about what's right and correct for this office?"

"It's about Donovan, and what's good for our future here," Talina insisted. "It's about libertarian versus Corporate. About creating an independent third entity on the planet. Port Authority? Corporate Mine? We both need Mundo Base and what it has to offer. You heard about Dya Simonov's medical miracles?"

"Yep. Something."

"That's the tip of the iceberg." Talina hooked a thumb at Rebecca. "But it's theirs. They did the hard lifting. Paid the price in lives, sweat, and blood to keep that place and to make it pay. Yesterday Aguila tried to whisk it out from under them by claiming Mundo is Corporate property. So you tell me, madam libertarian, is protecting their claim worth a couple of days? And what does that mean in the fourteen-billion-year history of the universe?"

Yvette coolly appraised Rebecca. Then she asked, "You've been there the entire time?"

"Since the beginning."

Yvette closed her eyes, looking pained. "Tal, if we do this . . . Damn it. If we compromise here, where do we compromise next? Yes, I agree, it's theirs. But what difference does it make if we file the papers today? The documents are still binding and—"

"I told Spiro it was already a done deal. You can bet it was recorded. Kalico will have reviewed those tapes."

"Fuck." Yvette shook her head. "Talina, why do you put me in the middle of these messes?"

"Because it was the right thing to do," Rebecca said. "Sometimes justice—or true justice as the case may be—

requires a bit of latitude in the application of the rules. Corporate philosophy is absolutely rigid in its approach to governance. Where does your libertarian philosophy stand in comparison?"

"Embrace a lie just because it serves the common good?" Yvette crossed her arms.

Rebecca shrugged. "I lied yesterday in a desperate bluff to avoid a firefight and save my family and home. But for Spiro's need to strike out, it almost worked without anyone getting killed. What's a peaceful resolution and our freedom worth? How do you value that against your own sense of morality and ethics?"

Yvette closed her eyes, muttered, "Shit!" under her breath. For a long moment she considered, lips pursed.

Tal finally added, "At risk of unleashing all that dharma and Taoist crap, should we ask Shig what his opinion would be?"

"God no." Yvette opened her eyes. "He'd wax on about the quest for sattva until we were all foaming at the mouth."

Rebecca lifted an inquiring eyebrow as she studied Dushane.

Yvette crossed her arms. "You know there's a filing fee. SDRs or trade?"

Rebecca reached in her pack, producing a small box, about ten by ten centimeters.

"And what's that?" Yvette asked, taking the box.

"Blueberries and blackberries. Had the kids pick them before we left."

The tall woman opened the box. Stared in green-eyed disbelief. She took one of the large blackberries. Popped it into her mouth.

Like the breaching of a dam, Yvette caved. "Yeah, well, let's take a stroll to the records room. Seems to me we filed those papers what . . . ? Couldn't have been more than a couple of days ago."

Talina smiled wearily. "Yeah, that's my recollection, too."

To Rebecca, she said, "Let's get this done and I'll buy you a beer. You had a beer recently?"

"Not for years."

An hour later, Talina was seated in her chair at Inga's,

elbows braced behind her as she instinctively scanned the tavern's clientele for potential trouble.

Beside her, fingers laced around a ceramic mug full of Inga's pale ale, Rebecca asked, "Okay, so now that the gloves are off, what does this really mean? What do you and Port Authority expect to get out of my family?"

"Trade." Talina reached back for her stout.

"You've got it." Rebecca winced. "We owe you. But you'll have to help protect us from Aguila. We can't stop her if she comes to take Mundo." She made a face. "It hurts me to say, but we'll need your armed troops to defend—"

"You don't understand. It's not about Port Authority against Corporate Mine. We *need* Aguila and her people to succeed, and she needs us. Good old Kalico is still learning to think in Donovanian terms, but she's coming around. She knows she's losing down there. I think you are the key to keeping that mine and smelter running." She paused. "It's all about those pine trees."

Rebecca glanced sidelong at her. "But give me a single damn reason why, after what that woman has done, we should give her anything?"

"One word: Survival. Mundo's falling apart. I know it. You know it. More importantly, Mundo's condition is prophetic for Port Authority and Corporate Mine. We're flush for the moment. Lots of new equipment and supplies that we're going to use up faster than anyone can anticipate. But ultimately, we're abandoned."

"And just because of that, we should forgive her for Rocket? For trying to take our home?"

"Spiro shot Rocket. Not Kalico." Talina smiled as she sipped her stout, then added softly, "And you've forgiven me for acts even more odious."

Rebecca shook her head. "It'll be up to the family. But don't count on it. Not after Rocket. They're going to want a payback, and as the old saw says, payback's a bitch."

61

This was fixing to be a good night. From Dan Wirth's perspective as he walked the floor, The Jewel was in fine
form. Not only that, but it was raining outside. His businesses did better on nights when it was raining. Gave the
locals an excuse to be indoors, not standing around on
the streets enjoying the evening and gossiping with their
neighbors.

"Raise you fifteen," Deb Spiro's strained voice carried
above the chatter.

Dan glanced her way as she tossed a couple of SDRs
onto the table. She'd taken to The Jewel like a chamois to
the bush. Turned out that poker was a pastime in the marine barracks, and according to now-ex-Private Michael
Chavez, Spiro was noted for winning.

She was certainly taking Szong Sczui—a farmer from
the south side—for every SDR he had. Wye Vanveer was
holding his own, and Tad Johnson was losing the last of his
recent hoard of SDRs. All paid out by the tannery for the
load of chamois hides the hunter had brought in from beyond the Blood Hills up north.

Art Maniken, keen-nosed as he was for trouble, had
taken a position just back from the table. Art wasn't the
kind to fear any man, but he was damned respectful of Deb
Spiro. And not just because of the shooting in the tavern.
The Marines didn't just hand out the rank of lieutenant. It
had to be earned. Usually because someone was tough
enough, hard enough, or deadly enough to engender the
respect of his or her superiors.

Not that Spiro was particularly smart. But as Art's instinct and Dan's experience suggested, her calling to command had come from the ruthless application of force to a
problem. Not the sort of woman anyone with brains would
cross over a card table.

Not to mention that she'd shown no hesitation when it came to shooting somebody dead.

Dan watched her rake in yet another pot.

"Shit," Szong muttered, shoving back from the table and pocketing the few SDRs he had left. "I'm outta here."

"Sure you don't want a chance to win at least part of this back?" Spiro called.

"Naw. I got just enough for a roll with young Manzanita over at Betty Able's. Think I'd like to take the memory of her hitting a high C back out into the bush with me."

"Think you can get her to reach a high C?" Vanveer asked. "Heard that the best you can do with a woman, given that little, hand-stroked stiff of yours, is a B flat. Even when she's paid to sing like Manzanita."

That brought a round of chuckles and guffaws.

"Aw, to hell with all of you," Szong growled as he headed for the door.

Spiro's gaze didn't so much as flicker as she watched him go. Only after the door closed behind him did she smile slightly and turn her attention back to the table.

Art met Dan's eyes, nodded, and wandered off, apparently having figured the only potential troublemaker had pulled stakes.

"I'm out of here, too," Vanveer said, raking in his chips. "Time to cash out. Catch one last beer at Inga's. Big day tomorrow at the mine. Trying a new excavator that Montoya's got running from the *Turalon*'s hold."

Tad Johnson, too, laid his cards to the side. "Me, I'm headed home. See what Clara and the little one are up to."

Spiro arched a mocking eyebrow as she flipped the deck of cards back and forth and quoted Mechalander's play: "Alas, but there's no guts, nor sense for glory, among the whole damn bunch of them."

Dan pulled up a chair, seating himself, and sighing before quoting Tybalt's rejoinder from the classic old VR: "And such, good lady, is the curse of the talented and proud."

Spiro's lips twitched and she indicated the cards. "You want to try your luck?"

"Sure. Five-card draw."

From long practice, Art shifted his course, subtly am-

bling back until he slouched against the wall, just behind
and to Spiro's left. Ostensibly the man was keeping an eye
on the room, his arms crossed, fingers tapping his elbows.

Spiro shuffled and dealt.

Dan tossed in a ten-SDR chip for the ante.

As Spiro studied her cards, Art's fingers traced patterns
on his elbows. His index, middle, and ring fingers on the
right hand were held level; they tapped his elbow three
times.

Okay, Spiro had three eights.

Dan had nothing. "I'll fold, Lieutenant."

"That quickly?" Spiro gave him a sour look as she raked
in his ten.

Wirth took the cards, shuffled, knowing she was watching him like a hawk. He dealt, took a look at his hand, and
tossed in another ten.

Art's fingers danced on his elbow.

This time around all Spiro had was a jack high.

"Raise you ten," Dan told her, holding two queens.

She chipped in, said, "Take two."

Art's fingers telegraphed a pair of eights.

"So, what's the story on this Mundo research base?"
Dan asked, tossing out another ten.

"Quite the place." Spiro, deadpan, watched him through
predatory eyes. "Huge dome, lots of land under cultivation.
Almost nobody there. Well, but for a dead quetzal, some
women and children, and a deserter."

He won the hand, saying, "No wonder Aguila was interested. Rumor is she wanted it bad."

"They laid an ambush. Had us outgunned."

Oh, prickly. Best not to push her. "Shit happens. Heard
that the woman Rebecca was up here, double-checking
with Yvette that her deed was registered."

Dan played her for three raises, and took the hand.

"Yeah, that back-shooting slit, Perez, had a hand in that.
Every time that toilet-sucking bitch has done me rotten,
she's done it from behind. The day's gonna come when she
has to meet me face-to-face." Spiro smiled grimly. "And on
that day, I'm going to finally kill her for the cowardly cunt
she is."

Dan gave the woman a flat-eyed appraisal, expression neutral. "Others have tried."

He let her win the next hand.

"Sure. I'm not saying the locals don't have guts, and maybe some talent, but none of them were marines. Let alone marines who've been in the shit."

"You take out Perez," he told her, "you'll be a hero to more than just me. But I'd say it might make your life tougher in some corners."

Spiro shuffled, dealt. "I'm tired of taking shit from people. I don't care who they are. Mosadek? Dushane? Something tells me they're just walking sacks of skin without Perez to back them up."

"So, what's the real story behind The Corporate Mine? I hear she's solved her mobber problem. Still, rumor is that Aguila's just hanging on down there."

"Sure, she shot the hell out of the mobbers." Spiro studied her cards, two pair. Fours and sixes according to Art's signals. She discarded and took one card. A ten.

Dan had her with his three deuces, but folded diplomatically when she raised.

"Trees are going to shut her down in the end," Spiro added as she tossed out a five to ante for the next hand. "That's a battle she's slowly and surely losing. In the end, she can mine all the rich ore on Donovan, but if the forest overgrows that smelter, what damn difference does it make?"

"The trees can't move that fast, can they?"

"Oh, yeah. But what's she going to do? Spend every waking hour beating back the forest? It just keeps coming. Like a relentless damn tide. Five meters a day from every direction, like a noose being drawn tight. Her crews have taken to hauling the trees they kill off and dumping them. But that's wasted resources. What happens when the saws wear out? Circuits in the laser cutters fry? They lost another four acres just over the slowdown during the mobber scare."

"So it's a matter of time? Maybe she's not feeling too high and mighty now." Dan had Spiro at ease now, talking, so he skillfully dealt her three kings. Let her win big.

"Her? She'll feel high and mighty until Hell's colder than Pluto."

Guess we'll see about that. Ah, the snakes in our dens.

"What about you, Lieutenant? What do you see yourself doing now that you're retired from the Corps?"

She gave him that hard, dangerous stare. "Whole planet for the taking, wouldn't you say?"

"Oh, indeed I would." He gave her the slightest conspiratorial wink. "Opportunity everywhere. No telling where a tough, motivated woman like yourself could end up. Maybe even running your own operation. Got anything in mind?"

Spiro narrowed an eye. "Mundo'd be nice. Didn't get much of a look around, but what I saw looked like it had real potential. Fucking Aguila did it all wrong. Show of force? Hell, they knew we were coming. Were ready for us. But if a small party landed without them knowing? A team of five could take the whole place without a shot being fired."

"I see." He glanced at her. "Where are you going to get this team? My people tell me that the only marine who'll back you is Chavez."

She scowled at her cards. "Nashala's a sorry piece of work, isn't she? Took a job as security out at the clay pit. I'd need reliable people."

"I might have some." He carelessly bid a twenty.

"What's your interest in Mundo?"

"Power, Lieutenant. Same as yours."

"You have such a team?"

"I do." Now he matched her gaze for gaze. "But I'd want guarantees. Like the knowledge that Talina Perez wouldn't waltz right in and take it back."

"I can handle Perez," Spiro promised. "But what about Aguila? She's still got loyal marines, a shuttle, and enough people to back her."

Dan smiled as he cocked a knowing eyebrow. "Poor Aguila. The Supervisor doesn't know it yet, but the lady's about to find out that a very sharp blade is hovering within bare millimeters of her precious balls. And she can either acquiesce to common sense, or lose 'em."

"You can do that?"

"With a flick of my wrist."

Spiro grinned, slapping down her hand. "You know, I think I could come to enjoy playing cards with you, Mr. Wirth."

"That just leaves Officer Perez."

"Yes," she told him, eyes seeming to catch fire. "It does."

62

Some things just couldn't be kept quiet. No one had paid much attention after Ituri told Rita Valerie's crew chief that the woman had been reassigned to another job in Port Authority.

But with Petre Howe's very public poisoning, everyone at Corporate Mine was wondering about just where Valerie had been "reassigned." Especially a particularly distraught Ashanti Kung.

At this stage, Kalico had Corporal Abu Sassi admit that both Valerie and Howe had been murdered. That Valerie's death had been suppressed as part of the investigation into the killer's identity. They'd taken Kung into protective custody, and the growing camaraderie among her people had been substantially shaken.

Kalico fingered the healing scar on her cheek and stared woodenly at the cafeteria walls, wishing she had more of Talina Perez's wonderful breakfast on her plate and fewer problems at Corporate Mine.

They'd lost another acre to the trees over the last couple of days. Photoimagery showed no difference in the spacing between the encroaching trees. The forest could have been likened to water pouring into a hollow. None of the molecules were any farther apart. The whole forest was flowing in from all sides to reclaim her precious farm and smelter.

And then there was the mine. The mucking machine in Number One had broken. One of the gears that drove the conveyor had given way with a bang, leaving the machine useless.

This morning she was dispatching an aircar with Stryski aboard to see if Toby Montoya could machine a replacement.

Damn it. If only they'd thought to ship a machine shop aboard *Freelander*. Corporate, for whatever reason, hadn't thought another machine shop worthwhile.

So once again, Kalico found herself reliant on Port Authority. And it galled the hell out of her.

Not to mention the debacle down at Mundo. And what to do about Spiro.

"She shot a man in Inga's," Aurobindo Ghosh had told her after a quick trip to check the *Freelander* cargo for a crate of overalls. "Fair fight. The other guy shot first."

So which problem was more pressing? Spiro's growing reputation for shooting people, or the fact that her folks were working in patched clothing that was ever closer to rags?

If anything alleviated the near hopelessness, it was the four-day rotation into Port Authority. She'd had Ituri schedule the rotations so that crews worked ten days, then took four days in Port Authority. After which they helped load the shuttle with supplies and food purchased from the farmers, then flew back.

Not that it's done me a bit of good, she groused.

The constant problems had kept her shackled to Corporate Mine. One minor crisis after another. No sooner did she deal with one than another popped up. Equipment, personnel, the murders, technical problems at the smelter, decisions at one of the mines, medical emergencies, shortages, maintenance.

God, I'm tired.

Images of Talina Perez and Shig Mosadek formed in her memory. Fragments of conversation replayed. Kalico imagined herself sitting at Talina's breakfast bar, eating that magnificent breakfast, bantering with Shig about life, about government. Even hearing him lecture about religion while Talina chafed and shot back snide comments.

Wouldn't that be a welcome relief?

Kalico shook her head, blinking back to the reality of the cafeteria and the cup of tea before her.

"Get a grip on yourself, woman. What does it say about the rest of your life when all you can think about is wasting time with people you don't even like?"

She rubbed her face, massaging her eyes. Damn it, she was supposed to be a Corporate Supervisor. All of her life she'd been trained for higher purpose than mere existence. More had always been expected of her. Anything else was proof of weakness. The mere notion of socializing with inferiors unthinkable.

"God, Kalico, you're a vacuum-sucking mess."

"Supervisor?"

She looked up, seeing Abu Sassi where he'd stopped a couple of paces short so as not to startle her.

Shit. What had he heard?

"What is it, Corporal?"

"Sorry to interrupt." He looked distinctly uncomfortable.

"Go ahead."

"It's the woman. Ashanti Kung."

"Corporal, I know she's unhappy. I've already been appraised of her complaints. She's not getting out of that room until we've figured out who hung Valerie and poisoned Howe."

Abu Sassi winced. "Um, that's just it. Private Michegan went in to take her breakfast. Thought the woman was asleep on that cot we set up. That's when she noticed that last night's meal hadn't been eaten." He took a deep breath. "She's dead, ma'am."

"Dead?" Kalico stiffened, her tea forgotten, any refreshing thoughts shredded by this new reality. "How?"

"We'll need an autopsy, but Dina thinks someone broke her neck."

"Who? How? Damn it, she's been under surveillance, hasn't she? Check the cameras, Corporal."

Kalico stood, shoving her chair back. "Come on. This is like a slap in the face. As if we're completely incompetent. She's in the middle of the admin dome. Right down the hall from my room. How could it be more secure?"

"Easy, ma'am," Abu Sassi soothed. "Whoever got in there, we've got them. Sure, they might have gotten past building security, might even be an inside player, but they can't have managed to get past the cameras. Paco put 'em up. He's the best we've got."

Despite the frustration, Kalico knotted a fist. "As soon as we know who it is, I want them taken quietly, by surprise. We're going to have to deal with this publicly. Reassure people that we don't tolerate murderers. And we're going to need a confession as to who's really behind all this."

"Dan Wirth?"

"Got to be. Sending a message to the rest of his people. Don't make trouble. Grin and bear it. You know it's him."

"What if the murderer won't rat him out?"

"I ratted out," Kalico said thoughtfully. "That's what was scrawled on Rita Valerie's chest. I finally understand."

"Is that good enough to file charges?" Abu Sassi asked.

"No. Think, Marine. We've got to have a confession that ties the murderer to Wirth. Something concrete. The moment we get that, we go in, arrest the slimy son-of-a-bitch, and bring him here for trial."

They were in the hallway now, headed for the radio room with its security monitors. She led the way in, nodded to the woman at the radio, and watched Abu Sassi seat himself at the small side table.

The marine wasn't exactly greased electrons when it came to operating the holo projectors, accessing the right files, and bringing up the displays, but he finally managed to isolate the images taken by the security cameras outside Ashanti Kung's door.

Working backward, Abu Sassi ran the images starting with Dina Michegan finding the body, fast-tracking back. Each time someone entered the frame, it slowed to real time, showing everyone who entered, the time, and the duration of their visits. During the night, no one entered.

At 23:15 hours, it showed Paco Anderssoni escorting Kung to the women's room, and then locking her door behind her.

"I don't get it," Kalico muttered. "She's alive. Run it back farther."

Abu Sassi did. For the next hour they ran and reran the footage. In the end, the result was the same: From the time Paco locked a living Ashanti Kung into her room until Dina Michegan found the woman's corpse that morning, no one entered Kung's room.

"Could it have been Dina?" Kalico wondered, disbelieving that the private could have betrayed them all so.

"No," Abu Sassi told her reluctantly. "Look. She's not in there for more than three minutes before she's out in the hallway. That's at 07:05. I'm there with Tompzen by 07:13."

He looked up at Kalico. "I checked for a pulse immediately. Kung's body was stone cold. If Dina had gone in, broken her neck, and called me, Kung would have still been warm."

Kalico felt her stomach sour. "So it has to be someone on the inside." She glanced at the radio operator, a petite brunette woman. "What time did you come on duty this morning?"

"05:00, ma'am." The operator turned around in her chair. "Tam logged out last night at midnight. I found the door locked this morning. Um, that's five hours where this place is unoccupied."

"Five hours?" Kalico slumped back against the door.

"What do you want to do about this, ma'am?" Abu Sassi asked.

Kalico rubbed her forehead, the beginnings of a wretched headache beginning to stab at the back of her right eye. "Call Port Authority. See if Cheng can fly down. Maybe he can get something. A fingerprint. DNA. Some fiber or hair. And meanwhile, fly Ashanti's body up to PA. Maybe Raya can find something on the body that will give us a clue as to who killed her."

"You got it, ma'am," Abu Sassi told her with resolve.

Somehow, however, she already knew what they'd find: nothing conclusive.

Dan Wirth would have covered his tracks.

That meant she didn't have quetzal shit for proof.

Wirth was going to slip away like a slug through mud.

63

Rebecca had radioed in to announce the shuttle's arrival. Mark, Dya, and Su, along with all of the kids except the comatose Kylee, were present just beyond the shuttle perimeter to watch the silver delta sweep in from the sky to the north.

This time was different, but no more pleasant in its way than the last time. This shuttle might belong to Port Authority instead of Supervisor Aguila, but it represented a sort of death all its own.

Like a lethal raptor, the shuttle backed air, its thunder filling the mostly cloudy sky. With a rending of the heavens, the thing banked, slowed, and settled onto the recently cleared pad. The blast of deflected gases sent them ducking and scrambling.

"Shit," Dya cried over the earsplitting whine of the turbines as the thrusters spooled down.

Mark draped his arms around Dya and Su's shoulders as they straightened and started forward. Could feel the tension in his wives. Su sniffed, trying to wipe away her tears.

The hot, acrid stench of the great machine's engines washed over them.

"Su, I'm scared," little Tuska said as he clamped a death hold on his mother's hand.

"It'll be all right, baby," she told him in what she no doubt believed was an outright lie.

"Me, too," Taung chimed, holding back. The little boy looked on the verge of tears.

"Do you think they brought any young people our ages?" Damien asked.

"Probably not this time," Mark told him. "This is just Rebecca, Officer Perez, and probably a collection of technicians who can fix some of the broken things around the base."

He tightened his arms around his wives' shoulders, half urging them forward now that the great beast had gone silent.

Mark and his small troop had just passed the tractor up on its blocks when the shuttle's ramp dropped.

"God," Su whispered, "I prayed that this day would never come."

"It's the end of an era," Dya told her. "It was this, or Kylee."

"And look how that worked out," Su said bitterly. Then winced. "Dya. I'm sorry. I didn't mean that the way it . . . Ah, hell. You know I'm just as heartbroken as you are."

Mark shot a sidelong look at Dya, seeing the pain and flaring anger. "Sure, Su. It's all right. This is just a hard day for all of us."

Rebecca descended the ramp, a curious mixture of emotions reflected from the set of her lips: both grim resolve and a weary acceptance. At sight of them, she broke into a smile, trotting forward to hug them, one after another, and then scooped the children into her arms.

"How did it go?" Dya asked, struggling for composure as Perez led a group of three men and a single woman down the ramp. The group carried shouldered bags filled with various tools and equipment.

After Rebecca had fawned over each of the children, she took a final swipe at Damien's hair, ruffling his dark brown curls with a loving hand. Then she straightened and said, "We've got the best deal we could get. The base is ours."

"To do with as we will?" Su asked.

"That's right," Rebecca told her.

"Then tell those people to get back on the shuttle and leave us the hell alone," Su snapped.

"Not that easy," Dya told her. To Rebecca she said, "They'll fix the lift?"

Rebecca nodded, but her dark eyes didn't leave Su's. "Cable's in the shuttle." Turning she called, "Come meet my family."

Mark finally let go of Dya, but gave Su one last hug, adding, "It will be all right. You'll see."

"Yeah," his youngest wife whispered bitterly. "The end of everything we've loved."

"Not each other," Mark reminded.

Su shot him a disbelieving look, then turned on her heel, stalking away and dragging Taung and little Ngyap with her.

"Thought she'd take this better," Rebecca mused as she watched the younger woman stalk off.

"She's convinced herself it's going to end in disaster," Dya said. "After what happened the last time . . ."

"Yeah, well, we're not Corporate," Perez declared as the others walked up. "The first of these guys with me is Tyrell Lawson; he builds things. This big, thumb-fingered fellow is Toby Montoya. If it's broke, Toby can fix it. Hofer here is a sour-assed, hard-to-deal-with, opinionated pain in my ass, but he's the best structural builder on the planet. And finally, Sheyela Smith is the brains who keeps the lights and power working in Port Authority. She's here to check out your electrical."

One by one, they shook hands, going through the awkward ritual of introductions.

Mark, who should have felt at least a little at ease, had the feeling that something wonderful had just died. Like a beautiful bloom, a delicate flower had just gone brown and lifeless in his chest.

"Don't mind Su," Rebecca was telling them. "She's just taking this harder than we thought."

The remaining children—now face-to-face with strangers—looked abashed, each wide-eyed as they were introduced. Even Damien, so eager to meet other people, looked like he'd swallowed his tongue.

"How's Kylee?" Talina asked.

"No change," Dya told her dully.

"Damn it," Talina said through gritted teeth. "Mind if I go see her when we get everyone situated? Don't know that I can help, but maybe this quetzal inside me . . . ? Hell, it's still a chance."

"Sure," Dya told her easily.

To the newcomers, Rebecca said, "We're going to put you up in the old crew dormitory. It's not pretty. Only one light panel works. It's ground level so it'll save you another trip of having to climb up and down the stairs."

Tyrell Lawson told her, "Don't worry about us, Rebecca." He glanced around. "Um, what about protection? Didn't see any fences coming in. It's, like, nothing between the forest and us."

Sheyela winced, looking around skeptically. "Something tells me we don't set foot outside without being ready for a fight."

"We don't have much trouble here," Rebecca told him. "But since Kylee and Rocket . . . Well, this is a whole new world for us in other ways, too."

"Just keep your eyes open," Mark told them. "We have invertebrates, roos, and hoppers. If the death fliers, what you call mobbers, come through, just throw yourselves flat, don't move. Most definitely don't run! They don't know that humans are food. Don't let them learn on you."

"Yeah," Montoya said, voice dripping with worry as he looked around. "Teaching is the last thing I'm good at."

Sheyela jabbed Montoya's shoulder. "Don't worry, if they come, we'll feed Hofer to them. Couple of bites off his rancid carcass and they'd never touch humans again."

"Very funny," Hofer groused. To Rebecca, he said, "Let's see what the lodging looks like. Then let's get a look at the lift. And don't worry, for a plate of blueberries and some of these other goodies you been talking about, we'd be willing to sleep in the mud and shoot quetzals all night long."

Mark and his wives immediately bristled.

"*Not* funny," Talina told him. "Not here."

Hofer's eyes narrowed, and he nodded a grudging acquiescence. "Right. Tal, you brought us down here to fix things, not talk all day. Let's get to it."

"This way." Rebecca led them off to the small dormitory just back of the tower base.

"That didn't go so well," Mark admitted, glancing uneasily at Dya.

"Sorry," Talina said with a sigh. "Having Hofer around is like having sand deep in your knee joints. You know it's going to be gritty and painful. Problem is, no one knows buildings like he does."

"We'll deal," Dya said, and slapped hands to her thighs. "We're going to have to adapt. Accept changes."

Talina gave her an amused, sidelong glance. "Sure, Dya. But don't think it's all one-sided. You're sitting on a miracle here."

As she spoke, Manny Bateman, the shuttle pilot, came striding down the ramp followed by Sun-Ho, his copilot. "Hey, Tal?" he called. "Want me to button it up?"

"Better do so," Mark told her. "Otherwise it will be full of hoppers, and you wouldn't like that."

"Keep her tight, Manny," Talina called back. "You and Sung-Ho will have to stay on station. The others are probably going to be in and out for tools and supplies, not to mention that roll of cable."

"You got it, Tal." The hazel-eyed pilot snapped a short salute.

"Wasn't he one of the more infamous of the deserters?" Mark asked. "Like he was the first. Started the whole rush from *Turalon*?"

"Yeah, Trish farmed him and his shuttle crew out to the Briggs' place. Kind of nice when it was all said and done. We could space a starship with the kind of crew that ran off."

"Hard to believe," Mark whispered, taking Dya's hand. "Once upon a time I'd have been happy to have shot them both for running out on the Supervisor."

"See?" Dya told him with a smile, "We do learn new things."

"Yeah." Talbot gave his wife's hand a squeeze. "Let's go get these people lined out. The sooner they fix what's broken, the sooner we can load them up with delicacies and let them fly home."

Talbot turned, leading the way, attention fixed on the coming days. He might have just been a marine, but he damn well knew that Mundo was in bad shape. And it wasn't just the lift.

"What about Aguila?" Dya asked as they walked. "What have you heard from her?"

"Quiet as a mouse," Talina told her. "Spiro deserted, resigned, whatever. Rumor is that Kalico told her to bring back Talbot, here—and to do it without a ruckus—or don't come back herself."

"She made a ruckus, all right."

"Yeah, and she's been making more in Port Authority. Shot a man in a fair fight. And she's been blasting her mouth off about me. But getting back to the Supervisor, I think the reason you haven't heard from her is because Spiro really, truly irradiated the waters. And Aguila understood just how much Rocket was part of your family."

"So she's going to leave us alone?" Mark asked hopefully.

"For the time being," Talina answered. "But here's the underlying reality: She needs Mundo."

"She's *not* getting it," Dya snapped.

"No. We've got her boxed with the deed and titles." Talina walked with lifted chin, eyes slitted as if thoughtful. "That doesn't negate the fact that she needs what this place offers: pine trees. Your expertise in how to plant them and keep them alive until they can hold back the forest. She needs your produce until her own fields are producing. And in the long run, you, here, need her smelter and metals. We all do. We all need each other."

"After Rocket," Mark said, "we're not in a forgiving mood."

Talina put out a hand, stopping them. The woman's expression had gone deadly serious. "You have to be. We all have to be."

"Why?" Dya demanded. "What she did to Rocket—"

"What *Spiro* did to Rocket," Talina snapped. "Sure. Aguila sent her here. The woman's not without fault in this. She still thinks too much like a damned Boardmember: Always use a sledgehammer when all it takes is a feather to get the job done. But damn it, Dya, no one's coming for us. With Mundo, Port Authority, and Corporate Mine, we've got a lot better than even chance to make it. A real good chance."

"How can you be so positive?" Talbot asked.

"Because you and your family live here without fences, Mark. You've brokered a truce with Donovan. Something new. The die was cast at Port Authority when that first quetzal ate Donovan. We've been warring with the planet ever since, and Aguila just followed suit when she blasted Corporate Mine out of the forest."

"And you're saying that in a war, Donovan will win?" Dya asked thoughtfully.

Damien had been standing, lips pursed, listening thoughtfully. "But, Dya, we buried a lot of our people here. When we could find their remains, that is. It only changed when Rocket came."

Talbot saw the familiar narrowing of Dya's gaze. "That fact wasn't lost on us. Never saw another quetzal this side of the tree line after Kylee came waltzing in saying she had a new friend who was a quetzal. Everything changed."

Talbot arched an eyebrow. "Damn, I wish we could talk to her about this."

"She's still unresponsive?" Talina asked.

"She's not exactly in a vegetative state," Dya told her, stressed just by the saying. "She'll chew and swallow when I put food in her mouth. Drink when I put a glass to her lips. But otherwise she just stares at nothingness. Catatonic."

Talbot added, "We were thinking of flying her back to Dr. Turnienko. Just to get her thoughts if nothing else."

Talina squinted up at the high dome, as if seeing through the walls to the little girl. "I shared spit with Rocket that day. Maybe there's some molecule he left with me. Something my own quetzal hasn't told me about."

"Shared spit?" Talbot asked. "That's a bit . . ."

"Graphic?" Talina finished for him. "Yeah. I still haven't quite got my own brain wrapped around this yet. Trust me, you haven't lived until you've had a quetzal stick its tongue in your mouth."

"See if you can help her," Dya pleaded. "I've tried everything in the book."

"Yeah." Talina took a deep breath, reshouldering her rifle. "She's a most remarkable kid. I'll see what I can do."

What if she fails? Talbot wondered. What do we do then? Just watch Kylee waste away into a skeleton? Try and live with ourselves as she dies a little more each day?

64

Mark Talbot found Su sulking in her room. His youngest wife was sitting cross-legged on her bed, pillow clutched against her stomach in a manner reminiscent of the girl she had been not so many years ago. Her long black hair hung in silky waves down her back; a reflection of misery lay behind her eyes.

From her window, the nose of the Port Authority shuttle could just be seen where the silver monster stood on the pad.

"Hey, wife," Talbot greeted, stepping in and closing the door behind him.

Su remained silent, not even blinking to acknowledge his presence. Damn, that was all he needed. Two catatonic women in his life.

Talbot seated himself on the bed beside her, leaning forward to brace his elbows on his knees. "It's the blueberries, you know."

"The what?"

"Once word spread that Rebecca had taken blueberries to Port Authority, nothing could have prevented our discovery here."

"They're just fucking berries. Thousands rot on the bushes every month."

"They won't. They will feed people. Help everyone survive. You can dole them out along with all the other treats that grow here. Heard there was a new scanning atomic microscope in the *Turalon* cargo. That, and some data recording and analyzing gadgets that not only collect and categorize, but collate at the same time."

"God, Mark, what's stuff? Gadgetry? When everything we have here is dying before our eyes? I've had to swallow my hatred for that Perez woman. Had to have her *in my house*. And now our home is swarming with strangers."

As if in response a loud thump could be heard and felt through the floor. That had to be Hofer. The crude bastard had all the social graces of a diamond-bit rock saw, but Talina hadn't lied about his skills when it came to structural analysis.

"Did you really think that it would last forever, darling girl?"

"I had hoped." Su tightened her grip on the pillow, as if to comfort an ache deep in her gut. "And then you came along, and it was all so perfect. Some of the hole Paolo's death left inside me was filled. We had a chance for a future. All of us. Just family."

"You got lucky, you know. The three of you and the kids. If the lift had broken six months ago with all of you in it? If that second joist had rusted through under the floor where the water's been leaking in? If the pump had given out?"

"We'd have moved to the ground."

"You still might have to. Depends on what Hofer finds under the floor."

Her soft, dark gaze had gone moist on the verge of tears. "This isn't going to end well. I can feel it. Something's coming, Mark. And it isn't going to be good for us."

65

The change in Kylee shocked Talina when she finally stepped into the little girl's room. Kylee's face had hollowed, taken on a gray cast. The girl's vacant eyes had sunk into her skull and her hair had lost its luster. She sat rigidly on her bed, thin hands crossed on her lap. A pinched bitterness marked her bloodless lips.

"Kylee?" Talina asked, settling down beside her. "It's Talina. How are you doing?"

The girl might have been in a different universe for all the attention she paid.

Talina sighed, looked around the little girl's room. The walls were covered with pressed and dried plants; a small microscope stood on an end table. Rocket's bed of mussed blankets still lay on the floor, his memory so haunting that Talina could almost see him there. Tail curled around him, colors streaming down his sides as he chirred and stared up with his three curious eyes.

Even as she imagined it, her mouth began to salivate. A wet rush that surprised her.

"*Do it.*" Her quetzal's words came as a subtle whisper.

Talina made a face.

Would it help? Just the thought of it sent a quiver of unease through her. She hesitated, feeling the quetzal in her guts shifting. The thing was definitely irritated by her reluctance.

Well, shit. What would it hurt?

Talina winced, glanced back at the door to make sure that no one was watching, and bent down.

She placed her mouth against Kylee's. The girl might have been a corpse, so cold and unresisting was she. The notion sent a shiver down Talina's spine.

She felt the wet rush of saliva increase. Let it flow past her lips. Nothing.

The memory flashed through her of the times she'd

been face-to-face with quetzals. How that first one she'd encountered at Briggs' had acted. Or the one that had tried to kill her in her house.

Talina nerved herself. It took all of her will to force her tongue past Kylee's pinched lips. Felt the girl's teeth.

In that instant her saliva changed, tasting of a bitter peppermint so strong her eyes began to water. She knew that taste. Quetzal taste.

Adding to her unease was the knowledge that it had come from her.

"Yes," her quetzal told her.

Talina pulled back. Desperately she searched for some reaction. The girl just sat there, still rigid. Not even a flicker of her eyes betrayed any hint of returning consciousness on Kylee's part.

"Makes me feel like a fool," Talina whispered. "Come on, kid. Snap out of it. You have people here who love you. Your mom, Talbot, Rebecca, and the rest."

Nothing. Kylee's gaze remained empty. Her face expressionless.

"Kylee," Talina tried again, wondering if the girl could even hear her. "People lose loved ones all the time. It's part of life. I've lost people I loved with all my heart. You're tough. I know you. You'll come through this. Rocket would want you to."

Or would he? How would Talina know? Hell, she didn't even know what she might have communicated to the kid through that quetzal spit. Given her relationships with quetzals, she might have been telling Kylee to pick up a hammer and beat her to death.

"Kylee? Can you hear me? Anything?" She snapped her fingers before the girl's eyes. Still nothing.

Maybe the girl was so far gone not even quetzal spit would reach her.

Talina kept trying. Was still talking, patting the girl's hand when Dya leaned in, asking, "Anything?"

"No." Talina sighed in defeat and stood. "I tried everything I could think of. Damn Spiro for this. I wish that woman had never been born."

Dya gave her that glass-hard look the woman seemed to adopt when she was remembering the past. Then she slapped a hand to the doorframe and said, "Hofer and Lawson want us all in the great room. Something about the dome."

"Yeah." Talina bent down, staring into Kylee's eyes, to add, "You just tough it out and come back to us, all right?"

Dya let her pass, taking a final look back at her daughter, and calling, "We love you, Kylee."

Talina led the way, her heart like a stone in her chest. Surely there'd been something of Rocket that she'd taken in that day he died. She remembered the way the little quetzal's tongue had flickered on her lips. If Raya and Cheng were right, some message should have been in the twerp's TriNA. If nothing else, that should have broken Kylee out of her funk.

In the big main room, Hofer was sucking down a glass full of tea, Lawson standing to one side, arms crossed as he talked to Talbot.

Rebecca and Su were already on the couch, and Dya stepped over to join them. The little kids were playing in the corner next to the window; Tuska was reciting a list of amino acids to Shine and Ngyap. The older kids, however, were all outside, tackling their various chores.

Talina retreated to her now accustomed place by the curving window where she could listen and stare out at the compound and forest beyond.

"Okay, you're all here," Hofer said, fingering his empty glass. "It ain't good. In fact, I'm a bit nervous just standing here."

"What did you find?" Rebecca asked.

"The dome rests on a foam-steel frame. A radial construction cast in vacuum. Foam steel's great stuff. Three to four times stronger than regular steel at a quarter the weight. And the dome base folds up. Think of splayed fingers that rotate around a central hub. Perfect for transportation in a ship's hold from Solar System."

"So, what's the problem?" Talbot asked.

"Problem is that the dome was supposed to sit on the ground," Hofer said. "Not up here a hundred meters in the air atop a tower. Not that that wouldn't have been okay, but the dome hasn't been kept in repair. There's cracks in the shell. Most of the windows leak. And it rains just about every day here."

"Corrosion?" Lawson asked.

"Oh, yeah." Hofer squared his shoulders. "Water's been running down the inside of the walls, pooling around the steel. And that's what it is: steel. An iron-based metal. Iron oxidizes in the presence of water and oxygen."

He paused. "There's places under your floor where I tapped the rusted joists, and my hammer went clear through. That's why the floors are sagging across the dome."

"How bad is it?" Dya asked.

"I told you: I'd rather be someplace else having this conversation. If every day were like today, you'd be lucky if the underlying steel lasts another year. But ma'am, you get a high wind? Bad storm that buffets this place? My guess is that it's all going to come tumbling down, and you and the kids don't want to be inside it when it does."

Talina watched the expressions as Rebecca, Su, and Dya turned ashen.

"This is our home," Su whispered. Then she looked up, expression expectant. "Can we fix it?"

"Sure," Hofer told her. "With the proper reinforcing, a heavy-lift shuttle could lift the dome off and set it on blocks. The old subframe could be cut out and a new one bolted on. You got another subframe laying around someplace I didn't see?"

The women looked uneasily at each other, the answer obvious.

"So, what do we do?" Rebecca asked.

"Pack your gear," Hofer told them. "And pray that you can get it down before this thing comes crashing down. My bet is that the west side collapses first. When that happens, the dome slants in that direction. The tower might hold, or the shift in mass might pull it over. If it falls to the west, it's going to crush the buildings on that side. Best case is if, when the west side goes, the rest of the joists let loose. If that happens, the tower punches right through the top of the dome, and it all slides down to the ground like a donut around a spear."

"Just a matter of time, huh?" Talbot asked.

"Hey, I'm sorry, Mark. But, yeah, that's it." Hofer spread his arms in apology.

Talina's stomach churned, and it wasn't the quetzal this

time. She almost couldn't take the expressions on the women's faces.

Su whispered, "But this is our home."

Rebecca closed her eyes, reached out and gripped her younger wife's hand. "Not anymore. At least, the dome isn't. Believe me, Su, this hurts me more than you. I helped build this place. I was here when Weed, Max, and the rest lifted the dome atop the tower with a heavy-lift shuttle. Weed lost his arm in the process. Crushed when the dome was lowered."

"How do we get everything out of here?" Dya asked. "Fix the lift? Even knowing it's short term?"

"Use the Beta," Talina told them. "It's got a one-ton lift capacity. Take your equipment and appliances out through the roof hatch." She glanced at Hofer. "They probably want to remove their possessions carefully? Uniformly relieve the stress on the substructure?"

"That'd be smart," Hofer agreed. "You can recharge the Beta from the shuttle, which will save time when the power pack runs down. Speaking of which, I'd move the shuttle. Granted, it's to the east of the tower, but that's one piece of equipment we really don't want damaged if everything goes to shit."

"What about the dormitory?" Lawson asked. "It's on the north side, but to tell you the truth, I ain't sleeping there tonight."

"There's room for everyone in the shuttle," Talina told them. "And we can move it down to the field, even if it crushes some of the crops."

Tears were streaking down Su's face. Dya's jaw had gone tense, the muscles in her cheeks knotted as she ground her teeth. Rebecca just looked worn, old, and defeated.

"It's almost dusk," Hofer said. "We might want to at least get the bedding out. Take tonight and figure a plan for how to tackle the rest come morning."

Talina watched the three women, sitting as if paralyzed, thinking: *So this is how a dream dies.*

66

It wasn't until just before dusk that Dya came charging down the stairs inside the tower. The way her feet rang on the rickety stairs caught Talina's attention long before the woman came panting and leaping down the last flight.

"What's up, Dya?" Talina called, straightening from where she'd been packing tools at Rebecca's request.

"You seen Kylee?" Dya was panting, frantic, eyes a glazed blue.

"No."

"She's gone."

"What do you mean, gone?"

Dya swallowed hard. "She's not in her room. Not anywhere in the dome. Did you see her come down the stairs?"

"No. Not that I've been here the entire time. People have been in and out."

"Help me. I've got to find her!"

Talina put a soothing hand on the woman's shoulder. "It's all right. We'll find her. Were her crutches still in her room?"

Dya nodded, forcing a panicked swallow down her throat.

"Well, in her condition, she can't have gone far," Talina told her. "Let's alert the others. It's still an hour before dark. We'll find her."

But even with everyone looking, by the time night fell, Kylee might have vanished into thin air.

And even worse, Rebecca and Shantaya, who'd volunteered to search the fields to the south, hadn't come back either.

Just to be sure, Talina had used the shuttle's speakers to call out, ordering Kylee, Rebecca, and Shantaya back to the shuttle. Then she'd gone out on her own, using night vision, as she searched for the missing woman and girls.

Several times she thought she caught flashes of images

at the edge of the trees. Moving fast, the things had looked suspiciously like quetzals, which made the one in her gut hiss with delight.

In the end, she'd returned. Buttoned up the ramp, and called it a night.

But damn it, it didn't make any sense. Why would Rebecca, of all women, take silly chances?

And what would have possessed Kylee to leave the dome in the first place?

Talina had been on Donovan too long, been involved in too many missing persons searches, to think this was going to end well.

67

"**D**efinitely a quetzal." Trish stood just outside the shuttle field gate, binoculars to her eyes as she watched the creature duck along the edge of the distant tree line.

"Yeah, that's what I thought," Smit Hazen, the young guard who'd been on duty at the gate replied as he watched through his own binoculars. "Why's it parading like that? White and red stripes, flashes of orange. It's acting like it wants us to know it's here."

"Maybe that's the plan." Trish lowered her optics, took in the shuttle field where Kalico's A-7 sat no more than one hundred meters away, the ramp down. A couple of completely clueless crew lounged beside the ramp telling stories in the shade of the aft tail section.

"Two Spots?"

"Go, Trish," her implant answered.

"Got a quetzal hanging out just at the edge of the tree line beyond the shuttle field."

"Roger that."

A moment later, Two Spots' voice called through the loudspeakers, *"Attention. We have a quetzal sighting at the edge of the bush just east of the shuttle field. This is just an alert."*

Trish grinned as the two crew leaped for the ramp, drawing it up after them.

Out by the containers, Pamlico Jones and his crew moved with considerable alacrity, scrambling up into one of the loaders and heading for the gate.

Trish checked her watch, seeing that it was almost quitting time anyway. The distant quetzal had stopped, and was studying them as Trish raised her glasses and returned stare for stare. The thing had spread its collar, now shooting rainbow patterns along both ruff and sides.

To her com, Trish said, "Keep your eyes open, people. This might be a decoy. Might be another one or two trying to sneak in from another direction. On your toes and don't be shy using the thermal gear. That's what it's for."

"Roger that."

"The farms are all shutting down," Wejee Tolland reported. *"Everyone outside the fence is on alert."*

"Roger that," Trish replied, searching past the distant quetzal, looking for any others that might be accompanying the first. At that distance, a quetzal could only be seen if it wanted to be. As masterful as they were at camouflage— Trish had almost stepped on them in the past—this was highly unusual behavior. Like it meant something.

A rifle banged on the afternoon air. Banged again. Then came the crackle of pistol shots.

Trish turned. "That was inside the fence. Sounded like the middle of town."

"I'll lock the gate behind you," Smit called as she charged through the small man gate.

She didn't look back, figuring that at any moment . . .

"Trish? Got shots fired." Two Spots' voice echoed in her ear. *"Main avenue. Just out front of The Jewel."*

"On my way."

Shit. And Kalico Aguila's people were all over the place. They hadn't been in town for more than two hours.

Trish rounded the admin dome, rifle gripped as she called, "Coming through!" Not that so many people were in the street, but they were all looking toward the north where the shots had come from.

Just about everyone had a rifle or pistol in hand. Shots coming that close to a quetzal alert? What the hell were they to think? Wouldn't be the first time one of the beasts had slipped into the compound in broad daylight.

The only reason everyone wasn't flocking toward the shots was that they halfway expected to hear the siren blare for a lockdown.

A knot of people was gathered in the street in front of The Jewel. Some were crouched over a sprawled body. Lieutenant Spiro stood to one side, hip cocked, hand on the butt of her pistol.

The lieutenant had a crooked but amused smile, her dark eyes flashing. The breeze flipped insolently at her shoulder-length black hair.

Dan Wirth stood in The Jewel's doorway, arms crossed on his quetzal-hide vest, a grim amusement betrayed by his wry expression. His people crowded the door behind him, heads bobbing as they tried to see.

"What's going on here?" Trish demanded, pushing her way through the crowd. "Oh, shit. What happened?"

Trish bent down. Shan Strazinsky lay facedown in the avenue's packed gravel. Three gaping wounds in the middle of his back leaked blood into the fabric of his bright blue shirt. More was pooling under his chest; bright crimson, it flowed around the angular chunks of gravel. From the looks of things, he'd fallen face-first onto his rifle. One arm was flung out, the dirt clawed at, as if he'd been reaching for something when he died.

Trish felt for a pulse in the man's still-warm neck, but wasn't surprised to find nothing. Not shot through the chest like he was.

Trish slowly stood, looking around. Spiro was grinning at her, the woman's left hand lifted as in a "so what" gesture. Her other hand remained suggestively on her pistol butt, as if it were a dare.

"The guy just started shooting," Spiro said. "Never seen him before in my life. He called out, 'Hey, you, Deb Spiro,' and I turned. That's when he shot. Bang."

Spiro fingered a frayed spot in her uniform about midway down her right arm. "Fucker came that close. Can you believe? I'm just walking along, minding my own business, and this guy starts shooting."

"It's Shan, you idiot," Friga Dushku called from where she watched at the edge of the crowd. Two of her kids were peeking around her skirt with wide eyes.

"Who's Shan?" Spiro asked. "And why would he care to kill me?"

"Shan Strazinsky," Trish told her, stepping forward. "Felicity's husband. You murdered his wife with that bomb you set for Talina."

A muttering of anger broke out in the crowd behind Trish.

Spiro's smile, weirdly, stupidly, grew wider. "Whoa now. Don't you go laying that on me. That was Talina's fault. I told the woman. Shouldn't be leaving explosives lying around the house."

"You did it, bitch!" someone called from behind.

Spiro's smile went deadly. "You come out here, you piece of shit. You look me in the eye when you shoot your lying mouth off like that!"

"Hey!" Trish yelled, turning, seeing Rude Marsdome, the boot maker, looking like he'd just swallowed a slug. "All of you, shut the fuck up. Now, anyone see this?"

"I did," Friga said warily. "Shan hasn't been doing well. Him and the kids. Alone in that house. Said he was going to fix things. That it wasn't right that some bitch like Spiro could just walk free after what she'd done to Felicity."

"Done what to Felicity, bitch?" Spiro started forward.

Friga went pale, swallowed hard, but stood her ground.

Trish pointed a finger at Spiro. "You don't want to so much as look mean at that woman, Lieutenant, or these people will shoot you into hamburger on the spot, and I'll step back and let them do it."

Spiro's crazy smile was back. "Ohhh. I'm so scared, Officer Monagan."

"What happened next, Friga?"

"Shan was coming from the Mine Gate. Saw Spiro from behind. Recognized the uniform. He called out 'Hey, you, Deb Spiro.' That's when I stopped."

"And when Spiro turned and said yes," Rude declared, "Shan pulled up his rifle and shot."

"Shan shot first?" Trish asked just to be clear.

Nods and mutters of assent came from around the circle. Trish's gut sank. "No provocation? Spiro didn't taunt him? Didn't challenge him?"

"Fuck, no!" Spiro almost spat the words.

Around the circle of witnesses, everyone shook their heads.

"Self-defense," Spiro told her. "Hey, the bastard got off two shots. Look at this friggin' hole in my uniform. That the best you scum-suckers can do with a rifle at twenty paces?"

"Shan wasn't a hunter," Trish said softly. "Mostly he took care of the kids. Especially during the hours when Felicity was called away. He did most of the sewing in their clothing business. But for quetzal drills, the man probably never held a rifle in his life."

"Maybe he should have," Spiro offered with a shrug, her

predatory eyes on Trish. "Can I go now? Or do you want to try and pick up where good old Shan, here, left off?"

"Self-defense," Trish said wearily. "Sure can't call it murder." But just for once, couldn't Shan have let honor slide? Just shot Spiro in the back and saved them all a world of grief?

"Sure you don't want to try me?" Spiro hinted, a crazy gleam of anticipation in her black eyes. Her fingers were tapping suggestively on her pistol butt.

Trish pursed her lips, slowly shook her head, and realized she was afraid like she'd never been in her life.

Her heart pounding, her mouth dry, she watched Deb Spiro turn on her heel and stride purposefully for the door of The Jewel, acting for all the world like she owned the place.

Dan Wirth backed out of the way, gesturing for the lieutenant to pass. After she'd strode inside, Wirth shot the shaken Trish a smile, then flicked a sort of mock salute and vanished into his lair.

This was the way it was meant to be. Dan Wirth prowled his tables, enjoying the dealer's calls, listening to the prattle of the faro dealer as he exhorted the marks. The clinking of chips and glasses, the bustle of a busy night, were all the hallmarks of success.

Especially since the personnel rotations from Corporate Mine had resumed. Nights like this? Wealth flowed into his coffers like a river into a sea.

Dan glanced back where Art Maniken exchanged chips for SDRs and plunder back in the cage. The big man wore a genial smile as he slid stacks through the barred window.

Allison, much to Dan's delight, was profitably engaged in her plush room in the back. Desch Ituri had arrived within minutes of the shuttle's arrival. He'd strode in, his coveralls washed, a curious and somewhat self-conscious smile on his lips.

At the cage, he'd thunked down a golden ingot before the startled Allison, and asked, "Will that buy me the whole night?"

She had glanced sidelong at Dan, who'd nodded. Had to be a twenty-pound ingot if it weighed an ounce. To Allison, he'd whispered, "And drop a little eros in the man's drink, angel. Then ride him like he's never been ridden in his life. Leave him weeping for more. Whatever it takes."

She'd nodded and given him a conspiratorial wink. "I'll give him everything I've got."

"That's my girl!" He'd smacked her on that wonderful tight ass of hers as she led the short engineer back to her lair.

Ituri. Aguila's right-hand engineer. Dan hadn't known the man was even aware of Allison's existence, and then he wanders in and drops a chunk of gold like that?

Under his breath, Dan whispered, "Played right, who knows where this will end?"

"Fuck me!" Spiro disrupted his thoughts as she cursed

loudly enough to be heard over the entire room. Some of the patrons glanced back toward where she sat in the corner next to the bar, her back to the wall.

The lieutenant had been drinking ever since the shooting. While she'd had a trickle of people who dared to play poker with her, the only one left was Michael Chavez as she'd grown more surly. Even the ex-marine was looking owly and unsure. Drunk as she was, Spiro was squinting at the cards, her head wobbling.

Not a good sign.

Dan caught Vik Schemenski's eye where the man poured drinks behind the bar. Gave him the cut-off sign, and indicated Spiro.

Schemenski flicked a finger along the line of his jaw in acknowledgment.

Not thirty seconds later, Kalico Aguila herself stepped in, stopped, and slowly took in the busy room. As her eyes met Wirth's, they seemed to turn a glacially cold shade of blue. A faint and distasteful smile bent her lips.

She wore a form-fitting black jumpsuit that did little to camouflage her marvelous body. To Dan's appreciative eye, she might have lost some weight. Maybe ten pounds if he were to guess. Not that the rail-thin look didn't suit her well. The healing red scars on her cheeks, however, rather than mar her appearance, added a menacing quality. Word was her entire body was crisscrossed with a patchwork of scars now. Made her, if anything, more exotic.

All the way back to the days on *Turalon* Dan had speculated what it would be like to take Aguila to bed. True, she came off as an overindulged prig, but what if she dropped all those Corporate inhibitions and really turned herself loose? Allowed herself to unleash all that subsumed passion and fuck a man like God had intended?

"Might even give Allison a turn of competition," he mused to himself. Then he plastered that boyish smile on his lips. Inclined his head graciously, and stepped forward.

"Why, do my eyes deceive me? Can that be Supervisor Aguila come to share her company with us? And yes, indeed, it really is. Welcome. We are not only honored, but delighted. Come, do step inside. And what, good lady, might we do for you this fine evening? Perhaps a game? A turn at the tables? Or might we just offer you a drink, a simple token of our appreciation for all that you've accomplished down at Corporate Mine."

He turned, calling, "Vik! A glass of our best for the Supervisor!"

"Coming up, boss!"

As Dan turned back, it was to find Aguila's smile even more icy, were that possible. He kept his in place, radiating hospitality and delight as he pondered the slit's true purpose in walking through his door.

Perhaps something related to Spiro's shootings?

No. Had to be the *Turalon* deserters.

A fact she confirmed the moment she said, "You killed them all, didn't you?"

"Why, dear lady, I have no idea to what you refer." He took the drink Vik offered him, extending it toward Aguila. The room had gone eerily quiet, every eye on him and Aguila as they faced each other between the craps table and the door. "Do try the whiskey. Cost me an arm and a leg, as Inga drives a hard bargain, and this one's been aging for about a decade now."

She reached out—eyes never leaving his—and took the glass. "Valerie, Howe, Kung. You got them all. Paid them back for the temerity of charging you for being the bit of bipedal walking dung that you are."

Dan took a deep breath, kept his smile in place. "Surely someone has pointed you in my direction for some nefarious purpose. If you'll recall, I was shocked, alarmed, and more than mortified at the revelations they professed about that despicable Tosi Damitiri. Wonder where he's vanished to, or I'd deal with him myself. Odd, don't you think, how a man like him could so completely disappear? Poor sap was known for a fondness for drink. Maybe, deep in his cups, he wandered out into the bush."

Dan waved it away as if a trifle. "But I digress. No, far from wanting those poor deserters punished, it would have been my humble duty to offer them every remedy in the book! What happened to them out at Tosi's? In *my* name? Call it what you will, but I call it un-fucking-conscionable!"

"Indeed?" she asked softly, a dangerous clarity in her cerulean gaze.

"Indeed!" Dan shot back. "And I would have made every restitution in the . . . Ah! But wait! Don't I recall that it was the good Supervisor . . . waving a contract as if it were a holy charter blessed by God . . . who reclaimed the three poor innocent victims and marched them off to her shuttle?"

He waved a hand grandly toward the south. "Hauled them off to Corporate Mine, far beyond my ability to offer them suitable recompense for the indignities that bastard Damitiri inflicted upon them. And now you tell me they're dead?" he ended on an incredulous note.

"Drop the act," she told him coldly. "You and I need to make something clear. I *will* figure out who your agent is at Corporate Mine. And when I do, I will put a bullet through his head. And if you *ever* try something like this again, I will follow through by putting another bullet right between your eyes. Are we clear, Mr. Wirth?"

Dan felt that cold calmness settle around his heart. That growing focus and narrowing of purpose. He let the smile fade, let the promise burn in his eyes as he coldly said, "Supervisor, don't come here blaming me. I offered those people everything. Rather, could it be *your* aims which were best served by their unfortunate demise? A warning to the rest of the *Turalon* deserters? Your way of stating: 'Beware all ye who have crossed me in the past! Heed this, in the event you might think of doing so in the future. For your fate shall be as is the fate of these unworthy wretches. If you ran out on me like Valerie, Howe, and Kung did, you're all dead.' "

Aguila's smile thinned. "You think anyone will buy that?"

"Oh, most assuredly I do," Wirth told her with special emphasis. "I didn't need to harm a hair on their heads. By crying, 'Contract! Contract!' you had already dissuaded any of the other *Turalon* folks from turning themselves in."

He let the smile expand again. "Or, despite your announced clemency, have there been floods of them washing up on your shores down at Corporate Mine begging to be brought back to The Corporation's bosom?"

"You are warned, Mr. Wirth," she told him, coldly. "It will not be repeated."

Wirth suffered a moment of irritation as Spiro, weaving

on her feet, appeared at his elbow, asking, "Got a problem here, Dan?"

"Nothing the good Supervisor and I haven't come to a satisfactory conclusion on, Lieutenant."

"Hey, Deb." Chavez was pulling at Spiro's arm from behind. "Come on. You don't want to get into this."

"Good ol' Kalico's givin' my comrade Dan a hard time. Can't have that." Spiro had that silly grin on her lips, her half-lidded and drunken eyes fixed on Aguila's.

Oh, fuck.

Dan turned, waving Spiro back. "Deb. There's a free drink back at the bar. Just waiting for you. All is fine here. Trust me."

"Come on." Chavez was tugging Spiro back. "Let's go get that drink. Dan can handle the Supervisor."

"Yeah, right," Spiro gulped, as if on the verge of puking. "Leave it up to Dan to handle the silly slit."

Aguila's expression, her pinched lips, the disgust she could barely contain, amused Dan as he turned back to her. "My, Supervisor, you do inspire loyalty from your people, don't you?"

Aguila lifted the glass of whiskey Vik had brought. Turning it, she poured the contents out to spatter onto the floor. Then she dropped the glass onto the chabacho wood planks.

"To all Corporate employees. This place is off limits until further notice. Any of you who doubt my word can take it up with Corporal Abu Sassi. You have three minutes to collect your winnings and be the hell out of here!"

She turned on her heel and stalked out the door.

In the silence that followed, Dan slapped his sides, and cried, "You have got to love that woman. Talk about spirit." Then he turned, adding, "Well, come on. All you Corporate types. Pack your shit and trot your asses out of here! Move it!"

He was laughing as he said it. Making light. As if he thought the whole thing amusing.

But, Supervisor, you have just declared war.

69

The shuttle seats hadn't been designed to be slept in. Talbot realized he was getting a kink in his neck, and his butt was numb. But then, none of the adults in the passenger section were really sleeping. More like they were dozing, waiting for the night to end.

The kids, however, were so deeply asleep they appeared comatose. That was the thing about kids. When they ran out of energy, they switched off. Dropped into that alpha-wave pattern. Didn't seem to care if they were cramped, jammed into a chair, or what absurd position they were bent into.

Even Damien, for all of his distress and hurt, had surrendered to oblivion.

For Talbot it was just one nightmare after another, playing over and over in his head. How had Kylee managed to get out of the dome? Where had she gone? What happened to Rebecca and Shantaya?

Surely they hadn't walked off into the forest.

Or, if they had, why? Was it the abandonment of the dome? Had losing the security of their high and comfortable home been such a shock that it completely unhinged Rebecca? Enough that she'd seek suicide in the forest rather than live in a hovel on the ground?

But that didn't explain her taking Shantaya with her. Or why Kylee would have suddenly snapped out of her funk enough to sneak away.

None of it made an atom's worth of sense.

Which left him to imagine. He'd lived so many of Donovan's horrors. Smart as Rebecca was, he couldn't imagine her, Shantaya, and wounded Kylee out in the darkness. Where would they have gone? How would they stay safe?

In the dim light, Talbot saw Su get up and walk forward toward the cockpit.

He sighed, climbed to his feet, and rubbed the back of his neck as he started forward.

He stepped through the hatch to find Su standing behind the pilot's seat, staring out at the darkness. Light from the instruments silhouetted her slender body. Glowed around the edges of her long black hair.

"Can't sleep?" He asked the dumbest questions.

"Scared. Heartsick. Frustrated. You name it." Su shook her head sadly. "This is like a nightmare that doesn't end. The worst thing is what I keep imagining."

He stepped up to put an arm around her shoulders. "Rebecca is the best of us. She's been here from the beginning. If anyone knows her way around the forest, it's her."

"It had to be the girls," Su said stubbornly. "Kylee must have come to. Maybe Shantaya told her we were abandoning the base. They're best friends, you know. Same age. Kylee wasn't quite sane. Decided to run rather than give up her home. Somehow Rebecca discovered what they were up to. Saw them as they disappeared into the trees and . . ."

"Why didn't she call the rest of us?"

"I don't know. Maybe she didn't have time."

Talbot hugged his wife closer against his side. Memories kept flashing through his mind: Kylee, grinning as she teased him about being a pedophile. Shantaya, dirt on her nose, laughing as she picked blueberries and plums. That wry, somewhat amused look in Rebecca's eyes as she told Talbot she was pregnant with his child.

How could a man who loved so much be so helpless?

"I'm a marine. I should be out there."

"In the dark?" Su asked. "Have Dya, the kids, and me scared to tremors over you, too?"

He bit his lip, fought for a breath. "It's the waiting. The not knowing. Damn it, if my armor still worked, I could be searching right now, using the thermal sensors in the heads-up. Wouldn't matter what Donovan threw at me, I could be keeping our people safe."

"Kylee's behind this," Su whispered. "Has to be."

"Hey, don't. She's a little girl who lost her best friend. If it's anybody's fault, it's the lieutenant's."

"I wish . . ." Su swallowed hard. "I wish that woman were dead."

"If I ever get the chance," Talbot promised.

"Mark? What if something's happened to them? How are we going to heal? It's going to destroy Dya, Damien, and the kids. On top of losing our home, it's just too much."

"Rebecca knows what she's doing. You'll see."

He wished that were true as he looked out at the black night. Couldn't even see the buildings under the cloud-dark sky. If Rebecca and the girls were out in the forest? Damn. The darkness would be so thick they couldn't see their hands in front of their faces, let alone a sidewinder or chokeya.

Su nodded.

But he could tell she didn't believe it.

Neither did he.

Please, let them be alive, he prayed to the universe. Prayed like he'd never prayed before.

70

Talina glanced up at Talbot, Su, and Dya as they followed her down the shuttle's ramp and onto the hard-baked ground. Saw the worry in their eyes as they glanced around, half desperate, half afraid. The damp air carried the perfumed smells of forest mixed with the green scents from the agricultural fields.

The chime was rising as if in response to the pinkish-orange glow of morning as Capella's first rays tinged the highest treetops on the eastern horizon.

Talina looked back where Lawson, Hofer, and Sheyela Smith stood at the top of the ramp. "You continue with the removal of the dome's lab equipment. Keep an eye out in case we need the aircar."

"Sure you don't want us to come along?" Sheyela asked.

"You don't know the property," Dya answered. "And someone has to keep an eye on the kids. We've already lost two, don't let any more wander away. Food's in the kitchen. Damien will help."

"Just find them," Damien called where he stood beside Hofer. "I've got the rest."

Good kid that Damien. He was doing his best to look like he wasn't frightened half out of his mind.

Talina turned, saying, "Okay, as per the plan: Talbot, you and Su take the north end, Dya and I will take the south. First one to find anything, fire a shot."

Talbot had the old bolt-action rifle over his shoulder. Talina had her pistol and service rifle.

"Let's go," Dya told her. The woman took off at a crisp walk, a grim set to her jaw.

Talina gave a final wave to Talbot and Su, had to trot to keep up with Dya as she led the way past the old tractor and between the shops.

"Think they might have made it back after that final

pass I made last night?" Talina asked. "Should we check the shops again?"

"Went through them just before sunset," Dya replied. "If she got that close, Rebecca would have headed for the dome. If she's there, Hofer and Lawson will find her as soon as they take the aircar up."

"You really think they went into the forest, huh?" Talina kept shooting wary glances to each side. Checked every shadow cast by the buildings. She couldn't get over the notion she'd caught glimpses of quetzals the night before.

Now she was vigilant. Over the years, she'd developed an eye for the slight wavering edges of her vision where a quetzal, bem, or skewer might be lurking. As good as Donovanian beasts were at camouflage, it was always the edges that gave them away. Or the smell.

"I don't know," Dya's near-cry was tinged with exasperation and fear. "I've been trying to think this through all night. This isn't like Kylee. And it sure as hell isn't like Rebecca, let alone Shantaya."

Dya hesitated, her face contorting in the pale morning light. "I'm scared like I've never been in all my life."

"We'll figure it out," Talina told the woman with more assurance than she felt.

They passed between the last of the sheds and slowed. The fields looked blue-green in the half light, leaves silvered from the morning dew.

As the chime rose and fell, nothing moved in the fields. They looked perfectly still, peaceful. The sort of bucolic image therapists projected on the wall of a mental institution to reassure and soothe patients.

"Rebecca!" Dya shouted. Her voice carried across the fields, the chime rising in response.

Nothing.

"Come on," Dya said at last, leading the way down the causeway that separated the fields.

Talina eased her rifle from her shoulder, left hand supporting the forearm, index finger of her right on the rest above the trigger as she flexed her hand around the grip.

Her senses tingled, every sound coming to her ears, her nose taking in the rich morning air, catching just a trace of . . .

"*Yes,*" the quetzal in her belly whispered.

Even as she identified it, she stopped short, pointing with the rifle. "Dya? Stop. See them?"

Dya froze, eyes on the moist dirt. "Tracks. Quetzals. Two of them."

"Full adults," Talina added as she squatted, head cocked to study the tracks. But no. Could it be?

"Got a girl's tracks here. Real faint, see? Like a heel strike. And here's a rounded toe print. Kylee wears those soft-leather boots."

"She's walking between them?"

"That or she either went this way first and they followed, or they went first and she followed them."

Dya stared around, cupped her mouth, and called, "Kylee? Rebecca? Shantaya? Where are you?"

The chime shifted its tremolo, as if in response.

Talina's heartbeat picked up as she straightened, trying to see in all directions. "You see a lot of quetzal tracks around here?"

"Just Rocket's. Haven't seen an adult since Rocket and Kylee bonded." Dya was pulling at her hands, her nervous eyes scanning the tree line.

"And then you suddenly get two?"

Her quetzal wiggled where it lurked down by her spleen. She could feel the thing's anticipation. But what was it waiting for?

"If those are Kylee's tracks, this is the way she went," Talina said as she stood and started down the causeway. Step by step, she led the way. The hair on the back of her neck prickled. She was experiencing that eerie sensation, the intensity of being watched by unseen eyes. She shivered from a tickle of premonition. The danger was close.

Where?

To either side the tangle of intermixed crops stretched away like a green mat; they changed color as the first of Capella's rays topped the eastern forest and cast shadows from the leaves.

Two quetzals. They could have taken Kylee, used her as bait, knowing any rescue would come this way. And if they were hiding down in the squash, beans, okra, and cabbage? It would be the edges, the three gleaming dark eyes, that would give them away.

Come on, Tal. They're quetzals. You should be able to sense them.

"*Yes,*" her quetzal whispered, and she could feel its elation.

"Waiting for me to get killed, you piece of shit?" she asked under her breath.

"*Soon now.*"

"Fuck you."

"Talina?" Dya asked unsurely.

"Talking to my damn quetzal. They're here. The ones who took Kylee. They're close, Dya. You be ready to get behind me. Understand?"

"Yeah," the woman breathed, fear heavy in her voice.

Step by step. Talina's mouth had gone dry. She tried to see everything, desperate to know where the danger would come from. The prickling of her scalp was almost an itch.

"*Close.*"

"I know."

They were approaching the end of the field where the causeway ran between the berry bushes, through the fruit trees and under the interwoven pines.

"If there's a place for an ambush, this is it," Talina said through a dry mouth. Her heart might have been a hammer as it pounded in her chest. Adrenaline and fear had every muscle in her body charged.

She slowed, rifle up, advancing a step at a time. In the dirt before her, the maddening tracks were clearer. Two quetzals and a little girl. Kylee? Or Shantaya?

Talina took two attempts before she could swallow. Her nose picked up the scent. Richer. Two quetzals, their odors intermingled.

It might have been forever. Probably no longer than a couple of minutes, but Talina made her way through the tree band. The muzzle of her rifle swept in time with her gaze as she searched every shadow, every inch of the pine duff and lower branches.

And then they were through, passing out into that narrow gap between the pines and Donovan's native forest. It loomed up into the sky before them, implacable, like a wall between worlds.

The ripped fabric lay there on the red-brown dirt. Torn. Bloody.

Dya bent down, lifting what was left of a shredded dress. "This is Rebecca's. Look. See the stitching? This is the one she was wearing yesterday."

Almost frantically, Dya plucked up the smaller garment, bloodstained, damp from the dew.

"Kylee's?" Talina asked, her heart sinking.

"Shantaya's. See the little squash flower? She embroidered it on all of her clothing." Dya seemed to waver on her feet, looking sick. "Dear God, please. But . . . but where would their bodies be? I mean, look around. You don't see them, do you?"

"No. No bodies." Talina swallowed hard. Too many times she'd seen clothing like this. Quetzals didn't eat cloth.

This is going to be bad.

Her quetzal flexed itself where it lurked just under her ribs. The beast sent a flood of energy through her muscles. Talina's heart began to pound.

"Sending me a warning, huh?"

"Close. Beware."

"It's not Kylee's. They took my little girl," Dya whispered miserably. "Walked right in and stole her out from under us. We've got to find her."

"Yeah, we'll find her. These aren't the first fricking quetzals I've hunted. Haven't had one yet that . . ." Talina stopped short, no more than two paces into the forest.

She froze, rifle up, finger hovering over the trigger.

"Oh my God!" Dya cried, starting forward. "Kylee!"

"Dya," Talina snapped. "Don't fucking move! Not another step!"

To her surprise, the woman obeyed, whether from Talina's order or the recognition of the two huge quetzals who stood in the shadows to either side of Kylee.

But there they were. Maybe two meters tall, their triangular heads were lowered for the attack, front claws extended. The expanded collar ruffs kept pulsing with patterns of indigo and orange. The beasts had fixed their three-eyed stares on Talina. Sensing, no doubt, that she was the dangerous one with her raised rifle. The tongues kept flicking out like lashing snakes.

Talina squirmed, feeling as if the damn things were looking right through her like lasers.

Can I kill them both before they can hurt Kylee? Am I that fast?

"Kylee?" Dya whispered, one hand to her breast. "Sweetie, are you all right?"

Talina spared a good look at the little girl. She was wearing the same homespun dress, blonde hair hanging around her shoulders in tangles. Her face looked fuller now. The vacancy had gone from her eyes to be replaced with a feral, half-manic glitter.

"You have to go now," Kylee said, her voice sounding bruised.

"Come here," Dya coaxed. "Just ease your way forward, baby. It's going to be all right."

Dya took a step toward her daughter; the quetzals bristled, hissing, their collars flaring crimson in threat.

"Dya, don't," Talina warned. "They're a heartbeat away from killing us all."

Talina almost leaped out of her skin when a third quetzal hissed from behind.

She whirled, barely kept from firing as the beast—even bigger than the two at Kylee's side—blocked any retreat. Not more than four meters away, the huge quetzal flashed orange, blood-red, and indigo through its collar and down its sides.

Talina watched it hunch down, digging in with its rear feet. She knew that posture. The beast was preparing to spring.

"Baby?" Dya asked, glancing back and forth between her daughter and the surrounding quetzals.

"You have to go," Kylee repeated, her voice taking on that old tone, the one that brooked no argument.

"Kylee, we'll work something out. You need to come back with me. We have to find Rebecca and Shantaya. We're going to have to—"

"We're tasting Rebecca. Trying to learn her," Kylee said.

"Learn her?" Dya asked as she wadded the bloody dresses in her hands. "I don't understand." Dya was craning her neck, staring back into the inky-shadowed depths of the forest. "Is she with you?"

Talina's quetzal uttered that amused chitter.

And as quickly, a terrible realization sent a shiver through

Talina. Tasting? Learning? She felt sick, understanding, and wishing she didn't.

"Dya, step back." To Kylee Talina said, "Rebecca? And Shantaya, too? Both of them?"

"They must have seen us leaving. Came after us. We wanted to know why the experiment failed. Maybe learning Rebecca would tell us."

Us?

Talina lowered the rifle slightly to lessen the threat, hoping it would be enough as she forced herself to ignore the quetzal behind her, and took a step Kylee's way. "It doesn't work that way."

Talina glared at the quetzals watching her from either side. Then to Kylee she said, "You're a biologist? Like your mother? Then you know that quetzals share molecules. Like Rocket shared with you. Like I shared my quetzal's and Rocket's with you. That's how they taste and learn, but it only goes one way, Kylee. Our molecules are different. You can't share a human's knowledge, or their experiences, with a quetzal. They can taste all they want, but they can't process our DNA. They're not going to learn anything from Rebecca or Shantaya."

Talina took a halting breath. "Kylee, Rebecca and your sister Shantaya are dead. And worse, they died for no reason. You should have known."

The little girl didn't even flinch. "You're wrong. You have to go now. All of you."

"Kylee?" Dya asked in growing horror as she worked out the meaning behind the girl's words. "Listen, you come home with me now, and we'll—"

"The experiment is over." Kylee reached out, fingers tracing the quetzal's hides on either side of her. Patterns of rainbow colors seemed to flow from her touch.

"You're leaving now," Kylee said. "You are no longer welcome here."

Dya protested, "Rocket wouldn't have wanted—"

"Rocket's *dead*!" Kylee screamed in a wounded little girl's voice. "Those people *killed* him. Now leave, or we'll taste you all!"

"Kylee, please!" Dya cried, knotting the bloody cloth and reaching out.

"This is no longer your place," Kylee said as she turned. "You had your chance."

The quetzals whirled, impossibly fast, and vanished into the shadows. The way they whisked Kylee away with them might have been magic.

Talina whirled, rifle up, only to find the quetzal behind her, too, had disappeared. How silent? How un-fricking-nerving?

Talina just stood there, fought to catch her breath, and tucked her rifle close. The forest gloom might have been lifeless, dark, and empty.

"Kylee!" Dya shrieked, starting forward.

Talina leapt, grabbed the woman by her arm. "Let her go! Damn it, Dya, you heard her. If you follow, they'll kill you. Eat you."

"She's *my daughter*," Dya pleaded, tears leaking down her face. "She's my little girl."

"Yeah, I know," Talina relented, glancing around nervously. "They're watching, waiting, seeing what you're going to do."

"I *have* to go after her."

"Tusk and Shine need you. So do Damien and Tweet. Rebecca's dead. So's Shantaya. Along with your death—assuming you charge off into that forest—you going to drop that entire load on Su's shoulders? On Mark's?"

Dya was staring into the gloom. "But she's . . ."

"Theirs now." Talina stepped close. "Think it through. They sent Rocket. You heard Kylee's words. 'The experiment is over.' From their perspective, it died when Spiro shot Rocket."

Dya swallowed hard, closed her eyes as she struggled with herself.

"I understand," Talina said softly. "It's a shitty choice. You go in there, they'll kill you. Dead, you still don't save Kylee. You come back with me, you'll regret it for the rest of your life, wondering if you could have saved your daughter. But by coming back with me, you'll save Mark, Su, and your remaining children from mourning for the rest of their lives."

Dya nodded her understanding, but still stood, torn between her imperatives as a mother and her responsibilities to the rest of her family.

"Your people need you. They're already dealing with the loss of the dome. How are they going to feel when they learn Rebecca and Shantaya are dead? That they have to abandon the base as well?"

Dya glanced unsurely at Tal. "Do we really have to leave? I mean, Kylee's here. She might be coming back. And there's the experiments and research. We can't just—"

"You can't hold this place, Dya. Not just you, Mark, Su, and the kids. You and I just survived being surrounded by three adult quetzals. Intelligent alpha predators that can come and go, hunt you day in and night out. You don't even have a fence."

"But we've been able—"

"Stop *lying* to yourself. You're a scientist. Look me in the eyes and tell me how long your family can last if those quetzals really want to kill you?"

Dya fixed her miserable gaze on Talina's. Struggled with herself, arguments rising and falling in her quick mind. And in the end, she nodded in defeat. "Nothing we can do, is there?"

"Nope." Talina took a deep breath, staring woodenly into the forest's dark shadows. "Donovan just struck back. Get used to it."

"But Kylee . . ."

Talina ground her teeth, turning. "Yeah, I know. Rebecca, Shantaya, and Kylee. Three people you love. Gone. In one way or another."

"Maybe it's just a matter of time. Maybe Kylee's human half will eventually win out and she'll come back."

"Maybe."

Bitterly, Talina led the way back across the gap between Donovan and Mundo Base, knowing as she did that each step was a symbol of defeat.

71

Talbot had wept himself dry. He sat sideways in the shuttle seat, Tweet's petite body partly on his lap. The little girl finally slept. Su was clinging to his arm, little Ngyap asleep on her lap. Across from them, Dya was cuddled with Tuska and Shine. Damien huddled by himself, sleep finally granting him relief from the grief and anger. Only so much pain could be packed into a body.

Only so much misery.

They'd buried Rebecca's dress in a shallow grave in the cemetery beside Rondo's marker. The same with Shantaya's little dress. Those bloody, rent garments were the closest they could come to their loved ones' last physical remains, which, after all, the blood and dried fluids were.

For most of the day, Talbot and his family had puttered around in shock, going through the motions while the folks from Port Authority did most of the packing, listlessly directed by Dya and Su.

Load by load, they used the Beta to haul belongings and materiel from the dome down to the shuttle where Talina stood guard at the ramp, her rifle chambered.

In the shuttle, Manny Batemen and Sun-Ho kept a constant eye on the sensors, wary of an approach by any thermal source. They got hits, of course. Faint readings as quetzals appeared at the edges of the trees, apparently to look, and then faded back into the forest.

As night had fallen, the last of the loads had been packed into the shuttle's cavernous hold.

In the end, the ramp had been raised, and the shuttle had blasted its way into the air, leaving Mundo Base abandoned to the night. Devoid of any human presence for the first time since its founding so many years ago.

Was this all my fault? Mark wondered as he clasped

Tweet's delicate body close. The little girl's eyes flickered in REM sleep, her rich brown hair curled around her face.

Had he not come to Mundo, the lift would still have broken. Maybe it wouldn't have been Kylee who'd been injured. It might have been someone else. Or, if it had been Kylee, and the women were unable to fly her north to Port Authority, the little girl would have lived as a cripple. But she'd have been alive. With Rocket. And the quetzals would have remained mollified.

Rebecca and Shantaya would be alive. Damien and Tweet would still have a mother. A home.

Spiro came to Mundo looking for me.

He shook his head, feeling the guilt. Wondered what would have happened if the dome's subframe had let loose in storm.

That might have killed his entire family. They didn't understand how precarious their home had become.

And if they'd figured it out. If they'd had a chance to move to the ground?

"Stop it, Mark," he whispered to himself. A hundred ifs were just ifs. Speculation. He had to figure out what to do next.

Dya shifted, blinked awake. She stared blankly at the shuttle floor for a moment, then rearranged Tuska and Shine. As only kids could do, they slept through their mother's extrication, and curled together on the seat.

Dya pushed her hair back, stood, and walked back to the toilet.

Talbot eased Tweet off his lap and deposited her on the seat as she mumbled something under her breath; he was waiting when Dya stepped out of the toilet a couple of minutes later.

"You all right?"

She shook her head, hopelessness in her expression. He pulled her close, and she settled her head on his shoulder. "I keep thinking of her. Out there in the forest with those creatures. Did she see them kill Rebecca and Shantaya? Did she watch them eat . . ." She shivered. "God, Mark. What happened to her?"

"I don't know. This is more than just Rocket's death."

"The molecules. TriNA is what Talina calls them. They're screwing with her brain, Mark. Knowing that, is there any way to rescue her? Bring her back and deprogram what they've done to her?"

"I don't know."

"Damn. Talina was right. I *hate* myself for leaving her with those fucking beasts."

"Kylee said they'd kill you if you followed. No reason not to believe her."

"Doesn't make it any easier."

He kept her close. Let her cry on his shoulder. "One day at a time, Dya. That's how we have to deal with this. If we do. If we're smart and dedicated, maybe we can go back someday. Reclaim Mundo. That's the goal. We just have to dedicate ourselves to reaching it."

She pushed back, wiped at her tears, and stared up at him. "I couldn't do this without you. You know that, don't you? None of us could. Especially Su. She's going to be the hardest hit by this. She's going to need you the most."

"We're all going to need each other." He gave her a reassuring smile as he pulled locks of her blonde hair back in a caress. "We're family."

She smiled faintly. "What happens when we get to Port Authority?"

"Talina says she's got her people making a dome ready for us. Hell, we're landing in the middle of the night. No telling how this is going to work out."

"What are we going to do? How are we going to make a living? What about the kids? Will they let us educate them the way we want? How do we pay for things? Where do we get food?"

"One day at a time, Dya. But if we do this right, work hard, the time will come when we can go home again."

"Back to Mundo."

"That's right."

But even if they did, it would never be the same. Spiro had killed paradise with a single bullet.

72

The rise and fall of voices in Inga's actually had a calming effect on Talina as she settled in her chair. Inga must have seen her coming, for no sooner had Talina seated herself than the woman thunked Talina's old glass mug onto the bar. The stout was blacker than the hubs of Hell, and an inch of rich foam floated on the top.

"Heard you've had quite a time down south," Inga greeted, waving off Reuben Miranda's demands for service down the bar. She told him, "Just sit there and hold your balls for a second. Willy will get to you as soon as he can."

Inga turned her attention back to Tal. "You wouldn't believe the rumors floating around since you landed with that bunch. Is it true? The little girl ran off to live with the quetzals?"

"It's true." Talina tasted the stout. "Damn, I've missed this."

"So, Mundo's abandoned?"

"No way they could have held it." Talina wiped the foam from her upper lip. "So, yeah. The quetzals have taken it back. Made their point by killing a woman and little girl. Think of it as a sort of exclamation point."

"Hofer was in last night. Said the place was on the verge of disaster anyway."

"Yep."

"Any way we can take it back? I heard they had blueberries, raspberries, plums, cherries, a whole lot of things."

"I don't know, Inga." Talina set her mug down. "We don't have the materials to build the kind of fence they'd need. And it's deep forest. Not bush like we have here. Security would be a full-time job."

"Ain't it a pisser? Didn't know we had it, and as soon as we got it, we lost it." The big blonde woman sighed, slapped the towel she kept on her shoulder down, and polished the bar.

"That's it in a nutshell. Oh, yeah. Speaking of which, they had walnuts, too."

"Shit." Inga glanced up. "Don't look now, but here comes the Supervisor."

Talina didn't look. Wished the woman would leave her alone, but unwelcome as the plague, Kalico Aguila placed herself on the stool next to Talina, calling, "Wine if you would, please."

"Coming up," Inga called back.

"Haven't seen you around." Kalico stared thoughtfully at the back bar. The healing scars on her face wove an interesting pattern, and she absently ran a finger along the one lining her jaw. "The story is that Mundo's a disaster. That you had to pull everyone out."

"That's pretty much it. Hofer figures the dome is coming down with the next big storm. But Spiro killing Rocket was the end of everything. Not that anyone knew, but he was the reason the quetzals left Mundo alone. With him dead, all bets are off."

"Spiro." Kalico said it with such distaste.

"She's your problem."

"Not anymore." Kalico received her wine with a smile, tossing an SDR coin onto the bar. "Where are Dya, Talbot, and her people?"

"One of the domes down in the residential section. Spent most of yesterday moving Dya and Rebecca's lab equipment into the back of the hospital. Raya and Cheng made a room available. They have already adopted Dya. On top of her research, she's manufacturing her salves and medicines. Shig grabbed up Su in a heartbeat, has her collating data in the admin dome when she's not working to recreate Rebecca's research for Iji. It's like cross-fertilization."

"And Talbot?"

Talina chuckled. "Mostly taking care of the kids. Says he'd like to talk to you. Says he's willing to run survival classes for you and your people." Tal lifted a finger. "Here's the thing: He says if he's going to be an instructor, he wants to be paid like one. That he has a family to provide for."

Kalico shook her thick black hair back. "Maybe I'll talk to the women, too. See if they'd be—"

"I wouldn't if I were you. They blame you. Not for pulling the trigger. That they lay to Spiro. But you were the one who sent her. You were going to take their husband away. As they see it, you were the cause of their calamities."

"Damn Spiro!"

"It's trees."

"What is?" Kalico shot her a mystified look.

"The answer to your problem. Specifically, pine trees. Something about the pine resins. Southern pitch pine and loblolly pines planted alternately in a row. And behind them you plant black walnuts, oaks, and other southern temperate species. Then a belt of fruit trees followed by berry bushes."

"And that's it? That's the secret to Mundo Base?"

"That and Rocket. The trees kept the forest from advancing. Something in the fallen needles and the defenses terrestrial trees have developed. And as long as Rocket was alive, the quetzals weren't going to bother them."

Kalico took a deep breath. "I'll send a shuttle down first thing. Dig up enough trees to—"

"Whoa there, it's their property."

Kalico gave Talina a "you've got to be kidding" look. "The place is abandoned."

"They still hold title. Those trees belong to Dya, Su, and Talbot."

"You already said that they blame me. I *need* those damn trees, Perez."

Talina extended a soothing hand. "My advice? Talk to Talbot. He's really a reasonable guy when you're not threatening his family in one way or another."

"Think that would work?" Kalico was staring thoughtfully at the back bar, her brow furrowed.

"And another thing. Offer to buy the damn trees. Same with the berry bushes and other crops you want to take for Corporate Mine."

"Buy?"

"Yeah, radical term, huh? Sort of like charging a half-SDR for breakfast down at Corporate Mine. So I think you get the idea."

"Perez, give me one good reason why I should pay for a

fucking thing down there. That was Corporate property after all. They wouldn't have been there, wouldn't have had those trees in the first place, if it hadn't have been for—"

"And you'd have jack shit if they hadn't stuck it out, bled, and died to keep it. Kalico, you're making progress, but there's still that stubborn Corporate streak inside you. Let me drop another, even more radical term on you: co-operation. It might actually get you better results than that other word you like so much: coercion."

Kalico shot Talina a hard look over the rim of her wine glass. "Say I'm dense. Give me another reason."

"All right." Talina cocked an eyebrow. "Dya Simonov is doing a lot of Felicity's work at the hospital. Raya's training her to be a nurse. Says the woman has an aptitude given her background in biology. This being Donovan and all, the day may come when you're hurt again, lying on that table bleeding. Now, knowing Dya like I do, I suspect she'd take just as good care of you as anyone else. Still, wouldn't you want her feeling kindly disposed toward you while you're in such a vulnerable position?"

"I see."

"Yeah. I know firsthand how someone's ill will can work out in the hospital. Someone didn't feel kindly toward Cap while he was lying in one of those beds."

Kalico's mouth had pursed. "You're right. I'll buy the damn trees and crops."

"Talk to Talbot. I think they said they had a patch of pine seedlings somewhere along the west side. I never got over there to see." She paused. "And be damned careful. Those quetzals were serious when they said to stay away."

"What if I see Kylee?"

"If you can get her back, Dya would probably forgive you everything."

"Makes you wonder how many other research bases are out there, doesn't it?" Kalico fingered her glass.

"Now that we have shuttles, it might be worth doing a survey, don't you think?"

"Might indeed. If you think about the strides Mundo made, there could be a wealth of knowledge out there. Perhaps enough to make a difference in our survival. Especially if we never see a Corporate ship again."

"After all these years, don't expect the Wild Ones to welcome you with open arms. And if you pull that Corporate Supervisor shit—"

"Don't push your luck, Perez." Then Kalico shot her a wry smile. "I only learn one word a day. I'm still working my way around 'cooperation,' but after Mundo, I may be getting the idea."

"Miracles do happen, don't they?"

73

Talbot was drying dishes when the knock came at the door. Drying dishes? Could you believe? That was the contradiction of Port Authority. Some of the most complicated technology in the universe working side-by-side with what was essentially a Neolithic culture. And everything in between thrown in for good measure.

"I got it," Talbot called, seeing as how Su was in the middle of a reading lesson with Tuska and Taung. She had the kids spread out in a ring on the floor in the front room. Hard as this new life was, they'd agreed to keep the schedules as close as they could to the old days at Mundo.

Talbot crossed the room, opening the door to Dina Michegan. The marine was dressed in fatigues, her short black hair slicked back. She gave Talbot a quick smile, saying, "Hi. Just got off duty. Figured I'd drop by, see how you were doing. Some of us have been wondering."

"It's home. Or so they tell me. Tough time for us. Come on in."

"No. I . . . Could we talk?"

Talbot cocked an eyebrow, knowing his old friend too well. "Want a beer? Got a couple of bottles. Something called a housewarming gift. Never heard of the like, but some of the local women put together a case of food and stuff. Anyway, the wives don't drink beer, so I've been saving them."

"Sure. Maybe I'll just sit here on the step 'til you get back."

Talbot nodded, left the door open as he retreated to the kitchen and grabbed the bottles out of refrigeration. He gave Su's questioning glance a shrug, stepped outside, and closed the door before he settled on the step beside Michegan and popped the tops.

"Wives," she said. More of a statement than a question.

"That notion causes a bit of hesitation here. Not that it's

unknown back in Solar System. Especially in some of the stations." He shrugged, took a swig of the pale ale. "Just sort of the way it happened."

Michegan sipped her beer. "What did happen? We're all wanting to know. I sort of volunteered to hear your side of the story."

So he told it, leaving nothing out.

"You didn't desert?"

"Not in the beginning. As to where I am now? I don't know, Dina. Somewhere in the meantime I've found myself. For a time down at Mundo, I was happy like I've never been in my life. Dya, Su, they're pregnant. And I lost another child when the quetzals killed Rebecca. That's a sobering realization for a man to make."

"Don't know if we should be jealous or pity the shit out of you."

"Dina, what's wrong with just wishing me the best? People used to do that, you know. Hell, took me until I was lost in the forest to realize what a waste my life had been. And now, here, I've seen how close to the edge we all are. The only thing we have on Donovan is each other. And, like Mundo, we could lose it so easily."

She sniffed, nodded, took another swig of beer. "Yeah. Listen, were you really going to hose the shuttle engines with AP that day down at Mundo?"

"Naw. Like I told you. I've only got one round for the rifle. It was all just a bluff to get Aguila to leave us alone. Would have worked if Kylee hadn't sent Rocket down to see what was happening. When Spiro shot him, that pretty much screwed the whole deal."

He blinked back tears. Hoped Michegan didn't see how close he came.

"I've been standing duty at The Jewel. The Supervisor's serious about the place being off limits. That doesn't mean we don't hear things through the door when the place gets loud."

"Anything interesting?"

"Yeah. Listen. Mark, I think you're all right. You didn't let us down like some believed. Thought I'd come see for sure. So here's what you should know: It's Spiro. She's been shooting her mouth off. She and Chavez. Says she's going after Talina Perez this afternoon. Says she's going to shoot her down. Then she says she's coming after you. That you betrayed us all. That it was your fault she's in the fix she is. That you're a traitor and a coward for running out on us."

Talbot took a deep breath. "It never stops, does it?"

"I thought you should know. Have a little warning. She's been drinking. Chavez, too. He says he'll kill you if the lieutenant doesn't. And he's a back-shooter, if you get my meaning."

Talbot felt a chill run down his spine. "Yeah, I think I do." He swallowed. "Shit."

"Hey, lay low. Maybe keep out of sight for a couple of days. Let her cool off."

"Dina, what if she comes here? Drunk? She might just bull her way into the dome. Start shooting. Just like that day at Mundo when she shot Rocket. I've already lost a woman and two daughters I loved."

"Mark? Don't try and stand up against her. This is Deb Spiro we're talking about. You've seen her in action. Maybe you haven't heard, but she's killed two men already. Men who were shooting at her first. You're not in her league when it comes to killing."

"It's my family," he said simply.

And he had only one round left for his rifle.

74

"**T**alina Perez is at Inga's," Shin Wong reported. The faro dealer had just wandered in the door.

Dan Wirth sat at his table in the rear, leaned back with one foot up on a chair. The cards fluttered and snapped between his fingers as he practiced his shuffle. Practice made perfect, and perfect meant he could deal out whichever cards he wanted to a mark. And that meant profit in the end.

Maybe not monetarily, but through obligations.

Just as it had with Tompzen.

That—as the centuries-old saying went—was Dan's ace in the hole. And with the abdication of Deb Spiro, the Supervisor was relying ever more on Corporal Abu Sassi and the corporal's good friend, Kalen Tompzen.

Now Wirth shot an evaluative glance Spiro's way where she sat in the corner, a half-full glass of ale at her elbow. She and Chavez had been rattling dice in a can as they played ship, captain, and crew for beer money.

"It appears the lovely Officer Perez has finally come out of her hidey-hole," Wirth observed with enough volume to make his point.

Spiro grunted, her attention on the dice as she spilled them onto the table and muttered, "Damn."

It was Chavez who said, "Might be worth sending a message, don't you think?"

"Who you got in mind to deliver it?" Spiro swept up the dice, dropped them in the can, and handed it to Chavez.

"Hey, Shandy!" Chavez barked.

The cargo specialist looked up from where he was playing a hand of stud with Schemenski. "Yeah?"

"I'll give you a fifty-SDR piece if you take a message to Talina Perez at Inga's."

Shandy was on his feet so fast he almost toppled his chair backward. "What do I tell her?"

Spiro said, "Tell the lying slit she's a coward . . . a back-shooting bitch. Tell her that she either walks down here and looks me in the eyes while I shoot her, or I'll have to run her down and shoot her in the back like she'd shoot me, given half a chance. You think you got all that?"

Shandy gulped. Nodded, his loose brown hair flapping in time with the jerking of his head.

"You say it loud. I mean loud enough that everyone in the room hears. You got me?"

"Sure. Loud."

Chavez, not even bothering to straighten, flipped Shandy the gold-and-platinum coin.

Shandy caught it and was out the door like a shot.

"Easiest money he ever made." Chavez laughed, shook the can, and tossed the dice to rattle on the table. "There's my captain."

"You cheat," Spiro groused, turning. "Shin. Bring me a whiskey. The good stuff."

"Comin' up, Deb."

Wirth fanned his cards, studying Spiro from under lowered brows. "You think she's going to come?"

"Hey, this is make or break for her," Spiro answered as Shin Wong set a glass full of Inga's good stuff on the table beside her. Spiro didn't hesitate, but took the glass, knocked it back, and drained it.

She uttered a deep-seated sigh as the whiskey hit home. Then came the mocking smile as she said, "Call it lubrication for my joints, Dan. God, I hope she comes. I've been waiting for this. Ever since that fucking day in the hospital. Especially after the cheating cunt targeted me with that heat-seeking round. Time's come for that snot-sucking bitch to get what's coming to her."

"Don't miss," Dan told her dryly. "You're worth a hell of a lot more to me alive than dead."

Chavez stood. Stretched. "Me, I might slip out the back door. Maybe find a cool place in the shade where I can watch this go down. Sort of like insurance, you know? Never know about Trish Monagan. It'd be just like her to show up at the wrong moment. Think she might have something to prove."

Wirth raised an appreciative eyebrow as Chavez re-

trieved his service rifle from where it had been leaning
against the wall and slipped silently out the back door.

"Think the marines outside the front door will interfere, boss?" Art Maniken asked from where he was stock-
ing the bar.

Lowering his voice, Dan said, "Our good friend Kalen
is out there. I suspect that, as ordered, they'll just stand
there keeping the good Supervisor's people from entering
our fine establishment. No sense in them getting in the way
of a bit of local trouble."

"As if they'd interfere with me," Spiro growled. "Naw,
they won't so much as bat an eye. Not even when I go after
that fucking Talbot. What a maggot-gagging slit he turned
out to be. Family man? My ass."

"Lot of people on your list, Lieutenant," Dan noted as
he dealt out four kings and an ace, the cards slapping the
table like automatic rifle fire.

"Yeah, but have you noticed?" Spiro's smile had gone
flaccid. "With each passing day, there's fewer and fewer of
them."

"How long do you figure before we know if Perez is
coming?" Maniken asked.

"Five. Ten minutes," Dan guessed.

"If she shows," Spiro bit off the words in disgust. "Vik?
Bring me another whiskey."

Oh, she'll show.

He knew Talina Perez. But more than that, he'd seen
Deb Spiro in action. And after she'd killed the good Officer Perez, Spiro would be even that much more valuable to
him. Not that he'd miss Perez when she was gone, but the
world would be just a bit less interesting.

75

Inga's tavern went stone-silent as Shandy called out Spiro's challenge. Talina sat through the whole spiel, back rigid, her hand clenching her mug. She couldn't help but note Kalico's audible gasp where the woman sat beside her.

Talina took a deep breath, sighed, and climbed down from her chair.

The Supervisor reached out, laying a hand on Talina's arm. "You don't want to do this. This is a setup, and you know it."

Every eye in the tavern was on her as Talina carefully lifted Kalico's hand off of her forearm. "The woman's a walking menace, Kalico. Since the day Cap left the Corps she's been on a downward spiral. She could have stopped the riot that night outside the shuttle field fence. But she didn't, and people died. Since that day she shot up the hospital, she's been out of control. She's got people gunning for her, and she's killing people. Damn it, she lost Mundo for us. Maybe forever. Killed Rocket. Ruined Kylee. And for that, if nothing else, I owe her."

"Talina," Kalico's voice dropped, firm, deadly serious. "She's combat trained. The reason she's so fast? It's the implants."

Talina smiled, a deadly calm inside. Her quetzal was slipping around in her guts like an eel. "Kalico, I appreciate that but—"

"Don't go." A faint smile bent the Supervisor's lips. "I . . . I guess I'd miss you."

Talina chuckled, touched. "Doesn't mean it has to end in a shooting. Let me see if I can talk her out of this madness."

She stood, hitched her belt around so the butt of her pistol rested at the perfect angle. She was aware of the people, maybe fifty of them, scattered around the tables. These were her people. They understood.

Shandy was standing with his hands out defensively, saying, "I was only paid to deliver the message. Don't take it out on me."

Talina considered. "Spiro pay you?"

"Chavez did."

"Hope you got it in advance." To Inga she called, "Keep my beer cold. I'll be back to finish it."

"See you then, Tal," Inga called with forced joviality. "And Tal, you be careful with that woman. She's a damn quetzal if I ever saw one."

"Not even close. Quetzals have saving graces," Talina whispered as she strode for the aisle. Every head in the place turned to follow her. And as she trotted up the steps, she could hear the chairs and benches being pushed back, the rustle of feet as the room began to empty behind her.

Well, hell, so what if she had an audience? As she stepped out into the late-afternoon sun, she began flexing her fingers, loosening them up.

Her quetzal hissed and chattered inside, sending an electric pulse through Talina's muscles.

"You ready for this, you piece of shit? Normally that bitch shoots for the heart, but if she's a little low, she's going to blow a hole right through you."

"*Scared.*"

"Damn right I'm scared. What you've got to understand is that she's going to kill me. Somehow, I've got to get her, too. She's like a poison. Felicity. Shan. Rocket. Kylee. Rebecca. Shantaya. They'll just be the beginning."

"*Rocket?*"

"Might have been a bridge between people and quetzals. Spiro needs to die just for fucking that up. Plus, I really liked the little twerp. Broke my heart when he died."

Just remembering the pain she'd felt as Rocket died in her arms bucked her up with a wooden resolve. Yeah, one way or another, Spiro died today.

She was passing the foundry now, aware that the crowd was lining out behind her. Damn it, if it came to shooting, didn't the fools know they could be shot down just as quick?

She could see the front of The Jewel, watched as Spiro stepped out into the sunlight. Even across the distance, the woman had a weird smile on her lips, as if idiotically amused.

"Hey," Talina turned. "You people get out of the way. I don't want anyone getting hurt if this goes sour."

"We got your back, Tal," Terry Mishka called where he stumped along on his healing leg.

"Fine. Just stay the hell under cover while you've got it. Shots can go wild."

To her slight relief, people were slipping to the sides of the street, as if that would really keep them safe.

"What kind of fools want to see a shooting?"

Even better, how the hell was she going to take Spiro out? The woman was supposed to be faster than a spark.

Talina, you're not up to this.

She took a deep breath, her heart beginning to hammer. So this was what it all came down to? A sunny afternoon in the street? All the dangerous hunts, the times she'd faced down mobs on Clemenceau's orders. The close calls in the bush. Even the time she'd faced the mobbers, stared into one of the deadly creature's eyes. Or the times she fought quetzals. She could have died at any instant. Could have been shot in the back, could have been looking the other way when a quetzal leaped.

"It's been a hell of a life," she decided. "But no one lives forever."

Just got to take Spiro with me.

She flexed and rolled her shoulders, frantic to loosen the tension. One thing was sure: the adrenaline was pumping.

Word is she wants her opponents to fire first.

That was the key. Center punch Spiro right off. Don't go fast. A rushed shot was a missed shot.

Even if I'm heart-shot, there's a couple of seconds to aim, fire, and fire again.

"That's all that matters. She *can't* walk away."

And what the hell, Cap was dead. Trish had turned against her. She had a quetzal in her guts. It wasn't like she had anything outstanding to live for.

With that realization, a humorless chuckle rose to her lips. The fear seemed to have hit its high, and now ebbed.

Talina locked eyes with Spiro, watched the woman's gaze burn a glistening black in her blocky face.

Talina kept walking. Closing. Stopped right in front of
the woman, not more than two paces away. Close enough
she couldn't miss.

"How's this for face-to-face?"

Spiro's flaccid smile went wider. "You're a lying piece of
shit, Perez. What are you going to do about it?"

"What do you think, you miserable . . ."

Spiro's hand blurred.

One instant Talina was talking. The next she was staring into the black muzzle of Spiro's pistol. It hovered no
more than six inches from Talina's forehead.

"Thought I'd let you shoot first? Different story now,
isn't it?" Spiro asked. "I wanted you to feel it. What it's like
when a back-shooter puts a gun to your head. What it's
like when a sneaking cunt like you lights up a hot spot on
a person's cheek and targets a heat-seeking round. Enjoying the feeling? Getting that runny sensation down in your
guts?" The smile went oily. "Nice, isn't it?"

Talina froze, eyes fixed on the black emptiness inside
the muzzle of Spiro's pistol.

"There's one difference," Spiro told her pleasantly. "I
shoot people from the front. And I'm . . ."

"Now!"

The quetzal did it. Instantaneously.

As Tal ducked, Spiro's pistol blasted at the top of her
head.

The move wasn't conscious. Wasn't even hers. She had
no memory of the decision—let alone the action. One instant her hand was gripping the holstered pistol's butt. The
next it was level and firing into Spiro's chest.

Shot after shot. Like the crashing of hammers on planks.

And then it was over: Spiro falling away, collapsing as if
her spine had been cut. The woman's pistol came slashing
down before Talina's nose as the arm that held it went limp.

Spiro toppled backward, her eyes oddly bugged, mouth
open. As if in slow motion, the woman's body slammed
into the hard-packed gravel, the impact rolling through her
chest, arms, and legs. Spiro's head hit hard, bounced, causing her cheeks to jump and her eyelids to flicker.

Talina blinked, still crouched low. Aware that her eyes
burned. The world had vanished in a wailing, high-pitched

ringing. Her pistol remained at the ready, gripped for a follow-up shot.

Her forehead felt funny and her scalp was on fire.

Talina fought for air. Struggled. But filling her lungs seemed impossible.

All around her, people were staring around, pointing off across the street.

At what?

Then Trish was there. Carefully she reached out, laid her hand on Talina's, and guided the pistol back into its holster. Then Trish's reassuring grip pulled Talina's arm up over the young woman's shoulder, supporting her.

All the while, Trish's mouth was working soundlessly. Damn that horrible ringing. It drowned the whole world.

"Can't hear!" Talina bellowed.

Trish stopped short, peered into her eyes, then leaned close to shout through the ringing. "You're deaf from the gunshot! It'll pass!"

People were running, still pointing as they called to each other, heading off toward Sheyela's repair shop. Others were crowding around, staring in awe at Spiro's bleeding body.

"What's that all about?" Talina bellowed, pointing toward Sheyela's.

Trish leaned close. Shouted through the ringing. "Talbot just shot Chavez! The fucker was going to shoot you for shooting Spiro!"

"Talbot?"

"Chavez!"

"I don't—"

"Shut up, Talina! I've got to get you to Raya."

Which was when the first of the blood began to drip down her forehead and onto her nose.

And to her surprise, it was Kalico—immaculate in her black suit—who came to take her other arm. And together the three of them went plodding up the street, heedless of the people clapping and cheering.

Not that Talina could have heard them through the ringing.

76

Cherries were wonderful things. Trish must have tasted
something similar—but it had been so long ago in the
past she couldn't remember. Nor would they have been real
cherries, but some processed juice, or dried concoction
that had come off one of the ships.

These were the genuine article.

As Trish stepped lightly down the hospital corridor, she
plucked another one from the sack, popped it in her mouth,
and artfully chewed the seed from the fruit. With two fingers she removed the pit and placed it with the rest in her
pocket.

Pocket? Well, it wasn't like she was going to spit them
on the hospital floor. And hell, they were seeds. She wondered what they'd be worth in trade to Szong Sczui, Terry
Mishka, or one of the other farmers.

It had been almost two weeks since the shooting. The
whole town was still talking about it. Hell, if Trish hadn't
seen it with her own eyes, she wouldn't have believed it
either.

She'd been coming at a run, hadn't been more than
twenty paces away when Talina stopped short in front of
Spiro. Trish hadn't seen the lieutenant's draw. Just a blur
and the pistol appeared pointed at Talina's head.

Faced with the momentary death of her friend, Trish had
been in the act of drawing her own weapon. Had seen Spiro's
pistol discharge, had known that Tal was shot through the
head.

And then Talina's pistol flashed, three thunderous shots
ringing out. Impossible as it seemed, Talina was crouched
down, her weapon leveled, and Spiro was falling.

Trish hadn't made more than ten steps when another
shot rang out. Deeper, the boom of a rifle, and Michael
Chavez had tumbled from the roof of Sheyela's electronics

repair. The man's body had made a smacking sound as it hit, bones popping.

Moments later, Talbot had emerged from where he'd taken a position behind a hauler's front wheel, his service rifle in hand as he walked carefully toward the fallen marine.

"Couldn't let that fucker shoot Talina from ambush," he'd said later. "That's not how a marine conducts himself. In the Corps, or out of it."

Word was that he'd only had a single round of ammunition.

Man like that? Maybe he had a future in Port Authority security. It was worth having a word with Shig, Yvette, and Talina.

With a left hand, Trish pushed the examining room door open to find Dya Simonov unwrapping Talina's bandage. Tal sat on the bed, looking for all the world like she wanted to kill something.

"How's the patient? Still butt-ugly for a toilet-sucking excuse of a security officer?"

Talina's black eyes flashed. "My hearing's been back for days, Trish."

"Yeah, too bad, huh? I liked you better the other way. Deaf and bleeding. And I gotta say, that new hairstyle you've adopted just flat will stop a bem in its tracks."

"It will grow back," Dya said reprovingly as she removed the last of the bandages.

"How bad is it?" Talina asked with a wince.

Dya leaned forward, looking carefully. "I think we can pull the stitches. Probably better do it now. Especially with your hair coming back in."

"And the powder stippling?"

"That was mostly surface. It's peeled. Raya excised the deeper speckles."

"So, Tal's going to be, well, like normal again?" Trish asked.

"She'll hardly have a scar. Another couple of months for the hair to grow back, and you won't know the difference."

"Ooh. Too bad on all counts."

Talina glanced sidelong at Trish. "You got a reason for being here?"

"Yeah, I got a reason; Kalico sent you a sack of cherries. But if you don't want them, I can just turn around and—"

"Cherries?" Dya and Tal asked in unison.

"Kalico went down to Mundo?" Dya asked first. "Did she see Kylee?"

"Nope. They definitely kept their eyes out. Broadcast your message on the loudspeakers. Left a radio like you requested and instructions on how to use it. Used high resolution scan, thermal, IR, LiDAR, you name it. They had hits on plenty of quetzals. Well, six at least. No little girls."

Dya's eyes closed, and she took a deep breath. "I should go down there."

Talina laid a hand on the woman's wrist. "And do what? Feed a quetzal?"

Dya tried to smile. Couldn't.

"And Dya, you better brace yourself. Word is that the dome's fallen. Just like Hofer said it would."

Dya nodded, looking as if her heart was tearing in two.

"Kalico got her trees," Trish said. "Took the seedlings like you and Su agreed. Left the mature trees to hold the line. Took armored marines to do it—quetzals popping out of the forest as they were—but they got a good harvest from the farm. Including these cherries."

She popped another in her mouth.

Talina's eyes narrowed. "Thought those were my cherries?"

"Hey, who's been all over town looking for your chapped ass? I'm doing you a favor. You think I'm going to pass up cherries? And if I wasn't a true friend, I'd have sat down on the other side of the fence and eaten the whole sack. You'd never have known."

Talina looked thunder and mayhem at her. Trish smiled. Handed over the sack.

As Talina took it, Trish asked, "So, Dya? Want some help pulling them stitches? If we can get Tal to pass out, I'll share the rest of those cherries with you."

"Pass out?" Dya asked. "It's just a furrow through her scalp. Barely touched the outer table of her skull. She'll barely feel the stitches being pulled as it is."

"Some friend," Talina groused.

"Hey, into every life a little rain must fall, and I'm your thunderstorm."

"Yeah," Talina agreed. "You're the rain, and I'm the lightning. But eating my cherries? That's going too far."

Then Talina shot her wicked wink, popped a cherry into her mouth. Having done so, she offered the sack to Trish. And the world was once again a fine place.

77

Call it a good day. They'd have four acres. Four, miserable, tiny, but inviolate acres. From the original land they'd cleared, that was all that remained.

But, for Corporate Mine, it was a definite start.

Kalico had participated in the planting, all taking place under Su's critical eyes. They'd had to leave bare ground between the forest and the seedlings. Ground they'd have to defend through out-and-out hard work and savage cutting. But it would buy time for the little pines to take root. In addition, they'd scattered pine needles raked up from beneath the trees at Mundo.

And behind that first line of seedling pines had been planted the first of the black walnuts and oaks. And then a line of fruit tree cuttings. And finally the berry bushes.

Kalico sighed, rubbed the back of her neck as she pushed past the double doors and into her admin dome. Makarov was still in the process of spooling down the shuttle after another trip to Mundo. They'd have more trees to plant tomorrow. The lights had turned on out in the compound, the sound of engines could be heard as the haulers and mucking machines were driven off to the mine by second shift.

Corporate Mine was running at an easy sixty percent production. She could have run the crews at one hundred. But what was the point? The smelter could only process what it could process.

I can have that tram up and running in a couple of months if I dedicate the labor to it.

That notion had its appeal. Especially now that the key to keeping the forest back had been found. It would mean braving the haunted decks aboard *Freelander*—maybe even overnighting as they built the equipment Fenn Bogarten said they'd need to spin the carbon fiber.

Just the thought of it sent shivers down her spine.

She considered stopping in the cafeteria for a cup of tea, decided against it, and checked in at the radio room, asking, "Anything I should know about?"

The woman looked up. "No, ma'am. Just routine chatter from Port Authority. Su Wang Ho was delivered safely back to PA. Aircar crew opted to stay the night in the PA dormitory rather than fly back in the dark."

"Smart of them. Glad to know they took my advice. Let me know if something comes up."

"Of course, ma'am. Oh, cafeteria wanted to know if you'd eaten?"

"Caught a bite down at the smelter. Just a ration bar, but it will do. Tell the kitchen they can shut down."

Kalico stopped, turned back. "And tell them I said thank you. That I appreciate it, and that I'm sorry they had to wait."

When did I start giving a damn what the kitchen staff thought?

"That will make their night, ma'am." The redhead smiled and bent back to her radio.

Radio. Not micrograv or entangled photonics. Just old, antique radio. Like the primitive set they'd left at Mundo should Kylee Simonov decide to sneak out of the forest and call home.

"Yeah, right. As if that would ever happen."

Kalico stepped into her room, locked her door, and peeled out of her jumpsuit. In the mirror she stopped short. Pus and buckets, she had a smear of dirt running down the side of her nose and across her mobber-scarred right cheek. A place where she'd rubbed with dirt-encrusted hands.

She'd taken part in the planting herself. The job was just too damn important. Hard to believe that was her, digging an actual hole in real dirt with a shovel. She had had to add her labor, symbolically bend her back and help stick those little pines into the ground. Pat the rich red dirt down around the roots and water it.

And she'd looked like this for the rest of the day? And no one had said anything? Hell, none of them had even so much as stared at her. As if she were one of them! Just an ordinary . . .

Kalico swallowed hard.

As if she were one of them.

She remembered Boardmember Taglioni back in Solar System. How he'd looked at her over a succulent, forty-course meal at his private table in Zekko's. "We're special in everything we do. In how we think. How we plan. How we eat. Even in the way we conduct our sexual unions. Those others, they will never catch so much as a glimpse, let alone an understanding of what elevates us above their tawdry little lives."

She grunted her amusement as she undressed. Her lean body was criss-crossed with angry red scars. Taglioni would have been horrified. "Maybe you better see if you can survive on Donovan for a couple of months before you believe that vacuum you used to spew."

So saying, she stepped into the shower, washed away the day's sweat, dirt, and grime. What would he say to that? This was the same body he'd taken into his gleaming white sheets. The one he'd fondled, explored so thoroughly with his tongue and lips. If she were to appear in his bed as she was now, could he stand to take her in another eros-induced rut, or would he puke his guts at the thought of her scarred flesh against his?

Same body. Remodeling courtesy of Donovan.

Raya could ameliorate the worst of the damage, of course. But Kalico would have to be back in Solar System for a complete cosmetic procedure that would return her skin to its previous perfection. For the time being, feeling reckless, she chose to wear the scars as a badge of honor.

Laughing, she dried with her antique-style towel and padded over to her bed. From the pitcher on her dresser, she poured a glass of water and tucked herself under the covers.

"Lights off," she ordered, and sank down onto the mattress. A fucking mattress. Not antigrav. Then she sighed in total victory. Pine trees. She'd found the key.

She'd saved the smelter. If the trees grew, she'd have her key to keeping the forest back. It wouldn't be overnight, but she'd reclaim the lost ground. As more pines grew, she'd scratch out more acreage.

Floating on that euphoric sense of accomplishment, she drifted off into the haze at the edge of . . .

From dreams, Kalico started. Blinked awake.

She checked the time. Middle of the night.

Fishing for her glass on the nightstand, she gulped down water. Gasped as something passed her lips with the last swallow. Spitting it out, she called, "Lights!"

There. On her blanket lay a small, round, black pebble. But how?

She glanced at the nightstand. The note lay there, perfectly placed so that the edges were parallel to the end table's.

The block letters were black on white: **YOU MIGHT JUST AS EASILY HAVE DRANK POISON. DON'T EVER CROSS ME AGAIN.**

But who?

She placed a hand to her throat, considering all of her people. And came up blank.

Spiro!

No. She was dead.

One of Spiro's . . .

Wirth! It had to be.

She frowned at the pebble.

But who was his agent here? Who could have gotten into her room?

And it hit her: "No one ordinary."

Someone close.

She smiled, that old predatory sense sharpening around her heart. "Oh, we're not through with this. Not in the slightest."

Call this the thrown gauntlet. And if Kalico Aguila was good at anything, it was winning.

78

Dan was coming in late to The Jewel, and to hell with the looks his people were going to give him. Allison had been magnificent that morning. It had been worth every second. He and Allison had dropped a tiny hit of eros, and buoyed on the drug, the sex had been fantastic. Maybe the best. Or at least the best until next time.

Just the thought of it, the memory of her sweat-glowing skin, the way she'd hammered herself against him, conjured a tingle at the root of his penis.

"Now that," he told himself as he strolled down the main avenue, "is as good as life gets."

He chuckled, glancing up at the morning sky. Partly cloudy. Patches visible of that curious turquoise blue that had so charmed him from the first day he'd set foot on Donovan. Already, he could read the signs: Rain tonight.

He passed the spot where Talina Perez had shot Deb Spiro. Stopped, stared at the hard-packed gravel. Still hard to believe.

Dan had been standing in his doorway, not ten paces away. He hadn't seen Spiro's hand move, so fast did she draw her pistol. One instant the weapon was in her holster. The next it was pointed at Talina Perez's face.

A sure thing. Just shoot.

But Spiro had to talk.

How the fuck had that slit Perez crouched and shot so fast? Again, though he'd been watching, Dan hadn't seen it happen. Hell, the way she dropped, he thought Perez was shot through the head. The first thought was that somehow, with a bullet in her brain, Perez had shot through reflex.

Only to find out it was a graze.

And then Talbot takes out Chavez.

"So much for insurance."

Damn it.

"Alas, poor Spiro. So today you rot up in the cemetery just downhill from good old Donovan, and I who could have so used your services am left high and dry. With nothing but my own wits. Of course, you're dead, and I'm still aglow with the greatest sex a man can stand.

"God, what a waste on your part. If you'd shot the bitch like we planned, just the threat of turning you lose on Mosadek or Dushane would have handed me the whole fucking town. And not a word of resistance uttered along the way."

So saying, he scuffed the gravel where Spiro had fallen. The blood, of course, had long ago washed away in the rains.

"Alas and alack."

He strode for The Jewel's door, opened it, and stepped inside. "How are we doing, Art?" he called. His heels rapped on the chabacho-wood floors as he passed the tables on his way back to the cage.

"Took hours, but we're cleaned up and ready for business again, boss." Maniken was seated in the back, a cup of mint tea steeping on the table before him. "Got to tell you, I'm so glad Aguila let her people come back. Pulled in a couple thousand SDRs last night."

"Yeah, well, the good Supervisor is no one's fool. She can understand the simplest of messages."

Dan stepped to the back of the bar, poured a cup of hot water from the pot on the hot plate. He crushed some mint between thumb and forefinger. God, he wished for coffee. Rued the day the last cup had been drunk. Word was the seedlings were still alive in the greenhouses, but it would be years before they bore.

"Um, boss? Found a backpack on the floor when we were cleaning up last night. Had Desch Ituri's name on it. I didn't know if you'd want me rummaging through it, so I set it on the counter in the cage."

"Ituri, huh? When was he in?"

"Beats me. I don't remember seeing him last night."

Dan used a spoon to stir his tea and stepped over to the cage door.

It sat on the counter as Maniken had said. A regular old backpack. Black. With Ituri's name stenciled in white.

"No telling what wonders might lie within. Plans? Construction info? Some secret to the good Supervisor's empire down at Corporate Mine?"

He did, after all, have the slit scared half to death. Tompzen reported that she'd found the pebble, drank the water. And the fact that she'd immediately reinstated crew rotations to The Jewel was proof enough that she understood exactly what her position was.

Dan unsnapped the restraints and lifted the flap, finding an envelope marked **To Allison**.

"Indeed." Wirth opened it. On the sheet of paper, it simply said, **Desch won't be coming to see you again.**

Well, not every goose continued to lay golden eggs.

Reaching into the pack, Dan removed a curious device that filled most of the interior. A plastic-wrapped square of what looked like clay was topped by a small power pack. On the front, a black duraplast screen flickered to life, the numbers **5, 4, 3, 2, 1,** flashing in countdown. Then the letters **BANG!** flashed on the screen.

"What the hell?"

A piece of paper had been taped to the side. This Dan pulled loose, reading: **I, TOO, HAVE AGENTS. SHOULD ANYTHING EVER HAPPEN TO ME, YOU AND THE JEWEL WILL BE A SMOKING CRATER.**

A curious tingling of fear raced around his guts. His hair was standing on end, and it was with difficulty that he forced a swallow down his throat.

He glanced at the fake bomb. Then considered the note again. Crumpled it up. Carefully he replaced the fake bomb and letter to Allison. Taking the backpack and his tea, he walked out.

"Art?" He set the backpack on his enforcer's table. "I want this delivered back to the Supervisor next time she's in town. You do it. In person."

"And what do I tell her, boss?"

"Tell her . . . Touché."

"I don't get it. Touché?"

"Trust me. She'll know what it means."

And with that, he raised his cup in salute. It was, after

all, a good morning. First Allison had gotten him off in a way that had left him wondering if his skull was going to explode, and now he discovered he had a most worthy adversary.

"Okay, so it's a stalemate. Makes the future a lot less boring place."

EPILOGUE

Yesterday, the shuttle came again. I heard its arrival from where I hid deep in the forest, and then its departure at dusk. They took more trees.

Flash and Diamond are worried. It's not like we didn't give them a perfectly clear message, right? Mundo is no longer theirs.

The fact that every time a shuttle comes back, it's guarded with armored marines means they've taken the lesson to heart.

"Actually, it's a good sign," I tell the quetzals. "Each time they've come, it's been to take equipment, different plants they need. If they ever come back and start fixing the buildings, bringing in new material, that's when we have to worry."

I'm not sure how I feel deep inside about Dya, Su, Mark, Damien, and the rest of the kids going away forever. There are a lot of things I'm not sure about.

Like why I ache on the inside when I think about how Rebecca and Shantaya died that day. It had to happen, right? I know that Flash and Diamond are looking for answers. It wasn't like they were being vindictive when they ate Rebecca and Shantaya. It was Rebecca, years ago, who told me, "Sometimes, Kylee, sacrifices have to be made in the name of science."

Flash and Diamond thought that by consuming Rebecca and Shantaya they'd gain an understanding of why the experiment went wrong. They were as upset as I was when they didn't get any answers from digesting the bodies.

That meant that Rebecca and Shantaya died for nothing.

Despite the ache and hurt that causes the human in me, I know it was part of the scientific method. Knowledge doesn't come without a little pain, regret, and a few mistakes.

And back then, I was still pretty broken apart inside.

The quetzal part of me was still growing, enraged at what they'd done to Rocket.

Part of me is Rocket. And I remain enraged. Unlike among humans, the desire to kill isn't muted over time. It can, however, be buffered by other stimulae. Like Talina desperately trying to keep Rocket alive. Communicating her desperation and hope as he died.

And she carried Rocket's last feelings, shared them with me through her saliva. But for her I would never have lived his fear, pain, and disbelief. Let alone his surprise that Talina cared so much that she held him as he died.

Talina proves that not all humans are beyond preserving. The problem is that too many of them are monsters like Spiro, the Supervisor, and the rest. In Flash and Diamond's eyes this makes saving the few not worth the effort.

The part of me that is Kylee would save the few.

Some days I teeter, but most days the quetzal perspective wins.

As the morning brightens in the eastern sky the old quetzal I named Flash and I walk out from the tree belt and across the seared surface of the shuttle landing pad.

Flash and the rest remain awed by the humans' ability to ride the skies. Technology perplexes them. It's beyond their conception. I constantly astound them by making the simplest of tools. Even to the point of using a stone to crack a walnut.

The buildings are looking a bit more shabby. Around the edges, sunflowers, amaranth, and lettuce are starting up.

I need Mundo's plants. None of Donovan's native plants are digestible in the human gut. Most are downright poisonous. Although the quetzal inside me can process heavy metals, the human part of me is still highly susceptible to toxicity. Almost all of my food comes from the fields here. A fact that ties me forever to Mundo.

Stepping around the side of the shop building, I stare with curious detachment at what remains of the dome; it collapsed around the main shaft of the tower. From the looks of things, the west side let loose first, tilting the whole, and then the rest of the floor gave way. As it plummeted down, the tower punched up through the roof.

Hard to believe that used to be our home. Rocket and me, we both miss it.

Flash chatters at the sight; yellow, green, and pink patterns of color paint the big quetzal's hide.

"It hurts," I tell him. "It was our home. We were happy here."

Flash makes a deep-chested clicking, his sides alternating in patterns of violet, mauve, and orange that communicates his curiosity. Especially about how the part of me that is Rocket could have been happy there.

"Humans feel things quetzals don't. And the other way around, I guess."

Flash clicks and chatters his confusion. Humans remain unfathomable to him. He asks if I will ever go back to the humans.

"Humans have a word: amputate. It means to cut off. They have another word: cauterize. Which means to seal by means of fire."

I lead the way, walking wide around the collapsed dome to the cemetery. Here I drop to my knees so that I can finger the dirt on Rocket's grave. "This is why. When they killed Rocket, they amputated the human part of me. Because it was purposefully mean, that cauterized it."

Flash half-flares his collar, his three eyes gleaming as they study me. A barely audible whistle sounds behind his serrated jaws.

"Of course I still love my mother. I love all of them. But they're not . . . us. Rocket made that clear as he was dying."

I close my eyes to better see the woman in my memory. "Ta Li Na. I always liked that name. She gave me Rocket's last message. He told me to get away. That's why I can't go back. They'd try to get what's left of him out of me. Wash him from inside. Make me one of them again." *I pause.* "I can't let that happen."

A curious chittering utters from Flash's mouth.

"Because I know how Turnienko, Cheng, and Dya think and work. They dissect what they don't understand. Experiment. Like Rebecca did with death fliers, roos, and hoppers. And you did with Rebecca and Shantaya. There's a cost to science."

Flash replies with a clicking, his hide dancing in golds and blacks mottled with tan that express his incomprehension and at the same time his distrust and contempt for human beings.

"Dya always used to tell me not to burn bridges. It's what she called a metaphor. Words that make a symbol. They would have killed Rocket in Port Authority. First Spiro, then the rest of the town. Talina is part quetzal. She got us away. And then they came all the way here and killed Rocket anyway. It's my fault. I sent him down to see what was happening."

I sniff, fighting back tears. But there have been too many of those already. "So, the bridge is burned. It's just us now. Rocket and me. He tells me not to, but I hate them."

Again the clicking.

"That last day, when we met Talina and my mother in the forest, Talina should have shot me. I'll grow up. And when I do, I am going to make them afraid like Rocket was."

I place a finger to my lips as the saliva flows in my mouth. "I can taste Rocket's death here. I've let you taste it. So you know what I mean. But what you can't know is how deeply my hate runs."

I knot a fist full of dirt from Rocket's grave. "But they will. One day, when I'm an adult, they're going to feel the same terror Rocket did."

Flash chatters a question.

"Because I swear it," I tell him. "Right here, on Rocket's grave."

And in my imagination I hear people screaming, see them dying in blood, with torn guts, and in fear. Just like Rocket did. My mother taught me to be a scientist, so I know just how to make it happen.

I stand, the dirt from Rocket's grave still clutched in my fist. I look to the north, far away, toward Port Authority. Too bad for them.

W. Michael Gear

The Donovan Novels

"What a ride! Excitement, adventure, and intrigue, all
told in W. Michael Gear's vivid, compulsively read-
able prose. A terrific new science-fiction series; Gear
hits a home run right out of the park and all the way
to Capella."   —Robert J. Sawyer

"Fans of epic space opera, like Rachel Bach's
Fortune's Pawn, will happily lose themselves in
Donovan's orbit."   —*Booklist*

Outpost	978-0-7564-1338-5
Abandoned	978-0-7564-1341-5
Pariah	978-0-7564-1343-9

and coming in 2020
Unreconciled
978-0-7564-1566-2

To Order Call: 1-800-788-6262
www.dawbooks.com

DAW 220

Tanya Huff
The Peacekeeper Novels

"Huff weaves a fast-paced thriller bristling with treachery and intrigue. Fans of military science fiction will enjoy this tense adventure and its intricately constructed setting."
—*Publishers Weekly*

"Anyone who has read any of Huff's previous books featuring Kerr . . . knows of her amazing ability to combine action, plot, and character into a wonderful melange that makes her books a joy to read."
—*Seattle Post-Intelligencer*

AN ANCIENT PEACE
978-0-7564-1130-5

A PEACE DIVIDED
978-0-7564-1151-0

THE PRIVILEGE OF PEACE
978-0-7564-1154-1

To Order Call: 1-800-788-6262
www.dawbooks.com

DAW 74

CJ Cherryh
The Foreigner Novels

"Serious space opera at its very best by one of the leading SF writers in the field today." —*Publishers Weekly*

"Her world building, aliens, and suspense rank among the strongest in the whole SF field." —*Booklist*

To Order Call: 1-800-788-6262
www.dawbooks.com

Cries from the Lost Island
by Kathleen O'Neal Gear

Set against the glory and tragedy of ancient Roman Egypt, a novel that brings to bring to life the greatest love story of all time...

Sixteen-year-old Hal Stevens is a budding historical scholar from a small town in Colorado. A virtual outcast at high school, he has only two friends: Roberto the Biker Witch and Cleo Mallawi. Cleo claims to be the reincarnation of Queen Cleopatra. She also believes she's being stalked by an ancient Egyptian demon, Ammut, the Devourer of the Dead.

But when Hal and Roberto find Cleo murdered in the forest near her home, it appears she may have been telling the truth. Her last request sends them journeying to Egypt with famed archaeologist Dr. James Moriarity, where it quickly becomes clear that Cleo has set them on the search of a lifetime: the search for the lost graves of Marc Antony and Cleopatra.

But they are not alone in their search. Cleo's murderers are watching their every move. And not all of them are human...

Available in hardcover March 2020

978-0-7564-1578-5